What people are saying about ...

NOT BY SIGHT

"*Not by Sight* starts a terrific new trilogy with the story of a father and daughter missing now for five years. Nonstop tension and danger, young love, and conflicts of faith make this a not-to-be-missed experience. Another winner for Kathy Herman!"

Lorena McCourtney, author of the Ivy Malone Mysteries and the Cate Kinkaid Files

"Prepare yourself for a roller-coaster ride. Kathy Herman's latest suspense doesn't deliver just one mystery but many twists and turns that will keep the pages flying! And all in another picturesque location. Don't miss this wild ride!"

Lyn Cote, author of *La Belle Christiane* and *Winter's Secret*

"As a longtime Kathy Herman fan, I know I can expect a top-notch mystery that will grab my attention from the very first page. *Not by Sight* exceeded those expectations, with enough dizzying twists and turns to leave me breathless. This book is an absolute gem—Kathy Herman's best yet!"

Carol Cox, author of *Love in Disguise* and *Trouble in Store*

NOT
by SIGHT

OZARK MOUNTAIN TRILOGY

KATHY
BESTSELLING
SUSPENSE NOVELIST
HERMAN

NOT
by SIGHT

A NOVEL

David C Cook®

transforming lives together

NOT BY SIGHT
Published by David C Cook
4050 Lee Vance View
Colorado Springs, CO 80918 U.S.A.

David C Cook Distribution Canada
55 Woodslee Avenue, Paris, Ontario, Canada N3L 3E5

David C Cook U.K., Kingsway Communications
Eastbourne, East Sussex BN23 6NT, England

The graphic circle C logo is a registered trademark of David C Cook.

All Scripture quotations are taken from the Holy Bible, New International
Version®, NIV®. Copyright © 1973, 2011 by Biblica, Inc.™ Used by permission
of Zondervan. All rights reserved worldwide. www.zondervan.com.

LCCN 2013933126
ISBN 978-0-7814-0804-2
eISBN 978-0-7814-0883-7

© 2013 Kathy Herman
Published in association with the literary agency of Alive Communications,
Inc, 7680 Goddard St., Suite 200, Colorado Springs, CO 80920

The Team: Don Pape, Diane Noble, Amy Konyndyk,
Nick Lee, Caitlyn Carlson, Karen Athen
Cover Design: Kirk DouPonce, DogEared Degisn
Cover Image: 123RF and iStockphoto

Printed in the United States of America
First Edition 2013

1 2 3 4 5 6 7 8 9 10

022813

To Him who is both the Giver and the Gift

ACKNOWLEDGMENTS

I love Arkansas! After moving to the rolling hills of East Texas from the front range of Colorado, I discovered that any time I missed the mountains, I could travel to nearby Arkansas to satisfy that longing. I chose the Ozark Mountains of northwest Arkansas to provide the backdrop for this new series and many of the images I describe in the story. However, Sure Foot Mountain, Angel View Lodge, Raleigh County, and the town of Foggy Ridge exist only in my imagination.

During the writing of this book, I drew from several resource people, each of whom shared generously from his or her storehouse of knowledge and experience. I did my best to integrate the facts as I understood them. If accuracy was compromised in any way, it was unintentional and strictly of my own doing.

I owe a special word of thanks to Retired Commander Carl H. Deeley of the Los Angeles County Sheriff's Department for helping me to understand when and how Miranda rights should be read; how SIM cards, bloodhounds, and helicopters are used to track criminals and victims; and how a command post is operated. Carl, you gave me such great information that, at times, I felt almost embedded with your officers! You're a joy to work with!

A big thank-you also to Paul David Houston, former assistant district attorney, for giving me clear direction regarding specific criminal charges in a rather complicated plot, and for helping me to understand Arkansas law regarding birth and death records that have not been filed. Paul, your prompt replies to my many questions is not something I take for granted. Thank you never seems like enough, but it is heartfelt.

A special word of thanks to Carolyn Walker, an ardent advocate for families and children who works with the Texas Foster Family Association, for offering helpful input based on her many years of experience with child protective services. Carolyn, thanks for answering a multitude of questions and enabling me to feel comfortable with my handling of this important element of the story.

I'm immensely grateful to my faithful prayer warriors: my sister Pat Phillips; dear friends Mark and Donna Skorheim and Susan Mouser; and my online prayer team: Chuck Allenbrand, Pearl and Don Anderson, Judith Depontes, Jackie Jeffries, Susie Killough, Joanne Lambert, Adrienne McCabe, Deidre Pool, Kim Prothro, Kelly Smith, Leslie Strader, Carolyn Walker, Sondra Watson, and Judi Wieghat; my friends at LifeWay Christian Store in Tyler, Texas, and LifeWay Christian Resources in Nashville, Tennessee; my church family at Bethel Bible Church; and my reader friends on Facebook. I cannot possibly express to you how much I value your prayers.

To the retailers and suppliers who sell my books, the church and public libraries that make them available; and the many readers who have encouraged me with personal testimonies about how God has used my words to challenge and inspire them. He uses you to fuel the passion that keeps me creative.

To my agent, Joel Kneedler, at Alive Communications for being such an anchor. Thanks that I never have to wonder if you're looking out for my best interests.

To Cris Doornbos, Dan Rich, Don Pape, and the amazing staff at David C Cook Publishers for allowing me to partner with you in "transforming lives together." I'm so pleased and proud that I'll be writing another two trilogies under your umbrella!

And to my editor, Diane Noble, ever-flexible encourager extraordinaire, for affirming, suggesting, instructing, and inspiring. This go-round was a challenge that pulled our hearts and minds together, page after page. Thank you for your gentle and seemingly endless patience! Your suggested enhancements to this story proved immeasurable.

And to my husband, Paul, my partner and soul mate, for understanding so well the commitment it takes to write one series after another while juggling overlapping edits and deadlines. Thanks for never complaining that we share our home with such a demanding boarder. Were it not for your support, I could never write professionally.

And to the God of all comfort, who collects our tears and uses them to water our seeds of faith, use the words poured out on these pages to remind us of Your goodness and faithfulness.

PROLOGUE

"We live by faith, not by sight." 2 Corinthians 5:7

Jimmy Dale Oldham had never killed anything bigger than a June bug. Hunting was supposed to come as natural as breathing to every Arkansas boy. Not him. At least if he could hit his mark, the kill would be quick and clean and the animal wouldn't suffer. That might be the best he could hope for.

He took careful aim through the scope of the Winchester 94 .30-30 caliber rifle he'd inherited as his birthday present. He slowly squeezed the trigger, and an empty soup can popped off a log about fifty yards away. He pretended it was a feral hog. He'd never shot one but was convinced he could do it now. Maybe. He didn't dare give in to the revulsion he felt every time he saw his dad shoot and butcher wild game. Or admit how disappointed he was that this birthday present was not the smartphone he had hoped for.

Dad said that turning twelve was a rite of passage. And being given a rifle passed down for three generations was something special—especially since Winchester had stopped making this model. Grandpa and Dad had hunted with this rifle and downed every kind of wild game that roamed the Ozark Mountains—and had wall mounts to prove it.

Jimmy Dale ran his fingers along the smooth, polished wood handle. He had always admired the look of Daddy's prize Winchester and the respect it had earned from less-successful hunters who recognized his father's exceptional marksmanship. He was proud to make the rifle his. He just preferred not to shoot anything that breathed.

He glanced up at a red-tailed hawk flying away with something squirming in its talons. He wondered how long he could put off going with Daddy and Uncle Jake to hunt the sounder of feral hogs that were ruining crops, burrowing into lawns, and eating up all the wild turkey. There were plenty of boys his age who could shoot a pesky porker without thinking twice about it. Maybe once he did it a few times, he would toughen up and be like them. Then his dad would be proud of him. His stepdad sure wasn't.

Jimmy Dale stood erect, the afternoon sun browning his bare shoulders, and lifted the rifle. He took aim and ever so carefully squeezed the trigger. Another soup can popped off the log. Perfect. No squealing. No bleeding. Nothing to butcher. His kind of "kill." He fixed his gaze on an empty gallon milk jug set on a big rock near the tree line about a hundred yards away. He hadn't hit one—yet. But there was a first time for everything.

He took off his red cap, wiped the sweat off his forehead, then put the cap back on and raised his rifle. He got the plastic bottle in his sights and squeezed the trigger. Missed. He cocked the rifle and took another shot. Missed again.

He spit out a curse word he knew was grounds for his mom to wash out his mouth with soap. He discharged the empty shell and dug his heels into the dirt. Holding his breath, he took careful aim, his index finger positioned on the trigger—and squeezed. The plastic bottle didn't move. He hadn't even grazed it.

He threw his hat on the ground. He stank at this! How come girls never had to prove themselves this way? It wasn't fair. He gripped his rifle tight and trudged through a field thick with larkspur, primrose, Indian paintbrush, and black-eyed Susans. He stopped at the rock and reached out to snatch the milk jug and move it back fifty yards just as a deep voice bellowed from nearby in the woods.

"That's some wild shootin', boy!"

Jimmy Dale jumped, his heart beating like a scared rabbit's, and saw a silhouette of someone in the dark woods—it appeared to be a bearded man, a little girl clinging to him like a monkey.

"I thought I was alone out here," Jimmy Dale confessed, his face scalded with humiliation. "I'm pretty good at fifty yards but can't seem to hit anything beyond it. Name's Jimmy Dale Oldham. Folks call me J.D. I live over yonder about a mile." He nodded toward the west. "What's your name, mister?"

The bearded stranger didn't answer. He said something to the little girl and set her on her feet, then reached down to the ground and started dragging something across the forest floor and out into the light. It was an injured man, the front of his shirt soaked with blood.

The bearded stranger let go of the man's wrists. The guy's arms fell to the ground like lead weights, his face hidden by tall clumps of Indian paintbrush.

"You killed him." The bearded stranger locked gazes with Jimmy Dale.

"Me …?" Jimmy Dale struggled for a moment to find his voice. "I … I didn't see a soul out here. I wasn't aiming for him. Honest. I was just shooting at that milk carton."

"You missed."

"It was an accident."

"So you say."

"Is he really d-dead?" Jimmy Dale's knees began to wobble, and he couldn't bring himself to look at the body.

"Ain't got a pulse."

"I … I didn't mean to do it."

"He's just as dead either way. The law'll expect you to *pay* for what you done."

"Please, mister. I'll tell the sheriff it was an accident. You saw everything. You can tell him."

"All I seen was a man shot! I don't know nothin' about the why or how of it!" The stranger's gruff voice made his little girl whimper, and he shot her an admonishing look, his index finger to his lips.

Jimmy Dale took a step backward. He remembered hearing about another boy who shot and killed a man, was tried as an adult, and went to jail. How could this be happening to him? What would his parents say? His whole life might be over before his voice even changed. Or he got his driver's license. Or a smartphone. He glanced out across the field and wanted desperately to run. But the stranger knew his name and where to find him.

"Sir"—Jimmy Dale felt urine soak the front of his jeans—"I … I don't know what to do. I didn't mean any harm. I'll swear to it on the Bible. Please … you have to believe me. This man probably has a family. We should tell someone."

"I know him. He don't have kin."

The bearded stranger was about his dad's age. Piercing eyes. He wore denim overalls and no shirt. His arms were hairy, his biceps big and lumpy like Uncle Jake's.

"Go on home, boy." The stranger spoke softly now. "What's done is done. I'll see to him."

"What're you gonna do?" Jimmy Dale's heart pounded so hard he was sure his accuser could see his bare chest moving.

"Ain't your concern. Don't never speak of this to nobody, or I'll be forced to tell the sheriff what I know, and they'll throw you in jail till you're an old man. Now go on. Git! Keep your mouth shut, and don't never come back here."

"I won't. I promise." Jimmy Dale turned on his heel, holding tightly to the murder weapon, and raced full throttle across the open field, wildflowers flattening under the thrusting blows of his Nikes, his rush of adrenaline fueled by fear and shame. If only he hadn't tried to hit the stupid target at a hundred yards! His birthday rifle had been used for decades to put food on the table and trophies on the wall, and now he'd put a man down with it. His dad would be devastated if he ever found out his son had killed a man. He couldn't let that happen.

Jimmy Dale fell on his knees when he reached the place where he had fired the fatal shot and retched until his lunch came up. He found his cap and put it on, then looked back at the tree line. The bearded stranger and the little girl were gone. So was the body. Nothing Jimmy Dale could say or do would bring the man back to life. All he could do now was try to forget it happened and hope the stranger did the same.

CHAPTER 1

Abby Cummings floated in the opaque gray fog that separated slumber from wakefulness. The buzz of her alarm clock would soon fill the silence. She would have to open her eyes and face the day she'd been dreading for weeks. Why was it still traumatic after five years? Everyone told her that time heals all wounds. Not hers. And especially not today.

She turned on her side and stole a glance at the clock before clamping her eyes shut again. Four forty-five. She still had thirty minutes. She hugged the same pillow that had faithfully muffled her anguished sobs and despairing cries, and had been pummeled with her blows of helplessness. Not that using her pillow to vent had ever made her feel better. Or stopped the torment of living without closure. But it had afforded her a private place to deal with raw emotion without feeling judged for it.

Her family seldom talked about what had happened anymore. But the past lurked in the shadows, uttering the same relentless litany of questions for which only God had answers. The anniversary always brought it back with bone-chilling clarity.

Abby sighed and sat up, rubbing her eyes and letting her legs dangle over the side of the bed. She turned on the lamp and glanced at the empty toddler bed across the room, still made up with a pink-and-white fitted quilt. She could almost see the tiny figure that once occupied it, cheeks rosy with sleep, a smile twitching the corner of her mouth as a sweet dream danced through her mind.

She ached for those tender moments of cuddling with her sister and singing lullabies. Riley Jo's curls always smelled like baby shampoo and seemed softer than the shared pillow that cradled their heads.

Abby swallowed the sting in her throat and told herself not to cry. She needed to be brave today. Her mother would be more fragile than usual—not that she would admit it to anyone.

Abby slid out of bed and onto the wood floor. She stepped over to her dresser, opened the top drawer, and carefully removed a small white-satin box. She took out the gold heart ring with a tiny diamond she'd received for her tenth birthday and held it in her palm. She pressed the ring to her cheek and closed her eyes, remembering the sound of her father's voice.

"You'll always be my princess," Daddy said, sliding the heart ring on her finger. *"Even when you're all grown up and some handsome and brilliant young man convinces you to marry him ... "*

The blaring alarm clock stole the sweetness of the moment, and Abby rushed over and turned it off. She let her racing pulse settle down and held the ring to the light once more, blinking back her tears. Finally, she returned the precious keepsake to the satin box and tucked it in the corner of her drawer. Not even happy memories would ease the angst of reliving this painful, life-changing day for a fifth time. She just wanted to get it behind her.

She picked up her khakis and Angel View staff shirt from the over-stuffed chair next to her bed and pushed herself toward the bathroom.

It would be a tough day to get through. Working would help. But she wasn't going to pretend it was just another day, even if the rest of her family did.

❧

Abby hurried along the glass wall at Flutter's Cafe, balancing a tray of empty breakfast dishes on one palm, the sadness in her heart soothed by the magnificent lava-colored sky visible as far as the eye could see. Sunrays fanned out from the golden rim separating earth and sky and turned the blanket of fog on Beaver Lake a glowing shade of pink—

Abby felt a jolt, and then the tray flew from her hand and landed with a deafening crash. Glass shattered. Silverware clanked on the stone floor. Her cheeks flushed as she stared at her mother.

Kate Cummings scanned the broken dishes, a look of realization replacing her blank stare. "That door really whacked you. Let me see." She gently brushed the hair off Abby's forehead and looked for any sign of injury. "You're going to have a bump, honey. But it's not bleeding. How do you feel?"

"My pride hurts a lot worse than my head." Abby felt her cheeks warm as she imagined customers staring. "What about you?"

"Yes, yes, I'm fine."

Her mother smoothed her neatly coiffed hair that was almost as gray as it was auburn, then straightened the Angel View owner-manager name tag she had worn ever since Abby could remember.

"Sorry, Mama. You can take it out of my paycheck."

"I'm not going to dock you." Her mother smiled, though her eyes looked tired and sad. "Just be careful."

"The sunrise was awesome, and for a moment I almost forgot … anyhow, it won't happen again."

Her mother seemed to go a little pale at the reminder. Abby ducked down to pick up the silverware and broken dinnerware.

"Don't fool with that, honey. You'll cut yourself." Mama reached for her arm and pulled her to her feet.

Abby avoided eye contact. It was impossible to hide her feelings, and it seemed obvious that her mother was working hard to contain her own.

Savannah Surette, her ponytail swaying from side to side, hurried over to them. "Here, boss," she said to Mama. "Let me get that. I'll fetch the broom and have this cleaned up in no time."

"Thanks." Her mother glanced over at the bustling dining room and then out the window at the June sunrise that painted the clouds covering the lake. "I'm sure the guests hardly noticed our little mishap—not with a view like *that*."

"That's fuh shore," Savannah said. "The bayou was pretty, and we had oodles of fog, but we didn't have Angel View Lodge. First time I've ever lived in a place where I could look *down* on the clouds. Takes my breath away."

"You and Benson are a great addition to our staff."

"You mean for a couple of crazy Cajuns who talk funny?" Savannah laughed. "We do love it here." She looked down at the mess again. "I'll be right back."

Mama put her arm around Abby. "I'm glad you weren't hurt."

"Sorry for the hassle. I'm a little *off* today." Abby waited, longing for her mother to say something—anything—to acknowledge the anniversary.

"Well, an Angel View sunrise can distract the best of us." Her mother's cheery demeanor belied the heaviness in her voice. She wet her finger and wiped something off Abby's cheek. "It's a good thing that Beaver Lake is beautiful in every season. Mother Nature draws the guests. All we have to do is make them comfortable."

"You sounded like Daddy just then."

"I'm surprised you remember details like that after all this time."

"I do. And I remember the last time I heard his voice was five years ago *today*."

Mama flinched ever so slightly, and Abby could almost hear the dead bolt slide across the door of her heart. "I'm well aware of what day this is." She seemed to stare at nothing, her eyes watering. "I'm glad you find comfort in remembering. I don't."

"Don't you ever wonder if Daddy and Riley Jo are still alive?"

"I accepted a long time ago that they're not coming back. Maybe one of these days we'll find out what happened so we can put it to rest."

Abby bit her lip. "People still gossip. Why don't you defend Daddy?"

Her mother ran her thumb across the diamond wedding band she still wore. "We've been through this, Abby. My being defensive won't stop the gossip. Or change anyone's mind. Gossip is pure poison, and there are always casualties."

"Well, I refuse to be a casualty." Abby folded her arms across her chest. "I'm the only one in this family who ever defends Daddy."

"And has defending him put a stop to the talk?"

"At least everyone knows where *I* stand."

Mama tilted Abby's chin and looked her squarely in the eyes. "There's a pain so deep in me, there're no words for it. But I don't feel obligated to discuss my private thoughts with anyone."

"Because you have doubts?"

"Because I *don't*. Now drop it."

"Yes, ma'am." Abby set her lips in a straight line and turned away.

"It's hard enough getting through each day without them," Mama said. "It doesn't help when my own daughter criticizes me for the way I handle my grief. I can only be what I am. I can't live in the past, even if people in town are still whispering about it. I've put it behind me the best I can."

Well, I haven't. Abby looked back into her mother's pretty face and sad blue eyes, wishing she hadn't brought it up.

Savannah came out of the kitchen, carrying a large plastic bucket, a broom, a mop, and a dustpan. "Benson said to tell y'all that he's making gumbo and cornbread for today's lunch special. That oughta make your taste buds stand up and sing."

"Everything he's made so far *has*," Mama said. "I'm enjoying adding a little Cajun flair to our Ozark cuisine."

As Abby left the conversation, she glanced out at the tinted fog on the lake, powerless to shake the heavy, ominous, unsettling feeling that she had anticipated would descend on this day. The only thing harder to bear than the unanswered questions was the fact that her mother had stopped asking them.

Buck Winters sat with a friend at Flutter's Café and observed his granddaughter taking the breakfast order of the folks at table six. Even though Abby was pleasant, he could tell that the smile she wore was strictly professional. She was probably embarrassed and upset about the earlier mishap.

Abby liked to please. And Kate had high expectations of everyone on staff, including her kids. Probably because Kate and Micah had built Angel View Lodge from the ground up and invested so much of themselves. Since Micah's disappearance, it had become almost a monument to his memory.

Buck's gaze followed his granddaughter as she tended to customers. Abby was so much like Kate at sixteen, her hair long and thick and the color of an Irish setter. Deep blue eyes. Fair skin and a natural blush to her cheeks. Cute figure. Sweet from the inside out. It was both a wonder and a blessing that she didn't have a serious boyfriend to complicate her young life. One more year of high school—and then she would be off to college.

"Where'd you go, Buck?" Titus Jackson said. "You seem miles away."

Buck lowered his gaze and peered over the top of his glasses at the retired history professor who reminded him of Sidney Poitier. "Sorry, Titus. I was thinkin' about Abby. Seems like yesterday she wore her hair in pigtails and I carried her on my shoulders down to our favorite fishin' hole." He chuckled. "And I'd hate to guess how many times I put the arms and legs back on that baby doll she just wouldn't part with."

Titus took a sip of coffee. "And now she's lost interest in the doll and the fishing?"

Buck smiled. "At least she's not boy crazy. That's one headache we don't have yet. She hangs out with Jay Rogers, a real nice kid from school, but they're just friends."

"I imagine it's hard on Kate, raising Abby, Hawk, and Jesse without the love and support of a husband."

"It helps havin' her dad livin' with her," Buck said. "I do what I can. But it's hard on those kids growin' up without a dad. I'd give anything to see Micah walk through that door with Riley Jo and put an end to this nightmare. In case you didn't know, it was five years ago today that they disappeared."

Titus ran his finger around the rim of his cup. "I didn't know y'all when they went missing, but it's easy to see the painful effects of it. Mind if I ask you a personal question?"

"Go ahead."

"Did the sheriff ever have a lead in the case?"

Buck shook his head. "Micah and Riley Jo just seemed to vanish. Micah's truck was still parked in the driveway. Kate was the only family member around that afternoon. I'd taken Jesse to a movie, and Hawk was workin' at the lumber company. Abby'd spent the night with a friend but called to check in that morning. I was sittin' in the kitchen at the time. Micah answered, and they had a right cute exchange. Before they hung up, Micah said he'd see her at dinner. Sure sounded to me like he planned to be home."

"So Kate was the last person to see Micah and Riley Jo?"

"As far as we know. Micah came into the office and told Kate he was takin' Riley Jo fishin'. Kate was busy and didn't see them leave. None of the guests did either, which I found kinda odd.

Sheriff's deputies searched the path to the lake and combed the woods around it. Never found any sign of them."

"Has anyone else disappeared?"

"Nope. I suppose you've heard the rumors."

Titus shrugged. "I've heard a few oddballs say Bigfoot got them—or aliens. And I've heard others say Micah ran off with another woman and took Riley Jo with him. I'd rather know what you think."

"Thanks for that. Speculation's been hurtful. Truth is, Kate and Micah had been fussin' at each other for a couple weeks over a business issue they disagreed on. The sheriff had to consider the possibility that Micah left her. Never rang true with me. But you never really know what's goin' on inside a person either."

"Any idea why he'd take his youngest daughter with him?"

Buck wrapped his hands around his coffee cup. "All I can figure is Riley Jo was the only one of his kids young enough to forget the past. She'd be able to adapt to his new life. But even if he wanted out of the marriage, I can't see Micah bein' cruel enough to take Kate's baby girl away from her."

"So this is what the rumor mill's been feeding off of all this time?"

"No. Kate and me and the sheriff are the only ones who know they were havin' a squabble." Buck stroked his mustache. "Gossip started flyin' after a couple town busybodies thought they *might've* spotted Micah and Riley Jo at the corner of Main and Cleveland, gettin' into a car with some blonde woman. Of course, neither of them can describe the car or the woman. And, at the busiest intersection in town, no one else saw them. But as time went on, the story got enhanced. I'm sure some folks believe it."

CHAPTER 2

Kate went out the front entrance of Angel View Lodge, the morning sun high and the fog now dissipated. She walked across the road and spotted her son Jesse on the porch of their two-story log house, his red wagon parked at the bottom of the steps and filled with plastic jugs.

"Hi, Mama!" Jesse bounded down the steps and ran toward her. "Hawk and I loaded the wagon with nectar for the hummingbirds."

Jesse came to an abrupt stop and threw his arms around her waist. "Thanks for trusting me with this. I won't let you down."

"I never thought you would." Kate brushed his fine dark hair out of his eyes, noting that the smattering of freckles across his nose and cheeks seemed to have multiplied from exposure to the sun. "I have every confidence in you, or I wouldn't have put you in charge of the hummingbirds for the summer. It's a big job. And I wouldn't let just anyone do it. You know how I love them."

"Me, too. I'll make sure they *never* run out of nectar. I promise!" Jesse's eyes were round and animated, the color of the summer sky.

"I'm proud of you for the effort you're putting into this."

Jesse puffed out his skinny chest, as if to show off the word staff embroidered above the pocket of his bright blue Angel View Lodge T-shirt. "I Googled so much stuff about the ruby-throated hummingbird, I should be able to answer any questions the guests ask me. I'm the go-to guy, right?"

"Absolutely." Kate smiled. Micah would be so proud of him. It broke her heart that Jesse could hardly remember his father.

"I'd better get going. I have a ton of feeders to fill." Jesse hugged her waist again and ran toward the wagon. "See you later, Mama."

"I love you," she called.

"Love you, too! Bye!"

Kate watched as Jesse took the wagon by the handle and headed for the hummingbird garden, looking oh-so-grown-up and responsible. Had she contributed to that, or was he just a great kid all on his own? She worried whether Micah and Riley Jo's disappearance would cause any long-term effects in Jessie, who had been just five when they went missing. Half his life, he'd been living with that loss and a mother consumed with grief.

Kate heard the screen door slam and glanced up. Hawk stood on the porch, slipping his arms into the straps of his backpack.

Kate walked up the steps. "Thanks for helping your brother. He is beyond excited."

"Doesn't take much to float *his* boat," Hawk Cummings said.

"Why the sarcasm? A word of encouragement from his big brother would go a long way."

"I did encourage him. I just think you're making too much of it."

Kate eyed her oldest son. "You sound *jealous*."

"It's nothing like that, Mama. But y'all are acting like Jesse's the only one who does anything around here."

"I'm sorry if I gave that impression. You've done so much, I wouldn't know where to begin. I'm not sure I would have survived the past five years without your help. You've stepped up and done your father proud. I *have* told you that."

Hawk hung his head, his expression sheepish. "I guess that sounded petty. Jesse's really jazzed about being a part of what we're doing here. He wants to prove himself."

Kate tilted Hawk's chin, still not used to the five o'clock shadow that matched his buzz cut. "It's not as though I'm creating busy-work for him. Having Jesse taking care of the hummers will help me immensely. I'd like to think we would all build him up."

"You know I will." Hawk glanced at his watch. "Gotta run. I've got three drivers already out there, and I'm scheduled to take out a dad and his two boys at ten."

"Hawk ..." Kate waited until he looked at her. "I hope you know I'm proud of you for pulling together the details to launch the jeep-rides operation. I would never have thought of such a thing, let alone that it would become a huge draw, even for folks who don't stay at Angel View. It's helped keep us in the black."

Hawk smiled with his eyes. "I love it. I can't imagine working for someone else and punching a time clock."

"You do better when you can set your own schedule. This suits you."

"Good. Because I'm never leaving Sure Foot Mountain."

She hoped that was true, more than she dared say. For some reason she couldn't explain, she felt vulnerable every time Hawk was away on a hiking or hunting trip. "Then you'd better marry a girl who loves it as much as you do."

"Marry?" Hawk cocked his head and flashed his father's grin. "I'm barely twenty-one. Don't be trying to marry me off just yet."

"*I'm* in no hurry. I think you have to start dating first anyway."

"I'm too busy getting the jeep business going. I've got plenty of time for that later."

"Not if you're interested in that cute little blonde at Bella's Bakery. Some other young man is liable to snatch her out from under your nose."

Hawk threw his hands in the air. "Did Abby tell you I had my eye on Laura Lynn Parks?"

"So it *is* true."

"I'd have to be blind not to notice her," Hawk said. "She wouldn't give me the time of day."

"How do you know if you don't ask her out?"

"Chicks like that can date any guy they want."

Kate put her hands on her hips. "And how do you know she doesn't want to date you?"

"Guess I'm too chicken to find out. I don't want to get shot down."

"Hawk Cummings, since when are you afraid of anything? So what if she says no? There are plenty of fish in the sea."

"Fish?" A smile tugged at the corners of Hawk's mouth. "We're talking mermaid here."

Kate and Hawk laughed at the same time.

"Granted, she's a beautiful girl," Kate said, thinking it should be Micah having this conversation with Hawk. "But don't underestimate yourself. You're handsome, inside and out. Smart. Creative. Hardworking. Polite. And, I dare say, a tad romantic like your father."

Hawk grinned and put on his sunglasses. "I've really gotta run, Mama. I'll be home in time for dinner."

"Be safe," Kate said, painfully aware that those were the words she had withheld from Micah before he and Riley Jo vanished.

CHAPTER 3

Abby left Flutter's Café and went down one flight of stairs to the outdoor cedar deck that ran along the entire length of Angel View Lodge. Guests sat at round tables, shaded by colorful green-and-white striped umbrellas, enjoying a postcard view of Beaver Lake and the rolling Ozark Mountains. The fog had burned off, and the lake sparkled in the noonday sun like a million blue sapphires. She only wished her spirits matched the brilliance of the day.

She descended another flight of stairs to the ground level, not surprised to see her friend Jay Rogers waiting for her, his smile warmer than the cedar railing, her gray-and-white cat perched on his shoulder.

"I see Halo thumbed a ride again," Abby said, running her hand across the ring of white fur on the cat's head.

"I never mind giving her a lift," Jay said. "So are you done for the day?"

"No. I'm working the dinner shift. It's catfish night, and the place will be hopping. But I'm off until five."

"I'm not scheduled in at Tutty's till four." Jay stroked Halo's tail. "You wanna take the paddleboat out? I know this is a hard day for you. We don't have to talk about it or anything."

"Thanks. I'd love to get my mind on something else." Abby held out her pale arms. "And I'd like to get a tan before the weather turns hot. I need to change clothes and grab something to eat first."

"Why don't I go get sub sandwiches and meet you at the dock?" Jay set the cat down. "You want your usual turkey, lettuce-and-tomato, black olives, and jalapenos on whole wheat?"

Abby smiled. "Don't forget the chocolate chip cookies."

"Or the Sun Chips?" Jay laughed, and Abby felt her burden lighten. Being with her best friend would help her get through the rest of the day.

Jay looked at his watch. "See you on the pier in about fifteen minutes?"

"I'll be there." Abby walked toward the log house and glanced over her shoulder. "Remember to have them put hot mustard on my half."

"Yes, ma'am. I'll make sure it's exactly as you ordered. I'll even get you the Coke you forgot to mention."

Abby grinned and kept walking.

❖

Abby followed half a dozen guests down the earthen path that led to Angel View Pier, a habit she had adopted five years earlier when her mother insisted there was safety in numbers, and it was unnecessary to walk it alone when there were dozens of guests coming and going all the time. Though her mother never said so, Abby knew she was afraid that whatever had happened to Daddy and Riley Jo could happen to any of them.

She spotted Jay standing on the pier and waved. She politely squeezed past the guests, skipped down the stone steps at the end of the path, and hurried over to him.

Jay held up a sack with the Sammie's Subs logo on the front. "I've got lunch. The paddleboat's ready."

Abby climbed in, and Jay settled into the seat next to hers. They pedaled in reverse until they were away from the dock, and then turned toward Egret Island and pedaled at a relaxed pace.

Jay's sandy hair blew gently in the breeze, his shadowy beard just visible enough to make him seem older than seventeen. "The lake's tame today."

"That can change on a dime."

Jay looked up at the bluebird sky, a silly grin stretching his cheeks. "Oh, I'm sure there could be a thunderhead out there *somewhere* between here and Jamaica. Why are you always looking for trouble?"

"Just habit," Abby said. "I was raised to be cautious."

"Yeah," he said knowingly. "Well, there's no cause for worry out here. It's just us, the birds, and the breeze, and the good Lord smiling down on us."

Abby breathed in deeply and let it out. "Did you happen to catch the sunrise this morning?"

"I wasn't up that early."

"I got so caught up in it that I ran smack dab into that swinging door to the kitchen just as my mother was coming out. Made a huge mess. Not exactly a great beginning to an already-hard-enough day."

"For both of you."

"Mama keeps her feelings in check better than I do." Abby shifted her gaze to the dragonfly that landed on the steering wheel. "Speaking of mothers, did yours ever decide when she's getting married?"

"Soon. She and Number Four are flying to Vegas on Monday. Guess I'll have to get used to the idea of her being Mrs. Richie Stump." Jay shook his head. "I'm just glad I don't have to change names every time she does."

"I can't believe this is the fourth time you've been through it. Has to be hard."

"What's hard is not having a close relationship with my real dad. We don't have much in common."

"You're his son. How much more 'in common' can you get?"

Jay looked out toward the island, his gaze intense. "I don't think he knows what to do with me. He's remarried and has three other sons that are more like him, into macho stuff. I feel like the odd man out."

"Do you get along with your stepbrothers?"

"I guess. I spend holidays with my dad's family, but I don't really belong. And Mom's life is a revolving door. About the time I get attached to a new stepdad, he leaves. And when I spend time with my real dad, I get the feeling he's just doing his duty."

"Dads are important," Abby said.

"I guess we both have a big void there."

This was too heavy a subject. Especially today.

Abby pulled the sandwiches out of the bag and handed Jay his half. She unwrapped hers partway, said a silent prayer of thanksgiving, and took a bite. "I'm glad you thought of this."

Jay tilted back his head and closed his eyes as if relishing the feel of the sun and breeze on his face. "There's no one else I'd rather be with. You're not like most girls."

"Is that supposed to be a compliment?"

"Yeah. I'm completely at ease with you. I don't have to be a jock. Or good-looking. Or say the right thing. Or impress your girlfriends. There's no real agenda, other than enjoying your company. Plus you're a good listener. I can just be myself when I'm with you."

"Same here. And we agreed not to spoil it by *what*?"

Jay laughed and opened his eyes. "Don't worry. I'm not going to come on to you. I like things the way they are."

Abby took a sip of Coke, glad she didn't have to worry about the boy-girl thing complicating their friendship. But despite Jay's welcome presence, the heaviness of the day hadn't left her—neither had the selfish fear she couldn't bring herself to tell anyone, not even him.

"You okay?" Jay said.

I doubt I'll ever be okay. Abby nodded and looked out toward the island. "I just need to get through today."

CHAPTER 4

The next day, just after noon, Abby parallel-parked her mother's blue Honda Odyssey in front of Salisbury's Supermarket. Foggy Ridge was bustling with activity. Neon signs had been turned on in shop windows. And the parking lots of eating establishments along Main Street were filled to overflowing with the after-church crowd.

Abby got out of the car, the words to "Above All" continuing to play in her head hours after she had attended the early-morning service at Praise Chapel. It hurt her to think of God's Son "like a rose trampled on the ground." It was that image that had softened her heart toward Him. It had been almost six months since she walked the aisle and made a profession of faith. Her mother had tried to be supportive, in a detached sort of way, but it was obvious she had abdicated the role of spiritual leader to Grandpa Buck. The days of the family going to church together had long passed. It was just Abby and her grandfather now.

Abby looked up and down Main Street. It was alive. Breathing. As if it had a heartbeat of its own. Magnificent shade trees lined the sidewalk on either side, branches intermingling overhead to form a green basket weave so thick that only glints of sunlight filtered through. On both sides of the busy boulevard stood a row of quaint two-story buildings, some brick and some natural stone, many with modern facades and creative signs designed to draw tourists.

She spotted Mrs. Sanchez, last year's Spanish teacher, across the street at Rocky Springs Park, pushing a baby carriage, flanked by two black-haired girls in pink dresses. Funny how seldom Abby thought of her teachers having a personal life.

Near a mossy rock wall, just inside the park entrance, about a dozen men and women stood in line, holding empty containers, waiting for their turn to fill up with pure spring water.

An African-American couple sat together on a park bench facing the carousel, with their three little boys, who were eating blue cotton candy.

Nearby, two pesky grackles played tug-of-war with a wrapper of some kind, seemingly oblivious to a pair of teenaged skateboarders who zoomed past.

A young woman and a blond, curly-haired boy, each carrying a rolled-up towel, turned into the park and walked in the direction of the public swimming pool. And coming from the opposite direction was Mr. Chang, proudly riding his power chair and throwing out seed for the pigeons.

Abby had no agenda, other than not letting yesterday's grim anniversary steal another day. She stuck her cell phone in the pocket of her sundress, hoping Jay would call and suggest they do something fun and adventurous. A sudden hankering for cookie-dough ice cream prodded her up Main Street toward Sweet Stuff.

Tourists moved in all directions, cameras strapped around their necks. Angel View Lodge was just minutes away, but it was like another world down here.

As Abby passed Murchison's Feed Store, she spotted a girl sitting on the bench next to the wooden Indian chief out front. The child appeared to be about six or seven. Braided dark hair and almond-shaped eyes.

Abby's heart nearly stopped.

The child was the spitting image of Riley Jo—only older. The little girl smiled shyly and waved. Without even thinking, Abby took her phone out of her pocket and snapped a picture. And then another. Her pulse surged.

She stood frozen in the middle of the sidewalk, people squeezing past her, grumbling for her to move. But she couldn't move. She could barely breathe.

Abby kept her gaze fixed on the little girl, who smiled at her again. Was it possible? Could it be?

The door to the feed store opened, and a fortysomething man with a mousy beard, dressed in overalls and a sleeveless T-shirt, came outside and grabbed the girl by the arm, swatted her behind, then pulled her inside.

Abby turned and walked briskly to her car, her heart racing. Shouldn't she have tried to get a closer look at the girl? Find out who the man was? Ask some questions? This was too important to dismiss without knowing more. Maybe they were still there.

She turned around and hurried back to Murchison's, pushed open the glass door, and breezed up and down every aisle—and then did it again. No sign of the little girl or the man.

Abby went outside and looked in both directions on Main Street. How far could they have gone so quickly?

She stepped off the curb and jogged over to the park, moving her gaze from person to person. They weren't there. She made her way up the block, looking in shops and eating places on both sides of Main Street. Finally she gave up and went back to her car and sat.

She took out her phone and looked at the two pictures she had taken. Only one had turned out, and she enlarged it to see what color the girl's eyes were. Blue! Abby felt chill bumps on her arms. The resemblance was uncanny.

Abby burst into the log house and shouted for her mother.

Hawk came out of the kitchen. "What's *your* problem?"

"Where's Mama?"

"Over at the office."

Abby turned and rushed out of the house, down the porch steps, and across the street. She raced over to the main building and felt a rush of cold air when she opened the door. She nodded at the day manager, went back to the offices, and stood in the open doorway, trying to catch her breath.

Her mother looked up from the computer, a puzzled expression on her face. "What is it, Abby?"

"I need to show you something." Abby hurried over to where her mother was sitting. "I was in town and saw this little girl. I nearly freaked out."

Abby held up her phone and displayed the picture of the girl.

Mama stared at the image on the phone without saying anything.

"Well …?" Abby said. "Don't you think she looks like Riley Jo?"

"Lots of little girls have similar features and coloring."

"Mama, look at that face. She's even the right age."

Her mother's eyes flashed a flicker of hope that was quickly extinguished. "Abby, you have to stop this. How many times has this happened? Twice? Three times? It's been five years. You need to accept that she's gone."

"But aren't you even curious? What if it's—"

"There's no way it's Riley Jo."

"I saw a man come out of Murchison's and swat her behind. He pulled her inside before I could get a closer look. As soon as I got my wits about me, I went into Murchison's and tried to find them. But they were gone. I looked in the park and every shop and restaurant along Main—all the way to First and back. But I didn't see them."

Mama turned a pencil upside down and bounced the eraser on her desk. "This isn't healthy. Maybe it's time you went back to see Dixie. There's no shame in getting more counseling."

"I don't need counseling," Abby said, more loudly than she intended. "I need the *truth*."

"Well, we're not going to get the truth! The sooner you accept that, the happier you'll be. What happened to Riley Jo and your father is a mystery and will likely never be resolved. We just have to accept it and move on."

"I can't," Abby said. "I won't!"

Mama threw her hands in the air. "I can't force you to accept it. But *I* have. And I simply can't be part of your false hope. I don't want to hear any more about this."

"Like you ever did."

"That's enough, young lady. One more disrespectful comment and you'll find yourself grounded."

Abby put her phone in her pocket. "Don't worry. I won't mention it to you again." *Ever!*

Abby turned on her heel and left the office. She went to look for Grandpa Buck.

"Why is everyone being so weird about this?" Abby looked across the kitchen table at her grandfather, who was studying the photo of the little girl. He handed her cell phone back to her.

"I didn't realize I was actin' weird," Grandpa Buck said. "But I agree with your mother, honey. The chance that it was Riley Jo is next to impossible."

"*Next to* impossible—not impossible. You said yourself that nothing is impossible with God. Now that I finally believe that, are you saying it's not true?"

"That's not what I'm sayin', Abby. And I think you know it." Grandpa stroked his white mustache. "Let's pretend for a moment that this was Riley Jo. What would she be doin' in Foggy Ridge?"

Abby shrugged. "Don't you think we should find out?"

"How?"

"Go to the sheriff."

"And tell him what?" Grandpa looked over the top of his glasses. "That you saw another girl that looks like you *think* your sister would look now? Where do you suggest he start lookin'? The sheriff's department has spent more money and manpower on this case than any in the town's history. They're not gonna take kindly to any more wild-goose chases."

"Is that what you think this is?" Abby's eyes burned with tears. "Grandpa, you should've seen her. The picture doesn't do her justice. It could've been Riley Jo. I can't just ignore that."

"And I'm not sayin' you should. But this has happened before, and I know that neither the sheriff nor the police chief is gonna start another investigation without somethin' more concrete to go on."

Abby heard someone laughing and turned.

Hawk stood leaning on the kitchen doorway, his arms folded across his chest, an irritating smirk curling his lips. "You're hallucinating again, Sis. The next stop is the loony bin."

"That's enough," Grandpa said. "Abby wasn't talking to you."

"How long have you been standing there eavesdropping?" Abby didn't bother to hide her annoyance.

"Long enough." Hawk came into the kitchen and stood holding the back of an empty chair. "All the wishful thinking in the world isn't going to bring Daddy and Riley Jo home again. And this kind of talk is really upsetting to Mama."

"You think I'm trying to upset her?" Abby handed him the cell phone. "Take a close look. Are you going to stand there and honestly say that if you had seen this little girl, you wouldn't have given her a double take—and wondered if it could be Riley Jo?"

"That's exactly what I'm saying." Hawk slid the cell phone back across the table to Abby. "Riley Jo's either dead or she's somewhere far away with Daddy. Either way, she's not going to show up in Foggy Ridge. You're the only one who doesn't get that."

Abby pushed back her chair and stood. "Laugh at me all you want. But I'm going to find out who this girl is."

CHAPTER 5

Abby sat cross-legged on her bed, staring at the cell phone picture of the Riley Jo look-alike she had seen at Murchison's and still stinging from Hawk's remarks.

A knock on the door startled her.

"It's Jesse. Can I come in?"

"I guess," Abby said.

Jesse opened the door and closed it, then flopped onto the bed. "Whatcha doing?"

"*Not* talking about the girl I saw."

"Hawk says it can't be Riley Jo."

"Hawk says a lot of things. Doesn't make him right. Why are you here?"

Jesse bit his lip and didn't answer.

Abby softened her tone.

"What's wrong? You can tell me."

Jesse toyed with the hem of his T-shirt. "Hawk said God is a joke, and the sooner I realize it, the better off I'll be." He glanced over at her. "Do you think that?"

Wow. She hadn't seen that coming. "You know I don't. It took me until six months ago to figure it out for myself. But God is real, Jesse. He's no joke. And He's with us every minute."

"Hawk said if God was good, He wouldn't allow all the suffering in the world."

"And I think if Adam and Eve had obeyed God, there wouldn't *be* any suffering. Evil changed everything, and lots of bad things happen now. But God is still good. He hasn't changed and never will."

Jesse slid off the bed and faced her. "So you don't think He's mean for letting Daddy and Riley Jo disappear?"

"I wish they hadn't disappeared. But I don't blame God. People—good and bad—make their own choices. Sometimes those choices hurt other people. But if God controlled every move we make, we would all be puppets. I wouldn't like that. Would you?"

Jesse pushed his hands deeper into the pockets of his khaki shorts. "Do you think Mama would be mad if I went to church with you and Grandpa?"

"I doubt it. I think she wishes she could trust God again."

"Do *you* trust Him?"

Abby paused to think, feeling totally unprepared for Jesse's probing questions. "I'm learning. The Bible says we should live by faith and not by sight. I think that means when we're in the dark, we have to take a step forward and trust that there will be light on the path in front of us."

Jesse cocked his head, his eyebrows furrowed. "What?"

"Okay, imagine God holding a flashlight so the beam shines on the ground in front of us. We can only see so far, but we keeping walking, trusting Him to move the light in front of us with each step we take. We get as much light as we need to keep moving, but we still can't see down the road."

"I get it."

"I'm thrilled you want to go to church with us."

Jesse flashed a toothy grin that would soon keep another orthodontist in business. "I was in the attic and found the Bible storybook Daddy used to read to me and Riley Jo. I took it to my room and read the whole thing. Did you know there was a donkey that *talked*? And water that turned into wine? My favorite story is the one about three guys with weird names who got thrown into a fiery furnace and didn't burn up because they trusted God. So cool!"

Abby nodded. "Shadrach, Meshach, and Abednego. I love that story too. What's also amazing is that they told the king they would trust God even if He *didn't* save them. I'd love to have that kind of faith. I don't yet."

"It only has to be the size of a mustard seed to move a mountain." Jesse smiled proudly. "Told you I read the book."

Abby stood and hugged her brother. "Go tell Grandpa what you just told me. I'm excited." And she was scared. She knew her faith might impact Jesse for the rest of his life. Had she said the right thing? Was she prepared to be an example? What if she failed?

Jesse raced to the door, then turned and looked at her, his eyes twinkling with trust and admiration. "Thanks, Abby."

He went out the door and pulled it closed behind him.

Kate glanced at the framed family portrait on her dresser, reality sending pain to every nerve in her soul. How different life had been back then, when Micah and Riley Jo were home and the Cummings family was whole and happy. It was hard enough dealing with the unknowns of the disappearance without Abby coming home again with a random photo of some little girl she imagined could be her baby sister.

Would this nightmare ever be over? Each time Kate thought she had moved forward, something would happen to drag her back into the grief and the aching loss that was almost paralyzing.

There had been no closure. No coffins. No headstones. No explanation. Her life was on hold—indefinitely. She couldn't go forward or backward. She was stuck somewhere in the middle.

She held out her hand and looked at her wedding ring. Was she still married—or widowed? Not that she could ever love another man the way she loved Micah. But if he was dead, she wanted to know, wanted to give him a proper burial and move on with her life. As much as she wished to believe her husband and daughter would come home one day, it hurt too much to cling to such hope.

Maybe they *were* in heaven with God—though she wasn't sure anymore if God existed. At least not the God she had once loved. The God she had walked with. Had worshipped and adored. If He was real, then He had repaid her devotion with cruelty. Kate sighed. Or was it possible that all things holy were mythical? And that evil was no respecter of persons? She didn't have the energy to figure it out. Her father had encouraged her to get into a support group. To what avail? The last thing she wanted to do was talk about the uncertainty she lived with every moment of every day. Either Micah and Riley Jo had fallen prey to some vile murderer or wild animal—or Micah had voluntarily taken their youngest child and chosen to vanish. Either truth was intolerable.

Her mind flashed back to that last time she had been with Micah …

Kate heard a knock on the open door and looked up from her desk.

"Sorry to interrupt," Micah said. "I'm taking Riley Jo down to the pier so she can catch some perch."

"Did you put sunscreen on her?" Kate asked.

"Total sunblock. No chance of sunburn on that delicate skin." Micah walked over and stood next to her desk. "Kate, I'm sorry I snapped at you earlier. But I think this potential investment deserves a closer look before you just slam the door shut on it."

"You know I'm not comfortable with *anything* risky."

"Chad's the one who brought it up," Micah said. "He's done a pretty sound job of putting together our portfolio up to now. Why so much resistance? He feels this is something we should do. We're only talking about moving fifteen percent for the short term."

"I don't feel good about it."

"And you base this on …?"

Kate felt her face get hot. "Call it women's intuition. Discernment. Gut feeling. Opinion. Fear. Common sense. Whatever name you want to put to it. I just don't think we should put that much money in a risky investment."

"Chad will watch it carefully. He's not going to mislead us. The lodge is barely breaking even, and we can't keep putting off making improvements. This is our chance to give the operation a shot in the arm *without* having to borrow."

Kate shook her head. "We've worked too long and too hard, just getting Angel View in the black. I don't want to take that much out of bonds."

"Even if we could double our investment?"

"What if we lose?"

"Chad feels this is practically a sure thing."

"*Practically* isn't good enough."

Micah came over to her and sat on the side of the desk. "No investment is totally safe, but when our financial adviser is telling us this is a timely opportunity, we should listen. Is there nothing I can say to get you to at least consider all the facts before you dig in your heels and turn into the Wicked Witch of the West?" He flashed a crooked grin and put his hands in front of his face.

Kate wadded up a piece of paper and threw it at him. "I hate it when you don't take me seriously."

"I take you very seriously. I just think you're casting your vote without fair consideration."

"You made that clear."

"We're running out of options, babe. We need working capital. It doesn't make sense to pay interest on a loan when we could be drawing dividends on an investment. And unless you have a better idea, those are the choices." Micah stood. "How about you think it over this afternoon, and we'll talk again after dinner? If you still don't want to do it, after you take an honest look at what Chad faxed to us, I'll stop pressing the issue."

"But it won't change your opinion that I'm playing it too safe."

Micah folded his arms and flapped them like wings, clucking like a chicken as he left her office ...

That was the last time she saw him. No kiss good-bye. No "I love you." No "Be safe." How she wished her last memory of her beloved was different. That her last moments with him had better reflected the deep love they shared instead of a disagreement they would surely have resolved.

Kate exhaled and felt as if her spirit deflated. She regretted being so harsh with Abby. But her daughter's naïveté could only bring more pain. Something Kate wasn't willing to risk.

CHAPTER 6

Abby clocked out at Flutter's. Maybe everyone else in the family thought she was wrong about the girl. But she had to find out. And she had a plan.

She slipped out the side door and skipped down the back steps. When she reached the bottom, she almost ran headlong into Hawk.

"Where are *you* going in such a hurry?" Hawk said.

"None of your business." He would only laugh if he knew. And there was no way she'd set herself up for that again.

Abby brushed past him and ran across the street to the house. She changed into shorts and a tank top, grabbed the bag she had prepared the night before, slung her purse strap over her shoulder, car keys in hand, and hurried outside to Mama's car. She drove it down the winding road into Foggy Ridge.

Traffic on Main Street had slowed to a crawl, and she looked for any available parking space along the street and didn't find one. She pulled into the parking lot behind Murchison's Feed Store, glad to find a spot, even if it was in the back row.

She sat in the car for a moment, thinking through what she planned to do and say. This was her chance to step out in faith—walk her talk—even though she had no idea where it would lead. She decided to trust God.

Abby got out of the car, the bag under her arm, and walked across the parking lot and into the side entrance at Murchison's. She walked nonchalantly past the customer service desk and down the hallway and stopped at the door marked Office, her heart racing. The worst that could happen was they would say no. What did she have to lose? She knocked, then turned the handle and went inside.

A woman with bleach-blonde hair and wearing a badge with the name *Maggie* looked up from her computer. "Can I help you?"

"Yes, my name's Abby Cummings. I found an expensive doll that I think belongs to a little girl I saw yesterday." Abby held up the cell phone picture. "I'm going around to businesses in the area, trying to locate her so I can return it." Misleading, but not really a lie.

"Beautiful child," Maggie said. "I can't say that I've ever seen her before."

"I was wondering if you would mind my asking your staff if anyone recognizes her."

"Our employees are not allowed to give out any customer information due to privacy issues."

"I understand. I just thought someone might know who she is and could have one of her parents call me. This looks like a very expensive doll." Abby removed Riley Jo's favorite baby doll—a gift from Grandma Becca and Grandpa Buck—from the bag.

"How lifelike." Maggie smiled warmly. "My girls loved their dolls growing up. I guess it couldn't hurt if you left your name and phone number with the staff. I hope you get this back to the little girl."

"Me, too. Thanks for letting me do this."

Abby went down the hallway and out to the sales floor. She waited until each clerk was free and then showed them the girl's picture one-by-one. No one remembered seeing her until she got to the last clerk, Henry Lawgins, who said he had waited on the parents.

"Yep, I seen her in here with her folks," Henry said. "Don't know who they are, though. I remember they paid cash. I doubt they're tourists, since they bought chicken feed."

"Can you describe her parents?" Abby managed to ask, relieved that her pounding heart didn't make her voice shake.

"Dad was tall and muscular. Had a beard. Looked like he works out. I'm guessin' he was mid to late forties. Mom was a lot younger, maybe thirty. Average height. Wore glasses and a dress down to her ankles. Had really long hair—plain brown—tied back in a rubber band. Oh, they also had twin boys—little, maybe two or three years old."

This was great information! "Anything else you can remember about them?"

Henry smiled. "The little girl's name was Ella."

Abby's heart sank clear down to her toes. "You heard them call her that? Are you sure?"

"Yep. I perked right up 'cause that's my granny's name."

"Have you seen them in here before?"

"Not that I remember. I hope this helps you find little Ella and she gets her doll back."

"Me, too," Abby said, not ready to put a period to the conversation. "Did she seem like a happy kid to you?"

Henry shot her a puzzled look and shrugged. "I didn't pay her much mind. Had my eye on the twins. I was afraid they was gonna knock over a display."

"Do you, by any chance, remember the twins' names?"

"Seems like one of 'em was Ronny, but I ain't sure about that." Henry glanced over his shoulder. "Look, miss, I probably told you more than I'm supposed to. I really need to get back to work."

"Of course." Abby reached in her purse and took out one of several cards she had made up. "Here's my name and cell number. If you see these people again, would you ask them to call me?"

"Sure thing."

Abby walked out the side door, her head reeling. The description the clerk gave of the dad fit the man she had seen come outside Murchison's, swat Ella's behind, and take her back inside. But a mom? Twin brothers? It was starting to feel less and less likely that Ella was Riley Jo.

Abby walked back to Mama's car, feeling as if a meteor had fallen on her heart, leaving a deep hole and dashing her hope to pieces. She sat for a few minutes, staring at Ella's picture. Why couldn't she just let it go? No matter how hard she tried, the connection she felt with this child was real. And magnetic. How could she just drop it before she knew why?

Abby gripped the steering wheel and laid her head on her hands. She took a slow, deep breath and let it out. She got out of the car and headed up Main Street, determined to talk to more people who worked with the public. Maybe someone else would recognize Ella from the picture and help her to piece together a more detailed description of this family.

❖

Abby walked into the living room and tossed her purse on the couch, the delicious aroma of Mama's homemade pasta sauce filling her senses. Hopefully her mother's cooking would dominate the conversation over dinner. She was not going to share her discovery with anyone in the family. She was on to something and was not letting them talk her out of it.

She went out to the kitchen, where Grandpa Buck sat, clipping coupons.

"There you are," Grandpa said. "I haven't seen you all afternoon."

"I was in town."

"Again?" Grandpa looked over the top of his glasses. "Wouldn't have somethin' to do with that girl you saw, would it?"

"I'm going to have a Coke. Want one?" Abby said.

"No, thanks."

Abby took a Coke out of the fridge and sat across from her grandfather at the table. "Find any great deals?"

"Buy one, get one on four-pound bags of sugar." Grandpa smiled. "*No* limit."

"Jesse's going to flip."

"You didn't answer my question, Abby."

"No. I guess I didn't."

"Is there a reason for that?"

Abby shrugged.

Grandpa's white eyebrows came together. "Since when won't you talk to me?"

"I don't want to be laughed at again."

"That's unfair, don't you think? I'm not the one who laughed. And I was all over Hawk for doin' it." Grandpa reached across the table and touched her hand. "I would never laugh when you're bein' serious about somethin'."

"I know. Sorry, Grandpa." Abby took a gulp of Coke. "I went back to Murchison's and talked to the people who work there." She told him the details of her conversation with Henry Lawgins.

"I'm sorry, honey. I'm sure that's disappointin'."

"At least I know her name now." Abby put her elbows on the table, her chin resting on her palms. "Why do I feel such a connection with Ella? Even after I found out this information, it didn't satisfy me. I went into lots of businesses and showed her picture. No one I talked to remembered her. But I left my name and cell number."

"How much proof do you need, Abby? Seems pretty obvious the child's got family."

"I can't explain it, but something doesn't feel right."

Grandpa stroked his mustache the way he did when he was trying to formulate a tactful reply.

"I don't believe this," Abby said. "You think I want it to be Riley Jo so badly that I'm imagining a connection."

"Don't presume to know what I'm thinkin', Abby. I know whatever you're feelin' is real to you, and far be it from me to say it's all in your head. I'm just lookin' at the odds, and you know as well as I do, there's a mighty slim chance that girl is Riley Jo."

"But a slim chance is still a chance."

Grandpa put the scissors down. "I can tell you're not ready to let this go. So what are you gonna do now?"

"I want to find Ella and talk to her, that's all." Abby sat up straight and took a long drink of Coke. "She might not be Riley Jo, but it feels so amazing, imagining that she could be. It's the first time in ages I've felt this way. I just want to enjoy it for a while."

"You could be settin' yourself up for a real hard fall, honey."

"Maybe." Abby leaned forward on her elbows. "But I love feeling that I could be on the verge of finding out something important. Can you even imagine how awesome it would be if ..." She exhaled when she saw the skepticism on her grandfather's face.

"If *what*?" Grandpa said.

"Doesn't matter. It can't hurt to hope, that's all."

"Have you told your mother what you found out about this girl?"

"No!" Abby heard the Coke can crinkle, and she loosened her grip. "I showed Mama the picture and told her what I thought. She shut me out and said not to mention it again. Don't worry. I won't. I'm not talking to Hawk about it either. Heaven forbid someone in this family should enjoy a flicker of hope without it depressing everyone else."

"They're weighin' the odds, Abby. All things *are* possible with God, but not necessarily probable. He doesn't always give us what we ask for."

"I'm going to find Ella and see for myself."

Grandpa nodded. "I figured as much. By the way, Jesse came to me this mornin' and told me about his conversation with you last night. As long as we're talkin' about all things possible, maybe your mother and Hawk will come around one of these days, and we can all go to church together."

"It's possible," Abby said. "Definitely not probable."

CHAPTER 7

Abby sat with Jay on the pier at Angel View, her legs dangling, her bare toes skimming the water. She watched as the sun slowly dipped below the western horizon, the sky painted with fiery swirls of crimson, purple, and hot pink. The June breeze was warmer than it had been earlier in the day, the humidity thicker, and the fragrance of honeysuckle sweet and pervasive.

Her thoughts zigzagged in every direction like the aquatic insects that shot across the top of the water. What if Ella turned out to be Riley Jo? Why wasn't she with their father? Was this just another wild-goose chase that would bring embarrassment and heartache to her family? Or was she on the brink of discovering the truth of why her father and sister had disappeared?

"You gonna tell me what happened today?" Jay said. "When you called and asked me to meet you here, you sounded upset. I assumed you wanted to talk."

"I didn't want to be alone." Abby glanced over at him. "You're the only person I'm comfortable being with even when I don't know what to say."

"Okay then." Jay lifted his cap and wiped his forehead. "I'm glad I'm here, in case you want to talk. Or even if you don't."

Abby sat wrapped in comfortable silence as the last vestiges of light faded away, leaving only darkness and bringing with it a chorus of crickets. She got lost in the moment but never did escape that nagging feeling in her gut that she needed to find Ella.

"Did you see that?" Jay said.

"What?"

"A lightning bug! There it went again."

Abby spotted a tiny yellow flicker. And then another. And another until the night seemed to come alive.

She heard herself giggling, her mind wandering back to one summer night when her family was camping on the Buffalo River. Neither Jesse nor Riley Jo was born yet, and Abby couldn't have been older than five or six …

Abby spotted a beam of light coming up the path from the river. Hawk came racing over to her and flopped down in the lawn chair next to her.

"Look what I found." Hawk held up a jar with several insects that seemed to turn on and off like lightbulbs. "Fireflies."

Abby drew back. "Will they sting me?"

"No, they're tame as anything. It's so cool how they light up the night." Hawk sprang to his feet and pulled her by the arm. "Come on. I want to show you something."

Daddy came out of the tent. "Did I hear you say you spotted fireflies?"

"Yeah, they're everywhere," Hawk said. "We need to get away from the lanterns so Abby can see them."

"See what?" Mama hollered from inside the tent.

"Come with us," Hawk said. "I'm taking Abby to the river to see the fireflies."

A minute later, Abby was covered in insect repellent and flanked by her mother and father, each holding her hand, her brother lighting the way with the flashlight.

Hawk stopped on a dry stretch of bank and sat cross-legged on the ground. "This is far enough."

Abby sat between her mother and father as Hawk turned off the flashlight. "Keep your eyes peeled," he said.

Within seconds, the inky blackness, near and far, was alight with hundreds—thousands—of tiny Tinker Bells, which seemed even more numerous because their flickering lights were reflected in the river. Abby had never seen anything like it. It was magical.

Daddy grabbed at something. "Gotcha." He rolled over on his knees in front of Abby. "Don't be scared. Fireflies won't hurt you. Let me show you."

He cupped his hands together and gave her a peek of the flickering light coming from the bug he had captured. "Here, princess. You hold it."

Daddy carefully transferred the firefly to Abby's palm and closed her hands around it.

Abby laughed. "It tickles." She opened her hand, and the firefly took flight, joining the magnificent festival of lights that made it feel like Christmas in summertime.

Mama reached up as if to touch the tiny bursts of yellow light that were all around them, her laughter like music. She seemed so alive and full of joy ...

Jay's voice brought Abby back to the present.

"I'm sorry," she said. "Did you ask me something?"

"I just wondered what had you so tickled. What were you thinking about?"

Abby told him about her first encounter with fireflies. "I've seen a million of them since then, but the light show has never been quite as spectacular as it was that night. I don't know if it's because it was the first time or because it was such a happy family memory." Abby exhaled. "I miss that so much. Our family doesn't really feel like a family without Daddy."

"But you've got your mom and grandpa and your brothers," Jay said. "That's a family."

"I guess. But there's a big hole that no one else can fill."

Jay nodded. "I get that. I still have my dad, but there's a big void when we're together, and I can tell he'd rather be somewhere else."

Abby looked out at the thousands of flickering lights illuminating the June night. "I miss mine so much. Part of me still thinks he's going to come home and all this will have been a nightmare."

She reached in her waistband and took out her cell phone. Why not go ahead and tell Jay everything? At least he wouldn't be dismissive.

"The reason I'm so somber," she said, "is I saw a girl at Murchison's Feed Store yesterday. She was the spitting image of Riley Jo. And about the age she would be now. Thankfully, I had my wits about me enough to take a picture of her." Abby pulled the photo up on the screen and handed her cell phone to Jay. "She even has blue eyes."

"Cute kid," Jay said. "She reminds me of Jesse. I mean, they could be related. Maybe it's the dark hair and blue eyes."

"Exactly. But no one else in my family thinks it's worth pursuing."

She gave Jay a complete rundown on everything she had done since seeing the girl, including going back to Murchison's and pretending she had found the girl's doll and wanted to return it.

"Wow, that's some detective work." Jay studied the picture of the girl. "So what does your family think now?"

"I only told Grandpa. Mama and Hawk don't care."

"I doubt that," Jay said. "Maybe they just don't believe it could be her."

Abby kicked the water, creating more splash than she had intended. "I'm sure everyone thinks I'm obsessing because we just passed another anniversary."

Jay rubbed the stubble on his chin. "Is that a possibility? It would certainly be understandable," he quickly added.

Nothing like an open and honest relationship. Abby snatched the phone from his hand. "Look, I saw what I saw. You said yourself the girl looks like Jesse."

"What do you think y'all should do about it?"

"I think we should find out more about Ella."

"How would you do that?" Jay said. "You asked around town."

"Only on Main Street."

"You think you can go up and down every street in Foggy Ridge and ask people if they know where this girl lives? Abby, do you know how desperate that sounds?"

"Well, maybe I *am* desperate! I'll regret it the rest of my life if I just blow it off. I have to try to find Ella."

"Why don't you go talk to the sheriff?"

"And tell him what—that this little girl looks like I imagine my sister would look now? Grandpa said the authorities won't start investigating again based on just that. Besides, Mama would freak if I did that without her permission."

"You don't think she'd go for the idea?"

Abby shook her head. "Absolutely not. She made it clear that she doesn't want to hear another word about it."

"Then what can you do?"

Abby shrugged. "I'll think of something. It's the first time I've felt hope in a long time. Maybe if I just step out in faith, God will help me find Riley Jo."

"You mean find Ella."

"Right now, they seem like one and the same to me."

Jay cracked his knuckles and was quiet for half a minute. "Abby, even if you could find Ella, how would you go about determining whether she was your sister?"

"All this just happened. I haven't figured it out yet, all right?"

"Hey, don't be mad at me for asking honest questions. This is pretty important. If this girl *is* your sister, then where is your dad? You have to deal with that, too."

"Jay, you're being a real pain. That's not what I need right now!" Abby blinked the stinging from her eyes. She was not letting him dissuade her from doing this.

"I'm a practical kind of guy. I think you should have a plan before you jump in with both feet."

Abby twirled a lock of hair around her finger. "My plan is to find Ella. I'm going back to town and ask around some more—places people would be likely to take children: ice-cream parlors, candy stores, gift shops, toy stores, pizza places, burger shops."

"People might remember her because of the twins," Jay said. "That's a good way to jog their memory. I could help you ask around."

"Thanks, but people are so protective of kids nowadays, I just think they'd be more willing to talk to a female."

"Whatever. I wish there was something I could do to help you."

"There is. Just listen and don't try to talk me out of it. Or tell me I sound desperate. I need to do this."

"Then go for it. I'll be the wind in your sails."

Abby felt a sting and slapped her arm. "Oh, great. I forgot to use insect repellent. The mosquitoes will eat me alive."

Jay stood and stepped into his Birkenstocks, then pulled her to her feet.

"How about I take you to Sweet Stuff and buy you a banana boat? As my aunt Clara used to say, 'Ain't nothin' that ails a body or mind that can't be fixed at Sweet Stuff.'"

"That does sound good," Abby said.

"And it's another place you can check to see if anyone working there recognizes Ella."

❦

An hour and a half later, Abby slid out of Jay's truck. She shut the door and leaned on the open window.

"I had fun," she said. "Thanks again for being a friend. It means a lot to me that I can tell you whatever's on my mind."

Jay smiled. "The nice thing about having a girl for my best friend is not having to do the talking."

Abby laughed. "You're a good listener. I know I talk too much."

"I'd say it's about right. See you tomorrow. Call or text me if you hear anything about Ella."

"I will. Good night."

Abby waved as Jay made a U-turn and headed back down the only road to town.

She walked up on the porch and opened the front door. Grandpa Buck was in his chair, watching a baseball game.

Her mother walked out of the kitchen, hands on her hips. "There you are. I was starting to worry. Hawk's down at the pier, fishing for bream. He called and said you and Jay weren't there."

"We were, until the mosquitoes drove us away. We went down to Sweet Stuff and had a banana boat."

"You have a cell phone." Mama came over and put her arms around Abby. "Just let me know where you are so I won't worry. That's the one rock-solid rule in this family."

"Sorry," Abby said. "I should have called."

Her mother squeezed her affectionately and then let go. "Now that we have that straight … how were the banana boats?"

"To die for. They haven't changed since I was little."

"Can't improve on perfection," Grandpa Buck said.

"Abby got a banana boat?" Jesse ran into the living room and came to a screeching halt in front of their mother. "Can we get one?" Jesse's round blue eyes were compelling. "Pleeease?"

Grandpa chuckled. "Sounds to me like we're going to Sweet Stuff."

Mama tapped Jesse on the nose. "All right. Go wash your face and put a shirt on."

"Yay!"

Abby smiled as Jesse turned on his heel and raced upstairs.

"You want to go with us and keep us company?" Mama said.

Abby shook her head. "Thanks, but I need to do my laundry. I don't have anything clean for work in the morning."

Mama stared at Abby as if she were probing her thoughts. "Honey, are we okay?"

Hardly. "What do you mean?"

"I'm sure I sounded harsh yesterday when you showed me the picture you'd taken of the little girl. I apologize if I hurt your feelings—"

"Don't worry about it. I said I wouldn't bother you with it anymore, and I won't."

Her mother sighed. "I'm doing the best I can to cope in my own way."

"So am I. We'll just have to respect the differences."

"Fair enough. But *respect* is the operative word here."

Abby started to say something and then didn't. She did respect her mother. But it was beyond comprehension that Mama could just blow off the girl's picture without any thoughtful consideration that it could be her daughter.

"If you have something to say, say it."

"I respect *you*"—Abby avoided eye contact—"but I just don't get how you can look the other way when the girl's face looks just like Riley Jo's."

"Abby, do you think you're the only one in the family who has done a double take of a man or young girl that reminds us of your father or Riley Jo?" Mama spoke softly, her tone void of anger. "We just don't talk about it. I've been through this dozens of times myself. I've learned the hard way not to let my imagination open that wound. They're gone. They're not coming back. You have to reach acceptance in your own way. But I *have*. And want to go forward now. I can't go back to false hope. I just can't."

Abby nodded. "I get it." She didn't. But she'd been lectured enough. "I need to get started on my laundry. Enjoy the banana boats."

Abby turned and walked toward her room, her heart flooded with doubt. What if Mama was right? What if this was false hope … and there really wasn't any hope at all?

CHAPTER 8

The next morning, Abby clocked out at Flutter's and left by the side door. She skipped down a flight of stairs and counted thirteen people on the deck, sitting at umbrella tables, enjoying the spectacular view of Beaver Lake and the rolling mountains beyond. She went down the stairs to the ground level and was walking across the street when her cell phone rang. She glanced at the screen. *Caller Unknown.*

"Hello." She heard someone breathing into the phone. "This is Abby. Who's there?"

"Listen carefully," said a muffled male voice. "Stop askin' questions about the girl, and don't tell nobody about this call. Or you're liable to go missin' too."

"Who *is* this?" Abby felt as if her heart had been dropped off a cliff. "Hello?"

The phone went dead.

Abby stood frozen in the driveway, her heart pounding, her mind racing wildly with the implications. Who would call and say such a terrible thing? Who didn't want her to find Ella …? And why …? What had she gotten herself into …?

Wait a minute—Abby's fear quickly turned to anger—this kind of mean prank reeked of Mason Craddock and his pathetic jock friends. She could just imagine them laughing and slapping each other on the back. And to think she almost fell for it!

Abby felt at the same time relieved and incensed. She kicked a pebble across the driveway. What a jerk. Mason was still mad at her for turning him down when he asked her to the spring dance. He must have gotten her cell number off one of the cards she had passed out around town.

Even if Mason and his brainless clones had gotten wind of Abby's search for the girl, why would they have automatically assumed that she was looking for her sister and using the doll story to cover up her real motive? Was she that obvious? Had other people figured it out too?

Abby felt heat scalding her cheeks. Why should she care what they thought? How could they even begin to understand the emptiness she lived with, day in and day out? Or how it felt not to know what had happened to your dad and sister?

She considered for a moment calling Mason and letting him know exactly what she thought of his sick joke. Then again, why give him the satisfaction of knowing that he'd finally gotten her attention? That's exactly what he wanted.

Abby looked at the picture of Ella on her cell phone. Why was she so inexplicably drawn to this child? Was it because she wanted more than anything for her to be Riley Jo? Or was there a true connection that defied words?

Either way, until she knew the answer, she wouldn't stop looking for her.

❖

Kate leaned on the wood railing on the umbrella deck at Angel View Lodge and looked out over Beaver Lake. The morning fog had lifted, and scores of sailboats and fishing charters were moving in all directions on the blue water. She spotted a number of Angel View paddleboats out there, as well as the three green-and-white houseboats she rented by the day or week.

A mixed flock of gulls and terns flew in the direction of Egret Island. The sky was azure and cloudless, the breeze mild. She never stopped being amazed that she owned this little slice of heaven, even though managing the lodge by herself was difficult. How she missed Micah—his entrepreneurial spirit. His innovation. His talent for fixing most anything. His friendly interactions with guests.

Her man had a passion for natural beauty evidenced by all the windows and decks he had designed to ensure that guests at the lodge could soak in the view from every side. Each task, project, or hobby he undertook, he did with exuberance. The word *boring* wasn't even in Micah's vocabulary.

Usually, when there was tension between them, he was the even-tempered half of the partnership. Slow to anger. Quick to forgive—and forget. Half the time she didn't even have to tell him what she was thinking. He could look past the exterior and read her heart. No one could bring Kate out of a bad mood like Micah. When she wanted to pout and hang on to her anger, Micah would pull her into his arms and just hold her. It was as though he could see her soul—flaws and all—and cherished her anyway.

Or so she thought. Sometimes she wondered if she had finally
pushed him over the edge of his patience with her stubborn unwill-
ingness to consider putting some of their money into a riskier
investment. They'd had arguments before but had never found
themselves at such an impasse. Despite all of Micah's wonderful
qualities, he was a risk taker and couldn't seem to understand that
Kate wasn't.

Outwardly, Kate rejected the notion that this man, who had
loved her so deeply and devoted himself to making her happy, would
have turned to another woman. But deep down, the fear tormented
her. For weeks before his disappearance, she'd been consumed with
financial worries. Their communication was often strained and their
lovemaking nonexistent, solely Kate's doing and something she now
deeply regretted. What she wouldn't give just to feel Micah's arms
around her again.

Kate looked out at the glistening lake. She had finally reached a
level of acceptance that made it bearable to move forward without
her husband and baby girl. But Abby's stubborn insistence that the
child she saw could be Riley Jo threatened to unearth the broken
dreams Kate had finally been able to bury. She would not bury them
twice. She refused to be deceived again by false hope.

Just seeing the picture of the little girl had been upsetting. The
child's face was sweet, her facial features dainty, like Riley Jo's. Was
it God's way of taunting her, rubbing salt in the raw wound that
would probably never heal? What did He want from her? She had
been a faithful follower when He broke His promise never to leave
or forsake her. Where was He during those agonizing days, weeks,
months, and years when she cried out to Him for relief from the pain

that tormented her? When she struggled to survive with the broken heart that He, in His sovereignty, had allowed to break?

It was difficult enough that He had repaid her faithfulness with suffering. But it was unbearable that He had left her to endure it alone. That He had removed His presence from her when she needed Him most. Every sympathy card she got encouraged her to reach out to Him for comfort. But there was no comfort. No loving arms to wrap her in the peace that passes understanding. If she learned anything from losing her husband and daughter, it was that God couldn't be trusted.

It would be disingenuous of her to encourage her children to put their faith in a God capable of such indifference. Though she missed that passionate longing for the spiritual. And the sense of being deeply loved by the God of the universe. Her father had it. So did Abby. Soon Jesse would. But not Kate. Never again. And she was not going to feel guilty for not buying into the religious hype. God was not what He claimed to be. And her faith had not withstood the betrayal. It was all a myth.

Kate felt a hand on her shoulder and jumped.

"Sorry if I scared you," Hawk said. "Could we talk privately for a minute?"

Kate glanced at the crowd of folks on the umbrella deck. "Sure. Let's go downstairs."

Kate walked down the steps to the ground level, then turned around. "What is it, Hawk? You look upset."

"Did you know Abby has been asking people in town if they know who the girl in the picture is?"

Kate bit her lip. "I did *not*. How'd you find out?"

"I went into Bella's to get donuts and saw Abby's name and cell number on a card at the register. I asked Laura Lynn about it. She said Abby and Jay were in there last night, asking if anyone knew *Ella's* last name and where she lived. And if they were uncomfortable giving out that information, would they contact her parents and ask them to call Abby. She showed Laura Lynn a doll and said it belonged to Ella, and Abby wanted to return it."

Kate dropped her head into her hands and shook it. "Okay, I'll take care of it."

"You have to make her stop."

"I *said* I'll take care of it, Hawk. That means you need to drop it and let me handle it."

"Abby's freaking me out. Why won't she let them go?"

"She just wants her father and sister back," Kate said. "She hasn't accepted the finality of the situation."

"Well, she'd better. She looks like an idiot."

"To whom?" Kate said. "She's just telling people she wants to return a lost doll."

"There are plenty of folks who know Abby's history and are smart enough to see through that. What're you going to say to her?"

"Let me worry about that. I would appreciate it if you'd just leave it alone."

"All right, Mama." Hawk kissed her cheek. "I'm heading out to take that couple from Illinois on a jeep ride."

"Be safe," Kate said.

"I'll be home for dinner."

Kate walked across the street, fighting back the tears that threatened to spoil her professional demeanor. She sat on the porch steps

of the log house and keyed in Abby's cell number. Halo came out
from under the porch and nestled next to her. The phone rang four
times.

"Hello, Mama."

"Where are you, Abby?"

"I'm at Tutty's with Jay. His boss is letting me sample the barbecue. It's incredible."

"I'd like you to come home. There's something I need to talk to
you about."

"Like what? I was going to hang out with Jay until he starts his
shift at four."

"Just come home. We'll talk then."

"Can't you give me a hint?" Abby said.

"Come to the house, not the office." Kate glanced at her watch.
"I'll see you in an hour."

"All right. I'm going to get off now. It's noisy. I can't hear you
very well."

"One hour, Abby."

Abby went in the front door and tossed her purse on the couch.
"Mama?"

"I'm in the kitchen."

Abby went into the kitchen and opened the fridge. "You want
something to drink?"

"I'm fine." Mama sounded stuffed up, her eyes red-rimmed.

Abby grabbed a bottle of spring water and sat at the table, facing her mother. "What's wrong?"

"Why are you going around town asking about the little girl whose picture you took?"

"You told me not to bring it up again."

"I'm bringing it up. Answer me, please."

"I want to know who she is, that's all."

"Abby, that's not all. You've been claiming to have a doll that belongs to her."

"It's Riley Jo's doll."

"So it's a lie."

Abby took a sip of water. "Not if I'm going on the premise she might actually *be* Riley Jo."

"But she's not. Her name's Ella."

Abby didn't flinch. How did her mother know that? "According to the clerk at Murchison's, the man and woman she was with called her Ella. But what if those people aren't her parents?"

"Your sister isn't coming back, Abby. Neither is your father. You've got to accept that. You're not living with reality, and I'm afraid it's going to hurt you."

"No, you're afraid I'm going to embarrass you again."

Mama's eyes welled with tears. "I've got a call in to Dixie. We need to nip this in the bud."

Abby felt hot all over. "Do you really think you can counsel away my hope? I don't get what you're afraid of. If it turns out I'm wrong about Ella, so what? But if I'm right, it would be amazing."

"This behavior is over the top," Mama said.

"Because I want to find out who she is?"

"You can't pester people in town."

"Not one person I've talked to seems to mind. I'm just getting the word out there that I want to return her doll, and I'm leaving my name and cell number. If someone knows who she is, they might tell her parents, and they'll call me."

"Then what?"

"I'll tell them that Ella reminds me so much of my baby sister who disappeared. I'll ask if I can meet her. That just seeing her up close would help me to let my sister go."

"No parent in their right mind would put their child in a situation like that, Abby. For all they know, you're a troubled teen."

"I'll let them talk to Grandpa. He'll convince them I'm harmless."

"You've talked to your grandfather about this?"

"No. But he'd do it. I know you won't."

Her mother took the wadded-up tissue in her hand and dabbed her eyes. "*I* know you're not a dangerous person, but Ella's parents don't know that. And I think Dixie would agree with me that searching for a child who looks like your sister on the off chance it might be her isn't healthy—for you or Ella. And it won't work anyway. After Ella, it would be someone else."

"That's not fair." Abby's eyes burned with indignation. "I have a strong connection to her I can't explain."

"She isn't your sister."

"You don't know that."

"I *do* know that!" Mama's quivering voice wasn't convincing.

"Well, I don't. Can't you just leave me alone and let me figure it out for myself?"

Kate buried her face in her hands. Finally she looked up and held Abby's gaze. "I don't suppose it would do me any good to forbid you to do this?"

Abby looked out at the hummingbird feeder attached to the window. "Mama, all I want to do is find Ella. You don't have to worry that I'm going to fall into some deep depression if she turns out to be the daughter of that man and woman she was with."

"And what if you can't find her?"

Abby shrugged. "Then that's just the way it is."

A long moment of silence made Abby shift in her chair. It was hard to tell if her mother was angry or just thinking.

"I'll make you a deal," Mama said. "I won't get in the way of your looking for Ella if you agree to go talk to Dixie—willingly and with an open mind."

"It's a waste of money."

"It's my money, Abby. I'll make the appointment. Deal or not?"

"Deal."

CHAPTER 9

Kate sat at a corner table on the umbrella deck at Angel View Lodge, watching the rental boats returning to the marina as dusk began to fall, her earlier encounter with Abby playing in her mind.

"Your sister isn't coming back, Abby. Neither is your father. You've got to accept that. You're not living with reality, and I'm afraid it's going to hurt you."

"No, you're afraid I'm going to embarrass you again."

There was no denying that she found her daughter's public search for Ella embarrassing. But that wasn't what Kate was afraid of. Abby's inability to let go of the past had stolen five years of her young life. It had to stop.

She heard footsteps on the stairs and looked up just as Savannah, carrying half a pitcher of lemonade, approached the table.

"I thought I might find you down here." Savannah filled Kate's empty glass to the brim with lemonade. "Tuesday nights are dead after the early crowd clears out. I've already stripped the tables and reset them for breakfast. I'll put fresh flowers in the vases in the morning. Carmen is watching for any last-minute customers, but I think we'll be ready to close up tighter than a tick at nine o'clock."

"Sounds like you're ahead of the game. Why don't you sit for a minute?" Kate said, hoping some girl talk would give her a sense of normalcy.

"Thanks. My feet could use a break." Savannah pulled out a chair and sat next to Kate, looking out toward the lake. "Incredible view from up here. All those years of living in Looziana, I don't think I was ever higher than a few feet above sea level. And now I'm living on a mountain. Isn't that a lick?"

"Sure Foot Mountain is only eighteen hundred feet high—not exactly Mount Everest."

"Well, this bayou gal feels on top of the world." Savannah laughed. "I could get a nosebleed up here. And just feel that cool evening breeze. Summer sure is different here."

"Wait until July and August. It won't be quite as humid as south Louisiana, but you can still fry an egg on the sidewalk. So are you settled in your new house?"

Savannah grinned. "Yes, but every chance I get, I end up outside on the covered porch, staring at these beautiful mountains."

"You and me both."

"Benson and I feel right at home here. Relocating was easier than we thought. And we couldn't ask for nicer people to work with. I was afraid the wait staff might resent an outsider being hired to coordinate things. But they're all so nice. Abby's a great asset, I can tell you that."

Kate took a sip of lemonade. "Does she seem okay to you?"

"Sure, why?"

"She's going through a thing right now. The five-year anniversary of her dad and sister's disappearance was last Saturday, and it's dredged up a lot of feelings. She really misses them. We all do. But Abby's having trouble letting go."

"Now that you mention it, she has seemed preoccupied," Savannah said. "But she's on top of her game with customers. You turned out one responsible young lady."

"Thanks. But Micah gets a lion's share of the credit." Kate coughed to cover the unwanted emotion that tightened her throat. "For the first eleven years of her life, Abby was a daddy's girl."

"So was I," Savannah said. "But me and my mama are real close now. Took me a while to realize what a positive influence she'd been on me."

"That's encouraging to hear, since Abby and I don't see eye to eye on much of anything these days."

Savannah waved her hand. "I don't think Mama and I agreed on anything till I married Benson. Once I didn't have to take her advice, I found myself asking for it. It'll happen."

Would it? Kate wasn't so sure.

"Don't you worry none about Abby," Savannah said. "I'll keep an eye on her. And if I see anything you should know about, I won't be shy about telling you."

❧

Abby sat with Jay on the pier at Angel View, watching the sun disappear below the horizon, the western sky the color of glowing embers and streaked with gold and purple.

"I can't believe Mama's making me go back to counseling just because I want to know more about Ella."

"She's just being a mother. They're all worrywarts. It's part of their job description."

"I don't need a shrink, Jay. I need to find Ella and satisfy this weird connection I feel."

"I know. But you have to admit, it's a long shot."

"Worth pursuing." Abby kicked the top of the water with her toes.

"How good a look did you get of the man you saw with Ella?"

"It was quick. But there were some things about him that stood out."

"Like what?"

"Bushy beard. Muscular arms."

"Did you see his face?"

"I did, but only for a few seconds."

"Do you think you could describe him enough for me to sketch him?" Jay said. "I'm pretty good at it."

"You mean like a police composite?"

Jay nodded.

"I'm not sure," Abby said. "Maybe."

"If I could sketch a good likeness of him, we could show the sketch around town, together with Ella's picture. Maybe someone would recognize them."

"That's a great idea," Abby said. "But we can't do it at my house."

"What if we met on the slope under that big shade tree around noon? I'll bring sub sandwiches and my sketchpad."

"Okay, but it's my turn to bring lunch. I'll get the subs." Abby glanced over at Jay. "Something else happened today. I haven't told anyone. I got a crank call on my cell. Some hick warning me to back off asking about Ella. I'm pretty sure it was Mason Craddock and his clones."

"How'd they find out you were looking for Ella?"

"I don't know. Maybe one of them works at one of the places where I left my card."

"What makes you so sure it was them?"

"Because the guy said"—Abby nudged Jay with her elbow and spoke with a drawl—"'Stop askin' questions about the girl, and don't tell nobody about this call. Or you're liable to go missin' too.' Now if that doesn't reek of Mason and his loser friends, nothing does. I'm sure they're all having a great laugh at my expense. Let them. I don't care what they think."

Jay turned to her. "Think you should be so quick to blow it off, Abby? What if the call was for real?"

"It wasn't. Mason's trying to get back at me because I won't go out with him."

"Maybe I should pay Mason a visit and tell him to back off."

"Please don't," Abby said. "They'll gang up on you. Just ignore it. I am."

"Shouldn't you at least tell your grandfather?"

"No!" Abby lowered her voice. "He'll tell Mama, and she'll tell the sheriff. Then they'll all make me back off looking for Ella. Besides, Mason will deny he knew anything about it."

"The jerk as much as threatened you."

"I'm sure he thought it was funny. Just drop it."

CHAPTER 10

Raleigh Country Sheriff Virgil Granger sat in the glider on the wraparound porch of his Victorian home on Puckett Street, holding a glass of sweet tea and listening to the happy chatter of neighbor kids riding their Big Wheels up and down the driveway across the street. They were still going strong, even though it was dark except for the glow of the streetlight.

It didn't seem that many summers ago that his own sons were outside doing the very same thing. Now that they were grown, he and Jill Beth didn't need all this space. But any time he hinted about putting the place on the market, she looked up at him with those sentimental puppy eyes that reminded him it was more than just a house—it was where they had raised their triplet boys from infancy to adulthood.

Virgil took a sip of tea. The house begged for paint. It was too much for him to tackle alone, and his sons had offered to come for a long weekend to help him get the job done.

Virgil chuckled, remembering the fiasco the first time he painted the boys' rooms. Robby, Ricky, and Reece were eight years old and eager to *watch*. Ricky stepped in the paint pan and ruined a new pair of expensive sneakers. Reece and Robby got into a tug-of-war over the dog's leash, and one of them finally let go. The other fell on his behind, knocking a half-full bucket of paint off a stool, the contents splattering both misbehavers—and the family's beagle—with a rich shade of yellow.

Virgil heard the front door open.

Jill Beth stepped out on the porch, dressed in her pink bathrobe and emitting the sweet fragrance of gardenia bubble bath. She held up his cell phone. "It's Chief Deputy Mann."

Virgil kissed her hand and took the phone. "What's up, Kevin?"

"Duncan, Hobbs, and I responded to a 9-1-1 call from a teenage couple that said they found skeletal remains in the woods off Smithville Road—up yonder on the mountain. Sure enough, there're remains up here. Way too decomposed to make any kind of ID—even gender. But judging by the size of the skull, it had to be an adult."

"Why were the kids in the woods?"

"Said they were *owl watching*." Kevin snorted. "Hey, I'm just the messenger. Anyhow, they were trudging through the woods and spotted the bones with the flashlight. They thought it was animal remains until they saw the skull. They ran back to their truck and called 9-1-1. They're still pretty shook up. Duncan and Hobbs are fixin' to take them to the station and wait for their parents to arrive. That'll give them a chance to calm down before we question them further."

"What about CSI?"

"On the way. Emergency responders are coming out of the woodwork. I'll bet you can see the lights flashing from down in Foggy Ridge."

"All right," Virgil said. "You're in charge. Preserve the scene. I don't want any missteps. It's hard to say what we're dealing with."

"Wouldn't it be something if this turned out to be Micah Cummings?"

"That's the understatement of the century." Virgil looked up into Jill Beth's wide, questioning eyes, his pulse soaring, his curiosity on tilt. Did he dare hope that this was the break they'd been waiting for? "You know what, Kevin? The media will be all over this like fleas on a hound dog. I'm coming up there."

❧

Virgil moved his flashlight across a swath of the forest floor that had been roped off with crime scene tape. Bones were scattered over an area of about twenty square feet, a human skull visible in the midst. It was sobering to consider that this might be all that was left of Micah Cummings. Virgil had imagined such a scenario many times in the past five years but didn't realize that the discovery would make him feel as if he had swallowed a lead weight. He had grown up on the same street as Micah. Knew him when he was a scrawny, runny-nosed little kid, always wanting to hang out with the big boys. He should've let him.

Virgil heard voices and spotted Kevin walking over to three crime scene investigators getting out of a familiar black Suburban.

Virgil raised his hand to acknowledge them, content to let Kevin fill them in.

Several minutes later, just as the red-white-and-blue van from KOMN-TV pulled up behind the long row of flashing lights, Kevin came over and stood next to Virgil. The chief deputy's carrot-red hair was unruly from the humid night air.

"The media didn't waste any time," Kevin said. "Want me to call Mrs. Cummings? She probably should know what's going on before it hits the news. The way these bones are scattered, could be more than one person."

"She doesn't need to hear that over the phone," Virgil said. "I'll drive up there and tell her myself."

Kevin nodded toward four Foggy Ridge police officers talking to Deputy Duncan. "PD's up to speed. Chief Mitchell's en route."

"Thanks." Virgil patted Kevin's shoulder. "I'll be back."

Virgil walked a hundred yards across a clearing. He got into his squad car and made a U-turn, avoiding the potholes in the crude dirt trail that led back to Angel View Road. He turned north and headed up the mountain to the Cummings' house.

Kate was sitting at the kitchen table, writing out a new recipe for herb chicken, when she heard the doorbell ring. She glanced at the clock. Who would come to the house at this hour?

She heard footsteps running across the wood floor, and then the door open.

"Evening, Sheriff," Jesse said. "Come in. Mom! It's Sheriff Granger!"

Kate came out of the kitchen, the recipe card still in her hand, and stood next to Jesse. "You need to come get me when we have a guest," she said softly. "It's not polite to yell."

Jesse nodded apologetically. "Sorry."

Kate turned her attention to Virgil. "So what brings you out this late?"

"I'd like to talk to you about something. Is there a place we could talk privately?"

"Sure, come out to the kitchen." Kate felt as if her pulse rate had doubled. Had Abby done something she didn't know about?

She walked across the living room and through the doorway to the kitchen, Virgil on her heels.

"Can I get you something to drink?" she said. "Coke, iced tea, lemonade, spring water?"

"No, thanks. I'm good."

"Let's sit here at the table." Kate pushed her recipe box aside. "Is this about Abby trying to find that little girl?"

"Actually, I don't know anything about that." Virgil pulled out a chair and sat. "I came to inform you of a new development that happened less than an hour ago. I don't know of an easy way to say this, so I'll get right to the point. A couple of teenagers stumbled onto human remains. The skull size suggests an adult."

The world stopped. Kate put her hand on her heart and struggled to find her voice. "You think … it's Micah?"

"We have to consider that possibility. CSIs are doing the investigating and will make sure the remains are sent for DNA testing." Virgil's expression looked somber.

"What aren't you telling me? Did you find other remains? A ... child's?" Kate refused to utter her daughter's name, as if not saying it would make her worst fear impossible. "Tell me!"

Virgil reached across the table and gently gripped her wrist. "We can't be sure the bones belong to just one person until the lab analyzes the DNA."

"But you only found one skull." Kate looked up at him, her mind processing the implications.

"It's just too soon to tell what we've discovered or what else is still out there. We're searching the area for any indication that this could be Micah *or* Riley Jo."

Kate blinked away the grisly images that invaded her mind.

"I hate dropping this on you," Virgil said, "but this is going to be breaking news within the hour. I wanted you to hear it from me—in person, not over the phone."

"Where did you f-find the remains?" Kate said.

"Just a couple miles from here—in the woods. There was no way to determine if foul play was involved. It's going to take the medical examiner for that."

"You said a couple of teenagers discovered them?"

Virgil nodded. "They're going down to the station now to give their statements. I'm headed back to the site. I'll keep you informed. If I learn anything significant, I'll let you know right away."

"Thanks."

Virgil withdrew his hands and folded his arms on the table. He spoke with a steady, compassionate voice. "We've both been dreading a discovery like this for a very long time. I can only imagine how much harder this is for you. Keep in mind we don't know that these remains belong to Micah *or* Riley Jo. We can compare Micah's dental records to the skull we found and get the results rather quickly. But it could take a couple months to get the DNA results back on each of the bones. I wish I could tell you I could speed up the process, but I can't."

"You said you were searching the area."

"We are. We're hoping to find some identifying article. Clothing. Watch. Jewelry. Anything like that."

"A gold wedding band?" Kate said, feeling as if her heart were breaking all over again.

"That certainly would have withstood the elements. If it's there, we'll find it."

"I should go out there in case you find something."

"I don't think that's a good idea. We're going to be searching all night. It's dark. We don't know that we're going to find anything. Why don't you stay home and rest? I promise I'll call you immediately if we find something."

"I don't care what time it is," Kate said. "I doubt I'll be sleeping."

Virgil gave her arm a gentle squeeze and stood. "I'll let myself out."

Kate couldn't have moved if she'd wanted to. She was vaguely aware of Virgil walking through the living room and out the front door and wondered how many times he had done that in the past five years. Was this finally the beginning of the end?

A wave of nausea swept over her, and she laid her head on the table. No matter how much she wanted an end to the ominous

unknowns that haunted her, closure wouldn't come without heartache. And even if her beloved Micah and Riley Jo were proven dead,
she would still be left wondering how they died.

Kate wanted to crawl into bed and fall into a deep sleep. But the
night was young, and she would spend it staring into the darkness,
waiting for Virgil's call.

CHAPTER 11

Abby, still groggy from being awakened from a sound sleep, shuffled into the living room behind Grandpa and saw that the rest of the family had already gathered. She sat on the couch between Jesse and Hawk. Her mother sat in one of two easy chairs facing them, her eyes red and puffy and her expression somber. Grandpa sat in the other chair.

"I called this family meeting," Mama said, "because I need to tell you the news the sheriff just brought. It's hard to hear, but it's important. In the woods, not far from here, a couple of teenagers discovered the remains of someone—an adult."

Abby put her hands to her face and sucked in a breath. "Daddy?"

"They don't know yet, but we have to brace ourselves for that possibility."

"What do you mean by remains?" Hawk said.

"They found human bones." Mama paused for a moment, her fist pressed to her lips. "And a skull. Virgil said it was an adult's, not a child's."

Abby listened as her mother shared with them everything Sheriff Granger had told her about the find.

"He really thinks some of the bones are Riley Jo's?" Hawk said.

Mama shook her head. "Virgil just said they couldn't be sure the remains belonged to only one person without DNA analysis."

"So when will *we* know?" Hawk's eyes had the same anxious look they had the night of the disappearance.

"DNA comparison on the bones could take a couple months." Mama paused and seemed far away for a moment. "But if they're able to match your father's dental records with the skull they found, those results would be back quickly."

"How quickly?" Hawk said.

"I really didn't get into all that with Virgil." Mama traced the floral pattern on the arm of the chair and seemed to be in a daze. "It was shocking news. I thought I was ready for anything."

"I don't see how we could ever be ready for this." Abby wiped a tear off her cheek, feeling as if someone had lanced her deepest wound all over again.

"Well, I am," Hawk said. "We've been in limbo for five years. I just want it over with. I want the truth, whatever it is. It's the only way we're going to get our lives back."

"We all want the truth." Grandpa Buck took off his glasses. "We're just hopin' it's not too hard to hear."

Hawk leaned forward, his elbows on his knees, his fingers laced together. He spoke softly. "I think it's time we accepted the worst possible scenario. Daddy knew the woods like the back of his hand. He and Riley Jo couldn't have gotten lost out there. Something—or someone—must've killed them."

"No one said they're dead!" Abby blinked the stinging from her eyes. "We should wait for the DNA tests. It might not be Daddy. And no one said any of the remains belonged to a child."

Hawk shot her one of his chiding looks. "That girl you spotted isn't Riley Jo. You'd better ditch your illusion and start facing the facts."

"I will," Abby said defiantly, "when we have *facts*. Right now we have remains." Even as Abby said the words, her heart sank. What if Daddy was dead? What if they found Riley Jo's remains too? What if her hope was about to be shattered?

"All right, everyone, listen up," Grandpa Buck said. "We need to pull together to get through this. The sheriff may have gotten a break in the case. Maybe not. But we need to support one another while we're waitin' to hear."

Her mother looked as fragile as she had that first long night after Daddy and Riley Jo went missing.

"The sheriff told your mama he'd call immediately if they found anything important," Grandpa Buck said. "We might as well try and get some sleep. There's nothin' we can do now but wait—and pray."

"You can do the praying, Grandpa." Hawk jumped to his feet. "Been there. Done that." He stepped over to where their mother was sitting and crouched in front of her chair. "Call me if anything happens or if you want me to drive you out to the search site."

Mama took Hawk's hand and held it to her cheek. "I will. Try to rest."

Hawk nodded and went upstairs.

Grandpa Buck set his glasses on the end table and leaned his head back in his chair. "I think I'll sit here a spell."

Jesse hugged Mama a long time, then ran upstairs without saying anything. Abby figured it was more painful for him seeing Mama upset than thinking the remains might be those of the father and sister he hardly remembered.

Abby got up and took her mother's hand. "I'll be in my room if you need me."

Mama didn't turn loose of her hand. "Honey, I know you want the girl you saw to be Riley Jo. If only that were possible. But I think deep down, you know it isn't. And with this new development, well … I just think we all need to be prepared for whatever Virgil finds."

Abby shook her head. "I'm not giving up hope they're coming home."

"But after all this time, it's nothing more than blind hope."

"Or blind faith." Abby pulled her hand away. "I've been praying that God would bring Daddy and Riley Jo home. The Bible says nothing is impossible with God."

"I know, Abby. But it doesn't say you should just ignore reality."

"We don't know what reality is yet. I still have faith that Daddy and Riley Jo are alive."

"All the wishing in the world won't bring them home, honey."

Abby exhaled. "Faith means more than *wishing* for something. It means trusting God. He may not answer my prayers the way I want, but praying is not a waste of time. I like feeling close to Him. It's a lot better than sitting here with no hope. And no one to talk to when you're sad."

"We have each other." A row of lines formed on her mother's forehead, and she spoke tenderly. "Isn't it possible that God has a bigger agenda than listening to one young girl from Foggy Ridge?"

"So now you're saying He's not even listening?"

The vacant expression on Mama's face said more than words ever could. Abby felt the sting of tears at the back of her throat and swallowed hard. She had to go on.

"Mama," she said in just above a whisper, "I figured out a long time ago how you and Hawk feel about God. It's pretty obvious."

A flicker of defensiveness flashed in her mother's eyes but never made it to her lips.

"I remember how hard you used to pray," Abby said. "At first, I mean. Every single day you prayed with us that Daddy and Riley Jo would come home." Emotion threatened to steal Abby's voice, but she had to finish. "And then something changed. You stopped praying. Stopped going to church. Stopped saying anything positive about God, the Bible, and Christians. You never want to talk about it, but I overhear things you say, especially to Grandpa. You're so wrong, Mama. God does listen. And He answers prayer. You have to have faith."

"I had faith, Abby. It didn't change a thing."

"You gave up. That's *not* faith."

Her mother wiggled out of the easy chair and rose to her feet, her face flushed. "I'm not going to argue with you about conversations that were never intended for your ears."

"Kate," Grandpa said softly, "your daughter's speakin' from her heart. It can only help to get it out in the open."

Mama stood still as a statue, her arms folded tightly across her chest, her stony, thin-lipped expression making it evident she was done listening. "Finish your thought, Abby."

"I did."

"Fine. I'm going to my room to be alone with my thoughts—and maybe get some rest. I would appreciate it if you and your grandfather would refrain from filling Jesse's head full of false hope right now. The best thing for him—for all of us—is the truth."

Abby sat in the window seat in her room and looked up at the night sky that sparkled like a showcase of diamonds spread out on black velvet.

God, are You up there? Can You hear me? Or is Mama right when she says that You don't listen to someone like me?

Abby moved her gaze across the heavens. She knew from the Psalms that God had not only created those stars but had also given each one a name. How hard could it be for Him to bring her dad and sister home? Or to make her family happy again? The search for Ella filled that vacuum with hope, and she wasn't going to let Mama or Hawk take that from her. Her mind wandered back to the last memory she had of Riley Jo …

"I go giddyup!" Riley Jo tugged at the back pocket of Abby's jeans. "Pweeze?"

Abby turned around and looked into her sister's pleading blue eyes and her angelic face. "Oh, all right. One more time. But then we have to stop. I'm going over to Staci's for a sleepover." Abby bent down and let her tiny two-year-old sister climb onto her back. She held tightly to the back of Riley

Jo's knees—the toddler giggling all the while—as she trotted across the backyard to the fence, and then came back to where they started.

Riley Jo nudged Abby with her legs. "Not stop. Go giddyup!"

"We have to stop now. Staci's mom will be here any minute." Abby let her sister slide off her back.

Riley Jo stood facing Abby, her lower lip protruding. "I go too."

"You can't. It's for big girls," Abby said. "I'll be home tomorrow. Let's go find Madeline, and you can keep her with you until I get back."

Abby took Riley Jo by the hand and went into the house. They walked back to the room they shared and over to the wooden cradle Daddy had made.

Abby picked up the beautiful, lifelike baby doll that Grandpa Buck and Grandma Becca had given Riley Jo for her second birthday. "Here. Madeline will sleep with you whenever I'm not here. You don't have to be scared. I'll be back." Abby kissed her index finger and pressed it to Riley Jo's nose, evoking a giggle.

Riley Jo held the baby doll, which seemed half as big as she was, to her chest and looked up, an elfin grin on her face.

Abby gently tugged her sister's pigtail, which was barely long enough to stay in the rubber band. "I'll see you tomorrow. I promise ..."

Abby felt an all-too-familiar aching in her heart. How ironic that it was Riley Jo who didn't come home. By the time Abby returned from Staci's the next afternoon, her daddy and sister had already gone fishing. They never returned. What she wouldn't give to take Riley Jo on another horsey ride.

Abby wiped her tears on her pajama top, her mother's words playing in her mind.

Isn't it possible that God has a bigger agenda than listening to one young girl from Foggy Ridge?

Suddenly Abby felt very small. Could she be wrong about God? What if her connection to Ella was nothing more than the manufactured hope of her own desperate emotions? What if God wasn't going to bring Daddy and Riley Jo home, and the remains turned out to be theirs? She didn't want to end up broken and bitter like Mama.

Abby pulled her knees up and hugged them. If God didn't do what she asked, did that mean He hadn't listened? Did that negate His being good and approachable and caring? She didn't have answers to any of her questions.

All she had was blind faith. Was that enough?

CHAPTER 12

Abby heard a ringing noise that kept getting louder and louder and finally realized it was her alarm clock. Groping the nightstand, she turned off the alarm, then sat up on the side of the bed, her legs dangling. She rubbed her eyes and groaned. Five o'clock was too early for any human being to have to get up.

She slid out of bed and walked down the hall and out into the living room. Her mother was curled up on one end of the couch, holding the phone.

"Mama," Abby whispered. "Are you awake?"

Her mother opened her eyes and sat up. "I was just dozing."

"Any news?"

"No, Virgil hasn't called. I'm assuming he hasn't discovered anything else."

Good! "I'm going to shower and then head over to Flutter's," Abby said. "If the sheriff does call, will you let me know?"

"Of course. What else are you planning today?"

"Unless we get bad news, I'm meeting Jay on the slope at noon so I can watch him sketch. He's an amazing artist. You should see his stuff."

"I'd like to. Have him bring some of his work to the house some-time." Mama seemed lost in a long pause. Finally she said, "You two are spending a lot of time together."

"It's nice being with a guy who's just a friend. I don't have to try and impress him. Or doll up every time I see him."

"You always look dolled up, honey. You're just naturally pretty. I'm sure Jay isn't blind."

Abby shrugged. "Doesn't matter. That's not the kind of friend-ship we want. Jay's mom is getting married for the fourth time, and he's lived with her ups and downs all his life. He thinks relationships just bring heartache. I agree with him."

"How can you say that, Abby? Your father and I had eighteen wonderful years together."

"And it nearly destroyed you when he disappeared."

"It would be a huge mistake to avoid loving someone because you might lose them. The joy I experienced with your father far outweighed the sorrow. I wouldn't trade those years for anything."

"Maybe not. But the pain of missing Daddy and Riley Jo is almost more than *I* can bear. Why would I want to be that vulnerable?"

"Not now," Mama said. "But someday. The grief will pass."

She wondered if her mother was saying that as much for her own benefit as her daughter's. "I need to get ready. I'm the only waitress scheduled until seven."

"Abby, about last night … I'd like to put it behind us. Can we agree not to get into spiritual discussions right now? I see things very differently than you and your grandfather. But I didn't mean to hurt your feelings."

"I didn't mean to upset you either."

Her mother squeezed her hand. "Let's forget it. You don't need to go to work with that burden on your back."

Too late.

✤

Buck sat at a table at Flutter's, his thoughts consumed with the implications of last night's visit from the sheriff. Savannah filled Titus's cup with coffee and then filled Buck's.

"It's a little crazy this morning," Savannah said. "I'll be right back to take your order."

Titus smiled. "We're not going anywhere."

Buck stroked his white mustache and waited until Savannah moved to the next table. "I guess you heard on the news that remains were found in the woods."

"I heard." Titus blew on his coffee, his round dark eyes peering over the top of his cup. "Wasn't sure you wanted to talk about it."

"Nothin' to tell yet, but if those remains turn out to be"—Buck swallowed the emotion that tightened his throat—"what the sheriff suspects, it'll sure change things in our family. At least it'd be closure."

The front door opened, and Sheriff Virgil Granger walked in with Chief Deputy Mann. They looked whipped.

Buck's pulse raced as the sheriff walked in his direction and stopped at the table.

Virgil bent down next to Buck's chair. "I just talked with Kate. We haven't found anything definitive. But if there's someplace we could talk privately, I'll fill you in."

"You can speak freely, Sheriff. Titus knows the situation."

Virgil's eyes were bloodshot, his face unshaven. "As I was saying, we didn't find anything definitive. Just some pocket change strewn across the area—and a 1967 class ring from Arthur Mixon High School. We're researching to find out where that school is. Also found a few buttons and a rusty pocketknife—tested negative for blood. We're combing the area again now that the sun's up. Dental records will tell us in a couple days whether the skull is Micah's. We'll have to wait a lot longer on the DNA analysis to know if any of the bones are Riley Jo's."

Buck tried to process what the sheriff had said, but it was as though the man had been talking about someone else. Micah's skull. Riley Jo's bones. It was difficult to think of people he loved in those terms.

"Thanks, Virgil," Buck said, shaking the sheriff's hand much harder and longer than he intended. "I know you're as eager to figure it out as we are."

"I'd sure like to find your family some closure." Virgil tipped his Stetson and stood. "I'll let y'all get back to your breakfast."

Virgil went over and sat at a table with his chief deputy.

Buck moved his spoon back and forth in his coffee cup. Bottom line: they still didn't know anything for sure.

"You okay?" Titus said.

Buck exhaled, looking into his friend's understanding eyes. "I'll be fine—as long as I remember that law enforcement can't possibly move fast enough to keep up with my expectations."

❦

Kate sat at the kitchen table, vaguely aware that someone was talking to her. She looked up and saw Jesse standing next to her.

"I'm going to go fill the feeders," he said.

Kate patted the chair next to her. "Sit with me for a moment."

Jesse, looking so grown up in his blue Angel View staff shirt, sat across from her, his arms folded on the table.

"I just spoke with the sheriff," Kate said. "He didn't find anything that would pinpoint that Daddy or Riley Jo had been there. This means we won't know anything until they do some tests on the remains."

Jesse looked up at her, his round blue eyes filled with compassion. "Mama, do you hope it *is* Daddy or Riley Jo?"

Kate brushed the fine dark hair off her son's forehead. "Part of me does. Five years is a very long time to wonder. That's half *your* life. But it's also hard to accept that your father and sister might be dead."

"Abby doesn't think they are."

"I know. But she's not basing her opinion on anything other than wishful thinking."

"She says she's stepping out in faith."

"Everyone has the right to hope, Jesse. But we have to be realistic."

Jesse squirmed slightly in his chair. "Can I ask you something?"

"Sure."

"Do you? Have faith, I mean?"

"First, tell me what you think faith is."

Jesse laced and unlaced his fingers. "Well … I *think* it means you believe something is true even if you can't see or prove it."

"That's a pretty good definition. So to answer your question, I do better believing in facts I can see than in something I wish were true."

"So … you wish it was true that Daddy and Riley Jo are alive. But you don't have faith that they are?"

"It's more complicated than that, Jesse. I don't want to think that hard today."

Jesse looked down and ever so slowly drew imaginary circles on the table. "I need to tell you something. But I don't want you to be mad."

"What is it? You can talk to me."

Jesse hesitated and then continued. "I was up in the attic, looking for the box of jigsaw puzzles, and I found the Bible storybook Daddy used to read to me and Riley Jo. Do you remember it?"

"Yes. I'm surprised *you* do."

"It's one of the few things I remember doing with Daddy." Jesse glanced up at her and then lowered his gaze. "I took it to my room and read all the stories. Are you mad?"

"Of course not." *It's just one more thing for me to worry about.*

Jesse's eyes looked like big blue buttons. "I see why Abby thinks God can do anything. Did you know He made a donkey talk? And saved Shadrach, Meshach, and Ben Dego from getting burned in the fiery furnace?"

Kate smiled without meaning to. "Yes, I knew that."

"He even came back from the dead! Isn't that cool?"

Kate just listened, hoping he wouldn't ask her to elaborate on or agree with anything he'd read.

"I feel a lot better now." Jesse wiped the perspiration off his face with the back of his hand. "I felt guilty sneaking around."

"You can never go wrong being truthful with me. But I need to be truthful with you, too. *I'm* not the go-to guy if you have questions about God or the Bible. I'm still working through my disappointment with God and wouldn't be much help. But you can always go to Grandpa."

"Okay." Jesse stood. "I'm going to pray that God helps you to trust Him again. I think you'd be a lot happier."

Jesse hugged her and left.

Her cell phone rang, and she glanced at the screen. *Virgil!* She took a slow, deep breath, reluctant to push the talk button. This could be the call that would change the course of her life.

CHAPTER 13

Abby hiked down a grassy incline on the east side of Sure Foot Mountain that she and Jay had named "the slope." She stopped at the giant oak tree that offered the only shady spot and spread a worn patchwork quilt on the ground beneath it.

She set the two sacks from Sammie's Subs on the quilt, then sat, hugging her knees, the warm breeze tussling with her hair. She looked down at Beaver Lake—nestled in the lush, rolling Ozark hills and dazzling in the noonday sun like a treasure chest of diamonds. Over twenty-eight thousand acres of sheer beauty, this pristine expanse never ceased to stir something deep inside her.

Abby spotted a fleck of white—an osprey. She watched the magnificent bird hover in midair before dive-bombing into the choppy water and flying off with a fish wiggling in his talons. "A master fisherman," Daddy used to say.

Daddy. She blinked away the image she had conjured up of the remains. Abby refused to believe the skull was her father's. He was alive. So was Riley Jo. She was sure of it.

A rather large sailboat caught her attention, the yellow-and-white mast crisp and colorful against the marine blue of Beaver Lake. The vessel seemed to glide effortlessly across the water as the skipper rode the wind.

Abby loved the feeling of the wind on her face.

She closed her eyes and just let the warm breeze flow over her. She imagined the spirit of God in the wind and relished His touch.

Father, I have faith even if Mama doesn't trust You anymore—

Abby heard a familiar whistle and turned around. Jay was making his way down the sloping hillside, carrying his art portfolio under his arm.

"Sorry I'm a little late," he said, sounding out of breath. "Traffic in town was backed up. I guess tourist season is in full swing."

"I haven't been here long."

"I got your text messages and have been following the news. When will you know if it's your dad and sister?"

"They're not finished searching," Abby said. "But you know I don't believe Daddy and Riley Jo are dead. My family's really stressed. I can't allow myself to think that way."

"What a shock, though." Jay sat cross-legged on the blanket and laid his portfolio next to him. "I'm sorry y'all have the uncertainty hanging over you. Frankly, I was surprised you didn't cancel this."

"It's too important to cancel. Now let's change the subject before I lose my appetite."

Abby passed him his sub, said a silent prayer of thanks, then bit into her sandwich, savoring every delectable flavor. "So what did you bring?"

Jay smiled, his five o'clock shadow looking both masculine and artsy. "Voila." He opened his portfolio and revealed a sketchpad and dozens of colored pencils. "I printed out some pages of facial features I found on one of those 'learn to draw' websites." Jay held up a small stack of images. "Eyes, eyebrows, noses, mouths, chins, cheekbones. Thought it might help you to look through them."

"Okay." Abby bit into a Sun Chip. "I kind of remember how he looked, but maybe once you start sketching it'll come together."

Jay took a bite of his sandwich, his dark eyes seeming to study her.

"What?" she said.

"You have the most amazing coloring, Abby. Especially up here on the slope. Your auburn hair and blue eyes are stunning against the green. Let me paint your portrait sometime. If you like it, I'll frame it for your mother."

"I'm flattered you want me for a subject, but I'm uncomfortable drawing attention to myself. People are always complimenting me about my looks. I want them to see there's more to me than that."

"They'd have to be blind not to. You're as pretty on the inside as you are on the outside. But there's no shame in being pretty. Beauty is something to be captured and enjoyed. At least think about it."

"Not today," Abby said, hoping Jay wasn't starting to feel attracted to her. "We've got work to do."

Abby brushed the crumbs off the quilt and stuffed the trash into the sacks. "Okay, let's get started putting a face on the man Ella was with."

Jay stuffed the last of his sandwich into his mouth and wiped his hands. He took out his sketchpad and selected a pencil, then thumbed through a stack of papers and pulled out a sheet that pictured a variety of facial shapes.

"Look over my shoulder so we can both see," he said. "Which one best fits the guy you saw?"

Abby knelt behind Jay and studied the faces and then closed her eyes and tried to picture the man. "It's hard to say since he had a beard."

"Look at the shapes and mentally put a beard on them. Which one?"

Abby pointed to the oval shape. "I'm not sure, but I think this is right."

Jay drew a big oval on his paper. "All right, let's build on that." He held out another paper with eye shapes. "Pick one."

Abby thought back to when the man came outside of Murchison's and grabbed Ella's arm. "His eyes were serious looking. I don't remember the shape and color, but they seemed dark. Brown maybe."

"That's a start." Jay drew the eyes and then held out a sheet with nose shapes.

"His nose was pointy." Abby perused the choices and selected one.

Jay drew it. "Is this starting to look like the guy?"

"It's too soon to tell. What else?"

Jay held up a sheet showing mouth shapes.

"The guy had a beard," Abby said. "How am I supposed to know what his mouth looked like?"

"If he was scolding Ella, you must've seen his mouth. Think."

"I just remember his teeth were kind of crooked."

"Can you be more specific? Were there spaces between his teeth? Were they protruding? Were they yellowish?"

"I don't know! I just saw him for a few seconds!" Abby sighed. "Maybe this isn't such a great idea. I don't know if we can do this."

"Yes, we can," Jay said. "We just have to work at it. What did his beard look like?"

"Reddish gray and bushy. It wasn't very long."

Jay drew the beard, and her heart skipped a beat. "Yes!" she said. "It's definitely starting to look like him, but now the eyes are wrong. I think they were more intense, sort of like an eagle's ..."

⚜

Kate picked a warm towel out of the dryer and folded it, then put it neatly on top of the stack. Doing laundry was therapeutic and the one chore she had always preferred to do by herself.

"There you are."

She turned around and saw Hawk standing in the doorway between the kitchen and the utility room.

"I have thirty minutes before my next jeep tour," he said, "and wanted to check in and see if Sheriff Granger found anything else."

Kate shook her head. "He called a little while ago and asked me to contact Dr. Silvers and authorize him to pull your father's dental records. Virgil seemed to think the pathologist could make a determination within a day or two."

Hawk exhaled. "Everything is a waiting game."

"At least it won't be long."

Hawk came over and put his hands on Kate's shoulders and looked into her eyes. "I almost hope it *is* Daddy. At least it would be closure."

"More like the finale." Kate turned and pulled another towel out of the dryer and began folding it.

"It's better than feeling like this for another five years—or ten—or twenty. Or *never* knowing."

"But you said yourself there's no way your father and sister got lost out there." Kate put the towel neatly on the stack, deliberately avoiding eye contact with Hawk. "If they're dead, something awful happened to them. We could have *that* unknown hanging over us, which would almost be worse."

"I don't know, Mama. I've already wondered about it a thousand times. If they're dead, I would rather know and get the grief out of my system than let it eat me up for the rest of my life."

Kate started to reach for another towel and then paused instead. "I suppose I would too. But it would be hard to accept that they're dead."

"Would you rather think Daddy ran off and took Riley Jo?"

"He didn't," Kate said. "He wouldn't do that to us."

"Something happened out there, Mama. Maybe a bear got them. Or wild hogs."

"I doubt just bones will tell *how* they died. So we'd still be left wondering. I'm not sure just knowing they're dead would bring closure."

"It would for me," Hawk said. "At least some. Maybe Abby and Grandpa will stop trying to cram their beliefs down our throats."

Kate pushed aside the stack of towels and turned to Hawk. "Don't be too hard on them for wanting to believe that God answers prayer. I used to believe it with all my heart. I'm just worried your grandfather and Abby are going to bottom out when they realize it's a myth."

"At least then Abby would stop embarrassing herself by trying to find that girl she took a picture of. How many times is she going to pull this before she starts living in reality?"

"I've got a call in to Dixie to get her an appointment." Kate looked over Hawk's shoulder and spotted the old family photo she couldn't bring herself to remove from the fridge. "But Abby may have to face reality when the pathology results are in."

❧

Abby studied the sixth sketch Jay had made using the facial features she chose that best fit the man she had seen with Ella.

"That's close," Abby said. "The eyebrows are still wrong. His were even fuller than that."

Jay glanced at his watch. "Why don't we take a break? There's still time for me to sketch a few more possibilities before I have to leave for work."

Abby sat next to him on the blanket. "I don't know if we're going to get any closer to what he looked like than this last one. The beard is perfect."

Abby's cell phone rang, and she felt tension tighten her neck. Was Mama calling to tell her that the sheriff had found something else? She glanced at the screen and saw only *Caller Unknown*. "Hello."

"I warned you not to tell nobody that I told you to back off lookin' for the girl."

"I didn't tell anyone." Abby mouthed the words, *It's him*, as she put the phone on speaker.

"You're lyin'. I know you blabbed to that Oldham kid. He ain't gonna tell nobody about the girl, and he knows why. But I'm warnin' you, stop askin' about her, or I'll make sure you go missin'—permanently."

Abby was rendered mute in the dead air that followed, her heart nearly pounding out of her chest. She stared at Jay, who looked as if he'd just seen a ghost.

Finally Jay began to pack up his art portfolio. "That was *not* Mason Craddock or any of his clones. That guy sounded middle-aged. Are you sure it was the same man who called you before?"

"I'm sure," Abby said. "I guess I was so positive it was Mason having a good laugh at my expense that I just assumed he disguised his voice. I wonder why the caller thinks I 'blabbed to that Oldham kid'? I don't know anyone by that name. Why are you putting your things away?"

"Because"—Jay stuffed the last colored pencil into the portfolio and zipped it—"he made it clear what's going to happen if you don't back off."

"But what is it he doesn't want me to find out? I know it's a long shot, but it's *possible* that Ella could be Riley Jo. I have to know for sure."

"Count me out," Jay said. "Some of these mountain folks can be dangerous. Paranoid. Who knows what kind of word's been spread because you were asking around about Ella."

"But I don't have anyone else. My family's turned me off. I'd go to the sheriff, but he wouldn't take me seriously either."

"You don't know that."

"Actually, I do." Abby took her finger and traced the star pattern on one of the quilt squares. What did she have to lose by telling Jay the whole truth? "I didn't tell you this before because I was afraid you would think I was crying wolf."

"Didn't tell me what?" Jay said.

"Two times in the past three years, I saw a girl who looked like Riley Jo. Once at the county fair, and once on the lake. The sheriff had his deputies searching high and low, and it didn't lead anywhere. They won't do that again."

"Guess you can't blame them."

"But this time is different," Abby insisted. "The phone calls prove it."

"All the phone calls prove is that someone threatened you." Jay was quiet for longer than Abby was comfortable. "I think you need to drop this right now."

"I can't. Not without finding Ella."

"Abby, you're chasing a rainbow."

"Maybe the sheriff would take me seriously since you witnessed the second call."

Jay reached over and gently held her wrist. "Look, even if I back up your story about what the caller said, the sheriff won't just reopen the case; he'll have to treat it as a kidnapping and get the FBI involved. Is that what you want?"

Abby considered how obvious the FBI presence was before in the search for her father and sister. "That's the last thing I need. If the caller's watching me, he'll know. And if he's the one who has Ella, he might take her away. Then I'll never find her."

"Maybe you're not supposed to." Jay rose to his feet, his portfolio tucked under his arm. "You're in over your head, Abby. You just got a death threat. This guy's not kidding around."

"Then help me find out who the Oldham kid is, since he apparently knows something. He might talk to us if I explained the situation."

"The caller told you to back off."

"I've come this far. I have to know the truth."

"Even if you end up dead?" Jay exhaled loudly enough to make his point. "I've got to go to work. I'll call you."

"Can I at least have the last sketch you did?"

Jay shook his head. "There's no way I'm helping you put yourself in danger."

"I'm going to find Ella, with or without you."

"Don't do this, Abby. Do you want your mother to lose another daughter? I don't want to lose my best friend."

"Then help me."

Jay walked past her and headed up the slope.

Abby sat on the blanket, her cell phone in her sweaty palm, and replayed the last few minutes in her mind. She had never once considered the threat to be real—until now. Jay was right. The caller was no high school kid.

A cold chill made her shudder. She got up and grabbed the quilt and the sacks, her mind spinning out of control.

"Come on …"

The male voice startled her and sent her pulse racing. She turned around, her hand over her pounding heart. "You scared me to death, Jay!"

"I'm not leaving you out here by yourself. I'll walk you to your car."

CHAPTER 14

Abby slipped into her room, the Raleigh County phone book tucked under her arm, and shut the door behind her. She flipped through the white pages and found the residential listings for the last name Oldham. There must have been over a hundred. She didn't know anyone with that last name except Mr. Oldham the pharmacist, and he was older than Grandpa Buck. Not that she knew what the caller meant by the Oldham *kid*. Was he talking about a child or a teen or a young adult?

Abby slammed the phone book shut. What good were all these phone numbers without a first name? Why would the anonymous caller make his threat seem less credible by accusing her of confiding in someone she'd never even met? If he was messing with her mind, it was working.

Abby flopped on the bed. She was getting close to something big. She could feel it.

Don't do this, Abby. Do you want your mother to lose another daughter?

Abby lay on her side and hugged her pillow. She would never want to put Mama through the agony of losing another child.

Lord, I don't know what to do if Jay won't help me. My family thinks I'm delusional. I can't go to the sheriff. But if Ella's in trouble—whether she's Riley Jo or not—how can I just walk away?

Abby watched the clock until 9:59, then called Jay's cell phone and got his voice mail. She hung up and called his work number.

"Tutty's Barbecue. Randy speakin'."

"Randy, it's Abby Cummings. May I speak with Jay before he leaves?"

"Could if he was here," Randy said. "He called around three and said he was sicker 'n a dog and could Philip take his place tonight. Said he was fixin' to stay close to the bathroom."

"Okay, thanks." Abby pulled up the keyboard on her phone and began typing a text message to Jay. *Called Tutty's. Home sick? Call or text me.*

Abby set her phone on the bed. She was with Jay until almost three. He must have called in sick right after he walked her to her car and they parted ways. Was he even more shaken by the caller's threat than she was?

She heard a knock on her door and put her pillow over the phone book. "Come in."

"It's me," Mama said. "I saw your light on. Just checking to see if you're all right. You seemed distracted at dinner, and I haven't seen you all evening."

Abby sat up on the side of the bed. "I'm fine. Just a little tired. You're not bringing bad news from the sheriff, are you?"

"No. I was just wondering how your afternoon with Jay went."

"Fine."

"Did you mention to him I would like to see his work?" Mama smiled. "I really would."

"It didn't come up. But I'll remember to ask him."

"Dixie just called back. She shuffled her schedule so she could see you Friday at one. I wrote it on the calendar so we won't forget."

Zero chance of that, Abby thought as her phone beeped. "That's probably Jay."

"I'll let you answer him." Her mother came over and hugged her. "Good night, Abby."

"Good night."

Mama glanced at Riley Jo's doll as she closed the door.

Abby pulled up one new text message from Jay.

Not sick. Need space.

Why space? Abby replied.

A minute later her phone beeped with his answer.

What you're doing is dangerous.

"So … you're … shutting … me … out?" she said aloud as she keyed in her reply.

Jay's response came quickly. *Weak signal. We'll talk soon.*

How soon? Abby shot back.

She waited ten minutes for a response and then put her phone on the nightstand. She wasn't going to play games with Jay because he couldn't handle the situation she found herself in. If he was going to abandon her when she needed him most, then he wasn't much of a friend.

❧

Sheriff Virgil Granger collapsed on the glider on his front porch, every bone in his body aching. He unbuttoned his navy uniform shirt and let the evening breeze cool his bare chest.

He closed his eyes and listened to a cricket choir fill the night with the sweet serenade he had loved since he was a boy.

The front door opened and closed, the fragrance of gardenia wafting under his nose and bringing a smile to his face. "Hey, sugar," he said.

Jill Beth came up behind him and gently massaged his shoulders. "You ought to sleep like a log tonight. It's been a long time since you were up thirty-six hours straight."

"At least we should know soon if Micah's dental records match the skull we found." Virgil shook his head. "Shoot, even after five years, it's hard to think that way. I can still see Micah as a scrawny little squirt wearing a Superman cape, wanting to hang out with the big boys. I'll always regret we didn't let him."

"You were kids, Virgil. Don't be so hard on yourself."

"I'm just glad we taught our sons better."

Jill Beth kissed his cheek and came around and sat next to him on the glider.

Virgil slipped his arm around her. "I talked to Kate just before I came home. Abby's at it again. She photographed a little girl she thinks looks like Riley Jo and has been making inquiries around Foggy Ridge."

"Poor kid."

Virgil cleared his throat. "It's hard to say this, but it'd probably be the best thing for everybody if the remains turn out to be Micah's. *And* Riley Jo's. At least the family could go to sleep at night knowing they're not coming home."

Jill Beth put her head on his shoulder. "They deserve to find closure."

"Thing is, even if we determine that Micah and Riley Jo are both dead, that might not be enough closure unless we determine how they died. This could open up a whole new nightmare for the Cummings."

"I'm sure it's nothing that hasn't crossed their minds a thousand times."

Virgil nodded. "But it's different when the truth of it looks you right in the eye. It really hit *me* today."

"I just hope Kate can move out of the past. I think Elliot Stafford is sweet on her. Of course, he's too much of a gentleman to admit it while Kate's situation is hanging in midair."

"Elliott, huh? I haven't paid much attention."

Jill Beth sat up straight and captured a yawn with her hand. "I'm not sure Kate will ever let herself fall in love with another man. She seems to have Micah on a pedestal."

"Some of it could be guilt," Virgil said. "Don't forget they'd been having a tiff for a couple weeks about some business thing they disagreed on."

"Yes, but all couples go through trials. That didn't have anything to do with what happened."

"Unless Micah was fed up and wanted out of the marriage."

Jill Beth looked up at him. "You don't really think that?"

"I don't want to," Virgil said. "But given the right circumstances, good people are capable of shocking choices."

"Kate needs the truth—whatever it is—so she can live in the present."

"I agree, sugar." Virgil ran his fingers through Jill Beth's thick dark hair, which was noticeably void of gray since her last beauty appointment. "The truth is in the remains. We just have to wait and see what pathology tells us."

✦

Abby lay wide awake in the dark, staring at the ceiling fan. The more she thought about it, the more scared she was about the caller's threat. The only way to find Ella was to ask around and show her picture. That had become dangerous.

Now what? Jay had left her hanging just when she needed him most. Not what she expected from a best friend.

Abby wiped away the tears that ran down the sides of her face. What if the remains turned out to be her father's? Could she let go of years of hope and accept the grim finality of it? At least if her father had died in the woods, he hadn't run off with another woman. Which meant he hadn't chosen to take Riley Jo because he loved her more.

Shame scalded Abby's face, and she wondered how her mother would react if she knew that, all these years, the biggest fear Abby had about Daddy and Riley Jo's disappearance was something so completely self-centered.

Abby sat up and blew her nose. She checked her phone to see if Jay had left a text message. Nothing. The last thing she wanted to do was go to the sheriff, but now that she suspected that Ella was a missing child, how could she keep the information to herself?

CHAPTER 15

Kate sat at the kitchen table, still dressed in her bathrobe and doodling on Thursday's to-do list, vaguely aware of footsteps moving in her direction.

"Good, you're still here," Dad said. "I was about to head over to Flutter's. Have you heard from Virgil?"

"I just got off the phone with him." Kate whisked a tear off her cheek. "There's been a new development."

Dad sat next to her and clasped her hand. "Tell me."

"Deputies got an anonymous tip and found what appears to be a mass grave in the woods—about a mile from where they found the first remains. Virgil said they've found skeletal remains of at least eleven people—five of them children. They're not finished looking."

"Dear Lord ..." Her dad's voice failed.

Kate swallowed the wad of emotion that threatened to throw her composure out the window.

"I'm sorry, baby. I really am. If I could take your pain myself, I would."

"I know, Dad. I'll be okay." *Will I?*

"You want me to tell the kids?"

Kate looked over at him, her vision totally clouded with tears. "I'll tell Jesse. Would you tell Hawk and Abby?"

"Sure I will." Dad leaned over on the countertop and picked up the box of tissues and set it in front of her. "Let's sit a minute and let this sink in."

Kate plucked a tissue and wiped her eyes. "I can accept that Micah and Riley Jo might be dead. It's something I've wondered a lot about. What's really difficult is wondering if they suffered. And now, a mass grave …? I have so many questions that no one can answer. We may never know the truth of what happened to them."

"Feels like we've been sucker punched," Dad said. "I didn't think there were many missin' persons cases still unresolved in Raleigh County."

"Virgil says there aren't. These are probably the remains of people from outside the area, or the remains of people never reported missing. Unless Micah's dental records match the skull they found Tuesday night, it could be another long wait before we know *anything*. I just want to lay them to rest. Is *that* too much to ask?"

Her dad didn't say anything. Why would he? He knew she wasn't about to ask God for anything. Not after all the times He had ignored her prayers—if He'd heard them at all. Faith was a bottomless pit she wasn't going to fall into again. Whatever courage, whatever strength she needed to get through this, she would find within herself.

Abby cringed as Hawk slammed the front door of the house hard enough to rattle the windows.

Grandpa Buck squeezed her hand. "You okay?"

Abby shrugged. "Not really. I understand why Hawk's so upset."

"We're all worn out with waitin'," Grandpa said. "But this is gonna drag out a while longer."

"How's Mama?"

"Scared. Sad. Anxious to know the truth."

"They're not going to find Daddy and Riley Jo's remains."

"What if they do, Abby? You have to prepare yourself for that possibility."

She shook her head. "I asked God to bring them home."

Grandpa looked at her with those kind gray eyes that seemed to speak even when he wasn't. "Honey, maybe He has."

"But that's not what I meant! I want them home alive."

"We all do," Grandpa said. "But like we talked about before, with God all things are possible, but not necessarily probable. He has a bigger plan than the one we can see, and we don't always get what we pray for. He knows what's best. We have to accept that."

"Well, I'm not accepting something that hasn't happened."

Grandpa stroked his mustache. "Are you still looking for Ella?"

"Yes. Mama promised not to bug me about it if I agreed to see Dixie."

"Your mother's worried about you."

"She doesn't need to be. I'm fine." Abby exhaled. "Look, I know Mama thinks my imagination's gone bonkers, but she's wrong. Ella looks so much like Riley Jo it's uncanny. I can't believe none of you see it."

"We see it, Abby. But we see her in a lot of sweet faces. Sometimes it's the big blue eyes. The elfin smile. The button nose. Heck, I've even thought I heard her giggling once. That's just part of the grief. Part of lettin' go."

"Then why do I feel such a connection to Ella? I've never felt that before."

Grandpa brushed the hair away from Abby's eyes. "Maybe you just want it so badly, it's got a hold on you. Hope is a powerful motivator."

"Then let me hold on to it while I can. It's a lot better than being depressed."

"Can't argue with that." Grandpa put his arms around her and held her tightly. "I talked to Savannah before I called you home. You don't have to go back to work today."

"But I want to," Abby said. "I can't sit around thinking about this, or I'll go nuts."

"Are you going to be with Jay this afternoon?"

Good question. "We haven't made plans. Maybe."

"It's probably better if you're not alone. How does *he* feel about your search for Ella?"

"Jay's been helping me. And he knows about the other two times," she quickly added, feeling guilty for deliberately not mentioning the threat to her life or Jay's insistence that she stop searching.

"Abby, I don't know whether looking for this girl is healthy or not. I'll leave that call up to Dixie." Grandpa stroked her cheek. "But I'm serious about this: you need to prepare—mentally and emotionally—for the possibility that your daddy and sister might be identified from those remains."

Abby pressed her lips together and forced back the tears. She wasn't going to think about possibilities. "I should get back to work. Savannah's going to be shorthanded."

⚜

Abby brought an empty tray back into the kitchen and heard her text message signal. She went into the restroom and locked the door.

She read the new text message from Jay. *Slope at noon? Eat before you come. This is urgent.*

Abby quickly keyed in her reply. *I'll be there.*

She put her phone in her pocket and opened the door. Savannah was waiting outside.

"You okay, honey?"

"Yes, ma'am," Abby said. "Did I do something wrong?"

"Heavens, no." Savannah smiled. "I'm just worried about you. Sure you don't want to go home?"

"I'm sure. I'll do better if I can stay busy."

Savannah put her hand on Abby's shoulder. "Truthfully, you're the best waitress I've got. Things run more smoothly when you're here."

"Really? Thanks."

"You have a great work ethic, kiddo. Not all that common in young people today."

"My parents taught me to finish whatever I started and to give it a hundred percent." *That's how I plan to find Ella.*

"Order two's up," Benson hollered.

Abby nodded toward the order shelf. "That's mine."

"You're a trooper," Savannah said. "If you change your mind about leaving early, let me know."

"Thanks, but I'll finish my shift." Abby arranged the order on a tray and walked toward table two, her thoughts turning to Jay's text message. What did he have to tell her that was urgent? He'd had all night to think about it. Maybe he had decided to help her find Ella.

Not that she knew where to start at this point. Whoever it was that didn't want her to find Ella was watching. It would be impossible to ask around without him knowing about it. Her only hope of making sense of Ella's situation was to figure out who the Oldham kid was and convince him to tell her. What were the odds of that happening?

CHAPTER 16

Abby drove Mama's Odyssey up Summit Road, winding through the tall trees toward the top of Sure Foot Mountain. She slowed the car and pulled onto an unmarked road, rocking and rolling over the rugged dirt terrain for about fifty yards until the narrow road dead-ended at the edge of a clearing. Jay's truck was nowhere in sight. She glanced at her watch. It was only eleven forty-five.

She rolled down the windows, comforted by the familiar sounds of Carolina chickadees flitting among the trees and a pileated woodpecker artfully drilling the side of the dead tree that marked the top of the slope.

Could the anonymous caller know she was here? Could he be watching? No one had followed her from Angel View. She rubbed her arms, which were suddenly like gooseflesh.

She checked her phone to be sure Jay hadn't sent another text. He hadn't.

A loud rustling noise caused her to freeze, her heart racing faster than the pair of rabbits that shot out of the brush and hopped down the grassy slope.

Come on, Jay. I feel exposed out here.

In the quiet that followed, she tried to relax. There was no place on Sure Foot Mountain where she felt safer than here at their secret place. She had rarely seen anyone else up here, other than occasional backpackers.

A crow began to caw, then several others joined in. What were they communicating? Abby rolled up her windows and locked the doors. She turned on the motor and let the cold air from the air conditioner blow on her face. How irrational was it to be afraid? The caller couldn't be everywhere. And she hadn't been out talking to anyone about Ella since his last call.

Lord, please protect me. I just want the truth of what happened to Daddy and Riley Jo. I know You hear me, and I believe You'll answer.

Abby heard the sound of a motor. She looked in the rearview mirror and saw a cloud of brown dust and Jay's white Ford truck approaching. She got out of the car and waved.

Jay pulled up next to the Odyssey and shut off the motor. In the next second she was at his driver's side window.

"Eat before you come?" she said. "Urgent? I hope you didn't get me out here to lecture me."

Jay turned as he opened the window, revealing his uncombed hair and the bags under his bloodshot eyes. "Don't worry, I didn't. Let's go sit under the oak tree."

He got out of the car and started walking briskly down the slope, his shoes and legs splattered with dried mud, his back soaked with perspiration.

"Why are you such a mess?" Abby said.

"I didn't have time to clean up."

"From what?"

"I'll explain in a minute."

"Why won't you look at me?" Abby said.

"Trust me, making eye contact with me is the least of your worries …"

❧

Minutes later, Abby sat cross-legged, facing Jay under the giant oak tree on the slope.

"All right, talk to me," she said. "Where have you been? You look like a bum."

"I told you I didn't have time to clean up."

"Will you at least look at me?"

Jay shook his head. "What I have to say will be easier if I don't."

"Well, if this is my Dear John Letter," Abby said, "just get it over with. I honestly thought we were better friends than that."

"We are. That's not what this is."

"Then what is *this*? Get to the point."

Jay held up his palm. "I will. Give me a minute. This is the hardest thing I've ever done."

"What is so hard?"

"I promise you, Abby, I never saw it coming. I …" Jay's eyes glistened, and he seemed to choke on the words.

"Saw *what* coming?"

"Something happened," he said. "I've never told anyone."

Abby put her hands to her temples. "I'm so confused. Can you start at some kind of beginning so I can figure out what you're talking about?"

"That's just it. No one would ever figure it out. It's the kind of thing you take to your grave."

"Jay, stop it! I am freaking out here. You look like something the cat drug in, and you're talking in circles. Have you been doing drugs or something?"

"I never connected the dots until yesterday," he said. "But now it's clear as anything. And I'm not sure what to do. I didn't pick up on Ella's picture. Or even the sketch. Until the voice ..." Jay's hands were shaking.

"The voice on the phone?" Abby said.

Jay nodded. "It's him."

"Who? You know him?"

"Yes. I mean no." Jay exhaled. "I don't know his name. But we've met."

"When?"

"I debated half the night whether to say anything to you about this. It'll cost us our friendship. I know that."

"You don't know that. I'm pretty loyal."

"No one's that loyal."

"When did you meet the guy?" Abby said. "Are you sure it was him?"

"I'm sure. I'll never forget his voice as long as I live."

"You didn't answer my question." Abby lifted his chin. "When did you meet him—where?"

"Across a meadow, at the edge of the woods—a few days after I turned twelve. My dad had given me a rifle that belonged to him and his dad before him. I was target practicing, trying to hit a plastic jug from a hundred yards. I kept missing and went to retrieve the milk jug and move it back to fifty yards. I … I heard this booming voice coming from the forest."

"*His* voice?" Abby heard herself say.

Jay nodded. "He said something like, 'That was some wild shootin', boy.' I saw a bearded man standing in the woods, holding a toddler—a girl. I was embarrassed that he had seen me miss my target. I told him I was pretty good shooting from fifty yards. I asked him his name and told him mine was Jimmy Dale Oldham, but that everyone called me J.D."

Abby gasped. "You're the Oldham kid?"

"Let me explain. That summer I'd started using my stepdad's last name and my initials. I thought it was cool. But when I started middle school, they said I couldn't legally use Oldham. So I went back to Rogers. And after I'd told the bearded guy I went by J.D., I thought it was smart to drop the D and go by Jay. I felt a lot safer being Jay Rogers, in case he ever told the sheriff what happened."

"You're not making sense. What happened? Who was this bearded man?"

Jay met her gaze. "He never told me his name. But the next thing I knew, he was dragging something out into the light, and I realized it was a person—a man. His chest was soaked with blood. The bearded man said that *I* killed him."

"When you missed your target?"

"Yeah." Jay paused to gather his composure. "I told him I didn't mean to. He said the guy was just as dead anyway. And the law would expect me to pay for what I did. I remember telling him over and over it was an accident and that he was a witness and could tell the sheriff. But he said all he witnessed was a man get shot and knew nothing about the why or how of it. I could tell he wasn't going to back my story. I was so scared I wet my pants. I'd heard of a kid who shot a man and was tried as an adult. They locked him up."

"How'd you resolve it?" Abby said.

"I kept saying I didn't mean any harm and would swear to it on the Bible, that he had to believe me. I said the dead man probably had a family, and we should tell someone. The bearded guy said he knew him. And he didn't have any kin." Jay wiped the tears off his face with his arm. "I thought I was going to jail, Abby. I thought my life was over. I thought my dad would disown me if he found out I'd killed someone—and with my birthday rifle that had been passed down for three generations."

"So what happened?" Abby studied Jay's face and saw that the agony was still fresh.

"Out of the blue, the bearded guy said, 'Go on home, boy. What's done is done. I'll see to him.' I asked what he was going to do. He said it wasn't my concern."

"Not your concern?" Abby said. "You had just killed a man!"

"He told me never to speak of it to anybody or he'd be forced to tell the sheriff what he knew, and they'd throw me in jail until I was an old man. He told me to keep my mouth shut and never go back there."

"What did you do?"

"I took off running across that meadow and threw up when I got to the other side. I went home and never told a soul. Never went back. But the guilt's eaten me up ever since."

"Why did you decide to tell me now?" Abby said.

Jay's face turned a funny shade of gray. He couldn't seem to push the words out and then finally said, "Because I think the man I shot … was your father. And the little girl with him was Riley Jo. The timing fits—so do the facts."

Abby felt dizzy. She leaned back on her hands, her palms pressed into the grass, her mind racing in reverse.

"I remember the little girl was whimpering," Jay said. "And seemed really scared. It never occurred to me in a million years that the victim was her daddy and she didn't know the bearded guy."

"Did you see her face?"

Jay shrugged. "Honestly, I was so stunned I couldn't tell you anything else about her."

Abby took a deep breath and then another and couldn't seem to get enough air. "What d-did the dead man look like? You've seen pictures of Daddy. Was it him?"

"I couldn't bring myself to take a good look at his face. But it was mostly hidden by wildflowers."

"What about the bearded man—can you describe him?"

"Yeah. He looks just like the sketch I drew of the man *you* saw. Certain things about him stood out. The beard for sure. Piercing eyes like an eagle's. Denim overalls and no shirt. Hairy arms. Big biceps. I'm sure we saw the same man, Abby. There's a good chance that Ella *is* Riley Jo. The question now is: what do we do about it?"

CHAPTER 17

Abby sat, staring at Beaver Lake, tears trickling down her cheeks, her temples pounding. She felt as if her bottom were cemented to the ground.

The thought that her father may have been accidentally killed by her now best friend, and his body "tended to" by a stranger, was shocking enough. But knowing that Riley Jo may have been taken by the same man who had made no effort to find out who she belonged to made her sick to her stomach. Why would he keep her and not contact the authorities?

"Abby, say *something*," Jay said.

"Like what?"

"Say you hate me. Say you're going to the sheriff. Say you want me to burn in hell! Anything is better than sitting here, watching you cry. I know I've caused you another heartbreak, and it's cost me our friendship. But you deserve to know the truth. I wasn't hiding it from you. I honestly didn't connect the dots until the guy called and you put your cell phone on speaker."

Abby felt as if her heart would burst wide open. She let more tears escape and finally looked over at Jay. "I don't hate you. You were just a kid. The guy told you the man you shot had no kin."

"I should've told my mom and stepdad what happened."

"Of course you should've. But you were just a kid. You were terrified of going to jail. And of disappointing your father and losing what little relationship you had with him. That's really heavy for a twelve-year-old to handle."

Jay wiped his tears with the bottom of his T-shirt. "At that moment, I'd have given anything to bring the man back to life. But what was done was done. I just wanted to forget it happened—but I never have. I'm so sorry, Abby."

"That's two of us." Abby hugged her knees tightly and rocked back and forth. "If we go to Sheriff Granger, what will he be able to do about any of it now? And if the man who has Ella gets the slightest hint that we've told the authorities, he might bolt, and I'll never know if she's my sister. Or he might come after me, and we'll both be missing."

"Not if I go after him first."

"How?"

"The reason I'm muddy is I spent the morning searching the woods near the place where I shot your dad. I figured if the man is a local like the sales clerk at Murchison's told you, then he's probably living on Sure Foot Mountain."

"He could be living anywhere," Abby said. "What makes you think that?"

"Because there are folks in those woods who are totally self-sufficient. They don't even send their kids to school. They live by their own laws and keep to themselves. That would be a perfect setting if he took Riley Jo. There would be no one to question whether she was his daughter."

Abby looked up and studied Jay's expression. "What makes you think you can find him?"

"Because I know my way around those woods. I know where the log cabins are. I'll search the area and see if I spot Ella—or the guy."

"Then what?"

"I'll take Ella and go to the sheriff. If her DNA matches Riley Jo's, we'll know."

"Do you think Ella is just going to go with you without a fight?" Abby rolled her eyes. "If the man catches you, he's liable to kill you. And even if you manage to pull it off, you could get arrested for kidnapping."

"I'll tell the sheriff the truth about what happened. I'm ready to accept the consequences, whatever they are. Frankly, at this point, it would be a relief."

Abby studied his face. He was serious. "There's no guarantee this will work," she said.

"There's no proof the guy is violent, Abby. Or even that his intentions are evil. I mean, he didn't turn me in when I was twelve. And Ella looked fine. He's got a wife and twin boys now. Maybe he just tried to scare you off because he loves the girl and is afraid of losing her."

"Too bad! She's not *his*!" Abby blinked away the stinging in her eyes. "When I think of the agony Mama's been through ..."

"I know. I know. I didn't say he was right to do it. But maybe he really thought the man I shot didn't have any family. And he took the girl and gave her a home. Maybe he found out we were asking about her and just wanted us to back off."

"That's a lot of maybes," Abby said. "If that child is Riley Jo, she belongs with her real family."

"Agreed. But we have to decide here and now how you want to handle this. If you want us to go to the sheriff instead, I'll understand. But I really do think I can find Ella without creating suspicion, if I do it my way."

"Then I'm going with you," Abby said.

"Absolutely not."

"You might need help."

Jay folded his arms across his chest. "It's a one-man job, Abby. You'll just be in the way."

"But if you actually do find Ella, I think she'll be less likely to be scared of a teenage girl than a guy."

"It's not like I'll have time to sweet-talk her," Jay said. "Any way you cut it, I'll have to force her to come with me. But I'll do everything I can to assure her I'm not going to hurt her. There's no way I'm going to make you an accomplice. I'm doing it alone, or you can go to the sheriff right now."

Abby felt her neck muscles tighten. "What if she's happy there? What if she'll hate us for doing this to her?"

"That's a possibility. But he had no right to take her like that. There's no painless way to get this done. So how do you want me to do this, Abby? It's your call ..."

Abby drove Mama's Odyssey past the Raleigh County Courthouse and turned onto Perkins Street, hoping she wasn't too late to sneak into the back of Jay's truck. She admired his courage. But the more she considered his plan, the less feasible it seemed that he could pull off snatching Ella by himself. He was going to need help. He might be mad at first when she made her presence known. But he would thank her when they had to move quickly and keep a scared seven-year-old calm and cooperative.

Abby slowed the Odyssey and parallel-parked in front of Lucy's Nail Spa. She got out and jogged across the street, then cut through two yards to the next block, excited when she spotted Jay's truck parked outside the Sycamore Apartments. Good. He hadn't left yet. The big tarp was still covering the bed of his truck, where he'd tied down an old easy chair he hadn't taken to Goodwill yet.

Abby looked both ways and didn't see anyone. She crossed the street and ducked behind Jay's truck. She unfastened the bungee cord closest to the bottom and crawled under the tarp and lay next to the chair. Now, if the other two bungee cords would just hold while they were on the highway ...

She heard someone talking and realized it was Jay.

"Mr. Sustern, it's Jay Rogers. Sorry to give you such short notice, but I'm still not up to par and won't be coming in to work this evening ... Yes, sir, I agree. I sure wouldn't want anyone else to catch what I've got. I'm glad you understand. I hope to be in tomorrow at four. Yes, sir, I will. Thanks."

The truck door opened, and a few seconds later the engine was running. Jay backed out and turned left.

Abby lay on the floor of the truck bed and held tightly to the chair, which was fastened securely to both sides, and tried not to roll with each turn. The last thing she needed was to make a thumping noise that might make Jay stop and take a look. The ride was hot and bumpy, and her arms were getting tired from gripping the chair.

She thought about what they were about to do. So many things could happen. So much could go wrong. She could even *be* wrong—again. Mama would probably ground her for the rest of her life for going along with Jay's plan to steal Ella.

It would be worth it if they were right. Her mind flashed back to the last image she had of Riley Jo, holding the baby doll that was half as big as she was, an elfin grin on her face.

Lord, when I left for Staci's that day, I promised Riley Jo I would see her tomorrow. I broke that promise. I can't change what happened to her. And I can't bring Daddy back. But with Your help, I can change the course of her future.

Abby was taking a leap of faith into the dark unknown. What happened next was out of her hands. Out of her sight. No matter what happened, she would never agree with Mama and Hawk that the God she had given her heart to would turn a deaf ear to her prayers.

Abby glanced at her watch as the truck slowed and came to a complete stop. Thirty-two minutes. She didn't move—or breathe—and listened intently.

Jay got out, his footsteps moving away from the truck. She waited half a minute and then crawled out from under the tarp. She peeked over the side of the truck bed and saw Jay walk into the woods.

Abby hopped out of the truck and followed him, stepping gingerly and surreptitiously in his footsteps on the muddy ground, glad she had thought to wear her jeans and Nikes instead of shorts and sandals.

The path was narrow, and she had to push overhanging brush out of the way to keep going. More than once a branch snapped back and whipped her bare arms or her face, and she couldn't see in front of her to be sure she was going the right way.

Terror seized her. What if she got lost out here by herself? No one would ever find her. Or even think to look for her here. She would make a tasty meal for a feral hog. Or a black bear. Or a mountain lion.

Abby shuddered and picked up her pace. Even if Jay found Ella, what would he do to keep her on a path like this one all the way back to his truck? A girl raised in these woods would likely have an advantage and know how to run into the trees and disappear.

Did he plan to intimidate her? Threaten her? Get rough with her? Abby couldn't see kindhearted Jay strong-arming a child for any reason. And yet, at the very least he would have to scare her into going with him.

Abby hated this! Getting Ella to the sheriff would probably be traumatic for all of them. And if the DNA test proved that she was Riley Jo, what then? It would break Abby's heart—and her mother's—if her sister begged to go home to the couple who had raised her, rejecting the family that had mourned her. Ella would probably end up with neither family and in a foster home until the court could sort it out.

Abby was hit with the gravity of what she was about to do. Their lives would never be the same. And what of Jay? Would there be an investigation into what happened the day he accidentally shot her father? And what if they were wrong about Ella's true identity? Jay would end up in jail for kidnapping, and Abby would probably be charged for conspiring with him. Mama would be devastated all over again—

Abby felt a hairy arm put her in a chokehold, a strong hand clamped tightly over her mouth. She struggled to free herself, to scream, to breathe …

"Girlie, you ain't as smart as I thought you were."

The man from the phone calls! His voice was unmistakable! Abby struggled in vain to break his hold on her, but he tightened his grip and held something sharp against her ribs.

"You just wouldn't leave it alone." Abby felt his breath in her ear. "Too bad. You shoulda done what I told you while you had the chance. I can't have you lookin' into things that are best left alone."

CHAPTER 18

Abby was pushed and prodded along the muddy path by the man whose voice she knew but whose face she still had not seen. Was he the man she had glimpsed that day at Murchison's? He had very convincingly threatened to butcher her and feed her to his pigs unless she did exactly as he told her.

"I seen that Oldham kid come up here," the man said, "but I lost sight of him. What's he want?"

"I'm not sure," Abby said. "I hid in the bed of his truck when he drove up here. I was following him when you grabbed me."

"How about you venture a guess?" He gave her a persuasive shove.

"I think he might be looking for you. He had some questions." Did this guy know Jay had come for Ella?

"Little ol' J.D. finally wants to talk, does he? Took him long enough."

Abby wondered why he sounded amused, but she was afraid to ask. "Where are you taking me?"

"This is your own doin'. You and that Oldham kid shouldn't have gone snoopin' into things that ain't your concern. I warned you what would happen if you kept it up."

"I haven't talked to anyone else about the girl—neither has Jay."

"Don't matter. You ain't gonna stop till you git what you come for. And I ain't lettin' that happen."

"Then you know Ella's my sister."

"Hogwash! She's my kin. Born to my late wife, Ella Jane. I was right there when the kid took her first breath and started wailin'. I don't know what you think you know, missy, but you're way off."

"Show me her birth certificate," Abby said. "And I promise I'll never bother you again."

"Oh, you ain't never gonna bother *me* again." The man laughed. "She's my kin, but I ain't obliged to show you nothin'. Keep walkin'."

"Why don't you just call the sheriff and report me? Get a restraining order or something?" She knew why.

"The law don't count for nothin' out here. I make the rules. I already tried restrainin' you. Now I'm shuttin' you up my way."

Abby's gaze flitted around the woods. She wanted to flee, but to where? The woods were ominous and dense and unfamiliar. He had the advantage. If she tried to escape and failed, she might end up as pig feed.

"You have to know it's not right to just take someone's child," Abby said softly, hoping not to provoke him. "If you give her back to us willingly, Mama would be so grateful that I'm sure the sheriff would go easy on you."

There was that irritating laugh again.

Abby wanted to slap him. "You think this is funny? Do you have any idea how torn up my family's been since my daddy and sister disappeared?"

"Don't know what Jimmy Dale Oldham's been fillin' your head with," said the gruff voice behind her, "but I didn't take nobody's kid. And *he's* the one who shot and killed a man."

"Well, that man was my daddy! And the little girl is my sister!" Abby started to cry. "You had no right to take her!"

"I told you, I seen Ella come into the world. And I don't know nothin' about your kin disappearin'."

"Then why are you treating me like this? What are you afraid of?"

"I ain't afraid."

"You should be," Abby said. "You can't prove Ella is yours—because she isn't. Jay told me about the accidental shooting that happened up here five years ago. The timing fits. You're not her real—"

Abby felt a powerful blow on the back of her head that collapsed her knees and sent her falling ... falling ... falling ... into a swirling gray vacuum. She was vaguely aware of her shoulder hitting something hard and the strong smell of wet earth ... and then nothing.

✿

Virgil sat at the desk in his office and glanced out the window, watching a pair of mourning doves in one of three red maples that graced the grounds in front of the Raleigh County Courthouse. The sun had moved to the western sky, hidden behind a billowy, gold-rimmed thunderhead. One of his deputies strolled across the grounds, hand in hand with his fiancée. Made Virgil wish he was home with Jill

Beth instead of getting ready to drive up the mountain to deliver the dental forensics findings to Kate Cummings.

He heard a knock on the door and turned in time to see Chief Deputy Kevin Mann walk in.

"I suppose you saw the DF findings on the skull we found?" Virgil said.

Kevin nodded. "Just did. Can't believe it's back already. Not sure whether it would've been any easier if it'd gone the other way."

"Me neither. It is what it is. I'm about to head up yonder and tell Kate in person. I owe her that. Then I'll call it a day."

"All right," Kevin said. "I'm fixin' to run out to the mass grave on my way home and see how the investigation's coming. I won't be hanging around long. Jenny's panfrying some of my white river trout for dinner. Been thinking about it all afternoon."

Virgil chuckled. "I know the feeling. Jill Beth's got a spicy meatloaf in the oven. I've had a hankering for it ever since she told me. See you tomorrow."

Kevin left the office.

Virgil stood and picked up the DF report, then set it down. Would it soften the blow if Kate read the report for herself? He decided it wouldn't.

He turned out the light and walked down the long, shiny hallway and out the side door. He crossed the street to the parking lot, glad that he had long ago opted to wear the navy department uniform every day instead of a suit and tie. Some of the other county sheriffs thought it would diminish the office if they dressed like the deputies, but he hadn't found that to be the case at all. And opting for a short-sleeved uniform shirt in this hot weather made sense.

He slid in behind the wheel of his squad car, started the engine, and pulled onto Commerce, then turned right on Main Street, glancing up at the white clock on the red-brick courthouse: 5:45. Kate had probably quit working by now. He didn't know whether this was the news she was hoping for, but it was what he'd been given. He just wanted it over with.

❧

Kate heard the doorbell ring. "I'll get it!"

She wiped her hands on a kitchen towel and walked out to the living room and opened the door, surprised to see the sheriff standing there holding his Stetson, looking even taller than his six feet three inches.

"Virgil," she said, feeling the muscles in her gut tighten. "Come in."

Virgil stepped inside and glanced over at Halo curled up on the hearth of the giant stone fireplace that took up one entire wall.

"Can I get you something to drink?" Kate said.

"Wouldn't mind some water."

"I've got spring water. Come out to the kitchen. We can talk there."

Kate led the way into the kitchen. She opened the fridge, filled a glass with spring water Hawk had brought home from Rocky Springs Park, and handed it to Virgil. "No ice. Right?"

"Right." He took a big gulp. "This is great. Thanks."

"Do I need to call the family together for this?" Kate said.

"Not really. Mind if I sit?"

"Of course not."

Kate followed Virgil to the table and sat facing him, her fingers laced together, her heart racing in anticipation.

Virgil cleared his throat. "We've already got the report back from dental forensics. Apparently their finding was obvious, almost from the get-go." Virgil paused. "Kate … the skull wasn't Micah's."

Kate clamped her eyes shut and brought her fist to her mouth. "Are they sure?"

"Absolutely sure. Didn't come close to a match. No chance it could be wrong."

She opened her eyes and looked over at Virgil. "What about DNA?"

"They're still working on that. Lots of bones to test from both scenes. That'll take a lot longer. We're not done digging and may not know anything for months. But, based on Micah's dental records, the skull we found at the first scene could not have been his."

"So he could still be alive." Kate wiped a tear off her cheek.

"There's always that hope. But we have at least six adult skulls from the mass grave we need to compare his dental records with."

Kate sat for a moment, realizing that, as relieved as she was, she was right back where she had been for the past five years. "I just want the truth, Virgil, whatever it is. My children need to move on. So do I."

Virgil nodded. "The mass grave was a huge discovery. It may be the key to solving this thing. We just don't know yet. And we might not know for a long time. We just have to keep going."

"Going where? My entire life is on hold." Kate felt her cheeks get hot. "Elliot Stafford has asked me out a few times—just as friends.

I would actually enjoy that. But I don't feel comfortable even entertaining the idea."

"I know. No one would fault you for it, though."

"But I would." Kate dabbed her eyes. "I need closure first. In my heart of hearts, I doubt Micah and Riley Jo are alive. I've grieved losing them until it's made me sick. I just want an end to the question mark—one way or the other."

❧

Abby was in a tug-of-war between sleep and wakefulness, aware of a throbbing pain in the back of her head. Where was she? She lay on her side and groped the area around her. *Dirt.*

She opened her eyes to a dimly lit pit. Fear seized her. She remembered being hit from behind and passing out. She reached to the back of her head and touched the aching spot.

"Ouch!"

Her hand was wet and sticky. *Blood!*

Abby shivered so hard her teeth were chattering. She wished she had on her sweats instead of just jeans and a T-shirt. She sat up, her muscles sore, and hugged herself to keep warm.

Was this her captor's idea of a meat locker? Was he going to butcher her and feed her to the pigs as he had threatened? She started to cry. *Lord, I'm scared. Help me.*

Her eyes adjusted to what little light there was, and she saw a trapdoor overhead—with a small metal grate for a window. She stood on her tiptoes and pushed on it, but it was securely in place.

She peeked through it and saw what appeared to be rustic metal shelves filled with canning jars. A single lightbulb burned overhead, but the wattage was so low she couldn't tell anything else about the room.

She sat against one wall, hugging her knees, lamenting her decision to hide in the bed of Jay's truck. He didn't know she had come up here. And neither would anyone else.

Abby heard a door open above. Her heart nearly pounded out of her chest. She curled up in a fetal position and didn't move. Or breathe.

"You awake down there, girlie?" said the man.

Abby didn't answer, but she was trembling. Surely he noticed.

"Don't matter. You ain't gonna be around long. How's it feel to lay your head on the ground where your daddy was? I put him down there after J.D. shot him—to preserve his body till I was ready to make good use of it."

Abby's tears fell onto the ground. Unless she made it out, her mother would never know what had happened to her either—or that Ella was Riley Jo.

The man laughed. "Soon as I find J.D., I'll make you both disappear. Them pigs is gonna be mighty happy."

"Wait!" Abby sat up and held her gaze on the silhouette of the bearded man, who knelt next to the grate. He appeared to be the same man she had seen at Murchison's. "When Jay was twelve, he shot my father by accident. That's when you found my sister and decided to raise her, right? You named her Ella. You and your wife also have twin boys—about three years old. One of them's named Ronny."

The man wore a stony expression and was quiet for a few moments. "You're too smart for your own good. Shoulda left well enough alone."

"Just tell me what happened," Abby said. "You're going to kill me anyway. Let me die knowing the truth."

"Not unless you tell me where J.D. is."

"I don't know. Honest. I hid in the back of his truck. I knew he was coming up here. I tried to follow him but lost sight of him when you grabbed me. I've got no reason to lie about it."

"Who else knows you were comin' here?"

"No one." The instant she said it, she wished she hadn't. "Okay, that's not true. *Lots* of people know where I am. My whole family does. And my friends. They'll have the entire sheriff's department coming up here any minute."

The man grinned. "You're a lousy liar. And J.D. won't tell nobody as long as he believes he killed your daddy. That'll give me time to round him up so I can git rid o' the both o' you."

Abby stood just as the man started to walk away. "What do you mean as long as he *believes* he killed Daddy? Jay shot him by accident. He told me all about it."

The man laughed and opened a door. "No one's ever gonna know nothin' about it once the two o' you up and vanish—like your daddy and sis."

CHAPTER 19

Kate called Abby's cell phone as she'd been doing every five minutes for the past hour. It rang and rang. She hung up, torn between
irritation and concern. Why would Abby turn off her phone? Why
wouldn't she call if she was going to be late for dinner?

Kate sent a text to Abby's phone. *Call home NOW! I'm worried
about you.*

"Did you get through to her?" Dad said.

Kate jumped, her hand over her heart. "I didn't hear you come
in. No. Her phone just rings off the hook. I sent another text."

"Maybe she's out of cell range up there."

Kate glanced at the clock. "She knows what time we have dinner.
She's never late."

"Are you sure Savannah didn't schedule her to work?"

"Positive."

"Well"—Dad laid his hand on her back—"Abby's on edge like
the rest of us over the remains that were found. Maybe she's not
thinkin' clearly. My granddaughter's a very responsible young lady.
I'm sure she'll be home soon."

"Dad, she knows not to worry me this way. I need to know where she is all the time. We look out for each other. All of us! That's the commitment we made after—"

"I'm sure she's fine, honey."

Kate chewed her lip. "I don't even know exactly where the slope is. Somewhere off Summit Road. If I knew where, I'd drive up there myself and look for her."

Buck scratched his chin. "Did you try callin' Jay?"

"I don't have his cell number."

"You know where he works. Doesn't he go in at four and work till ten?"

Kate nodded. "That's right, he does. Thanks, Dad."

Kate flipped through the phone book until she found a listing for Tutty's, then keyed in the numbers.

"Good evenin', Tutty's Barbecue. Randy speakin'."

"Yes, this is Kate Cummings. May I please speak to Jay Rogers?"

"Ma'am, Jay's not workin' tonight. He called in sick."

"Oh, I didn't realize that. I thought my daughter, Abby, might be with him. Sorry to have bothered you."

Kate disconnected the call. "Jay called in sick. So where's Abby?"

"Maybe she went to his place to sit a spell," Dad said. "To keep him company, since he's feeling bad."

"That's a thought. Abby told me Jay and his mother live at the Sycamore Apartments. But I don't know his mother's name. She's been remarried a few times, and her last name is different."

"I know where those apartments are," Dad said. "If it'd make you feel better, I could drive down there right now and look for the Odyssey—or Jay's truck."

Kate shook her head. "I don't want to overreact and embarrass her. Let's go ahead and eat dinner. If Abby's not here when we finish, we'll drive down to Foggy Ridge and check the apartment complex and see if my Odyssey is parked outside."

"Don't worry, honey," her dad said. "I'm sure she's fine."

No, you're not, Kate thought. *You're as uneasy as I am.*

❧

Abby stood on her tiptoes and pushed and pulled on the iron grate that allowed her a glimpse of the room above. The grate wouldn't budge. Not even slightly.

She was stuck in some dank, dark hole, and not a soul knew where she was.

Lord, I don't want to die! Mama can't handle it. Please … I know You hear me. Help me!

She yanked the grate one more time and then pulled herself up by her arms, her feet dangling. It was no use. She let go and dropped to the ground, brushing her hands together.

Abby sat on the earthen floor, her back against the wall that felt as if it was made of sod and held together with some sort of metal mesh. What possible reason would anyone have for digging out a room like this?

She ran her fingers across the dirt floor, thinking about her father lying there lifeless and without dignity. Her captor said Jay shot him but then implied he hadn't. Jay could not have faked that gut-wrenching confession.

Abby thought back to the last time she had been alone with her father—the day before he disappeared …

"Don't cry, princess," Daddy said. "Let me take a look at you."

He carefully lifted her up onto the bathroom counter. "Don't let the blood scare you. I'll fix you up. How'd you scrape your knees and elbows?"

A tear trickled down Abby's cheek. "I was running down to the dock to tell Hawk that Mama wanted him to come home—and I tripped on a tree root."

Daddy tilted her chin. "You've got a scrape there too. You never do anything just a little bit. You always do it up big."

"Mama says I'm a drama queen."

"You're just sensitive. That's part of what makes you special. Does it hurt?"

Abby nodded. "A lot."

"I'm going to need to flush those abrasions with an antiseptic."

Abby clutched his arm. "No, it's going to hurt!"

"It'll sting." Daddy wiped away her tears with his thumbs. "But only for a few moments. It has to hurt some in order to get better. Don't be scared. You can hold on to me. You trust me, don't you?"

She did trust him. Abby studied his face and his kind eyes. If he had told her to jump off a bridge and he'd catch her, she would have done it. Daddy always told her the truth without sugarcoating it. And he had never given her reason to doubt anything he said …

Abby blinked to clear her eyes. When her father lay wounded and bleeding, no one was there for him. Had he died right away? Or had he lain where he fell, in pain and unable to move—and afraid for Riley Jo?

She curled up on her side, her cheek pressed to the ground. "I'm so sorry, Daddy," she whispered. "We tried so hard to find you."

Losing her father was the biggest hurt of Abby's life. But there was nothing she could pour on that wound to make it better except maybe the truth of what really happened. But whose truth? Just when she thought she had solved the mystery that had consumed the last five years of her life, she was left to die alone with even more questions.

$$\maltese$$

Kate rode in the passenger seat of her dad's Toyota Corolla and perked up as they pulled into the Sycamore Apartments in Foggy Ridge.

"You try to spot Jay's truck," Kate said, "and I'll look for my Odyssey."

Kate searched carefully as her father drove slowly around each of the three buildings and then back to the entrance.

"Nah, Jay's truck isn't here," Dad said.

"Are you sure? My Odyssey isn't here either."

He nodded. "I'm sure. But there're plenty of empty parkin' places. They could just be out somewhere together."

"Why would Jay be out? He called in sick."

"I don't buy that any more than you do." Dad looked over at Kate. "Maybe they're still up on the slope. It won't be dark for a while yet."

Kate folded her hands in her lap. "I know Abby was upset about the remains and adamant that her father and sister are still alive. But I didn't sense that she was angry with me. I don't understand why she doesn't call or answer my text messages."

"Now don't you go thinkin' the worst."

"Why wouldn't I?" Kate said. "Every time one of my children is two minutes late, my heart is in my throat. I don't think I will ever feel comfortable with them out of my sight until Virgil figures out what happened to Micah and Riley Jo—if he ever does."

"Have to trust the Lord."

Kate stared out the window and let the silence speak for itself.

"It's not God's fault, Kate. It's nobody's fault. Whatever happened, happened. There's nothin' you could've done differently that would've prevented it."

Her dad's comment caught her off guard, and she felt surprisingly defensive. "I never said I could've prevented it, but *the Lord* could have. Forgive me, Dad. But I'm not having this conversation with you again. You know how I feel, and you're not going to change my mind."

Dad pursed his lips and started to say something, then didn't.

Kate glanced over at the clubhouse. "Why don't I go over to the office and see if anyone there knows where Jay lives? Maybe his mother is home and knows where the kids are."

"Good idea." Dad pulled over in front of the clubhouse and into a parking space.

Kate opened her door. "I'll be right back."

She walked up the steps and through the front door. She saw an arrow directing her to the office and found it just as a bottle brunette in a red dress was locking the door.

"Sorry, the office is closed," the sixtysomething woman said. "You can call the night number. There's always someone on duty."

"I'm not a resident," Kate said. "I'm looking for my daughter. She's late coming home, and I'm a little worried. I believe she's with one of your tenants, Jay Rogers. I was hoping you could help me locate him or his mother. His mother has a different last name. I'm sorry, I don't know what it is."

The woman raised an eyebrow. "Is Jay on the tall side? Nice looking. Sandy hair. Five o'clock shadow. About eighteen—give or take?"

"Yes," Kate said. "Can you tell me where he lives?"

"No, sorry. That would violate our privacy policy. But I can call and convey a message."

"Would you?" Kate said. "It's really important."

The woman opened the door and turned on the light. "By the way, I'm Betty Wilber, the day manager."

"I'm Kate Cummings. I manage Angel View Lodge."

"Nice place. My parents stay there when they come to visit."

Kate paced in front of the window and saw her dad waiting in the car.

"Ah, here it is." Betty picked up the phone and keyed in some numbers.

Kate could hear it ringing and listened intently.

"*Hey, y'all. You've reached Sue Ann, soon to be Mrs. Richie Stump. Me and the groom are in Vegas. If it can't wait, Jay can reach us. If it'll keep, leave a message at the sound of the beep, and I'll get back to you when we return."*

Betty handed Kate the phone.

"Jay," Kate said, "this is Mrs. Cummings. I'm looking for Abby, and she's not returning my calls or texts. Would you please call me as soon as you get this message, even if you don't know where she is? I'm really quite concerned." Kate gave him her cell number and then hung up. "Thank you, Betty. I guess all I can do now is wait."

Betty studied her for a few seconds. "You know what? I've got teenagers and know how upset you must be. I'm going to turn my back, and if you should just happen to see Sue Ann's apartment number, there really wouldn't be anything I could do about it, would there?"

"Thanks." Kate looked at the information on the Rolodex and wrote it down. "I really appreciate this. My daughter has never done this before, and I'm beside myself."

"Good luck," Betty said. "I hope you find her."

"So do I. Thanks again." Kate left the office, pushed open the door to the main entrance, and hurried down the steps. She got into her dad's car. "Pull around to building three."

Dad drove around to the building marked with a large numeral three, and Kate got out. "I'll be right back."

Kate walked inside and up the steps to apartment 3C and rang the bell. She put her ear to the door and didn't hear anything. She rang the bell again and waited. Finally, she took a notepad out of her purse and wrote a message for Jay.

I came looking for Abby. I've left messages for her and for you. I'm very upset and worried. Please call me ASAP. Kate Cummings.

Kate added her cell phone number, then folded the note and pushed it under the door. What more could she do?

She started to leave and noticed someone in the apartment across the hall, looking through a crack in the door.

"Excuse me," Kate said. "Do you happen to know where Jay is? I believe he's with my daughter, and I'm trying to find her."

The door opened wider, revealing an elderly woman wearing a floral house dress. "He goes to work at four. Some barbecue place."

"Have you seen my daughter?" Kate held up a phone picture of Abby.

The woman smiled. "She's pretty, that one. I haven't seen her since Sue Ann and her beau went off to Vegas to get married. They're fixin' to be back on Monday."

"You don't have any idea where Jay might've gone—other than to work?"

The woman shrugged. "Had on hiking boots. Doesn't usually wear those to work. Come to think of it, he left about an hour earlier than usual."

"Have you ever heard him mention the slope?" Kate said.

"Can't say as I have. We don't talk much."

"Well, if you happen to see him, would you tell him to call Kate Cummings right away? Here's my number." Kate tore off a sheet from the notepad and jotted down her name and number and handed it to the woman.

"My name's Clara Bresden. If I see Jay, I'll tell him to call. I might even knock on his door later and check on him. He's usually home by ten thirty."

"Thanks." Kate shook Clara's hand and then went down the stairs and out the door and got in the car.

"Jay wasn't there," Kate told her father, "but I left a note with the neighbor across the hall." Kate relayed the short conversation she'd just had with Clara.

"Maybe those kids *are* on the slope," Dad said, "seein' as how Jay left the apartment in hikin' boots and hasn't come back yet."

"But from the way Abby described the slope, it's just a grassy clearing. Why would he bother with hiking boots? And what's he doing up there if he's sick? And if he's not sick, why'd he call in sick?" Kate tucked a runaway lock of hair behind her ear. "You don't think Abby lied to me about the nature of her relationship with Jay, do you?"

"Kate"—Dad gently took her arm—"don't go jumpin' to conclusions. Abby's never given you reason not to trust her. There's gotta be a logical explanation for everything."

"What if they're hurt? What if they can't get a signal to call for help? Maybe we should drive up Summit and see if we can spot their vehicles. I remember Abby saying the slope was near the top."

"Yes, but off road," Dad said. "Doubt if we could spot their cars from Summit."

"I can't just sit at home and wait, or I'll go stark-raving mad."

Dad nodded knowingly. "All right. Let's head up that way and nose around. It's premature to think of callin' Virgil, but I'm uncomfortable with doin' nothin'."

CHAPTER 20

Abby's stomach rumbled, and she regretted having skipped lunch in her haste to meet Jay. But she was miserably thirsty and wondered how long she could go without water before she died of dehydration.

She had been wrong about her father still being alive. But she wasn't wrong about God being good. He might not do everything she wanted, but He was listening to her prayers. He had promised.

Lord, I can't see how You're going to get me out, but I have faith You will. I won't stop loving You, even if You don't. But I really need Your help.

Abby stood on her tiptoes and held her watch up toward the lightbulb burning dimly in the room above her. *8:05.* It would be dark soon. Her mother must be worried and had probably surmised that Abby and Jay were together. She would check every place they could possibly be—but not this one. How long would she wait before she called Sheriff Granger? And even when she did, what could he do? No one knew what she and Jay were trying to do. No one—except the man who was out to make them disappear.

Abby grabbed the grate and swung from it, pulling with all her weight. "Let me out of here!" she hollered. "Somebody let me out!"

Her arms started to cramp, and she dropped to the ground, out of breath and out of ideas. No one was going to come to her rescue unless Jay figured out what had happened and went for help. But he was being hunted.

Kate squinted and looked into the woods that lined Summit Road, hoping for a glimpse of her Odyssey—or Jay's white truck. The sun had settled on the western horizon, turning the sky overhead a glowing shade of hot pink.

"She has to be up here somewhere," Kate said. "Where else would they have gone?"

Dad shook his head. "I don't know, honey. I just don't see any sign of them. Can you get a cell signal?"

Kate keyed in the number to the Angel View Office, and it rang. Once. Twice. Three times. Four times … *Hello. You've reached the offices of Angel View Lodge* … She disconnected the call. "The signal seems fine. If Abby needed help, she could've called for it. Dad, I'm scared."

"I don't like it either, but she's only been missin' for a couple hours. She and Jay might've gone on some adventure and lost track of time. Or just stayed up here to watch the sunset."

"I'm beginning to think she lied about her relationship with Jay," Kate said. "Maybe they're in love. Maybe Abby was afraid to tell me because she knows I wouldn't approve of her getting involved at such a young age."

"I think you're jumpin' the gun," Dad said. "I've watched those two together. They seem like two peas in a pod, but I never got any kinda vibes that Abby was keen on him."

"Maybe she was afraid to tell me. Afraid that I'd resent her finding someone when I had lost Micah. Abby's sensitive that way. She wouldn't want to cause me more pain."

"I think you just need to hold your horses and give this time to play out."

"How much time should I give it, Dad? Jay is missing too."

"Just because he wasn't home doesn't mean he's missin'."

"Well, Abby is! Any time my kids are out of touch, I don't see how I can afford to assume anything else."

Dad pushed his glasses up higher on his nose. "I still think there's a logical explanation for it. Let's not get ahead of ourselves. We can't afford to ask the sheriff for help until we're sure it's warranted."

"As far as I'm concerned, it is. I'm going to call Virgil at home and ask his advice. He can be objective. We sure can't."

Virgil rinsed the roasting pan, dried it with a towel, and handed it to Jill Beth.

"There you go, you sweet thing." He pressed his lips to hers. "Dishes done. Anything else I can do for you, ma'am?"

Jill Beth giggled. "Down, boy. You need to take out the trash, and you promised we could take Drake for a walk."

Virgil looked over at the handsome mutt they had adopted from Animal Rescue last year—part German shepherd and part Australian sheepdog. Drake was like an overgrown kid and had already broken several picture frames with a swish of his happy tail.

"Why don't we walk up to Icy's and get frozen custard?" Jill Beth said.

Drake barked and ran in circles, then sat under the hook where his leash hung, his tail wagging beneath him as he whined, looking as if he would lunge at any moment.

Virgil laughed. "I swear this dog understands English." He took the leash off the hook and attached it to Drake's collar just as his cell phone vibrated. He looked at the screen. "Darlin', it's Kate Cummings. I need to take this." He handed the leash to Jill Beth and hit the Talk button. "Kate, it's Virgil. Anything wrong?"

"I'm not sure. I need your advice."

"What is it?"

Kate exhaled into the receiver. "I don't want you to think I'm crying wolf. I know we've cost your department a lot of time and money ..."

"I'm a public servant, Kate. Tell me what you need. You sound stressed."

"I can't find Abby."

"What do you mean—can't *find* her?"

Virgil listened as Kate told him everything she knew about the slope and Abby's plan to meet her friend Jay there, as well as about Jay's calling in sick and the neighbor seeing him leave the apartment earlier in the afternoon.

"Virgil, I'm scared."

"What time was Abby supposed to be home?" he said.

"Six. That's when we have dinner. It's the only time we're all together. She would've called if she wasn't coming. Something's wrong."

"Maybe not," Virgil said calmly. "She wouldn't be the first sixteen-year-old to go off with a friend and lose track of time. Maybe she's out of cell range."

"Dad and I have been up and down Summit Road. The cell signal is strong up there."

Virgil glanced over at Jill Beth, who was struggling to restrain Drake and trying to keep from being dragged to the front door. "Where else have you looked?"

"I had Hawk check the pier, Sammie's Subs, Sweet Stuff, and some of Abby's other favorite places. No one has seen them."

Virgil paused and cleared his throat. "You say Abby and Jay are just friends?"

"Best friends, according to Abby. It's possible she's not telling me the full extent of their relationship. But she had no reason to deceive me, especially since I've never objected to her seeing Jay."

"Does she seem depressed to you?"

"Not at all," Kate said. "Abby's had a burst of new hope since spotting the girl I told you about and seems consumed with finding out more about her. I promised not to interfere if she agreed to go back and see her therapist. Abby's running on false hope, but I don't think she's depressed."

Drake began to bark, and Virgil motioned to Jill Beth that he was stepping out on the porch. "Kate, listen ... I understand why you're concerned, but it's only been a couple hours. I have a feeling that Abby will be home soon and all this will get worked out."

"So you don't think I should file a missing-person report?"

Virgil switched the phone to his other ear. "It seems premature. But if you think Abby's in trouble, we need to act on it."

"That's just it"—Kate began to cry—"I don't know what I think right now. I just want her home."

"What would you like me to do?" Virgil said softly.

"I don't know. Nothing we haven't already done, I guess. I'm just scared. If anything happened to Abby, I'm not sure I would survive it. I can't lose another child …"

Virgil breathed in slowly and let it out. He couldn't allow himself to get emotionally enmeshed in this. He had to stay objective. "It's your call whether you want to file a missing-person report."

There was a long moment of dead air.

"Kate, you still there?"

"I'm here," she said. "I think I'll go home and wait a while longer. I'm probably overreacting. Abby will call home any minute, and I'll realize all the worry was for nothing."

"You sure?"

"As sure as I'm going to be under the circumstances. If I change my mind I can always file a report later."

"Keep me posted," Virgil said.

"I will. Thanks for listening. I feel a little better. Good-bye."

Virgil stood on the porch, his mind racing. Teenagers! He was glad his boys were grown. How many times had they pulled stunts like this and worried their mother and him for nothing?

The front door opened, and Jill Beth poked her head out. "Everything okay?"

"I think so. Come on. Let's take that walk, and I'll fill you in."

Abby, emptied of tears and filled with dread, lay shivering in the dark pit that might well end up being her grave. Minutes seemed like hours now. Helplessness threatened to steal her hope. How she missed the cozy home she had taken for granted. And the family she had failed to appreciate. Would she ever see them again? She regretted arguing with Hawk. And being rude to her mother. What would their last memory of her be? What kind of a Christian witness had she been?

Abby heard muffled male voices. She curled up in a fetal position, her eyes clamped shut, her heart nearly pounding out of her chest. Seconds passed, and then the squeaky door opened in the room above. Abby held her breath, her temples throbbing. Had her captor come back to kill her?

Lord, You are my protector and defender. My only hope. Help me!

She heard footsteps coming down the wood stairs, her mind barraged with graphic images of what awaited her. She wanted to scream but couldn't find her voice.

CHAPTER 21

Virgil and Jill Beth walked hand in hand toward Icy's, Virgil holding tightly to Drake's leash and wondering how an animal that size could be so strong.

"I feel bad for Kate," Jill Beth said. "If I'd been through what that woman's been through, I'd never let my kids out of my sight."

"It's understandable that she panicked when Abby missed dinner and didn't call." Virgil stopped on the sidewalk as Drake watered one of the tree trunks along Puckett Street. "But my department gets these kinds of calls on a regular basis. The kids almost always show up within a few hours."

"Kate didn't need this on top of everything else," Jill Beth said. "Waiting on the remains has to be torture."

"So was having no leads at all. I'm sure Kate has considered every possibility imaginable. I just want to solve it and put an end to all the unknowns."

"Well, if anyone can, it's my man."

Virgil smiled and slipped his arm around her. "From the lips of the woman who thinks I hung the moon."

"And the stars."

"By the way"—Virgil pulled on the leash to redirect Drake's attention to the sidewalk—"you were right about Elliot Stafford. Kate mentioned that he's shown an interest in her."

"Did she elaborate?"

"Just that she would enjoy his company but not while Micah's fate is still up in the air. Heaven knows, she loved Micah. But five years is a long time for anyone to be unsure of their marital status."

"If you were missing, I'd wait forever."

Virgil sighed. "So would I. Let's hope Kate doesn't have to."

⚜

Abby lay frozen in the darkness, the hammering of her heart so forceful that she thought she might die of heart failure.

Lord, help me! I'm so scared!

"Git down there!" commanded the all-too-familiar voice.

Abby's eyes flew open just as the trapdoor opened above her. She rolled over and sat up in the far corner, letting her eyes adjust to the light.

"Jump, or I'll push," her captor said. "But if you break a leg, I'll hafta put you down." He laughed.

Abby heard a loud thud and felt a gust of wind as someone hit the ground a couple feet from her.

"Y'all have a nice chat. The clock's tickin'."

The overhead door slammed shut, and she heard a bolt lock slide in place and the man go back up the wooden stairs and out the creaky door.

"Abby?"

"Jay!" Abby threw her arms around him and didn't let go.

"You're shivering," he said. "How did you get here?"

"I h-h-hid in the b-b-back of your truck and tried to follow you. But you got t-t-too far ahead of me, and I got lost. He hit me on the head with s-s-something and knocked me out."

"You okay?"

"My head really hurts. I'm sore. And c-c-cold. But I'm okay. Are you?"

"Yeah." Jay held her tighter and rubbed her arms. "He snuck up behind me with a rifle and pressed the barrel against my back. I decided not to resist. The creep's name is Isaiah Tutt."

"How do you know that?"

"I looked in his mailbox."

"How did you know it was his mailbox?"

"As I was sifting through the mail, I saw a woman and little girl coming, and ducked behind some trees. I'm sure the girl was Ella. I'm assuming the woman was Mrs. Tutt. I wanted to grab the girl and run, but the missus had a rifle. I didn't think I could overtake her without Ella running away. So I followed them back here."

"What kind of woman carries a rifle to the mailbox?" Abby said.

"One who's expecting trouble or is just plain paranoid. I waited until it got dark to snoop around some more, but Tutt caught me red-handed and brought me here."

Abby let go of Jay and sat on the earthen floor. "He was out looking for you."

Jay dropped down next to her and put his arm around her.

Abby relished the warmth and told Jay about her conversation with Isaiah Tutt that led to his hitting her on the head.

"Isaiah wasn't about to show me Ella's birth certificate," Abby said, "because he doesn't have one. I caught him in a lie, and he didn't like it."

"Now that he knows we're on to him, he's not letting us go. We've got to find a way out of here."

Abby paused for a moment, then looked up at Jay. "He said something that's really bugging me. He said that he wasn't worried you'd tell anyone about Ella as long as you believed you had killed Daddy."

"I did kill him, Abby. It was a horrible accident. Why would I say it if it wasn't so? It was the worst day of my life. I'd like to erase it."

"Why do you suppose he told me that?"

"Beats me. Why would he steal someone's kid? Why would he throw two teenagers in a hole and threaten to feed them to his pigs? Who knows what drives a man like that? The guy plays by his own set of rules."

"What are we going to do?" Abby said. "Did you tell anyone you were coming up here?"

"No one. Did you?"

Abby shook her head. "He must've taken my cell phone. Did he take yours?"

"Yeah. He took the battery out and tossed it into the woods. The last call I made was to work, telling them I wasn't coming in tonight. Even if they pull my phone records, it's not gonna tell them anything."

"Mine either," Abby said. "The last time I used my phone was to text you this morning."

"Of all times for my mom to be gone. She's not even planning to check in with me until the weekend."

"But mine will. And she knows we're together."

"Abby ... unless someone figures out where we are—and fast—Isaiah's gonna kill us."

✣

Kate sat on the couch, vaguely aware that her father was sitting in his easy chair, thumbing through a magazine.

"You really oughta get some rest," he said.

"So should you." Kate barely had the strength to unfold her hands.

"I'm just turnin' pages, waitin' for the phone to ring."

"Dad, it's ten thirty—where *is* she?"

"I wish I knew, honey."

"Abby's scheduled to work the morning shift. She's always in bed by now. She's too responsible for this." Kate wiped a tear off her cheek. "Do you think they've run off together? Be honest."

"I don't know what to think. I didn't notice any sparks between them. Abby said they were just close friends. I believed her."

"They both have cell phones." Kate got up and paced in front of the fireplace. "At least one of them should have called by now. Do you think it's time to file a missing-person report? We've already checked the ER and every place Abby likes to hang out. I don't know what else to do."

"It's your decision, Kate. I'll support whatever you decide."

"Tell me what to do. I'm so confused." Kate flopped on the couch, her face in her hands. "No one at the sheriff's department will take this seriously—not after Abby ran them in circles, not once but twice."

"Virgil will, and he's ramroddin' that outfit. They'll follow his lead."

"Once I open this door, there's no turning back."

Dad got up and sat next to Kate, his arm around her. "Have faith, honey. God's got everything under control."

I wish I could believe that. Kate laid her head on her father's shoulder and linked her arm with his. "Dad, I know you're trying to help. And I love you for it. But I *had* faith, and look where it's gotten me. So please … let's not talk about trusting God. Or His plan. His timing. Or His faithfulness. Not now. Not tonight." She kissed his stubbly cheek. "I need to handle this my way."

But I'm not handling it! I'm completely helpless to stop this madness!

Kate's heart raced faster than her thoughts. She got up and walked over to the fireplace mantel and picked up a framed photograph of Abby. She traced her daughter's face with her finger, her mind assaulted with visions of horror, of all the terrible things that could have befallen her child. She fluttered her eyelashes, the image of Abby turning into a blur. She was aware of her father standing next to her, putting her cell phone in her hand.

"Honey, call Virgil."

Kate nodded. "I can't lose her, Dad. I just can't."

Abby lay in Jay's arms, praying for help and glad to finally feel warm.

"You awake?" Jay whispered.

"Wide awake. I'm praying for a miracle. Maybe there's a way out of here we aren't seeing."

"It was stupid of me to think I could just take Ella and go to the sheriff."

"We still might."

"Abby … face it. We're in real trouble here. No one knows where we are or even where to begin looking."

"God knows."

"He's not telling!" Jay loosened his embrace. "Sorry. I didn't mean to raise my voice. I'm just frustrated. I don't want to die."

"Me, either. But I'm not giving up. I'm not letting Isaiah Tutt break Mama's heart all over again. At least not without a fight." Abby was quiet for a few moments. "Jay, did Ella seem happy when you saw her?"

"She skipped down the path to the mailbox. So I suppose so. But Mrs. Tutt was stonefaced. Reminded me of my sixth-grade math teacher."

"I don't know what I would do if we got the chance to take Ella and she started crying," Abby said, "and begged us to let her go. She doesn't know any other life than this one, and leaving it would probably be traumatic."

"You would rather she end up like Mrs. Tutt," Jay said, "marrying some backwoods hillbilly and toting a rifle to the mailbox? She belongs at the Cummings house. She has the right to grow up at Angel View. And your mama has the right to have her baby girl back."

"I know. I just wonder if Ella would ever get over it. If she would ever love us like we do her."

Abby felt a tear fall on her arm, and it wasn't hers.

Jay held her tighter. "I'm sorry I brought this on you, Abby. I'm sorry I shot your father. I'm sorry I didn't know Isaiah had kidnapped Riley Jo. I'm sorry I never told my mom and stepdad. It never occurred to me the little girl with Isaiah wasn't his daughter. I just never connected the dots until I heard his voice on the phone."

"Why would you?" Abby said. "And there's no point in beating yourself up. You were just a scared kid."

"Old enough to know that I should've reported the shooting."

"And just old enough to be terrified of going to jail and losing your father's love. You didn't do anything malicious, Jay. And, if it helps, I forgive you for shooting Daddy. I get that it was totally an accident."

Jay sobbed quietly.

Abby let herself cry with him for a few minutes, then forced herself to stop.

"It's important that we stay clearheaded," she said, wishing she had a box of tissues. "There might be a way out of here if we just think it through."

CHAPTER 22

Abby nestled next to Jay, her body aching and sore from having fallen to the ground, and her head throbbing where Isaiah had hit her. She had never been more scared in her life.

Lord, unless You help us, we're not going to get out of this alive.

How ironic it was that she had grown close to the young man who had accidentally killed her father and started the chain reaction that had left her family devastated. She refused to blame Jay. This was Isaiah Tutt's fault. He was the adult. Kidnapping Riley Jo was unconscionable. And he was about to steal another daughter from Kate Cummings. Did the man have no conscience? No soul?

"Abby, are you awake?" Jay whispered.

"Uh-huh."

"Isaiah's probably gone to bed."

"Or is out digging our graves," Abby added, immediately wishing she hadn't.

Jay didn't respond for perhaps an entire minute. Finally he said, "Abby ... I want you to know how much your friendship has meant to me. I've never had anyone in my life I could open up with. I'd give anything to not be the one who took your father from you."

Abby covered his mouth with her hand. "Don't do this. I told you I don't blame you."

A tear trickled down the side of Jay's face. He gently took her wrist and removed her hand. "No matter what happens, I want you to know I don't regret one minute of the time we've spent together."

"You're talking like it's over," Abby said. "We're getting out of here. Have faith."

"I'm trying. But face it, we're trapped. And Isaiah's calling the shots."

"Shh. Did you hear that?" Abby held her breath and listened intently.

"No. What'd it sound like?"

"Footsteps. Someone's coming."

The squeaky door slowly opened and closed, and then the light came on in the room overhead and footsteps descended the wooden stairs.

Jay pulled Abby to her feet. She held so tightly to him that her fingernails were pushing into his arm.

Seconds later, a face peered through the grate in the trapdoor. "Y'all down there?"

"Ella?" Abby whispered.

"How come you know my name?"

"I know all about you," Abby said. "Can you get us out of here?"

"Yep. But if Pa finds out, he'll be hoppin' mad, so you hafta be really, really quiet."

Abby heard the bolt lock slide back and Ella grunting as she strained to open the door.

A few seconds later, the trapdoor was wide open, and the girl, the spitting image of Riley Jo, stood staring at them. She bent down and grabbed something and let it slide down one wall. Abby touched it and realized it was a flexible rope ladder.

"It's kinda wobbly," Ella said. "But Pa's got it hooked real good up here."

"You go first." Jay helped Abby get her foot in the bottom rung. "I'll be right behind you."

Abby pushed past her soreness and tried not to groan as she climbed out. She reached out to Jay as he neared the top and pulled him up.

"Come on," Ella said. "I brung a flashlight so y'all could see to git outta them woods."

"How'd you know we were down there?" Jay said.

"I heard Otha and Pa talkin' 'bout it. He ain't lettin' you go. I don't understand why, but I know it ain't right."

"Aren't you afraid he'll know you let us out?"

Ella shrugged. "Pa's always mad at me. I git whippin's all the time, whether I done somethin' or not. I heard him tell Otha I've been like a rock in his shoe since my real ma died. When I'm fourteen, he's makin' me marry Bobby Lee Hoover."

Abby's heart sank. It was all she could do not to reach out and hug her sister.

"Come on," Ella said. "You best git movin'."

Abby and Jay followed Ella down a narrow aisle between shelving filled with jars of home-canned goods. They climbed the wooden steps, and Ella opened the creaky outside door and stopped abruptly. Abby heard her gasp.

"Pa!"

"Whaddya think you're doin'?" Isaiah Tutt's voice sent a chill up Abby's spine. "Did you think I wouldn't hear you sneakin' outta the house?"

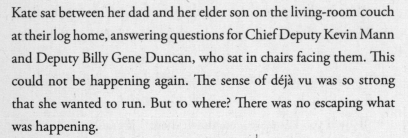

Kate sat between her dad and her elder son on the living-room couch at their log home, answering questions for Chief Deputy Kevin Mann and Deputy Billy Gene Duncan, who sat in chairs facing them. This could not be happening again. The sense of déjà vu was so strong that she wanted to run. But to where? There was no escaping what was happening.

"I don't know what else to tell you," Kate said. "Now you know what we know."

"And you're sure Abby isn't involved romantically with the Rogers boy?" Mann said.

"As sure as I *can* be." Kate turned to her father. "Dad doesn't think so either."

"That's right," Dad said. "And I've paid attention. I've been watchin' out for Abby."

"Abby told me she wasn't ready to open her heart to anyone," Kate said. "That she'd had all the pain she could handle, dealing with her father and sister still missing. She seemed fine with just being friends with Jay."

Mann twirled a pencil in his hand. "And you believe her?"

"Mama already told you she did." Hawk shifted his weight, his arms folded across his chest. "Maybe y'all should be out looking for Abby instead of asking us the same questions several different ways."

"Sorry if it seems tedious," Mann said. "We're just being thorough. We get calls all the time from worried parents whose kids are late coming home. Most of the time there's a logical explanation."

"I can't think of any logical explanation for this," Kate said.

Mann wrote something on Duncan's notepad. "Try not to worry, Mrs. Cummings. The sheriff called me back in this evening so I could personally look into it. We'll find your daughter. The girl that Abby saw in town … what can you tell me about her?"

"Just that she had the same coloring and features as my missing daughter, Riley Jo, who would be seven now. I told Abby I didn't want to hear any more about her. We made a deal: I said I would stop bugging her about looking for the girl if she would agree to go back to her therapist."

"Abby needs a shrink, all right," Hawk said.

Kate elbowed her son in the ribs to silence him. "I held up my end of the bargain and stayed out of it."

"I can add some details," Dad said. "Abby took the cell phone picture of the little girl back to Murchison's to see if anyone who worked there recognized her. One male clerk—I don't recall his name—said the girl's name was Ella. That she'd been in there with a man and woman and twin boys about three years old. The clerk figured the family lives in the area somewhere since they were buyin' chicken feed. But they paid cash, and he didn't have a name or address."

"Any idea what these folks look like?" Duncan asked.

Dad shook his head. "I avoided delvin' into it with Abby. We've been there before with her. It seemed obvious to me at the time that the girl had a family and Abby should leave it alone."

"You think this is relevant?" Kate said.

"I'm not sure, ma'am." Mann moved his gaze from Kate to Hawk to Dad—and back to Kate. "But we have to look at everything in Abby's life as relevant while we're fixin' to commit all our resources to finding her. Any of you know what Abby's been doing to find this Ella?"

"I do," Hawk said. "Abby and Jay left flyers in businesses on Main Street and in some of Abby's favorite hangouts. She told people she had a valuable doll she wanted to return." Hawk rolled his eyes. "Her cell number was on the flyer."

"Do you know if she got any responses?" Mann said.

Hawk shook his head. "No, sir. I don't. But I'm the last person Abby would confide in about this. I agreed with Mama and Grandpa that she should drop it."

Duncan wrote something on his pad.

"Do you know if Abby backed up her SIM card on her server?" Mann said.

Hawk nodded. "She usually does."

"Any idea what her password is?" Mann said. "With that, we should be able to check her SIM card and see who she's been talking to."

Kate linked her fingers together. "I have it written down."

"Great." Mann glanced at Duncan's notes. "Okay, just to recap, the last conversation with Abby took place this morning when she told you she was meeting Jay on the slope at noon?"

Kate nodded. "That's right."

"But none of you know where the slope is?"

"Only what I've already told you." *At least three times*, Kate thought.

"Anything else Duncan and I should know about Jay Rogers?"

"Just that his mother is in Las Vegas right now," Kate said. "And at some point, I suppose you're going to have to locate her and tell her he's missing."

Missing. Saying the word out loud sent terror through every fiber of Kate's being. Seven dreaded letters that had haunted her for five torturous years. A single word with the power to steal her joy, her peace, and her future. Not this time! She wasn't hanging that word on the empty grave of another loved one. She wasn't giving up until they found Abby—no matter what.

Abby clung to Ella as Isaiah shoved the door open with his foot, holding a sawed-off shotgun in his hands.

"Well, ain't this a lick?" Isaiah said, his gaze moving from Abby to Jay to Ella.

"I heard you talkin' to Otha." Ella hung her head. "I wanted to see what was down here."

"Curiosity's one thing. Turnin' them loose is another! That makes you worse than a sneak. You're a traitor."

"I'm sorry, Pa." Ella held her palms in front of her face. "I was wrong to do it."

Isaiah grabbed her arm and slammed her against the wall. "Git over there and shut up." He looked at Abby and Jay. "Git back in the hole. Now! I ain't ready to finish you off just yet. But you give me one reason, and I'll shoot you dead right here, right now."

Abby backed up and climbed down the ladder. Jay jumped.

"As for you," Isaiah shouted at Ella, "that's the last straw. You ain't been worth a plug nickel from the git-go."

Abby heard the sound of a hand slapping flesh, and Ella whimpered. *Lord, help her!*

"I'm sorry, Pa. I promise I won't do it no more."

"I ain't givin' you the chance."

Abby heard scuffling, and a few seconds later, Isaiah stood looking down at them, holding Ella by her hair. She was crying.

"Please, Pa. Don't throw me down there," Ella begged. "I'm sorry. I … I know I did wrong."

"Sorry ain't good enough. I can't trust you no more. Go on now. Git!" Isaiah gave her a hard shove, and Ella fell into the hole.

Abby gasped as Jay scrambled and caught Ella with his arms, the force of her fall knocking them to the ground.

"I'm done with all o' you." Isaiah pulled up the ladder, slammed the trapdoor shut, and slid the bolt lock.

Jay let Ella get up and then stood, rubbing his arm.

"You wanted your sister back," Isaiah said mockingly. "She's all yours—for the rest o' your life. But you best talk fast. It's gonna be a short reunion."

Abby kept her eyes on Jay, unable to find her voice as Isaiah walked back up the wooden steps and out the creaky door.

Ella stood facing the wall, sobbing quietly into her hands.

Abby thought her heart would break. She put her hand on Ella's shoulder, glad that the child seemed receptive to her touch. "It's going to be okay, sweetie."

"No, it ain't." Ella shook her head. "Pa's really mad. You don't know how he gits."

"Otha will come looking for you," Abby said. "She's your step-mother, right?"

Ella nodded. "Why did Pa say I was your sister? I ain't never seen you before."

"Not since you were old enough to remember. But I used to give you piggyback rides, and tell you stories, and rock you to sleep."

Ella turned around, her eyes wide. "So he's your pa too?"

"No, my father's dead."

Ella cocked her head. "Well, if we don't have the same ma or the same pa, why are you my sister?"

Abby looked over at Jay and then at Ella. "Isaiah hasn't told you the truth."

"He lies to Otha sometimes. She pretends to believe him so he won't git mad. But I know she don't."

"Sit with us and let me explain some things." Abby sat on the ground next to Jay, not surprised when Ella remained standing.

"You don't have to be afraid of us, sweetie. My name is Abby Cummings. This is Jay Rogers. We came to find you."

Ella dropped to the ground and sat facing them. "Why? I ain't lost."

"This is the only home you remember," Abby replied, feeling as if someone else were talking, "but you lived somewhere else until you were two. Your real name is Riley Jo Cummings. Your parents are Kate and Micah Cummings. You have two big brothers, Hawk and Jesse. And I'm your sister, Abby. You disappeared when you were two years old, and so did our daddy, Micah. Your family's been looking for you ever since, and Mama has been very sad and misses you terribly. We all have."

"I don't know nothin' about none o' you." Ella's voice shook. "That ain't what Pa told me."

"You said yourself that he lies," Jay added.

Ella rocked, her arms folded tightly across her chest. "I got twin brothers, Ronny and Donny. Them and Pa and Otha's my only kin. Well, 'cept for Uncle Walter and Granny Faye."

"I'm sure you love them," Abby said. "I'm not trying to take that away from you, sweetie. But it's important to know where you came from. You want the truth, don't you?"

Ella kept rocking and avoided eye contact. "Why does Pa want y'all dead?"

"Because"—Abby cupped her sister's chin in her hand—"we know the truth, and he's scared of getting into trouble. Isaiah broke the law when he brought you here to live and kept the sheriff and your real family from knowing about it."

A tear spilled down Ella's cheek. "Pa don't want me. Why didn't he let me live with my real ma? Why'd he lie?"

"I don't know," Abby said. "But I *do* know that your real family loves you and wants you. We've been trying to find you since you and Daddy went missing."

Ella put her hands over her ears and started to cry.

Abby got up on her knees and pulled her sister into her arms, rocking gently from side to side, crying with her and thinking how sad it was that they were both going to die without their mother ever knowing the truth.

CHAPTER 23

Virgil glanced out his office window at the Raleigh County Courthouse and, through the maple branches, saw that dawn had turned the Friday morning sky a simmering shade of hot pink. Why hadn't Abby Cummings contacted Kate? Was she playing games? Or was she in trouble?

There was a knock at his open door. Virgil looked up just as Kevin walked in.

"Still haven't found the Rogers kid's mother," Kevin said. "We've got the Vegas PD checking out hotels for Mr. and Mrs. Richie Stump."

"You need to go home and get some shut-eye," Virgil said. "I appreciate that you were so willing to pull a double shift. I wanted my best man on this."

"Just wish I had a clue where to go with it," Kevin said. "Abby's SIM card records didn't raise any red flags. The last time she used her cell phone was yesterday morning, when she sent Jay a text. We compared her day-to-day calls and texts over the past month, and most of them were between her and Jay. Also a few with her family members. There were two calls, both under a minute long, from a prepaid cell, the last one day before yesterday. That could be significant—or simply the wrong number. There's no way to know. I hate to say it, but it's almost as if Abby and her friend vanished, same as her dad and sis. Raises serious questions about whether the same person or persons is at it again."

"But why wait five years?"

"I dunno, Sheriff. Maybe this Ella's the real deal and someone didn't want Abby getting any closer."

Virgil rubbed his chin. "But what are the odds? Abby's got a pattern of doing this. And if someone had Riley Jo, why would they stay in the area? Seems far-fetched. "

"I'm not convinced that's what happened. But Abby and Jay are nowhere to be found. And since they seem to be responsible kids, I think we have to consider everything."

A knock on the door caused Virgil to turn.

Billy Gene stood in the doorway. "Sir, we found Mrs. Cummings's Odyssey. It was parked on Perkins, a block over from the Sycamore Apartments, where the Rogers kid and his mom live. It was parallel parked, nice and neat. Left unlocked. Nothin' looks fishy. We're gonna start collectin' evidence. You wanna tell Mrs. Cummings, or should I?"

"I'll do it," Virgil said.

"Looks like I'm gonna have to wait on that shut-eye," Kevin said. "I'll head over to Perkins Street and make sure we don't miss a beat."

Virgil nodded his approval. "Thanks. I'll call Kate and meet you over there in a few minutes. Keep looking for Jay's truck, and try the apartment again. It's possible those two kids have been in there all night and didn't want to be discovered."

⚘

Abby sat nestled between Ella and Jay, her arm around her sister. The only sound she heard was the rumbling hunger of their stomachs.

Lord, we need wisdom to get out of here. But if Jay and I don't make it out, please get Riley Jo home to Mama. Don't let me die for nothing. Don't let Mama lose both of us. It'll break her heart all over again.

"What are you thinking?" Jay whispered. "I can feel the wheels turning."

"I'm praying," Abby said. "We need wisdom on how to get out of here."

"I wish Custos would come git us out," Ella said. "He's humongous. And strong."

Abby's gaze collided with Jay's. "Who is he?" she said.

"My angel. I seen him once."

"Oh." Abby's hope of being rescued rose and fell in an instant. "When?"

Ella looked up at Abby. "When I fell outta the weepin' willer tree and landed in the pond. I swallered a big gulp o' water and was coughin' and coughin' and couldn't breathe. I couldn't touch bottom neither." A pretty smile lit up Ella's face, and Abby's heart melted. "All of a sudden, I was standin' up on the bank. Custos wiped the mud off me with his wing, and I wasn't coughin' no more. He promised he was always watchin' out for me. And then he was gone. I didn't even see him go."

"When I was your age," Jay said, "I had an imaginary friend named Ko-Ko. He was a dragon. He had wings too."

Ella's eyes grew wide. "Did real fire come outta his mouth?"

Abby looked over at Jay and ever so subtly shook her head, hoping he would get the hint not to encourage this line of conversation. "Ella, what is this room used for?"

"Pa said it was a storm cellar, but we ain't never used it."

Except to dump our daddy's body, Abby thought. "Jay, what time is it?"

Jay pushed the button on his watch, and the face lit up green. "Eight twenty-two. What I wouldn't give for a plate of eggs and bacon and hash browns."

"You must be so hungry," Abby said to Ella.

"I'm used to it. When Pa gits mad, he sends me to bed with no supper. And Pa's mad a lot." Ella linked arms with Abby and nestled closer. "He's gonna kill us like he said. He ain't makin' that up just to git us afraid."

"You seem awfully sure about that," Jay said. "Has he killed someone before?"

Ella clutched more tightly to Abby and didn't answer.

"It's okay, sweetie." Abby stroked her sister's cheek. "You can tell us."

Ella shook her head. "I ain't sayin' nothin'."

❦

Virgil watched investigators go through Kate Cummings's Odyssey, and an ominous sense of déjà vu came over him. He blinked it away. He could not allow himself to fall into the trap of assuming that Abby's situation was related to Micah and Riley Jo's disappearance. But neither could he ignore it.

He saw Billy Gene pull up and walked toward him, arriving at the squad car just as the deputy was getting out.

"Any luck at the apartment?" Virgil said.

Billy Gene shook his head. "No, sir. The maintenance supervisor went in under the guise of needin' to change the furnace filter. The place was empty. Beds hadn't been slept in. No dirty dishes. We still haven't spotted Jay's truck."

"Have you talked to any of the neighbors?"

"Everyone in the building. The last one to see him was the lady across the hall."

Virgil's cell phone buzzed, and he glanced at the screen. It was his administrative assistant. "April, please tell me you have good news."

"I do," April Cox said. "I've got Jay's mother, Sue Ann Stump, on the line. Should I patch her through?"

"Yes. Thanks."

Virgil waited for the beep. "Mrs. Stump? Sheriff Granger here."

"Thank heavens," she said. "The Las Vegas Police came to our hotel room and told us what's going on. Jay can't be missing. It's just not possible. My boy's very capable and responsible, or I would never've left him by himself. There has to be another explanation."

"We're certainly hoping so. But right now, we can't think of any. Can you remember the last time you talked to your son?"

"I know exactly when it was," Sue Ann said. "Tuesday morning, the day after we arrived in Vegas. I called Jay to tell him Richie and I had tied the knot and were fixin' to stay all week and fly back next Monday. I said I'd check in with him this weekend. But he knows my cell number."

"Did Jay hint that he might be going somewhere?"

"Absolutely not. He was gonna follow his normal routine. He goes to work at Tutty's at four and works until ten. When he's not working or sleeping, he's usually with Abby Cummings, which I'm sure you know."

"What's his relationship with Abby?"

"She's a doll, but Jay says they're just friends. Abby's been to the apartment a few times. I've played Scrabble with them and watched a few movies. I didn't see any sparks flying."

"Is Jay dating anyone?"

"Not lately. He's shy with girls. It's just as well, or he might could end up like me. I had Jay when I was barely eighteen. I'm only thirty-five, and it's taken me four tries to find my soul mate." Sue Ann sighed. "I've finally found him. And before I can even get home from my honeymoon, there's already a crisis."

"I'm not sure whether this is a crisis," Virgil said. "But you need to be aware that Kate Cummings thinks it is and has filed a missing-person report. Is there any other family member who might know where your son is?"

"Not really," Sue Ann said. "Jay's grandparents've passed on, and he isn't really close to any of his kin, not even his dad. He would've sent me a text message if he was fixin' to go somewhere overnight. I guess it's possible that Jay and Abby are sexually active and he lied about it. But even if that's true, why wouldn't they just use the apartment to be together? He knows Reggie and I won't be home until Monday. He's got the place all to himself."

Virgil leaned on the squad car and noticed that a group of curious onlookers was beginning to gather. "Mrs. Stump, are you aware that Jay and Abby have been looking for a girl that Abby thinks could be her missing sister?"

"No … this is the first I'm hearing about it. Tell me more."

Virgil told her everything he knew about Abby and Jay's search for a little girl named Ella.

"We haven't been able to locate this child yet," Virgil said. "We're doing everything we can to track her down."

"And you think she's the reason Jay and Abby are missing?"

"We think there might be a connection, ma'am. We just don't know yet. But I assure you, we're doing everything in our power to find out."

"Should I be concerned enough to cut my honeymoon short?"

"That's your call," Virgil said. "Jay and Abby could surface at any time with a logical explanation. But right now, we're acting on the missing-person report that Mrs. Cummings filed on Abby. And we think it's likely that Jay's with her."

There was a long moment of dead air.

"Mrs. Stump, are you there?" Virgil said.

"Of course I'm here. I need a minute, okay? I'm about to go tell Richie the honeymoon's over. I can tell you right now, that's not gonna sit well."

"I'm sorry."

"Not as sorry as I am," Sue Ann said. "We'll catch the next flight home. But if Jay went somewhere and didn't tell me, I'm gonna wring his fool neck."

"Call us when you get here. In the meantime, we know how to reach you."

Virgil disconnected the call. He probably should have given Jay's mother a heads-up about the mass grave they found. But why worry her when there was no indication that discovery was related in any way to Jay and Abby's disappearance?

❧

Abby held her sister's face and looked into her eyes. "*Did* Isaiah kill someone?"

A tear trickled down Ella's cheek. "I ain't supposed to talk about it."

"He won't know," Abby said. "It might make you feel better to tell someone."

"No, it won't!" Ella buried her face in Abby's chest. "I swore I wouldn't."

"Doesn't matter what he did before," Jay said. "He's not about to go to prison for kidnapping, and the only way to cover his tracks is to get rid of the three of us. We need to find a way out of here."

Abby wondered what her sister had seen in her young life to make her so afraid. In the long stretch of silence that followed, Abby figured everyone's mind was reeling with the realization that they had no options.

Finally Ella's voice broke the quiet. "Abby ... was my real ma and pa mean?"

"No. They loved you very much. Mama still does. She just doesn't know where you are. She's been very, very sad about that."

"How did my real pa die?"

Abby glanced over at Jay. "A shooting accident. Isaiah knew about it and must've taken you home with him. Raised you as his. But you're not his."

"I ain't Otha's neither."

Abby kissed the top of her sister's head and stroked her musty, tangled hair, remembering when it was soft as silk and smelled like baby shampoo. "You're ours. You're a Cummings. It must be confusing right now. The one important thing to remember is that there are lots of people who love you."

"Tell me agin my real name."

"Riley Jo Cummings."

"I like Ella Tutt better."

Abby wet her finger and wiped the smudges off her sister's cheek. "That's okay. Maybe your real name will grow on you after you get used to hearing it."

"How am I gonna get used to it if we're all dead?"

"Shhh, don't say that." Abby pulled her sister closer so she wouldn't have to look into her eyes. "We're still here, aren't we? And as long as we're here, there's hope. Father, You know where we are. Please send someone to find us."

Ella pushed back and looked up at Abby, her eyebrows scrunched. "Who're *you* talkin' to?"

"God."

"Granny Faye says He lives way up in the sky—in heaven—where Grandpa Clyde is. Only time Pa talks about Him is when he's hollerin' and sayin' bad words."

"Well," Abby said, "God is good. He never takes His eyes off us—not for a second."

"That's what Custos said, but he ain't doin' nothin' to help us."

"I believe God *will*," Abby said. "He's here with us. We can't see Him with our eyes. But I feel Him in my heart. And He's listening to my prayers. I know He is." *I'm trusting He is. If I'm wrong, we're dead.*

CHAPTER 24

Virgil looked through the missing-person report Kate Cummings had filed on Abby and the accompanying report from deputies investigating Jay's whereabouts. The fact that Abby told her mother she was meeting Jay on the slope, and the fact that Jay was seen leaving the apartment in hiking boots, led Virgil to wonder if the answers they were looking for were there on Sure Foot Mountain.

A knock at the door broke his concentration.

Kevin Mann came into his office and stood at his desk, the whites of his eyes almost as red as his hair. "We've got us a new development, Sheriff."

"Let's hear it." Virgil folded his hands on his desk.

"The mail carrier at the apartment complex where Jay Rogers lives saw our squad cars out front and inquired as to what was going on. Come to find out, yesterday afternoon, he spotted a pretty girl standing in back of a white Ford pickup parked outside the apartments. She seemed to be looking for something and then crawled up under the tarp covering the truck bed. He thought it was odd but blew it off. Figured it was her truck and she was looking for something. Said the girl was young, shapely, dressed in jeans and a pale yellow top and had long, copper-colored hair. That matches Abby to a T, right down to what Kate Cummings said she was wearing."

"What time was that?"

"He was running a couple hours late and guessed it to be around two-forty-five."

Virgil pursed his lips. "Maybe Jay was going somewhere and wouldn't take Abby with him, so she hid in the bed of his truck and took herself."

"That's what I'm thinking. She parked her mother's Odyssey on the next block and walked over to the apartment and hid in the bed of the truck. The neighbor across the hall said Jay was alone when he left. Abby was probably hiding in back, and he didn't know it. We're interviewing everyone Jay works with at Tutty's. Maybe one of them knows what he was up to."

Virgil nodded. "Good. Make sure Chief Mitchell is apprised."

"I will. So … you fixin' to bring in the feds?"

Virgil shook his head. "There's no indication that we're dealing with a kidnapping, or that Abby and Jay have left the state—or even the area, for that matter. Better if we keep the FBI out of it. If it turns into something bigger than this department and the Foggy Ridge PD can handle, we'll reevaluate. Kevin, why are you still here? I thought you were going home to get some shut-eye."

"I was." Kevin came around and sat in the chair next to his desk. "But I'm as caught up in this as you are. We've been working the case on Micah and Riley Jo Cummings from the beginning. I've watched Kate Cummings suffer through five long years, not knowing whether they're dead or alive. She sure doesn't deserve to lose Abby, too. And until I feel brain fog messing with my judgment, I'd just as soon keep looking for her—if that's okay with you."

Virgil studied his chief deputy. Tenacity was his strong point. No point in trying to squelch it. "All right. As long as you agree to step aside when you can't think straight. Or when I decide you can't."

"Fair enough." Kevin rose to his feet. "I'd better get back out there and do what I can to help."

"Heard any more from Jay's mother?" Virgil said.

"She called and said their plane was landing in Little Rock tonight at seven. She and her hubby were fixin' to drive home from there. Too bad she had to cut her honeymoon short."

"Sure was," Virgil said. "Let's try to find Abby and Jay before they get here."

❦

Abby huddled between Jay and Ella—hungry, thirsty, and out of ideas. No one had said a word for the past hour. Their lives were slipping away with every tick of the clock. Abby had made her petitions known to God. What more could she do?

The sound of Jay's voice startled Abby. "All right. There's one thing we haven't tried." Jay turned around and sat on his heels, facing Ella. "Call for your angel friend. Maybe he'll come get us out."

Abby shot Jay a disapproving look, but he held up his palm.

"We're out of options, Abby. Let her do it."

"What if he don't come?" Ella said.

Jay shrugged. "We won't know unless we ask. Can't hurt. Come on, Ella. Call him."

Ella hesitated for several seconds, looking from Jay to Abby and then back to Jay. Finally, she clamped her eyes shut. "Custos, can you help us? Pa threw us down in this big ol' hole, and we can't git out. We're powerful scared."

Abby didn't move in the pin-drop stillness that followed.

"Pleeease?" Ella pleaded. "Or bring us water and somethin' to eat?"

No one stirred for half a minute.

Finally Ella said, "We ain't gittin' outta here."

Jay spun around, faced the far wall, and began wildly kicking the metal mesh with the heel of his hiking boots. "Come on ... *break*!" Some of the dried sod crumbled and fell through, but the mesh stayed secure. After a minute or so of repeated blows, he lay with his back flat on the dirt floor, his knees bent, and let out a sigh of exasperation. "Why'd you have to hide in my truck? Why didn't you go home like I asked? We're not getting out of here, Abby!"

"You don't know that."

"Yes, I do, and so do you! I just wanted to make things right. That's all I was trying to do. If I could die in your place, I would. I'm sorry I got you into this."

"You didn't," Abby said. "I'm the one who ignored Isaiah's threats."

"But if I hadn't shot your dad, *none* of this would've happened." Jay's voice shook, sounding more angry than frightened. "Isaiah's nuts! It's not a matter of *if* he's gonna kill us—it's a matter of *when*."

"Stop yelling, Jay. It's not helping."

NOT BY SIGHT   213

Ella began to cry and then cry harder, seemingly inconsolable, her face buried in Abby's chest.

"It's okay, sweetie." Abby tightened her embrace and rocked back and forth. "Shhh ... it's going to be okay." Ella's tears soaked the front of Abby's shirt as the child continued sobbing.

Lord, help us! Abby looked over at Jay, and he turned away, his chin quivering. It took every ounce of willpower to keep the dam of her own emotions from breaking through her defenses. She thought of her daddy lying dead in this hole, robbed of dignity, and his baby girl kidnapped by a mountain man with no set of rules but his own.

Anger rose up in Abby, and she welcomed it. As long as she stayed mad, she would have the will to fight.

CHAPTER 25

Buck stepped into the cedar gazebo on the back lawn of Angel View Lodge and leaned on the railing, looking down at miles and miles of glistening water and the green, rolling mountains beyond. Cloud puffs hung in the baby blue sky and a balmy breeze tickled the wisps of hair left on his nearly bald head.

About a hundred yards down the hill, he spotted Angel View Pier and counted eleven paddleboats on the lake—and a pontoon. His mind wandered back to when Abby was little. How that girl loved to fish!

"Carry me up, Gam-pa!" Abby looked up at him with eyes that matched her bright blue ribbons and pigtails the color of O'Shea, the neighbor's Irish setter.

"Okay, all aboard." Buck bent down and got Abby situated on his shoulders, then trudged down the path to Angel View Pier, which he and Micah had worked together to build the previous summer.

"I'm gonna catch a *whopper!*" Abby declared.

Buck set her on the dock, then reached in the pontoon boat and grabbed her yellow life jacket. "Listen, punkin'. We're goin' out after crappie for our fish fry. Whatever you catch'll be just great. Doesn't have to be big."

Abby held up her index finger, her face animated. "If I say it, I'll do it."

Buck chuckled, tightening the straps of Abby's life jacket. She was repeating what she'd heard him say the day before.

He pulled the boat next to the dock. Abby climbed in and sat on the passenger bench, and he stepped in after her, taking his seat at the wheel.

"Here we go." Buck put the boat in reverse and slowly backed away from the dock, then headed off to Egret Island.

"Hey, you said *I* could drive, Gam-pa!"

"Are you sure?" He winked at Abby. "All right. Come over here and give it a little gas."

Buck took Abby's hand and steadied her as she walked over to him and stood facing the wheel.

Buck put his hands around her waist, holding her tightly as she pushed fearlessly on the throttle, sending the boat into high gear. She giggled above the sound of the motor, her pigtails fluttering like flags in the wind.

"Whoa, girl. Let's not get in too big a hurry!" Buck pulled the throttle back to a respectable cruising speed and turned the boat so they were headed straight for the island and away from other watercraft.

"All right, Cap'n," he said. "Let's go fishin'."

Abby's tiny hands gripped the wheel as the pontoon seemed to glide over the light chop, the wind blowing in their faces. "Look out, fishies," she hollered gleefully. "We're gonna catch you!"

Buck let go and allowed his granddaughter to take the helm, her expression pure bliss. He memorized the moment, hoping that one day she, too, would look back, remembering the magic of their time together ...

Buck felt Halo rubbing his leg and was startled back to the present. The possibility that Abby might not come home suddenly overwhelmed him. He wrapped his fingers around the railing, his heart pounding. That girl was something special. He loved all his grandchildren, but he had a powerful connection with Abby. He couldn't imagine life without her.

Lord, help us. You know where Abby is. Please bring her home to us. Don't let any harm come to her. I'm trustin' You know what's best. But this is hard.

Buck thought about all the times he'd faced adversity and how God had been his Rock, his source of strength. Whatever happened, Buck could count on the Lord to see him through. But what did Kate and Hawk have to lean on? And Jesse's newfound faith was still fragile. Would he be turned off to God if his prayers weren't answered the way he hoped?

Lord, I'm not tellin' You how to do Your business. I'm just askin' for a little help down here. We got us a mess on our hands. I don't mind sayin' that I'm feelin' mighty helpless.

Buck reached down, picked up Halo and set her on his shoulder, then walked back toward the lodge. He spotted the yellow scarf Kate had tied on the railing of the umbrella deck to express her own quiet hope that Abby would be home soon. How much longer would it be there?

Virgil's cell phone rang. He put it to his ear. "Sheriff Granger."

"Hey there, handsome," said a female voice.

Virgil smiled. "Hey, yourself. What're you doing this afternoon?"

"At the moment, I'm standing outside your door with a Flutter's double cheeseburger and crispy shoestring potatoes. But if you'd rather I go away …"

Virgil jumped up and opened the door.

"That was quick." Jill Beth's infectious laugh echoed in the detective bureau.

He took the sack, the delicious aroma wafting under his nose, and let her inside, then shut the door behind him. "Let's sit at the table."

Virgil had the contents of the bag out and opened in a matter of seconds. He took a bite of the cheeseburger. "This is so great. How did you know I hadn't eaten?"

"You never remember to eat lunch when you're immersed in a case."

"Didn't you bring something for yourself?"

Jill Beth shook her head. "I had a Caesar salad hours ago. If I eat now, I won't want any of the honey-baked chicken I'm fixing for dinner. Not that I'm under any illusion that you might miraculously appear at the dinner table. I invited the boys, but only Reece can make it. He's coming at seven after he gets off work. I told him I wasn't sure about you."

Virgil smiled. "Stranger things have happened." He grabbed some shoestring potatoes and stuffed them into his mouth. "Maybe I'll come home and have dinner with y'all, and then come back here later. Then again, maybe we'll get lucky and find Abby and Jay before that."

"How's Kate?"

"Hanging by a thread. She was just starting to get a handle on her grief, and now this has her on the edge again."

"You think foul play is involved?" Jill Beth said.

"Too soon to say. We don't have much to go on." Virgil gave her a quick overview of what they knew for sure. "Shoot, Kate doesn't even know where the slope is."

"How many grassy clearings are there on Sure Foot Mountain?" Jill Beth's puppy eyes were wide and questioning. "That's like looking for a needle in a haystack."

Virgil nodded. "Fortunately, Kate remembered Abby saying that she and Jay had a great view of the lake from up there, so we're assuming the slope's on the east side of the mountain. The only way to get a good view of a clearing is by helicopter. Maybe it's premature, but I've asked the Benton County Sheriff to lend us their air search-and-rescue team."

"How could requesting a helicopter to search for a girl who didn't come home last night be considered premature?" Jill Beth said.

"Darlin', we're not even sure that Abby *is* missing. Her relationship with Kate has been strained ever since she started looking for

Ella. Maybe Abby's deliberately trying to worry her mother. Or just wants attention. She wouldn't be the first teenage girl to engage in passive-aggressive behavior. And if there's one thing I've learned about teenagers, it's that they're unpredictable on a good day."

"But that doesn't sound like the Abby I know," Jill Beth said.

"I agree. That's why I have an APB out on Jay's truck and have called in air support. I'd rather be guilty of doing too much, too soon than too little, too late."

There was a knock at the door, and it opened slightly. "Sheriff, it's Kevin. You want me to come back?"

"No, come in," Virgil said. "My sweet wife just brought me lunch."

Kevin walked into his office and nodded in acknowledgment at Jill Beth.

"What's up?" Virgil said.

"Great news: Duncan just found Jay Rogers's truck parked in the woods half a mile north of Fox Trail Road and Summit. It was unlocked. No keys in it. At first glance, Duncan didn't see any signs of foul play."

"Other than the truck's parked in the middle of nowhere?" Virgil said. "Is there a grassy slope nearby?"

"There's a meadow, but it's flat and not even close to the side of the mountain. The helicopter's on the way. Maybe search and rescue will spot something. I've dispatched investigators to go over the truck for evidence."

"Good," Virgil said. "We also need to get with Kate Cummings and Sue Ann Stump and fetch a piece of Abby and Jay's clothing. Maybe the hounds can pick up their scents."

CHAPTER 26

Kate had been sitting so long, she almost felt as if she were part of the living-room couch. She heard the front door open and close. Seconds later, her dad came over and sat next to her. They shared the silence for half a minute, and she felt no urge to fill it with words.

Finally Dad said, "How're you doin'?"

Kate tucked a flyaway lock of hair behind her ear. "I'm numb. I can't deal with any more pain. I just can't."

"Heard anything from Virgil?"

"Yes," she said. "He called about thirty minutes ago and said the Benton County Sheriff's office was sending their helicopter to search the mountain."

Dad took her hand. "That's a good thing. With all those capable folks out lookin' for Abby, they'll find her."

"Alive?" The instant Kate said the word, she wished she hadn't.

Her father squeezed her hand.

"You can't go thinkin' the worst. There's bound to be a logical explanation for this."

"Dad, we don't even know what *this* is. My mind is racing with a dozen possibilities, none of them logical. Abby wouldn't worry me like this on purpose. Something's wrong."

Her father didn't say anything. What could he say? He had to be as scared as she was.

"It's not like I don't have a valid reason for thinking the worst," Kate said. "I never thought anything tragic could happen to this family. Five years ago I found out it can."

Hawk came down the stairs and stood looking at them. "Did you get bad news?"

Kate reached out and clasped Hawk's hand. "No. Virgil is borrowing a helicopter from another department and is going to search the mountain by air."

"I passed my afternoon tours off to Eduardo," Hawk said. "I'm fixin' to take the jeep up yonder and look for Abby myself."

Kate gazed into her son's somber dark eyes. "Virgil's people are doing everything they can."

"Well, they haven't found her. I can't just sit around and do nothing like I did before." Hawk swallowed hard, his jaw set. "When Daddy and Riley Jo disappeared, I let everyone convince me to wait on the authorities. I'm not making that mistake again."

Of course you're not. "Promise me you'll be careful," Kate said.

Hawk kissed her cheek. "You know I will. I'll call you."

Kate's cell phone rang, and she glanced at the screen.

"It's Virgil." She felt as if her heart were falling off the side of a ridge. She breathed in slowly and put the phone to her ear.

"Hello, Virgil. I have you on speakerphone. Dad and Hawk are with me."

"Good." Virgil's voice sounded confident. "I'm happy to report that we found Jay's truck."

"Where?"

"Parked in the woods. About a half mile north of Fox Trail Road and Summit. I just got here. My investigators are going over it, looking for clues—fingerprints, DNA evidence, and anything to confirm that Abby was riding in the bed of the truck. There doesn't appear to be any sign of a struggle."

Kate exhaled. "Thank God." She lifted her gaze and looked squarely into Hawk's eyes, wondering how that cliché had slipped out.

"You might oughta thank the sheriff. *He's* doing all the work." Hawk started for the front door. "I'm going up there."

"Virgil, excuse me a moment …" Kate covered the receiver with her hand. "Hawk, do you really think that's a good idea?"

"I want to see what they're doing, Mama. That way I can call you with updates."

"Son, Virgil's already doing that. He's got things under control."

Hawk rolled his eyes. "Sorry if I don't trust the authorities to get this right. They aren't exactly batting a thousand. I just want to keep an eye on things. I'll stay out of their way. They won't even know I'm there."

Kate studied her firstborn. How could she not admire his tenacity? Or respect the fact that he was a grown man, capable of making his own decisions? "All right then."

"Don't worry, Mama. We're gonna find Abby. She's coming home—healthy and happy—and with her head in the clouds, same as always." Hawk opened the front door and left.

Kate locked gazes with her father, who hadn't said a word. He was probably silently praying.

"Sorry for the interruption, Virgil," Kate said. "What do we do now?"

"Sit tight and let my people and Chief Mitchell's people do their job. I've sent a deputy to your house to pick up an article of Abby's clothing. We're bringing in the hounds. If Abby was in the back of Jay's truck, the dogs should be able to track her."

⚜

Virgil stood leaning on his squad car next to Foggy Ridge Police Chief Reggie Mitchell, watching the first team of investigators search Jay's truck. The second team was combing the nearby woods. A third team, consisting of his deputies and Reggie's police officers, were gathered and waiting for the bloodhounds to arrive. Kevin Mann had already found a muddy trail and cast three distinct sets of footprints. But the trail stopped at a creek, and he couldn't tell where it picked up on the other side. They needed the bloodhounds for that.

"I appreciate your help with this," Virgil said.

"Glad to lend support." Reggie's dark skin glistened with perspiration. "I'm like you—I want to be out here where the action is so I can free up every available officer I've got. The Cummings family's had a tough go of it, and I want to find Abby as much as anyone. Plus I went to high school with Jay's mother. She dated one of my basketball teammates—first interracial couple at Foggy Ridge High School. Created quite a stir, as I recall."

"Thankfully, we've come a long way since then." Virgil lifted his Stetson and wiped his forehead. He spotted Kevin Mann and motioned for him to come over. "Where are we with the bloodhounds?"

"They're en route from Fayetteville," Kevin said. "About thirty minutes out."

Virgil glanced at his watch. "Make sure your team is briefed and ready to go the second they arrive. I don't need to tell you that time is everything if we hope to find those kids."

"No, sir. I know what's at stake here." Kevin pushed his wavy red hair off his sweaty forehead. "We're on it. But we've sure got our work cut out for us. The trees and ground cover are dense, and that canopy doesn't let in much light.

"It's a challenge. But if those hounds pick up a scent, we have to be prepared to go wherever they take us."

Kevin nodded. "We will be, sir."

Reggie perked up and seemed to be listening intently. "Hear that?"

Deep reverberations echoed eerily across the wide Arkansas sky, getting closer and louder.

"Search and rescue's here." Virgil turned to Kevin. "Be sure you maintain communications with them. Between air support and our teams on the ground, we ought to spot those kids if they're out here."

"Yes, sir."

Kevin jogged over to where the search team was standing, and Virgil turned to Reggie. "So have you kept up with Jay's mother since high school?"

"Some," Reggie said. "At reunions. Homecoming games. I run into her in town once in a while. Why?"

"I don't know. She strikes me as being a little strange. Seems more annoyed that Jay created a problem for her than she is about him being missing."

Reggie laughed. "Sue Ann thinks about Sue Ann first. Hasn't changed that much since high school."

"Well, I don't suppose anyone would be happy about having their honeymoon interrupted."

Deputy Billy Gene Duncan came out of the woods and hurried over to Virgil, carrying something in his gloved hand.

"Sir, I think I might've found Abby's iPhone. SIM card's gone. But the initials AKC are written on the back in white marker—like her mama told us."

"Where'd you find it?" Virgil said.

"In the woods. Not far from where Kevin found them footprints."

Virgil patted him on the back. "Good work, Billy Gene. Dust it for prints. Abby's SIM card records didn't tell us anything useful. But fingerprints just might."

❦

Abby nestled next to Jay, Ella lying with her head in Abby's lap. The only sound in the dark pit was the sound of their breathing ... and as long as they had breath, Abby wasn't giving up. She had prayed until she didn't know what else to say. What more could she ask for? Surely God had heard her prayers for help. Surely He would answer.

The thought that everything she believed about God might be a myth crossed Abby's mind, but she quickly dismissed it.

There was no way she had manufactured the joy that welled up in her after she got out of the pew, walked down to the front of the church, and made her profession of faith. That decision had been life-changing.

But God had never tested her faith until now. What if He didn't answer her prayers? What if he let Isaiah hurt her—or kill her? Would she still believe God was good?

Lord, I love You. I do. And I want to live with You in heaven— someday. I don't want to die yet. I've just begun to live my life. Mama needs me. She won't handle losing me, too. And my sister deserves a real life. It's so unfair that she had to live with Isaiah and Otha. Please ... just help us get out of here.

Abby heard the outside door open and close. Terror seized her and rendered her mute.

Ella squealed and sat up straight, clinging to Abby's shirt with both hands. She was trembling.

Abby and Jay shared a terrified glance as he rose, defiant and protective. His knees had to be shaking.

A few seconds later, a thirtyish woman with her hair tied back looked down at them through the grate in the trapdoor.

"Otha!" Ella cried.

"I come to git y'all outta there, but we ain't got much time. Isaiah's out sloppin' them pigs and can't see the root cellar. But you hafta take Ella with you. He's plannin' to kill her."

"We will!" Abby said. "That's why we're here."

"Isaiah said y'all was here to make trouble—to tell lies 'bout how Ella come to be."

"No," Abby said, "we—"

"Hush! It don't matter now. Ella ain't safe here no more." Otha slid back the latch and strained as she opened the trapdoor. "You tell the law her mama died when she was born and her pa never did take to her. That's the plain truth of it. They can find her a proper home."

"Isaiah lied to you!" Abby said. "Her mother didn't die in child-birth. Ella isn't even his. Isaiah stole her—kidnapped her. He led you to believe Ella was his by his first wife. But she's not. I know because she's my sister."

Otha slid the ladder down the wall. "What're you talkin' about?"

"It's true. I was there," Jay said. "Five years ago, I accidentally shot Ella's real father when I was out target practicing."

While Jay told Otha the short version of what had happened that day, Abby helped Ella get her foot on the bottom rung and pushed her up the ladder.

"I didn't know Isaiah wasn't her dad," Jay said. "I was just a scared kid who wanted to go home and forget it ever happened."

"Isaiah took my sister," Abby said, following Ella up the ladder. "He changed her name and passed her off as his daughter. I don't know where he buried my daddy. But my family's been grieving ter-ribly ever since. None of them know the truth yet."

"I've heard enough." Otha looked as though she'd seen a ghost. "Don't tell me no more. Just git Ella to a safe place where Isaiah can't find her."

Abby reached the top and climbed out, Jay on her heels.

"How do we get off the property?" Jay said.

"Go due south." Otha pointed to her left. "You'll come to a stone well. Keep goin' straight, on past them pear trees, till you come to the fence. Look for a big hole in the barbed wire. Slip through there and run like lightnin', else you're gonna end up full o' buckshot. The minute Isaiah sees y'all escaped, he's gonna hightail it after you with his shotgun—and he'll be fightin' mad. Now git! I gotta make up a story 'bout how you got out and hope he don't take it out on me."

Ella looked up at Otha with the saddest eyes Abby had ever seen.

"I'm scared," Ella whimpered, tears trickling down her cheeks.

Otha's face softened. She bent down and wiped Ella's tears with the hem of her long dress. "Things ain't always been easy, but I want-cha to know I care 'bout you. I wantcha to git better 'n you had here. What these folks say explains why your pa ain't never had no use for you. But you got real kin that wants you. You're gonna be okay. But you gotta go right now."

Jay opened the door and stuck his head out. He looked both ways. "The coast is clear. Come on!"

Ella threw her arms around Otha and clung to her, Abby not missing the angst in either.

"Thank you," Abby said. "This can't be easy for you."

"Just git Ella outta here and keep her safe. Go on now, child!"

Abby took Ella's hand, pulled her gently away from Otha, and then prodded her up the wood steps to the outside door.

Jay immediately grabbed Abby's other hand, and the three of them ran south past the stone well and into an orchard of pear trees. Now if they could just find that hole in the fence …

CHAPTER 27

Kate stood at the front door, the sound of a helicopter in the distance making her almost sick to her stomach with déjà vu. She wondered if she would have the strength to go on if Abby was found dead—or never found at all.

She spotted a familiar silver Lexus pulling up the driveway. *Not now! I'm trying to hold it together.* She was tempted to close the door and pretend she wasn't home, but the driver had already spotted her and waved.

A few seconds later, Elliot Stafford got out of the car, dressed in navy shorts and a white golf shirt, and walked up on the porch.

"I hope I'm not intruding." He met her gaze with eyes the color of bluish steel—a striking complement to his full head of salt-and-pepper hair. "I went over to the office to say hello and saw the closed sign on the door. Is anything wrong?"

Everything is wrong. A glint of sunlight bounced off the tiny silver cross pinned to his collar. "It's sweet of you to be concerned," Kate said. "I closed the office so I could deal with a personal matter."

Elliot's dark eyebrows came together. "I was just surprised no one was over there covering for you. I know how crazy the office can get on Friday afternoons. Would you like me to sit in for you? I could take messages. I'd be glad to do it."

Elliot's sensitivity was always comforting, like a pair of warm hands massaging her shoulders. Much more of this and she was going to cry.

"Thanks. But it'll be fine. Guests can use the answering machine." Kate swallowed hard and avoided eye contact. "I'll check it later. I'm sure there's nothing that can't wait until …" She choked on the words and couldn't find her voice.

Elliot gently took her wrist. "Kate … what is it? What's wrong? Let me help."

"Abby's missing!" Kate blurted out, then started to cry, trying in vain to stop the deluge.

In the next second, Elliot's arms were around her, her face buried in his chest. "It's all right," he said in barely more than a whisper. "Let it out. You've needed to do this for a long, long time."

Kate felt as if a fifty-foot wall of water had crushed over the side of her heart. It was all she could do to remain standing. She sobbed and sobbed until she finally felt the pressure subside, then wiggled out of Elliot's arms, wishing she could hide.

"I'm sure that was more than you bargained for," she said, reluctant to look at him.

"Kate, I'm your friend. I'm not here to weigh your baggage. I'd like to help you carry it. What's the situation with Abby?"

"Promise you won't tell me that God's in control, because that means nothing to me right now."

Elliot nodded. "Just talk to me."

Kate held open the door and let him go inside. "Let's sit in the kitchen. You want something to drink?"

"No. I'm fine."

Kate pulled out a chair and sat at the kitchen table opposite Elliot.

"Tell me what's going on," he said.

"No one's seen Abby since she got off work yesterday morning."

Kate started to talk and rattled off everything that had happened, starting with Abby's coming home with the cell phone picture of a girl she thought could be Riley Jo … and ending with Virgil's calls to Kate that they had found Jay's truck and then Abby's iPhone.

"A deputy came and got Abby's windbreaker so the bloodhounds can track her scent," Kate said. "They're using a chopper to search by air."

"Sounds like the sheriff is doing everything right." Elliot's voice was calm and comforting. "I'm so sorry you have to go through this—especially when you're already stressed, waiting for the results of the remains that were discovered. That's a heavy load for any person to handle."

"I don't have much choice."

"Does Virgil think Abby's disappearance is related to her search for Ella?" Elliot said.

"He doesn't know yet. But we have to consider it."

Elliot mused for a moment. "Would you like me to take you to where they found Jay's truck and Abby's iPhone?"

Kate shook her head. "I don't think I could bear seeing them carry a body bag out of the woods."

"I understand if you don't want to go up there. But don't give up hope that Abby and Jay are all right. I think it would be a big mistake to assume the worst."

Kate felt her neck muscles tighten. "It's so much easier to start with the worst and work backward, than the other way around. I've learned it's best to brace myself." She held up her palm. "Please … don't tell me I should pray and ask God to intervene."

"Since when have I tried to impose my beliefs on you?" Elliot's expression told Kate that he had already started praying.

It was a mystery to her why Elliot was so nice to her. He was the one friend who always seemed to show up at the right time with the right motive. He respected the uncertainty of her marital status and had never made a pass or acted inappropriately. He never even reacted defensively when it was obvious she wanted nothing to do with his Christian beliefs.

"Tell me what I can do to help." Elliot seemed to look into her heart. "We've been friends a long time. You've never asked me to do anything for you. *Ask*. I want to help."

"I wouldn't know what to ask help with," Kate said.

"You could start by letting me answer phones, take messages, or whatever else you need at the lodge office while you're awaiting news from the sheriff. If I can run a lumber company, I can certainly handle taking messages for a few hours." Elliot reached across the table and took her hands in his. "Don't try to carry this burden by yourself. You'll feel better if you know I've got you covered."

Kate felt her cheeks get hot, guilty at how comforted she was by his touch. "What about your Friday-afternoon golf game?"

"I'll cancel. The guys don't need me there to play."

Kate withdrew her hands and tented her fingers. "I've never understood why you're so nice to me."

"For one thing, I like you. You're a remarkable person. But my offer to help is just seeing a need and wanting to pitch in."

"Because you get points for taking care of the widows and orphans?" Kate said, instantly hating herself for her sarcasm.

Elliot's face went blank, and he dropped his gaze. "Kate, I just want to help you. I don't have any motive other than that." He glanced at his watch, then pushed back his chair and stood. "I'm available to do whatever you need. If you don't want my help, I probably should go. Tee time is in fifteen minutes."

Could she have been any more insensitive if she'd tried? "Elliot, please ... don't go. I'm sorry for my flippant remark. I believe you're sincere. And I could use your help."

Abby, flanked by Ella and Jay, stopped at the edge of the pear orchard and looked out across a grassy meadow. On the other side, she spotted a wire fence.

"That has to be the fence Otha told us about," Abby said. "How should we do this? We're going to be out in the open and easy for Isaiah to spot once we leave this orchard."

Jay nodded. "No kidding. We need to find that hole in the fence—and fast."

Before Abby could respond, Ella took off running.

Jay grabbed Abby's hand, and they raced across the meadow, full bore, not stopping until they reached the fence, wobbly kneed and completely out of breath.

Abby quickly scanned the fence line. "Oh, great. It's barbed wire. I don't see a hole."

"Otha risked … her neck for us," Jay said, still winded. "It's gotta be here."

"I found it! I found it!" Ella cried.

Abby turned to her left and saw Ella standing about twenty yards away. "Shhh …"—Abby put her index finger to her lips—"don't holler. We don't want Isaiah to hear us."

Abby and Jay ran to where Ella was standing and examined the large hole in the bottom of the fence.

"We should be able to fit through there," Jay said. "Abby, you go first and help Ella through from the other side. Be careful of the barbed wire. I'll keep watch. Go!"

Abby got down on her belly and gingerly put her arms through the hole, and then her head. She pulled her body slowly with her elbows—inch by inch. She felt her shirt rip and the barbed wire dig into her back, but she pulled harder until she was out. She turned and reached for Ella's hands and pulled her through unscathed.

"Come on," Abby said to Jay. "Hurry!"

Abby heard a deep vibrating sound that seemed to shake the ground. She listened intently as it got louder.

Ella clung to Abby's arm. "What's that?"

"Don't be afraid, sweetie. It's a helicopter! Probably search and rescue. I'll bet the sheriff's looking for us." Abby waved her free arm in the air, but the chopper never flew where she could see it—and quickly moved away.

"Don't! I heard Pa tellin' Otha the sheriff's mean, and he's fixin' to make me go live with strangers."

"That's a lie," Abby said. "The sheriff is a nice man who wants to help us. And you've got an entire family that wants you. You're going to live with us."

As the helicopter moved away, Abby heard the sound of rushing water. Her thirst was suddenly overpowering. "Hurry, Jay. I think there's water nearby." Abby nudged Ella. "See if you can find it."

Abby guided Jay through the hole, which was just barely big enough to accommodate him. She saw blood on his temple and bicep where he got nicked by the barbed wire, but he seemed otherwise okay when he finally emerged free and clear.

"Where's the water?" he said, brushing the dirt and dried grass off his clothes.

"Over here!" Ella cried.

Abby and Jay turned to her voice and jogged over to a creek bed. Water moved swiftly, rushing over the smooth rocks. Ella lay on her tummy, drinking from her hands.

Abby knelt next to Ella, plunging her cupped hands into the cool, clear water. She drank and drank and drank, wondering if she would ever get her fill. She couldn't remember a time when water tasted so good—or when she thought she might die for the lack of it.

Finally she stopped drinking and splashed water on her face and arms, aware that Jay was doing the same thing. "I'll never take water for granted again," Abby said.

"Me neither!" Ella got up on her feet, the front of her clothes muddy and her tangled hair now wet on the ends. At least her face was clean.

"Man, that tasted good!" Jay said.

"We've got to keep moving." Abby dried her hands with the bottom of her T-shirt. "Otha said that Isaiah wouldn't waste any time coming after us with a shotgun."

"He'll do it too," Ella said. "He's ascared y'all are gonna tell on him."

"He should be." Abby looked into the pair of blue eyes that were unmistakably Riley Jo's. "As soon as the sheriff finds out what he's done, he's going to prison."

"That makes two of us." Jay's expression was somber.

Abby put her hand on his shoulder. "There's no way anyone is going to press charges after all you did to help me."

"Doesn't matter," Jay said. "It's a relief to finally tell the truth. I just want to get you and Ella to safety. I sure hope that helicopter comes back this way so we can get out of here."

Abby tilted her ear. "Do you hear *that*?"

Jay nodded. "Sounds like a seal barking."

From behind them came a booming voice. "Them're bloodhounds, stupid! The law's lookin' for you."

The sound of Isaiah's voice sent terror through Abby. She grabbed Ella's arm and spun around, getting her first look at the evil Isaiah Tutt in broad daylight. He looked eerily like the sketch Jay had drawn. But now that she could see him plainly, his eyes looked dark and vacant—as if he had no soul.

"Why do y'all look so shocked?" Isaiah laughed. "Otha sent you the easy way. I took the fastest. I shoulda killed you when I had the chance. I come to finish what I started." He held tightly to his rifle with one hand and slapped Ella with the back of the other. "This is your fault, you little sneak! I shoulda got rid o' you years ago."

Abby stepped in front of Ella just as Jay lunged at Isaiah, got a fist in the face, and fell to the ground.

In the blink of an eye, Isaiah had pulled a hunting knife from his belt and stood pointing it at Jay. "Fight me agin, and I'll run you through, just like I did Ella's pa."

Abby gasped.

Isaiah's face went expressionless for a moment, as if he'd spoken out of turn. Then a smug grin revealed a row of stained teeth. "Guess it don't matter now if y'all know the truth of it. You ain't gonna be around long enough to tell nobody."

"Tell them what?" Jay said. "I shot him. It was an accident."

Isaiah snickered. "Nah, it was me that killed Ella's pa. I only said you shot him so you'd keep your fool mouth shut. You come along right after I done it, and I wanted to make sure you didn't say nothin' to nobody."

Jay's jaw dropped. "*You* killed Micah Cummings?"

"Stabbed him through the heart. He bled out fast. Didn't suffer long."

Abby's eyes burned with tears. If there'd been anything in her stomach, she probably would have thrown it up. "Why? Why would you do such a horrible thing?"

"I had my reasons."

"What *reasons*?" Abby said. "I deserve to know why you murdered my father."

Isaiah seemed amused that she had the courage to demand an answer. "You want the truth, girlie? Fact is, I couldn't git no woman to marry me. I figured at least one'd feel sorry for me if I was widowed and raisin' a kid on my own. When I seen that man in the woods with the little girl, I knew that was my chance to git what I needed. I tried to take her, but he fought me for her."

"Of course he did!" Abby said, her lip quivering. "He loved her. How could you? You're insane!"

Isaiah smirked. "Well, it done the trick. Otha took to us right away when I told her the sad story of how my wife died givin' birth to Ella." He flashed a grin so wide that it seemed to stretch his beard. "The law won't find a lick o' proof I done any o' that. And you three ain't gonna be alive to swear to it."

Abby's heart raced so fast she thought it would burst. "Do you have any idea how much Jay suffered all his life, thinking he killed a man?"

"He got to live, didn't he? If he done what I told him to, he'd still git to live. But the both o' you butt in where you don't belong."

"What about poor Ella?" Jay said. "She's an innocent victim."

Isaiah spit and then lowered his bearded face, his dark eyes looking into Ella's. "Ain't nothin' innocent about this one. She's a traitor."

"We told Otha *everything*!" Abby said. "You can't get away with this."

"Otha'll back me up." Isaiah wiped his mouth with the back of his hand. "I'm makin' you disappear while the sheriff still don't know nothin'." He pointed the rifle from Abby to Ella to Jay. "Put your hands on your head and start walkin'."

"Where to?" Jay got up on his feet.

"Turn around and start hoofin' it along the bank."

"Where are we going?" Abby said, clutching Ella's arm protectively.

"Wherever I tell you to." Isaiah pressed the rifle barrel against Abby's forehead. "Put your hands on your head and start movin'. Ella, you git 'tween them, and remember I got my rifle pointed your way."

CHAPTER 28

Kate walked faster than normal through the hummingbird garden at Angel View Lodge. Beds of wildflowers on either side of the winding stone walkway were raw and natural with hollyhock, Mexican Hat, cardinal flower, thistle, toadflax, and butterfly weed. The arched white trellises were woven with firecracker vine, morning glory, and angel trumpet.

All along the walkway, strategically placed hummingbird feeders hung on shepherd crook poles. A male ruby-throated buzzed in front of her face several seconds before flying off. She smiled despite her heavy heart and spotted Jesse up ahead, standing next to his wagon.

"Hey, Mama." He flashed a warm grin, his sweaty face dotted with freckles, his fine dark hair falling just above his eyebrows. "I'm just checking the feeders again. I already washed the dirty ones."

"That's great."

"You look sad." Jesse stared at her questioningly. "Did Sheriff Granger call with bad news?"

"Not exactly." Kate spoke with a calm, steady voice. "They found Jay's truck in the woods—empty. And they found Abby's iPhone not far from the truck. We don't know yet why Abby went there. They didn't find anything that looks like the slope she described."

"Maybe they decided to go hiking or camping."

Then why didn't Abby call and tell me? And why did she park my Odyssey a block over from Jay's apartment? "We'll see," Kate said. "The sheriff is using a helicopter to search by air. And bloodhounds to search on the ground. I just wanted you to know before someone hears it on the news and says something to you."

"Mama, Grandpa and me prayed hard this morning—for a really long time."

Kate didn't know whether to smile or cry. How disappointed her son would be when he finally came to the realization that religion was a crutch that didn't hold you up at all and let you fall flat on your face. Now was not the time to get into the pitfalls of blind faith.

"I have a *lot* of faith—in Virgil," Kate said, "to do everything possible to find your sister."

"*And* Jay," Jesse quickly added. "I like him. He's cool."

Kate stepped closer to Jesse. "I don't want you to be scared. This could turn out just fine, but the situation is serious. I want you to be prepared—in case the news isn't what we're hoping for."

Even as she prepared her son, she wondered if there was really any way to prepare for the worst.

Buck sat with Titus at Flutter's Café, gazing down at Beaver Lake and the vast expanse of rolling Ozark hills. The dining room was empty except for a couple from Kansas sharing a slice of Chef Benton's Muddy Bottom Pie.

Savannah, her ponytail swinging in time with her cheerful attitude, came over to the table, toting a platter containing a pitcher of lemonade and two glasses filled with crushed ice. "I thought y'all could use some fresh-squeezed lemonade."

"You're reading my mind." Titus's dark eyes grew wide.

"Mighty nice of you." Buck looked up and tried to smile, unsure whether he had succeeded.

Savannah set the glasses on the table and filled them with lemonade, then proudly set a plate of what appeared to be pralines between Buck and Titus.

"I promise you've never tasted prawleens like these here. My Benson makes them with extra pecans, raw brown sugar, and real cream. They'll melt in your mouth."

"Don't have to tempt me twice." Titus picked up a praline and took a bite. "Mmm. This is right tasty."

Savannah lingered a long time as if she wanted to say something. Finally she said, "How're you doing, Buck?"

"About as well as I can be, under the circumstances. The rumors are hard to handle. Some people already have Abby dead and buried. I try not to listen to any of it."

Savannah nodded, her blue eyes filled with compassion. "Can't say as I blame you."

"Don't know why folks make things up." Buck stroked his mustache. "False information isn't useful to anyone."

"Except the media folk," Titus said. "Rumors boost ratings by enticing people to tune in for details."

Buck blinked to clear his eyes. "Forget ratings. I just want my sweet Abby back home with her mama, safe and sound."

Savannah squeezed his arm. "The sheriff will find her."

Buck hoped he would, but Virgil hadn't been able to find Micah or Riley Jo. No one here was going to come right out and say it, but they had to be thinking the same thing.

The search-and-rescue chopper flew over Angel View Lodge and out over the lake, then circled back to the mountain. An ominous feeling came over Buck.

Lord, no grandpa should outlive his grandkids. It was hard enough with Riley Jo. But Abby and me—we've got somethin' special. I feel like part of my heart's missin'. I'm askin'—no, beggin'—with everything in my heart and soul that You bring her back to us alive.

Buck looked up into Titus's kind brown eyes and realized that Savannah had left. "You don't have to sit here with me. I'm sure you've got more important things to do."

Titus shook his head. "There's nothing more important, friend. I'm right where I need to be."

Abby walked briskly in single file behind Jay and Ella along the creek bed, her hands clasped behind her head. She could almost feel the cold barrel of Isaiah's rifle pointed at her back.

She listened to the sounds of water flowing over the rocks, bloodhounds baying, and Ella sniffling. It was all Abby could do not to put her arm around her sister and wipe away her tears. It wouldn't be long until the bloodhounds caught up to them. Isaiah had to know that. How much longer before he killed them?

The helicopter flew overhead, but Abby couldn't spot it through the tight canopy that let in only glints of sunlight. Perspiration trickled down her temples, but she didn't wipe it off, knowing that Isaiah might misread what she was doing with her hand and shoot her.

Suddenly the dogs' baying stopped. Muffled voices rang out in the distance.

"Well, I'll be." Isaiah laughed. "The dang stuff *does* work."

"What stuff?" Abby said.

"Just some powders I mixed up. Them hounds' sniffers've been disabled for a while. That'll buy me some time while I take care o' you three."

Abby shuddered at the thought of being fed to the pigs. What kind of monster was he? The temptation to run was stronger than ever. Even getting shot in the back would be less terrifying than what he planned to do to them.

"Pa, can I git me a drink?" Ella's voice was whiny. "I'm powerful thirsty."

"Ain't got no time to waste. Keep movin'. The law ain't gonna find no trace o' you when you're in the belly of them pigs."

"If you don't let her get a drink, she's liable to faint," Abby said. "Then you'll have to carry her."

Isaiah was quiet for a moment and then spit. "All o' you git over to the creek, down on your bellies, and keep your hands where I can see them. Drink your fill. You got thirty seconds."

�֍

Kate sat in the glider on the front porch of her log house, listening to the distant helicopter and wishing Virgil would call and say he had found Abby safe and sound.

Her mind drifted back sixteen years, to the day Abby made her entrance into the world …

"Come on, honey," Micah whispered tenderly in Kate's ear. "Just one more push." He brushed the hair out of her eyes. "Here we go …"

Kate bore down as hard as she could, her eyes clamped shut, and didn't realize their baby had been born until it began to cry.

Kate cried too, but her tears were joy spilling over.

Micah kissed her cheek. "You did great."

"Well," Dr. Boyer said, "you wanted the baby's gender to be a surprise." A smile appeared under his dark mustache. "You've got a daughter. She's a beauty."

The nurse handed Kate her baby girl, tiny and naked and vulnerable.

"Hello, angel. Oh, my, you're so beautiful. Your name is Abigail Katherine Cummings. And I'm your mama." Kate marveled as she looked at her daughter's face—the child's fair skin smooth like porcelain, her dark eyes the shape of almonds, her lips a perfect little rosebud. And though her hair was still damp, Kate saw the same red highlights so prevalent in Grandma Becca's.

Micah snapped some pictures, then knelt down beside them. "Hello, princess. It's Daddy. I think you already know my voice by now." Micah's eyes glistened. "I'm not sure yet what to do with a girl, but I couldn't be happier."

"I don't think you have to do anything differently with Abby than you've been doing with Hawk," Kate said. "Teach her to love the outdoors and let her choose the activities she enjoys. If she's anything like I was, she'll idolize her daddy, and wherever you go, she'll be your shadow."

Micah held up Abby's scaly, purplish foot and chuckled. "How can she have such a perfect little face and feet like a lizard?"

"You know that changes quickly." Kate smiled. "She's about the most beautiful thing I've ever seen."

"Me, too."

"We need to get her cleaned up, weighed, and measured," the nurse said. "I'll bring her to you as soon as we're finished."

"With one of those little pink hats?" Micah said.

The nurse winked. "That's the one. We won't be long."

Kate handed Abby to the nurse and turned to Micah, saying nothing, just relishing the feeling. It was magical …

I miss you so much, Micah. I thought I'd die when you and Riley Jo went missing. I don't think I can survive losing Abby, too. I really don't.

Kate sensed someone approaching and turned just in time to see Elliot stop at the bottom of the porch steps.

"I'm sorry to intrude on your privacy," he said, "but I thought you should know that your dad is handling things in the office. He insisted. I think it's helping him to cope."

Kate nodded. "He does better with a lot going on."

"And what about you?" Elliot said. "How are you coping?"

"Truthfully? I feel as if I'm going to break in two. But I've learned that I'm tougher than I think."

"You're about the strongest woman I've ever met." Elliot's face turned bright pink. "I hope you don't mind me saying that."

"I'm flattered. I just hate how I earned it." Kate patted the swing seat. "Come sit with me."

Elliot didn't hesitate. He climbed the steps and sat next to her, leaving a respectful distance between them.

"I thought when Micah and Riley Jo went missing I would never recover," Kate said. "And for a long time, it seemed that way. It's gotten easier to bear over time. But I just can't go through it again. I'm not sure I can live through losing Abby …" Kate put her fist to her mouth and choked back the emotion that had formed a knot in her throat.

Elliot took her free hand and squeezed it. "I don't pretend to know what you're feeling. But don't lose hope that Virgil is going to find Abby alive. While we're waiting to hear, is there *anything* I can do? Buck seemed right at home in the office and didn't need me to hang around."

"You're already doing it. I appreciate your kindness. You're a good friend."

Kate's cell phone rang. She jumped, her hand over her heart, and glanced at the screen. "It's Virgil." Kate breathed in slowly and exhaled, then pushed a button "This is Kate. You're on speakerphone. Elliot Stafford's here with me. Please tell me you've got good news."

"I wish," Virgil said. "The hounds picked up both scents immediately and were off and running, but we hit a snag. The dogs came to a gate in a barbed wire fence. It was unlocked, and the handlers took them through. The hounds got a big whiff of some kind of powder on the other side that seems to be playing havoc with their sense of smell. We're not sure what the substance is or how long it'll affect them."

"Are you giving up?" Kate said.

"Not at all. The dogs proved to us the kids had been in these woods. It's just going to be much harder to track them without the hounds. I've got search teams still moving in the same general direction. We're looking into who owns the property, but I'm declaring exigent circumstances and proceeding without a warrant."

"What does that mean?" Kate said.

"Simply put, it means that time is of the essence and we can't afford to get slowed down by red tape."

CHAPTER 29

Abby was on the verge of collapse but kept moving along the creek bed at the insistence of Isaiah's rifle at her back.

"That's it up ahead," Isaiah said. "I brung you back a different way so them trees'd hide us from the whirlybird."

Abby craned her neck and spotted a rather crude-looking log house nestled in the trees about fifty yards in front of Jay. And several small outbuildings, including what appeared to be a chicken coop and a smokehouse. She had never really seen the outside of the place where they'd been kept prisoner. But somewhere nearby was the root cellar. She glanced beyond the buildings to a pen—and spotted pigs. A chill crawled up her spine.

"You gonna throw us back in the hole?" Ella's voice was filled with dread.

"I already said what I'm gonna do with you."

Ella stopped and turned around, her arms folded resolutely across her chest, her jaw set. "I ain't lettin' you feed me to them pigs!"

"Too late. You shoulda thought 'bout that before you went up against me."

Abby shot Jay a knowing look. Without giving it a second thought, she swung around and kicked Isaiah in the gut, then grabbed Ella's hand and ran for the woods.

"Run!" Jay hollered. "Run!"

Abby, breathless with fear but fueled by determination, raced across the property toward the tree line, clinging tightly to Ella's hand.

A rifle shot ran out. Terror seized Abby, but she kept running faster and faster until they were hidden in the trees. She finally stopped, panting, and looked over at Ella.

"He killed him!" Ella cried. "Pa killed Jay! He's gonna get us, too!" The child's eyes were wide and brimming with tears, her body trembling.

Abby wanted to keep running. But she had to know. "Don't move. I'll be right back."

Abby moved closer to the edge of the woods and looked out, her heart pounding so hard she could scarcely take a breath, shocked and relieved that Jay didn't appear to be shot. He and Isaiah were rolling on the ground, engaged in a fistfight, the rifle not far from either.

"Jay, get the rifle!" she shouted. "Don't let Isaiah pick it up!"

Lord, help him!

Everything in her wanted to run out there and snatch the rifle. But if she failed, there was a good chance Isaiah would end up killing all three of them.

Ella came up next to her and clutched her arm.

"Father, we need You," Abby said aloud. "Help us. You're all we've got."

Jay, his nose and T-shirt bloody, struggled to his feet, only to have Isaiah get up and knock him to the ground, flat on his back.

Isaiah reached down and picked up the rifle, pointing it at Jay's chest. "You stupid kid! You shoulda left well enough alone!" He cocked the rifle. "That's the last time you're gonna give me grief!"

"Nooo!" Abby cried.

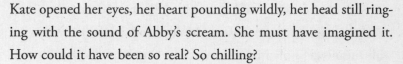

Kate opened her eyes, her heart pounding wildly, her head still ringing with the sound of Abby's scream. She must have imagined it. How could it have been so real? So chilling?

She got up out of the porch swing and stood at the railing, her pulse racing faster than a doe that bounded across the driveway and disappeared into the woods.

She listened intently to the quiet, which seemed to taunt her. The only sound was the distant reverberation of the helicopter, a haunting reminder that another member of her family might never come home.

There was a time when she might have felt some satisfaction in shaking her fist at God. Now she had neither the passion nor the energy nor even the assurance that there existed a God to blame. The more she suffered, the more convinced she was that nothing happened for a reason. It was all by chance. Chance that had victimized her again with no warning and no higher purpose.

She heard the screen door open behind her.

"You okay?" Elliot's voice was as soothing as his touch.

Kate had loved being held by him and was disappointed with herself for relishing the arms of a man other than Micah. "I'm fine.

I must have dozed off and had a dream. I thought I heard Abby screaming. It sent a chill right through me."

"I'm sure it did. You haven't heard anything more from the sheriff?"

"Nothing. I'm so afraid he's going to be too late. That Abby …" Kate's voice failed.

Elliot came up behind her and put his warm hand on her shoulder. "Don't say that. Don't even think it."

Kate turned around and looked into Elliot's understanding eyes, grateful he didn't tell her that she needed to have faith. Or hit her with meaningless platitudes. Instead, he simply pulled her into his arms and comforted her.

$\clubsuit$

Abby hid Ella's face in her chest and closed her eyes, waiting for Isaiah's rifle to fire. Would she ever feel joy that she had found her sister if Jay was killed because of it?

A single shot rang out, echoing across the Arkansas sky. She was pierced to the heart and paralyzed with dread, unsure whether it was she or Ella who was shaking.

Someone shouted a string of obscenities, and Abby's eyes flew open. Isaiah had dropped the rifle and was shaking his hand, shouting vile words that made her cringe.

A second later, a young man wearing a camouflage T-shirt and matching cap marched boldly out of the woods like a soldier on a mission, his hunting rifle pointed at Isaiah.

Hawk! Abby wasn't sure whether she had spoken his name or merely thought it.

"Don't you *dare* move," Hawk said, sliding the fallen rifle to Jay with his foot. "You okay?"

"Yeah, I think so," Jay said. "Am I ever glad to see you! Abby and Ella are safe. They ran into the woods."

Abby glanced over at the log house and saw someone close the curtain. She stood at the tree line, waving her arms. "Hawk! His wife's in the house! Be careful!"

Hawk turned sideways so he could see the house, his rifle still pointed at Isaiah. The front door opened slightly, and a broom with a white cloth hanging on the end slowly emerged through the crack.

"Don't shoot," Otha said. "I'm comin' out now, me and my babies. We's the only folk in here. Ain't got no firearm. I ain't gonna hurt nobody."

Otha came out, her hands in the air, her twins crying and clinging to her long dress.

"Don't you betray me, woman!" Isaiah shouted.

"You lied to me from the start," Otha retorted. "You stole that child from her kin. Whatever happens to you now, you're deservin' of it."

Abby looked at Ella, who seemed dazed. "It's okay, sweetie. No one can hurt you now."

But even as Abby said the words, she knew that the emotional hurt was immediate and deep, possibly even irreversible, as her sister was about to be separated from the only family—the only life—she had ever known.

❦

Virgil turned off his siren and got out of his squad car. He spotted a bearded man in the back of Kevin Mann's car, and Hawk and Abby standing with Jay and a little girl in the shade of a huge hickory tree.

Kevin jogged over to him. "Hey, Sheriff."

"Fill me in," Virgil said.

"Everything's under control. Hawk Cummings took care of business."

"Anybody dead?"

"No, sir. He shot the rifle right out of the perp's hand. The guy's name's Isaiah Tutt. He's a backwoods hick with his own mind-set—a real piece o' work. The bullet grazed his hand, but he's all right. I'll have the paramedics take a look at it when they get here."

"Has he asked for a lawyer?"

"Doesn't want one. He doesn't trust anyone connected with law enforcement."

"How're the kids?"

"Plenty shook up," Kevin said. "Cut and bruised. Dehydrated and hungry. Sore. I think Jay's nose is broke, and Abby's got a nasty gash on her head that needs stitching. Ella took a mean slap to the face. I gave them each a Gatorade, and they gulped it down right quick."

Virgil saw Billy Gene talking with a young woman clad in a long dress, her hair tied back, who sat on the porch steps with her arms around two little boys. "Is that Tutt's family?"

"Unfortunately for them." Kevin arched his carrot-red eyebrows. "Wife's name's Otha. The twin boys, Ronny and Donny, are three years old. The young'uns have been real quiet. I think they sense something bad happened."

"Was the wife an accomplice?" Virgil said.

"I don't think so. Abby and Jay said she rescued them from a hole beneath the root cellar and told them how to get off the property. She surrendered on her own after Hawk showed up. And judging by the way she lashed out at Tutt for telling her the girl was his, I think she was clueless. We're taking her in for questioning. An uncle is coming to pick up the twins and keep them until we sort this out."

"Good work." Virgil lifted his Stetson and wiped his forehead, then walked over to Hawk.

"Hey, Sheriff," Hawk said.

"I hear you took care of business." Virgil smiled and extended his hand.

Hawk clasped Virgil's hand and shook it, a twinkle in his eye. "I'd have waited for your deputies, but Tutt was about to kill Jay and I couldn't let that happen."

"How'd you know where to go?" Virgil said.

"I didn't really. I watched what was going on with your deputies and saw the direction the dogs were running. I remembered seeing a log house on this side of the property when I was out hunting over yonder. So I got in my truck and headed over here. I nosed through the woods around the property and didn't see any sign of them. I was about to leave when the dogs stopped baying. I wasn't sure what was going on. Next thing I knew, Jay, Abby, and a little girl came out of the woods. Some mean-looking dude prodded them with a rifle, so I hid in the trees and followed them. I saw everything. Tutt threatened to kill Jay."

"Where'd you learn to shoot like that?" Virgil said.

Hawk shrugged, his cheeks flushed. "It happened so fast I didn't have time to think about it."

"Hawk saved my life," Jay said. "Well, all of our lives. If Isaiah had killed me, he'd have gone after Abby and Ella."

Abby nodded. "He killed Daddy. And kidnapped Ella, I mean Riley Jo, and he admitted—"

"Hold on a second." Virgil held up his palm. "You say Tutt killed your father?"

"Yes," Abby said. "But Jay thought *he* did it by accident, and that was a lie. That monster let him believe it all his life, and he would've killed us all to keep the truth from coming out. He stole Riley Jo to get a wife, and—"

"Abby, wait." Virgil held up his hand. "Obviously this is complicated, and you kids have been through the ringer. After you get checked out at the ER, I'd really appreciate it if you'd come to the sheriff's department so we can get your statements."

"I'm ready to tell everything," Jay said. "I want that creep locked up."

Abby pulled her sister closer. "Me, too."

Virgil bent down next to the girl he had been trying to find for five years, surprised at the sudden surge of emotion that tightened his throat. "I'm Sheriff Granger, honey. There's no need to be scared."

Ella looked at him with the eyes of an abused puppy. "Are you gonna make me go live with strangers?"

"Well," Virgil said softly, "we have to take some tests that prove you really are Abby's sister. So for a little while, you'll need to stay with some very nice people. But I'm sure you'll be able to see Abby anytime you want."

"And my real ma?"

"Her, too. I can tell you this: she loves you very, very much. We've all been looking for you a long time."

"Can I see Otha and my brothers when I'm with the nice people?"

"I don't see why not. But let's take one thing at a time."

Ella's gaze was wide-eyed and disarming. "Mister Sheriff, is Pa goin' to jail?"

"I'm afraid so." *If I had my way, we'd throw away the key.*

"Good. I ain't never goin' back to him," Ella said.

"You don't ever have to worry about that. I promise." Virgil stood and looked at Abby. "Would you like to call your mother?"

"Yes!" Abby's face lit up. "Does she know?"

Virgil smiled. "She knows."

Kate hung up the phone after talking to Abby and stared out the kitchen window, unable to say anything.

She turned to Elliot, fell into his embrace, and wept. She couldn't yet grasp the cruel truth that Micah had been murdered the day he disappeared—and by a madman who abducted their daughter. Or that Jay had been saddled with false guilt much of his young life. That Hawk was a hero. And Abby was alive. And Riley Jo was finally coming home. None of it seemed real.

Finally Kate's tears turned to a trickle, and she pushed back from Elliot and looked up at him. "Did you catch everything Abby said?"

"Most of it. She was talking pretty fast." Elliot wiped her tears with his handkerchief. "Good news and bad news."

"I need to embrace the good news," Kate said. "I've feared for a long time that something awful happened to Micah and Riley Jo. I never expected to see either of them again. And I was beginning to wonder about Abby. So for now, I'm going to let my heart rejoice in the good news. And deal with bad news later."

"Why don't I drive you to the emergency room?"

Kate nodded. "I'd appreciate that. I'm not sure I could figure out how to get the key in the ignition at the moment. I'm so disappointed that someone from the Division of Children and Family Services has already taken Riley Jo. I would've loved a glimpse of her."

"They'll let you see her soon. Poor thing's been through so much."

Kate exhaled through her mouth, her nose stuffed up from crying. "I can't believe how cold and angry I was that Abby wouldn't let it go. Thank God she didn't."

Elliot smiled. "Amen."

Kate felt her cheeks get hot. "'Thank God' was just an expression."

Elliot didn't say anything.

"Do you really think this is going to make me trust God again? My husband was murdered, my baby's lived with a monster for five years, and my girls have just been through a reign of terror that my son ended by shooting the man's rifle out of his hand. Do you think that, just because Hawk found them in the nick of time, I should forget all the anguish it caused and simply thank God because it's 'all better now'? Well, I'm not. I'm thanking Hawk. And Virgil. And the teams who tracked them down."

"We may not agree on the *Source* of the miracle," Elliot said, "but you have to admit it's a bit miraculous how it came together."

Kate pursed her lips. "Well, it certainly defies coincidence that Abby and Jay ended up friends, neither of them knowing that Jay held the key to the truth about what happened to Micah and Riley Jo. But stranger things have happened."

"Come on," Elliot said. "You need to go talk to Buck and Jesse before I take you to the ER."

Abby waited with Hawk in a curtained cubicle at the emergency room of Foggy Ridge Medical Center, the gash on her head stitched and dressed. She took a big gulp of her third Gatorade.

"Guess you were right after all," Hawk said.

"I knew the first time I saw Ella that she was Riley Jo. Something just wouldn't let me give up finding her."

Hawk cracked his knuckles. "Sorry I came down on you. I said some pretty mean things."

Abby looked over at her brother and smiled. "You saved our lives. That's all I care to remember."

"Good. So what's she like?"

"Much different than she was at two," Abby said. "But she still has a sweet personality. She talks like she's from the backwoods. That'll change over time."

"Was she abused?"

"I don't know. But seeing Isaiah throw that child down in the hole like she was garbage was about the worst kind of abuse I've ever seen." Abby blinked to erase the image that popped into her mind. "Any man that could do that is dead inside. I can't imagine the deep wound that must've caused."

"What a creep." Hawk shook his head. "He's not gonna get out of jail anytime soon."

"He can deny killing Daddy all he wants," Abby said, "but I know he wasn't lying when he admitted what really happened. He just didn't think we'd be alive to tell about it."

The curtain opened, and Abby looked up.

"Mama!"

She slid off the examining table onto her feet and threw her arms around her mother.

"Oh, baby," Kate said. "I thought I'd lost you, too."

"We got her, Mama! We got Riley Jo."

"You sure did. It doesn't seem real yet. I've been so worried about you." Kate motioned for Hawk.

In the next instant, it was hard to say who was hugging whom.

"Hawk, you were so brave," Kate said. "It's a miracle you found them in time."

"I have no idea why I decided to drive around ahead of the dogs," Hawk said.

I do. Thank You, Lord. Abby enjoyed the emotional reunion, feeling no need to comment further.

But even as she celebrated the victory, something remained unsettled within her. Nothing would ever be the same. Life had changed again. One set of unknowns had been replaced with a whole new set of unanswered questions. There was no guarantee that Riley Jo would be able to adjust to the huge change in front of her. Or that she would grow to love her family the way it was obvious she loved Otha. And everyone remembered the adorable two-year-old. Would the seven-year-old Riley Jo live up to everyone's expectations?

Abby dismissed all the negative thoughts. She could not allow what she didn't know to spoil everything else. God had answered her prayer, though not entirely the way she had hoped. But this was not the time to stop having faith.

CHAPTER 30

Virgil stood outside interview room three at the Raleigh Country Sheriff's Department and watched through the two-way mirror as Deputies Julie Martinez and Roberta Freed finally got Otha Tutt to open up.

It had been evident shortly after Kevin Mann began the questioning that Otha seemed backward and shy and intimidated by the surroundings and the male presence. Virgil had decided then to call in both of his female deputies to question her.

Virgil studied Otha's features. She had a simple beauty not every woman who wore no makeup could claim. Her soft brown eyes were her most attractive feature. If only she would smile.

"Otha, what could we do to make you more comfortable?" Julie said. "We need to ask you more questions."

"I'm powerful thirsty," Otha replied. "I'd be grateful if you'd fetch me some water."

"Absolutely."

"While you're at it," Roberta said, "I'd like a Coke."

"You ladies keep talking. I'll be right back." Julie put on her glasses and got up and left the room.

Roberta leaned forward on her elbows. "I saw your little boys when their uncle Walter came to pick them up. They're adorable."

Otha stared at Roberta, as if she were examining her motives or maybe wasn't used to talking to African-Americans. Finally she said, "They's twins: Ronny and Donny."

"How old are they?"

"Three. I had 'nother one. Called him Luke." Otha's face grew taut. "He died in the night when he was three months old. He'd been cryin' a lot. I thought it was the colic, but he just stopped breathin'."

"I'm sorry," Roberta said. "My sister lost a baby with SIDS. Took a long time to get over it."

"You don't never *git over it*. You move on."

"That's a better way of putting it."

Julie came back in the room and handed Otha an ice-cold bottle of spring water, then sat at the table next to Roberta, giving her a Coke and keeping one for herself.

"Otha was telling me that her twins are three," Roberta said. "She also had a baby boy, Luke. He died in infancy."

"I'm so sorry," Julie said, maintaining eye contact. "Did this happen recently?"

Otha's eyes were suddenly brown pools. "It's been nigh onto a year now. Still gits me teary sometimes."

"Of course it does. We don't have to talk about it." Julie took a sip of Coke. "Tell us about Ella."

"Whaddya wanna know?"

"You said you became her mother when she was two. How'd that come about?"

"I married Isaiah. Met him through some kin o' mine that knew some kin o' his. He was raisin' Ella on his own and seemed kinda lost. Ella clung to me right off, and I took a likin' to her. Wasn't long before Isaiah was sweet on me and asked me to marry him." Otha's face turned pink. "I'd never been asked before that. I was always shy around menfolk. I knew we had a lot o' years 'tween us, but marryin' him seemed like the right thing to do. I was twenty-five and not gittin' any younger."

"How old was Isaiah when you married him?"

"He told me he was thirty-five, but I seen his driver's license. He was forty-three. Ain't the first time he lied to me neither. I figured out he tells me whatever he wants me to hear 'bout most everything. That's just the way of it."

"What did he tell you about Ella?"

"Said her ma died givin' birth to her, and he was havin' a rough time of it. That he weren't cut out for raisin' a girl by hisself. Ella wasn't no trouble for me. And I wanted kids o' my own, so I married Isaiah. We got along as man and wife, long as I didn't cross him."

"Did you ever see a birth certificate for Ella?"

Otha's face went blank. "Can't say that I have. I ain't sure what it is."

Virgil spoke into the ear mike. "She would've needed it to get her in school."

"What about when you registered Ella for school?" Julie said. "You would've needed it for that."

"Ella don't go to school. Isaiah don't want her learnin' city ways. We ain't leavin' her ignorant. I'm teachin' her to read. And she knows her numbers and can add 'em and subtract 'em."

"But you did register Ella with the local school district, right?" Julie said. "Even if you're homeschooling her, she has to participate in standardized testing. It's the law."

"But Isaiah said the law don't apply to folk like us."

"It does." Julie reached across the table and gently gripped Otha's wrist. "It's one more thing Isaiah lied about."

"I didn't know 'bout the law," Otha insisted. "And I ain't never seen Ella's birth certificate."

Virgil spoke into the mike. "Julie, it's a moot point. Move on."

Julie took a sip of Coke. "Okay, let's talk some more about Isaiah. How did you come to find out he had locked the two teenagers underneath the root cellar?"

"Isaiah was gone most o' yesterday," Otha said. "When he come home, he was hot and sweaty and acted real nervous. Said we had a problem. That two young folk had come on the property to make trouble, that they was spewin' crazy lies about him stealin' Ella from her real pa."

"Did he explain what he meant?"

"No. He just said they had to be stopped or the law would believe their lies and take Ella away from us." Otha bit her lip. "Isaiah told me he wasn't lettin' 'em go. And what he was gonna do to 'em wasn't my concern."

"What did you say to that?"

"I asked why he didn't just tell the sheriff the truth. He said the law folk don't understand our kind and want to change the way we do things. He told me to leave it alone and let him do what had to be done."

"And what did you think that meant?"

Otha stared at her hands. "I knew he wasn't never gonna let 'em off our property. I took it to mean he was gonna kill 'em."

"Did you think that was the right way to handle it?"

"O' course not. But I learned it don't do no good to go up against him. I decided to wait till Isaiah was off doin' somethin' else. Then I'd let them two kids go. I knew he'd be hoppin' mad."

"Otha, why didn't you call the authorities and let us handle it?"

"Isaiah said we can't never trust the law. And I was scared. I didn't want y'all takin' Ella from me. She's my kin, same as if I give birth to her."

"Julie," Virgil said softly, "find out how she knew Ella was being held."

Julie held up her palm. "Okay, let's back up a minute and clarify something. You say you planned to let the two kids go because you thought Isaiah would kill them. Correct?"

"Yes'm."

"At what point did you find out that Ella was locked up with them?"

Otha looked away, seemingly lost in a long pause. Finally she said, "In the night, I woke up when I heard the front door slam. Isaiah weren't in the bed. I looked out the window, and, under the moon, I seen him walkin' directly to the root cellar. I thought he was gonna kill them city kids. I was sick inside. But I was afraid to git in his way."

"When he came back, what did he say?"

"He was real quiet. And powerful serious. I never seen him like that before. He said Ella'd betrayed us. That she'd let the city folk out and they was all set to run back to the sheriff with their lies. Isaiah said he put Ella down in the hole with 'em. He said"—Otha choked back the emotion—"that she couldn't be trusted no more. That I should forgit all 'bout her now."

"How did you respond to that?" Julie said.

"I told him I couldn't, that I cared 'bout her like she was my own flesh and blood. He said she was gonna share the same fate as they was. That was the way it had to be, and for me to stay out of it."

"But you couldn't?"

"I cried and I pleaded with him!" Otha put her face in her hands. "He said if I opened my mouth, that he'd kill me, too. And Ronny and Donny wouldn't have no ma. I was so scared. I knew he meant it."

"So what did you do?"

"I couldn't sleep no more after that," Otha said. "I couldn't let Isaiah kill Ella and them other two. I waited till the next day when Isaiah was out sloppin' the pigs and went down to the root cellar. I let 'em outta the hole and told 'em how to git off the property."

"Even though you were afraid Isaiah would kill you?"

Otha's eyes glistened. "If I didn't do nothin' and they died, I'd be good as dead on the inside. I had to try."

"That was very brave of you," Julie said.

"Didn't feel brave. My knees was a knockin' the whole time. But I done what I had to do. I was relieved to git 'em out. What's gonna happen to Ella?"

"She'll be fine. The Division of Children and Family Services has picked her up and taken her to stay with some real nice folks until we can sort things out."

"Since I ain't her kin, does that mean I ain't never gonna see her again?"

Julie shook her head. "Absolutely not. You've been a mother to Ella most of her life, and we want to respect that relationship. The first thing that will happen is we'll test Ella to make sure she's actually Riley Jo Cummings, Abby's sister. If so, then she will be returned to her biological mother. But I'm sure you'll be allowed to visit her eventually."

"How long *is* that?" Otha said.

"Ella needs time to accept all the changes and get to know her biological mother. The folks at DCFS will determine when she's ready to see you."

"Am I goin' to jail?" Otha said.

"If you're telling us the truth, no."

"Is Isaiah?"

Julie's eyes grew wide. "Count on it. If Ella's test proves she's Riley Jo Cummings, he'll be charged with kidnapping—and possibly capital murder—and I seriously doubt he'll ever get out of prison."

"He made his own bed," Otha said. "I don't want nothin' more to do with him."

"Good work, Julie," Virgil said. "Go over her story again and make sure there're no inconsistencies, then get her to write it down. I'm going to go say good-bye to the Cummings and then sit in on Isaiah's questioning."

❦

Virgil took a minute to stretch and get a drink of water from the fountain, then walked across the detective bureau and into his office, where Kate, Abby, and Hawk Cummings sat at his conference table. He pulled up a chair and sat with them.

"Sorry to keep you waiting," he said. "It's a little crazy around here. I wanted to say how happy I am that Abby's safe. And that Ella might actually be Riley Jo. We'll know soon." He looked into Kate's eyes. "I'm so sorry about Micah. We're working on Isaiah to confess to his murder and tell us where his body is. Isaiah's an arrogant so-and-so and not cooperating yet. But he will."

"What if he *doesn't* confess?" Kate said. "Then what?"

Virgil wiped the sweat off his upper lip. "Abby, Jay, and Ella all heard him confess to killing Micah and kidnapping his daughter. And he told Otha that Ella's mother died in childbirth, so it's obvious he's hiding something. We've got enough to nail him on kidnapping, attempted murder, and a long list of other charges, even if he doesn't confess to killing Micah."

"Has he asked for a lawyer?" Hawk said.

Virgil smirked. "Doesn't trust them. Told us not to bother bringing one in."

"What if he sticks to his story about Jay being the one who shot Daddy?" Abby said. "It's believable. And Otha can't testify any differently. Until today, when we told her the truth, she believed him."

"Don't you worry," Virgil said. "We'll find a way to get him to confess to killing your father. I know it would help if we could find his remains and you could give him a proper burial."

"Can I take the kids home now?" Kate said.

"You're free to go. I really appreciate you giving us such detailed statements." Virgil turned his gaze to Hawk. "You did a brave thing, son. Your father would be mighty proud."

"Thank you, sir. I think he would be." Hawk's eyes glistened, and he took his mother's hand.

Virgil looked over at Abby. "Young lady, you stared death in the face. I hope you realize how lucky you are."

"I definitely don't want to do anything like that again," Abby said. "But I don't think it was luck."

❦

Kate sat arm in arm with Abby on the couch in the living room, listening intently as Abby and Hawk recounted their harrowing experience to Jesse, Grandpa Buck, and Elliot. The joy of knowing that all of her children would be together soon was numbed by the sorrow of learning that Micah had been murdered—stabbed in the heart—for trying to stop Isaiah from abducting Riley Jo. Kate wasn't ready to process that horrific moment when her husband lost his life. She had imagined worse. But the truth was overwhelming.

"I'm so grateful Abby's all right," Kate said. "But it's a bittersweet joy that Riley Jo's alive, knowing your father gave his life trying to protect her."

"It hurts to imagine it," Hawk said. "But I'm proud of him. Daddy was a hero."

"So are you." Abby nudged Hawk in the ribs with her elbow.

Kate smiled. "He certainly is."

"It's flat weird how I had the guts to stand up to Isaiah like that," Hawk said. "But something pushed me to step out and stop him. I didn't even think about it. I pulled the trigger and blew the rifle clean out of the creep's hand. I didn't even know I could shoot like that." Hawk started to say something else and then didn't.

"I hope y'all realize the terrible guilt Jay carried from the time he was twelve," Abby said, "believing he'd shot and killed a man. It was cruel of Isaiah to let him think it."

Kate clung more tightly to Abby's arm. "It was a heavy burden for a twelve-year-old to carry. And I can't even imagine his horror when he realized the man he thought he'd shot was your father."

"Jay was prepared to go to jail," Abby said. "He just wanted to tell the truth. Sheriff Granger said his guilty conscience was more punishment than he deserved."

"We should be pinning a medal on him," Hawk said. "He may not have chosen the wisest course of action, but it took a man to go up yonder and try to rescue Riley Jo, *especially* when he thought he was going to jail once he explained it all to the sheriff."

"Jay doesn't need to worry that I'm going to press charges," Kate said. "What Isaiah did to that boy was cruel. Yes, he should've told his parents, and I'm sure he'll always regret he didn't. But a twelve-year-old is simply not equipped to take responsibility for that kind of decision. He tried to make it right. When the dust settles, I want to talk to Jay myself."

"That would mean so much to him, Mama." Abby nestled closer. "You can't imagine how bad he feels."

"I wonder if Isaiah's ever gonna tell us what he did with Daddy's body," Hawk said.

Kate shuddered. That monster had threatened to feed Abby, Jay, and Riley Jo to his pigs. Did she want to know the truth?

"I think we oughta leave that to the sheriff for now," Grandpa Buck said, almost as if he could read Kate's mind. "Micah's spirit's with the Lord. We should dwell on that. That's what he'd want us to do."

Kate nodded. "He would." Not that she was confident that his spirit lived on. Or that heaven existed.

Abby looked over at Kate. "Mama, God *did* answer my prayers—and Grandpa's and Jesse's. He brought Riley Jo back to us."

"But not your father."

"And we'll never know why," Abby said. "But I felt God's hand on me the entire time we were being held captive. I wasn't sure if I was going to live or die. But I felt His presence. It helped a lot. Maybe because I knew if I died, I'd be with Jesus."

"Isaiah had free will," Grandpa Buck said, "same as us. He'll be held accountable for what he's done."

"That doesn't help us now, though, does it?" Kate hated that she sounded combative.

Jesse got up, walked over to Kate, and cupped her cheeks in his hands. "Mama, God didn't kill Daddy. Isaiah Tutt did it. And he's not getting out of jail—ever. Riley Jo's safe. Now you can be happy again."

Kate was moved by Jesse's sweet innocence and how much her sorrow must have weighed on him. "You're right, sweetie. There's a lot to be grateful for. We should concentrate on that."

Kate smiled at her youngest son even as her insides churned. She was not about to give God credit for bringing Riley Jo home. Not when Abby came close to losing her life. As did Jay. And Hawk could just as easily have missed when he fired his rifle and become a victim too. It was the sacrifice of her older children that won the release of her youngest. As far as she could tell, God was nowhere to be found.

CHAPTER 31

Kate lay on her side, staring at the empty side of her bed. She had grieved Micah's absence until she didn't have a tear left. It hadn't occurred to her that if the truth behind his disappearance was ever known, the gut-wrenching grief she had finally learned to manage would come back with a vengeance. How much more pain could she take before she simply shut down?

She blinked away the images that popped into her head of Micah fighting Isaiah to keep him from abducting Riley Jo. Did Micah agonize over his baby girl's fate as he lay dying of a stab wound? Did he think of Kate? Did he regret that last argument as much as she did? Or did he just lose consciousness and slip away? Haunting questions with no answers.

She hugged her pillow, her mind wandering back to one of her most cherished memories …

Kate stood in the bleachers at the Foggy Ridge High School football stadium, snuggled up next to Micah. The September afternoon was crisp and sunny as the Foggy Ridge Bobcats went back into the locker room at halftime, leading by four-teen points, and the marching band filed onto the field. The stands were packed with students and alumni, all anticipating a big win followed by the homecoming dance that evening.

"Not much has changed in five years," Micah said. "It almost feels as if we never left."

"Other than these students seem really young." Kate laughed. "Or is it just that we're older?"

"A little of both, I guess. We sure have some great memories of this place."

"There's never been a homecoming game like *our* last one, when you carried the winning touchdown in that stunning defeat against Fayetteville." Kate craned and spotted the floats pulling on to the track. "I'll never forget the sight of you being swarmed by fans and carried off the field with everyone cheering wildly. You were everyone's hero. But it wasn't until the homecoming dance when the band sang 'Endless Love' that I realized I was falling in love with you."

"I knew in the third grade." Micah flashed a boyish grin. "When Jason Longmont dipped your braid in blue acrylic paint—and you chased him into the boy's bathroom, wrestled him to the ground, and painted his face with it. I thought you were the coolest."

Kate nudged him with her elbow. "I got in big trouble over it. Dad never expected to be lecturing his daughter about not getting physical to resolve conflicts. I think he was more amused than mad. But he made his point in no uncertain terms."

"You were a little spitfire," Micah said. "Still are. It's one of the things I love about you. No matter what life throws at you, you hang tough."

"Tough, eh? That's not exactly the trait I'd like to exude."

"You're also beautiful, intelligent, feminine, compassionate, caring, fun—*and* sexy."

"How can I be all that and tough at the same time?"

"You are." Micah turned his gaze to the field and seemed distracted for a moment, then took her by the hand. "Come on. I want to show you something."

"I don't want to miss halftime. Where are we going?"

"You'll see."

Micah led her down the steps and out onto the field.

"What are we doing?" Kate said, realizing that a male voice was booming over the loudspeaker.

"We have two very special alumni with us tonight. Our homecoming king and queen of 1983, Micah Cummings and Kate Winters."

Kate felt her cheeks sizzling as they stopped on the fifty-yard line. "Why are they singling us out? I see lots of alumni here."

The male voice continued to echo across the stadium as a man quickly attached a lapel mike to Micah and ran off the field.

"Micah has something he would like to say and asked Principal Adams if he could have a couple minutes of the program to say it publicly."

"You knew about this?" Kate whispered.

In the next instant, Micah knelt down on one knee and took her hand. "Kate, I picked today—on the grounds of our alma mater and before all these students, past and present—to ask the most important question of my life. We've shared some wonderful times. You are my best friend and confidante. The love of my life. The other half of my heart." He pressed his lips to her hand. "I can't imagine living my life without you. Katherine Abigail Winters, will you marry me?"

Kate was suddenly so light-headed she thought she might faint. She had hoped he would propose but never dreamed he would do it with such flair.

"Yes!" she managed to say, aware that the stadium had exploded with clapping and whistles and feet pounding the bleachers.

Micah reached in his pocket and took out a tiny black case and opened it, revealing a delicate diamond solitaire. Kate felt him slip the ring on her finger but was so taken with the moment that she paid little attention to the ring and focused on the radiance of Micah's countenance.

Music began to play over the sound system: "Endless Love" by Lionel Richie and Diana Ross, which had been *their* special song since the homecoming dance where they reigned as royalty.

Micah took off the mike and rose to his feet, wearing a smile that would melt the polar ice cap.

Kate threw her arms around him, and he spun her around. "I love you," she whispered.

Micah set her down and looked at her as if she were the only person in the universe. "Don't ever doubt my endless love for you."

The stadium erupted again in whistles and applause and feet stomping the bleachers as the two hid themselves in a lengthy, tender, meaningful kiss …

A river of tears soaked Kate's pillow, an outpouring of grief she thought she had emptied years ago. Not that she ever expected to see Micah again. But the finality of his death—and her empathy for how he must have felt in those last horrifying moments—broke her heart all over again.

At least her girls were safe. That was the blessing. And Riley Jo would be home soon.

Kate was at the same time excited and terrified at the thought of being reunited with her younger daughter. Riley Jo's personality would be more evident now—and almost entirely without the influence of her biological parents.

Abby said her sister's grammar was terrible, but that was fixable. It was Riley Jo's heart that Kate worried about. Regardless of how much abuse had occurred prior to Isaiah's pushing her down in the hole, Riley Jo would need counseling to come to grips with being thrown away like a piece of garbage by the only father she could remember.

Kate couldn't shake the nagging fear that the child's DNA might not be a match. What if all this angst was for naught? No one had really proven that Ella was Riley Jo. What if another man, and not Micah, had fallen victim to Isaiah's heartless scheme? And some other little girl had been abducted?

Until the lab test came back proving Ella was indeed Riley Jo, Kate's life would remain on hold.

Kate heard a knock at her door. "Come in."

The door opened, and Jesse came in and crawled into bed next to her.

Jesse draped his arm over her and was quiet for a long time. Finally he said softly, "I'm sorry Daddy's dead."

"Me, too, sweetie. But your sisters are both alive. That's a wonderful thing."

"Maybe our family can be happy now," Jesse said.

Kate swallowed hard, all too aware that, for half of Jesse's life, their family had forgotten how to be happy. He had little recollection of the laughter and the playful times they'd had before his daddy and sister went missing. Most of the years he could remember had been spent with a mother and older siblings who were depressed.

"I hope so," Kate said.

"I wish I could make you happy, Mama."

Kate turned over and faced him, stroking his cheek. "Oh, sweetie, you do. I can be happy about some things and sad about other things."

"You never smile."

"I'm so sorry." Kate's eyes stung with tears. "I know it's been hard for you seeing me hurting all the time. And it might take time for me to get over the news about your daddy. But I promise things are going to get better now. We're going to be a happy family." *If I can just survive the grief.*

Virgil sat with Kevin across the table from a very arrogant Isaiah Tutt.

The questioning had become tedious, and Virgil was trying not to lose patience, lest Isaiah change his mind and lawyer up before they got him to confess to Micah Cummings's murder.

"Tell us again," Kevin said, "what happened the day Micah Cummings was killed."

Isaiah's eyebrows came together. "I done said it till I'm blue in the face."

"I'd like to hear it one more time."

"I was in the woods, tracking some feral hogs that was catin' up my crops. I heard shootin'. I seen a man on the ground and a little girl standin' next to him, cryin'. I hurried over to 'em. The man was bleedin' out. There was nothin' I could do for him. I looked out yonder and seen a kid with a rifle runnin' toward us. He stopped at a plastic carton set on a stump at the edge o' the meadow. I hollered at him. He said his name was Jimmy Dale Oldham and he lived over yonder. Said folks called him J.D."

"Tell us again how you responded."

"I drug the dead man's body out in the open and told the kid straight out he killed the man. He got all flustered and such and claimed it was an accident. I told him it didn't matter, that the law would make him pay, and he'd go to jail for it."

"Did you really believe a twelve-year-old kid would go to jail for an accidental shooting?"

"Killin's killin', that's all I knowed." Isaiah smirked.

"You really expect us to believe that you, a grown man and life-long citizen of the United States of America, didn't know that the law doesn't hold a child accountable the same as an adult, especially for an accidental shooting?"

"I weren't thinkin' that way at the time."

"How'd the boy react?"

"He was plenty shook up and said over and over it was an accident. I can't say one way or th' other. All I seen was a dead man and a kid holdin' a rifle. The boy pleaded with me to believe him. Begged me not to call the sheriff and not to tell nobody. I finally had mercy on him and told him to git, that I'd tend to the body. I knew I was takin' a risk he might tell someone and blame it on me. But I felt sorry for him."

Kevin looked Isaiah squarely in the eyes. "We've got three witnesses, one of them Ella, who say you admitted to stabbing Micah Cummings in the heart and abducting his daughter."

"Them kids got their fool heads together and made up a tall tale. I never said no such thing. Jimmy Dale, J.D., Jay—whatever name he goes by now—killed the man, pure and simple. He knows it too. If he said different, he's a liar."

Kevin stared at his hands for a long time. "Let's talk about why you tried to kill Jay."

"How many times do I hafta tell you? He come on my property and took Ella. He and that redhead. I was chasin' 'em down and had Jay cornered when someone shot my rifle outta my hand. Next thing I know I'm bein' accused o' all kinda things. I was just tryin' to git Ella back. I admit to takin' her home with me that day her daddy was shot dead. But I done it to be kind."

"Why didn't you just call the authorities and let us find her family?"

"I figured if I took good care o' her, I was doin' the right thing."

"You thought wrong. You have to live by the laws of the state. Being ignorant of the law is no excuse for breaking it."

"I ain't lookin' to make excuses. I took the girl 'cause she needed a pa. Anything else you read into it is your own doin'.'."

"What did you do with Micah Cummings's body?" Virgil said. "The kids told us you threatened to kill them and feed them to your pigs. Is that what you did with Micah?"

Isaiah stroked his beard. "Why does it matter? I took care o' the body, like I promised the boy."

Kevin lunged across the table and grabbed Isaiah's arm. "It matters to the man's wife and kids! You robbed them of two people they loved."

"I ain't talkin' about it no more. Jay killed that Cummings fella. He's the one you should hang it on. Not me!"

"All right. Let's move on." Virgil pulled the back of Kevin's shirt until he sat down. "Talk about today. Did you threaten Jay? Let me remind you that four other people heard the conversation."

"It could've sounded that way, I reckon."

"You reckon?" Virgil said. "Didn't you point a rifle at him and tell him that he should've left well enough alone and it was the last time he was going to give you grief?"

"Look, he run off with my daughter. I just wanted her back. The law says she ain't mine, but my heart don't agree. I raised her. I got feelin's for her."

"Oh, I see," Kevin said sarcastically. "*Now* you care about Ella? Even though you threw her down a hole, threatened to kill her, and walked away?"

"I did no such thing!" Isaiah pushed back his chair and started to stand up.

"Sit down," Virgil said. "Ella, Abby, and Jay all told us the same story."

"They got their heads together and made it up."

"When?" Virgil folded his hands on the table. "According to *you*, they grabbed Ella and took off, and you pursued them. When did they have time to concoct a story so perfect that every detail lines up? We're talking two scared teens and a seven-year-old."

"They're smarter 'n you think. They ain't tellin' the truth."

"Really?" Virgil said. "Because Ella's bruises are consistent with the kind of fall she had *and* a hard slap in the face. Jay's nose is broken, and his cuts and bruises are consistent with a heavy object—like a child's body—falling on him and knocking him to the ground. The gash on Abby's head required stitches and is totally consistent with her having been hit from behind—as she claims she was. Not only that, all three kids were severely dehydrated. There's no way that happened in the time frame you claim. Your story doesn't hold up."

"Your doctors'll say anything to take your side o' this."

"Okay. Explain the two phone calls you made to Abby. Jay heard you threaten her if she didn't back off looking for Ella."

Isaiah grinned. "I don't own no telephone."

"It was a prepaid cell phone, but it doesn't matter. Jay recognized your voice."

"The kid heard me talk one time—five years ago. You really think he could be sure of it?"

"*Otha* told us you planned to kill Abby, Jay, *and* Ella—and that's why she waited until you were sloppin' hogs, then let them go free."

"The woman was gonna leave me and take my boys. She'll say anything you want to git me put in jail."

"Isaiah," Virgil said, trying not to sound exasperated, "we can play this game all night if you want. Or you can ask for a lawyer. I really don't care. We're going to sift through every inch of your property until we have enough to nail you for the murder of Micah Cummings. But we've already got enough to put you away for kidnapping, child abuse and endangerment, and attempted murder. The testimony of Abby and Hawk Cummings, Jay Rogers, Ella, and Otha is enough to put you behind bars until you're an old man. The best thing you can do for yourself is to plead guilty and explain yourself to the judge. He might give you less time in jail if you cooperate."

"I ain't admittin' to what ain't true!"

Virgil stood, never taking his eyes off Isaiah. "I have a feeling you're going to change your mind."

CHAPTER 32

Early Friday evening, Kate was on hold with the Division of Children and Family Services in Bentonville, waiting to speak to Riley Jo's caseworker.

"DCFS. Who are you waiting for?"

"Stella Rhodes. This is Kate Cummings. I was told she's handling my daughter's case. I've been on hold for several minutes. Please don't cut me off. I don't want to start over."

"What is your daughter's name?"

"Riley Jo Cummings. Well, she may be listed as Ella Tutt. I'm not sure yet how she's being referred to. She was kidnapped five years ago and was just rescued today. I want to speak with her caseworker."

"Okay, I know the case. Please hold."

Kate tapped her fingers on the kitchen table, resisting the urge to verbalize her irritation. She moved her gaze around the table, where her family had gathered. Why should she have to jump through hoops to find out about her own daughter?

"Hello, this is Stella Rhodes."

"This is Kate Cummings. Did you get my message?"

"I did, Mrs. Cummings. Ella is fine. She's been temporarily placed in foster care, pending the DNA results. As of this moment, we don't have legal proof that she's your daughter. Until then, I can't really discuss the case."

"When do you anticipate the results being in?" Kate said.

"Sheriff Granger pulled some strings, but we're dealing with a weekend. I hope to know something by Tuesday afternoon. That probably feels slow to you, but it's actually fast-tracking it."

"I assume you've talked with Ella?"

"I have. She's been through the mill. But all things considered, she seems quite resilient."

"Does she know her biological mother wants to see her?"

Stella paused for several seconds. "To be honest, we're avoiding the subject for now. We prefer not to add another layer to her already confusing circumstances until we have the DNA results. I'm sure you can understand that."

"Is there any way I can see her? She wouldn't have to know I could be her mother. I just want a glimpse of her."

"I'm sorry, Mrs. Cummings. But no. It's best for Ella if we let the dust settle and do the DNA testing. If you are indeed her biological mother, I feel certain the judge will want to move as quickly as possible to release her to you."

"Assuming the DNA test proves she's my daughter, when can I see her?"

"I'll need to talk with Ella and see how ready she is for such an encounter. She speaks fondly of your daughter Abby. They seem to have developed a bond through their ordeal. The judge will take that into careful consideration. It could certainly make Ella's release happen faster."

"Assuming it's the best-case scenario, what kind of time frame would we be talking?"

"At best, two weeks," Stella said. "But don't count on it. We have a long way to go before that can happen. Ella will need to be examined by a pediatrician and a child psychologist. A lot of things can happen to slow down the system. You'll need to have patience."

"I've waited five years," Kate said.

"I can only imagine the pain you've been through." Stella spoke softly. "I remember when your husband and daughter disappeared. But we need to do this right. And my number-one concern has to be the child's well-being."

Kate sighed. "Of course. You're right."

"You'll be notified as soon as we have the DNA results. And if she's your daughter, I will make sure you're apprised of her medical and psych evaluations."

"I'm learning to hate the word *if,*" Kate said.

"I know this is difficult. But it won't take long to know for sure whether this child is indeed Riley Jo. Personally, I'm hoping she is. I would much rather see her go home to her flesh-and-blood family, especially one that will love on her, than to have her spend years in the system while we try to find out who she is. Just keep in mind there's more to making this work than merely establishing blood ties. Ella Tutt's world just crumbled. We have to be sure she's ready for a complete transition."

Abby sat with Grandpa Buck on Angel View Pier, after watching the sun set on the most harrowing day she had ever spent. Neither of them had said two words for the past thirty minutes, but she felt very close to him in the silence.

Finally Grandpa said, "You know, honey, I owe you an apology."

"Not really. I don't blame you and Mama and Hawk for not believing me, Grandpa. It's not like I haven't been wrong before."

"But you were right."

Abby wanted to smile, but she didn't have the strength. "Now we can stop wondering about the past and let it go."

"I expect it'll take a while."

"I guess." Abby splashed the water with her bare toes. "Mama seems so sad. I thought she'd be happy about Riley Jo."

"She *is*," Grandpa said. "But she just lost your daddy. And she hasn't gotten over bein' scared to death that she'd never see *you* again. I don't think she's really even processed that Riley Jo's alive. She hasn't seen her yet, like you have. Once she does, I expect some of the sadness she feels about your daddy'll ease up."

"I can't believe what Isaiah did to him," Abby said. "Poor daddy must've been so afraid for Riley Jo."

"Micah was a hero. He died tryin' to save his baby girl." Grandpa took her hand. "Better not to dwell on it. You've been through quite an ordeal. How're you feelin'?"

"Lost," Abby said without thinking. "And found. It's a weird feeling I can't really explain. I mean, it was sad finding out that Daddy was murdered. But it's a relief to be home and to realize Riley Jo will actually be with us soon." She sighed. "I was so sure God would bring Daddy home. But we don't even know where his remains are."

"We know where his spirit is, honey. God did bring him home."

Abby nodded. "I hadn't thought of it that way. Mama sure won't."

"She might could come around. She loved the Lord before your daddy and Riley Jo disappeared."

"Now she thinks everything spiritual is a crutch."

"Aw, I don't believe that," Grandpa said. "She's hurtin', that's all. Her life took a hard blow, but her pain's been worse because she won't let God comfort her. She has to let Him in on her own. No amount of pushin' by other folks'll get the job done."

"Elliot's tried." Abby turned her head and looked up at her grandfather. "I can tell he likes Mama."

"He's been a good friend."

"Do you think Mama likes *him*?"

"I don't know. Up to now, your mother thought she was still married. Elliot certainly has respected that."

"I kind of hope she *does* like Elliot," Abby said. "He's really nice. Maybe he can help Mama love God again. I want her to know that God was with me. He answered my prayers. Well … except for bringing Daddy home to Angel View. But like you said, Grandpa, He did bring Daddy home—to heaven."

"Micah's just fine. But it's still mighty hard on those of us who miss him."

Abby nodded. "It was so mean of Isaiah to let Jay think he killed a man and scare him into silence."

"We're gonna need to help Jay deal with it." Grandpa took off his glasses and wiped them with his T-shirt. "I expect he's got some powerful feelin's he's not sure what to do with."

Abby nodded. "He was devastated when he realized the man he thought he killed was my father."

"Jay showed real character when he owned up to it, not knowin' how you'd react. I suppose if he'd gone to Virgil, things might be different. One thing's for sure, God brought you home, safe and sound. And soon, Riley Jo will be with us."

"You know what's weird," Abby said. "If her DNA doesn't match, I'll still feel the same way about her."

A shrill whistle sliced through the stillness.

"That's Mama's referee whistle! Something's wrong!" Abby jumped to her feet and pulled her grandfather up. "I don't think I can handle anything else awful today."

Grandpa didn't let go of Abby's hand and began to pray aloud. "Father, give us strength, whatever it is. Go before us. We pray in Jesus's name."

Abby slipped her sandals on, then she and Grandpa Buck hurried up the path to Angel View Lodge, passing several guests as they made their way up the incline. In five years, Mama had not used the whistle except for family drills. What could possibly be happening?

CHAPTER 33

Virgil sat on the porch glider, wearing a pair of denim cutoffs, his shirt unbuttoned, his mind unloading the weighty burdens of the day. He took a sip of ice-cold sweet tea, his gaze on the neighbor kids across the street, who were catching lightning bugs and putting them in jars. Their innocence was refreshing after a day of dealing with kids whose childhoods had been marred by tragedy.

After hours of Otha being questioned by Julie and Roberta, Virgil let her go home, convinced she was telling the truth and had acted as lawfully as she knew how—and at great personal risk. Virgil told her not to leave town, that it might be necessary to question her again.

Isaiah stubbornly denied that he was guilty of kidnapping, child abuse and endangerment, *or* attempted murder. But he was starting to back himself into a corner with inconsistencies. Abby, Jay, Otha, and Ella were totally consistent in their statements. It shouldn't be hard to get a conviction on those charges. But nailing Isaiah for the murder of Micah Cummings would be dicey, especially without a body.

The front door opened, and Jill Beth came outside holding his cell phone. "I'm sorry to interrupt your peace and quiet, love. Billy Gene is on the phone. Says you'll want to take the call."

He kissed Jill Beth's hand and put the phone to his ear. "What's up?"

"Sir, we got us a situation. A 9-1-1 call came in from those foster folks that're keepin' Ella Tutt. She's gone missin'."

"*Missing*? How could that happen?" Virgil switched the phone to his other ear.

"They put Ella to bed and went in the den to watch TV. A short time later, they heard tires screechin' and looked outside. Never did see a vehicle. But they went and checked on the girl. She wasn't there. Her bedroom winda's open."

Virgil looked up into Jill Beth's questioning eyes. "I don't believe this! Are they sure? Did they search the house? The yard? Any place she might've wandered?"

"Said they did, Sheriff. We're fixin' to head over there right now. I'm thinkin' we should send a couple deputies up yonder to check Mrs. Tutt's place."

"Do it," Virgil said. "We also need a list from DCFS of everyone who knew where Ella was. I'll go up to Angel View and talk to Kate Cummings. Though I can't believe she or anyone in her family would pull a stunt like this."

"Mrs. Cummings already knows about it," Billy Gene said. "She called in right after we got the 9-1-1 call. Said she'd just gotten an anonymous call from a woman who told her that Ella Tutt'd been taken. Mrs. Cummings was real shook up. She might could use an encouragin' word from you."

"All right." Virgil rose to his feet. "I'm on my way."

Virgil disconnected the call, his mind buzzing with the implications.

"I overheard what Billy Gene said. This is surreal." Jill Beth seemed to be processing. "You don't think Hawk or Abby or Jay would've done something like that? I sure don't think Kate would jeopardize her chance of regaining custody."

"I hope not." Virgil opened the front door and let Jill Beth squeeze past him. "We had every reason to believe that the girl's DNA would prove she's Riley Jo and that she'd be returned to Kate very soon. A stunt like that would not sit well with the judge."

"You said Otha Tutt was fond of Ella. Maybe she did it."

"No way. It's not like DCFS would just cough up the name and address of Ella's foster parents and give it to her. That's protected information. Whoever took Ella must've paid someone off to find out where she was." *Let's hope it wasn't Kate.*

"This is really getting sinister," Jill Beth said. "There could be another layer to this no one's thought of yet. Maybe Ella isn't Riley Jo after all."

The thought pierced him. Just when he thought they had solved the crime, another dimension had been added. "We've got nothing to lose for now believing she is. The DNA test will tell us soon enough."

"Virgil, what are you going to do?"

"Get dressed and head up to Angel View. I want to eyeball every one of the Cummings. I need to know if any of them were in on it, but I just can't imagine it."

"Wouldn't it be awful if the girl's vanished again?"

Virgil went into the bedroom and turned around. "Darlin'"—he put his hands on her shoulders—"I can't think that way. Not after all that family has suffered and all those kids went through to get Ella out of there. My department has too much invested in this case to fail. If it's the last thing I ever do, I *will* find her."

❦

Kate opened the front door of her log home and invited Virgil inside and led him into the living room, where the rest of the family had gathered.

"Why don't you sit there, in the blue chair?" Kate said, all too aware of the numerous times Virgil had occupied that chair, discussing one dead end after another in his department's investigation into the disappearance of Micah and Riley Jo.

Kate, still shaking, sat between Abby and Jesse on the couch.

Virgil leaned forward in the chair, his hands clasped between his knees. "Let me start by saying how sorry I am that y'all have to go through this. I am committed to finding this child. And I won't rest till we do." He looked over at Kate. "Tell me about the phone call."

"*I* answered the phone," Kate said. "It was a woman. She sounded a lot older than me and spoke with a twang. All she said was, 'Ella Tutt's been taken.' Needless to say, I was on the phone with DCFS immediately. No one there could tell me anything, so I called the sheriff's department. Deputy Duncan told me about the 9-1-1 call."

Virgil moved his gaze from one family member to another and then back to Kate. "Just for the record, I'll need to know where each of you were this evening."

"Grandpa and I were down at the pier," Abby said. "We heard Mama's emergency whistle and rushed back to the house."

Jesse looked up at Kate. "I was in the kitchen making hummingbird nectar."

"What about you, Hawk?" Virgil turned to the fireplace hearth, where Hawk sat.

"I was up yonder on the ridge." Hawk fiddled with the bottom button on his shirt.

"Any particular reason?"

Hawk bit his lip. "Yes, sir. I needed to get quiet. I have a favorite spot where I go to think."

"Anybody see you there?"

Hawk's eyebrows came together. "No. But that's the whole point of going up there—to get away from everything."

"How did you know there was a crisis at home?"

"Mama called me on my cell."

"Did you tell her where you were?"

"I don't remember." Hawk looked at Kate and then at the sheriff. "You're acting like I'm a suspect."

"I'm just gathering the facts."

"It sounds as if you don't believe him," Kate said. "He was as shocked as I was to hear the news."

"It's my job to be objective. I'm sure y'all are disappointed that you're not allowed to see Ella until her true identity has been confirmed."

Kate's heart raced. "Virgil, none of us had anything to do with her being taken from the foster home. We weren't even told where she was."

"I'm not saying you did. But we both know the system can get bogged down with rules and regulations, and I could certainly understand you wanting to cut through the red tape."

"By kidnapping my own daughter?" Kate said. "Then what—hide her for the rest of her life?"

Virgil held up his palm. "Actually, I can't imagine any of you are foolish enough to complicate things by breaking the law. Especially when you're so close to finding out if this child is Riley Jo. But I'd be remiss if I didn't ask the questions. Kate, would you authorize us to check your phone records and see who the anonymous call came from?"

"Absolutely."

"I've got deputies checking the Tutt property," Virgil said. "We'll lean on Isaiah and see if he tells us anything. And we're gathering a list of everyone who knew where Ella's foster parents live."

Kate put her face in her hands. "Find her, Virgil. Please … I can't lose her again."

❧

A short time later, a handcuffed Isaiah, clad in his orange jumpsuit and leg irons, was brought into an interview room at the county jail, where Virgil and Kevin were waiting for him.

"You ain't got no cause to have me woke up and drug in here!" Isaiah bellowed as the deputy seated him at the table. "I told you all there is to tell."

"Not quite," Virgil said. "Where's Ella?"

"Well, she sure ain't with me."

Virgil leaned forward, his voice deep and threatening. "You *do not* want to mess with me on this."

"Your deputies give her to some foster lady, who drove off with her. I ain't seen her since."

"Who took her from foster care?"

A devious grin crossed Isaiah's face, turning his dark eyes to slits. "It sure wasn't me."

"But you know who did it."

"Don't be puttin' words in my mouth," Isaiah said. "Ain't my fault you can't hold on to her."

"You think this is funny?"

"Yep. Considerin' you treated me like I'm dumber 'n a bucket o' rocks, and now you're accusin' me of commitin' a crime in my sleep. I didn't do nothin'."

"Who did?"

"How should I know?" Isaiah faked a yawn. "I was sound asleep, sawin' logs. I ain't seen or spoke to nobody."

"But you know who took Ella," Virgil said.

"That's a powerful accusation, lawman. I weren't even told what y'all done with her. I ain't no magician."

Virgil studied Isaiah's arrogant expression, and it was all he could do not to grab him by the beard and get in his face. Instead he took a slow, deep breath. It was hard to argue with the fact that he hadn't had contact with anyone since he'd been arrested.

"Maybe one o' your deputies is in cahoots with Ella's real kin," Isaiah said. "I don't know nothin'."

"Sure you do," Virgil insisted. "And if I have to keep you up all night, you're going to tell me." *Please don't pick now to lawyer up.*

"Hope y'all brought your nightclothes." Isaiah looked down at his orange jumpsuit. "I'm all set."

Virgil could almost feel the heat of Kevin's seething anger, but neither of them showed any reaction to Isaiah's irritating remark. Kevin didn't want him to request a lawyer either. It was just a matter of time before the court appointed one, whether Isaiah wanted one or not.

Virgil folded his hands on the table. "An older woman, who didn't identify herself, called Ella's biological mother and told her Ella had been taken. Who's the woman? Give us a name. You know we're going to find out sooner or later. This is only going to get worse."

Isaiah pursed his lips. "You're wastin' your time. I can't tell you what I don't know 'cept to say I had nothin' to do with it."

"How about venturing a guess?" Virgil said sarcastically.

"I ain't in contact with other folk. Me and Otha and the young'uns keep to ourselves and mind our own bidness."

"Somebody took Ella from that foster home—and you know who it is."

"I'm sayin' I don't."

"I think you're lying."

Isaiah smirked, his arms folded across his chest, and didn't say anything.

"Sheriff, I can deal with him," Kevin said. "I know you've got things to do."

"All right." Virgil pushed back his chair and stood. "I'll go see where we are on that list of folks that knew who Ella's foster parents were. I'll send someone in to take my place. I don't care if you have to pry his eyelids open, this man doesn't sleep until he starts telling us the truth."

"Looks like you ain't gittin' your forty winks tonight neither." Isaiah laughed.

CHAPTER 34

Abby curled up in the window seat in her room, hugging Riley Jo's baby doll. The moon was suspended over Beaver Lake, its luminous reflection casting a soft golden glow that turned the ripples into diamonds and the islands and inlets into a mysterious shadowy maze.

Her father's death didn't seem real yet. But losing Riley Jo a second time did. It was both depressing and confusing.

Lord, it hurts so much that You let Daddy get killed. I was so sure he would come home. But it was amazing that we were able to get Riley Jo away from that monster. Why did You let us lose her again? I heard Mama crying in her room. She has too many things to be sad about.

Surely this setback would cause her mother and Hawk to be even more cynical toward God.

Abby heard a gentle knock at the door.

"It's Grandpa, Abby. Can I come in?"

"Sure."

Grandpa Buck came in, turned on the lamp, and sat on the side of her bed, facing her. "How're you doin'?"

Abby shrugged.

"I know how bad you must feel about Riley Jo. But as the sayin' goes, 'It ain't over till it's over.'"

"What if Sheriff Granger doesn't find her?" Abby said. "We'll be in limbo like we've been for five *long* years—only worse because now we *know* she's alive and we came so close to getting her back."

"We're still close to gettin' her back. Don't forget that."

"But Isaiah's in jail. He couldn't have taken her. Otha wouldn't do that, now that she knows the truth. How does anyone know where to start looking?"

"We best let Virgil work it out."

Abby rolled her eyes. "He doesn't know where to look either, Grandpa."

"Come over here," he said.

Abby walked over to her grandfather. He sat her on his knee the way he had done so many times when she was little.

"God knows where Riley Jo is," Grandpa said. "We have to trust Him."

"I know. I do. I mean, I want to, but ..."

"You feel like you're flyin' blind?"

Abby nodded.

"Well, I guess, in a way, we are. Isn't that what faith is? If we could see where we were goin', it wouldn't really be faith, now would it?"

"I guess not. But it's so hard."

"It takes practice. Maybe that's why so many trials come our way. Nobody ever said trustin' God was easy. I expect most everybody'd rather have control. I sure would."

"Me, too."

"But He's got a plan way bigger than we can grasp. And everything—even the difficult things—fits in to it somewhere. He's all about buildin' character, not keepin' us comfortable."

Abby mused, "So you *really* believe that all the sadness we've dealt with these past five years had a purpose?"

"Absolutely. Don't ask me what, because I couldn't tell you. But God doesn't waste anything, not even the suffering we believers go through. Some kinda good comes out of it. The Bible says so, and I believe it. Doesn't mean I understand it."

"It doesn't really make sense," Abby said.

"Certainly not to our natural mind. But somewhere deep in your spirit, it's actually a relief when we give in to it." Grandpa kissed her cheek. "You and me've got a real advantage over Kate and Hawk. We know God's sovereign. So there's no point in tormentin' ourselves with a lot of what-ifs. We have to trust Him, that's all there is to it. But since He's at the controls, it's okay that we're flyin' blind, if you know what I mean."

Abby nodded. "I get it, Grandpa. I'm just not very good at it yet."

There was a knock at the door. Hawk stood in the doorway, holding the portable phone. "It's Jay. He apologized for calling our home phone, but you don't have a cell phone anymore."

"I'm gonna scoot out of here and let you talk to him," her grandfather said.

Abby put her arms around him. "I love you, Grandpa. So much. I wasn't sure I'd ever get the chance to say that again."

Grandpa pulled her a little closer and stroked her hair. "I love you too, honey. I never want to come that close to losin' you again."

Abby took the phone from Hawk and thanked him, then he and Grandpa Buck left her room and closed the door behind them.

Abby put the phone to her ear. "Hey."

"Hey, yourself," Jay said. "I'm sorry for calling so late on this line."

"It's all right. We're all up."

"I figured." Jay exhaled into the receiver. "I'm sick about Ella. The deputies just left here. They asked me all kinds of questions— like *I* had anything to do with it. I can't understand how this could happen."

"Me, either. That's what Sheriff Granger is trying to figure out."

"How's everyone holding up?"

"Mama's a mess. Hawk's mad. Grandpa and I are praying like nuts. Jesse's trying to comfort everyone, but he hardly remembers Daddy or Riley Jo. How about you?"

"It was finally starting to sink in that we actually found your sister and escaped with our lives—and now this."

Abby fell back on the bed. "I know. Did you tell your mother the whole story?"

"Every detail. I think she was shocked that I had the guts to go after your sister. But she cried when I told her I thought I'd accidentally shot and killed a man when I was twelve and was scared to say anything. She remembers how moody I was as an adolescent, but she'd heard that it was normal and blew it off."

"I'm glad it's finally out in the open," Abby said, "and that you didn't kill anyone. I'm so sorry you carried the guilt all that time."

"Do you know if Isaiah's confessed?"

Abby stared at the ceiling fan going round and round. "I'm not sure. But last I heard, he was still blaming you. Sheriff Granger believes us. But he can't charge him with capital murder without more proof."

"What kind of proof does he think he can get? I can't prove his accusation wrong."

"I don't know. But he told us not to worry about it, that he already has enough to put Isaiah in jail for the rest of his life. And no one is going to prosecute you for the shooting."

"I should've told someone," Jay said. "If I had, maybe you would've gotten Riley Jo back five years ago."

"I wish you could stop beating yourself up for that. No one is blaming you for being manipulated by Isaiah's cruel lie."

"*I* blame me."

"But when you realized the truth," Abby said, "you risked your *life* to get her back. Shouldn't you give that equal time in your thinking?"

There was a long moment of dead air.

"Jay, you still there?"

"I'm here."

"Well, shouldn't you?" Abby asked.

"I guess so. Easier said than done."

"Well, I'm going to help you keep it in its proper perspective."

"Abby … can I see you tomorrow? I know this is bad timing with everyone waiting for news about Ella … or should I say Riley Jo?"

"Everyone in my family is saying Riley Jo now. But the sheriff can't until the DNA results prove it. Thankfully, they took a mouth swab before she disappeared again."

"I feel isolated out here," Jay said. "Can I see you?"

"I don't know why not. But I don't think I should go very far from home while we're waiting for a call from the sheriff."

"I'm not ready to face your mother yet."

"She wants to see you. But I agree that now is not the right time."

"Where do you wanna meet, then?" Jay said.

"How about on the bench under the sycamore tree? Mama never walks down there. It's a good place to talk, and I can also hear Mama's whistle if something important happens."

"Okay, what time?"

"Ten?"

"Great. I want to tell you about one really good thing that's come out of this, but I don't want to tell you over the phone. I'll see you then."

"Jay, wait … in all the craziness of today, I'm not sure I even thanked you for going after Riley Jo."

"By all standards, it was a really dumb thing to do."

"It worked," Abby said. "And you risked your life when you didn't have to."

"It was the least I could do."

"No. It was the *most* you could do."

"I'm no hero, Abby."

"You are to me."

Abby let the truth of her words sink into the quiet moment that followed.

Finally she said, "I'll see you in the morning. Be careful. I've been thinking about it, and I'm probably being paranoid, but you're the only one who saw Isaiah with Riley Jo when Daddy was shot. Your testimony holds a lot of weight. Maybe whoever took Riley Jo from her foster home isn't too happy about that."

CHAPTER 35

Kate curled up on one end of the living-room couch, clutching a throw pillow, a ribbon of moonlight bathing her face. Her mind jumped from one memory to another, her heart breaking all over again at the harsh reality of Micah's fate. She had come so close to having Riley Jo back in her arms, only to have her snatched again.

God, I'm desperate. I loved You once. I even trusted You. But You've proven to be cruel and unreliable, and now I wonder why I should ask You for anything. But I'm asking anyway. I have nothing to lose and nowhere else to turn. Please bring Riley Jo home to us.

Kate wiped a tear from her cheek. *I can't promise You my undying devotion. I'm not even sure I still believe You exist. But I'm helpless. And if You are the God I once loved and trusted, then this isn't too big for You. I'm not asking just for myself. I don't deserve anything from You. But Abby has that blind trust I used to have, and I can't bear to see her heart broken.*

Kate dabbed her eyes. Had she really just asked God to help her? Had she really prayed to the One who let her husband be murdered? Had she become that desperate?

Kate felt as if she were left sitting on the edge of a cliff after clinging frantically to Micah's hand as he ever so slowly, inch by inch, lost his grip and fell into nothingness. Now she held tightly to Riley Jo's hand, but she was slipping away too.

"Mama?" a voice whispered.

Kate looked up and saw Abby's silhouette standing next to the couch.

"I wondered if you were sleeping," Abby said. "I can't."

"Me, either. I'm wide awake. Come sit with me."

Abby sat on the couch and snuggled up next to her.

"I'm so glad to be home," Abby said.

"My head is still reeling at the thought of how close you came to dying. Gives me chills."

Abby laid her head on Kate's shoulder. "Mama … you haven't asked me anything about Riley Jo."

"I know." Kate hid for a moment in the awkward silence that followed. How could she explain her behavior to Abby when she didn't fully understand it herself? "The emotional roller coaster is overwhelming, honey. It's all I can do to deal with your father's murder. And frankly, I'm not sure if I can handle hearing about how cruel Isaiah was to her."

"I understand. But Otha was really sweet. I could tell they had a good relationship."

Kate blinked to clear her eyes. "That's painful too, Abby. I had absolutely nothing to do with forming Riley Jo's character or seeing her personality blossom. I'm glad Otha was good to her. But I'm just not ready to talk about it."

"Okay. But Riley Jo's really anxious to see you."

"She said that?"

Abby nodded. "I think deep down she's always known she didn't belong there, even if she didn't have words for it. She said she had an angel, Custos, that watched out for her."

"Interesting choice of imaginary friends."

"She told us she saw him once," Abby said. "She'd fallen out of a weeping willow tree into a pond and was choking on water. The next thing she knew she was on the bank, and Custos was drying her off with his wings. He told her he was always watching out for her, even when she didn't see him."

"Obviously she imagined him," Kate said. "If ever she needed rescuing, it was today. If this so-called angel was watching out for her, why didn't he help her?"

"Maybe God wanted Hawk to do it."

"Or maybe Hawk's good instincts got him there first. Is Riley Jo churched?"

"I don't think so. She said something about her granny Fay reading the Bible. But when I prayed out loud, she had no idea who I was talking to." Abby turned and looked up at her mother. "I know you don't believe God listened to our prayers. But how many times did we pray for angels to watch over her? Then when it sounds like they did, you try to explain it away?"

"I'm sorry, honey. It's more likely that she created an imaginary friend to make her feel safe. I don't mean to throw cold water on anything you believe. But you know I gave up relying on faith a long time ago."

"I know. But I'm still praying for angels to watch over her and bring her home."

God, I don't know whether Abby's right, but I'll take any help I can get to bring my baby home.

❧

Buck sat at a table at Flutter's Café and set aside Saturday's issue of the *Northwest Arkansas News*. He took a sip of coffee and looked up at Titus, who eyed him questioningly.

"I wonder why there's no mention in the paper that the little girl's gone missing," Titus said.

"There will be. Must've missed the deadline for goin' to press. It's sure all over the TV." Buck looked over the top of his glasses. "The authorities are still referrin' to her as Ella Tutt. But from what Abby told us, this Isaiah Tutt admitted to killin' Micah and stealin' Riley Jo right on the spot. Of course, he's denyin' it to the sheriff, but the kids all heard him say it. Can't see why he'd own up to doin' somethin' that low down if it wasn't so. I'd appreciate it if you'd keep that between the both of us for now—till the authorities sort it out."

"You know I will. Does the sheriff have *any* leads on who took the girl from the foster parents' place?"

"Not that we've been told, but he's questionin' everyone who knew which foster parents had her. Someone spilled the beans. The state doesn't make that information available to just anybody."

Titus put his hand on Buck's. "The sheriff will find her. I just know it."

"Sure hope so. I'm prayin' for it." Buck took a sip of coffee to hide the emotion just under the surface. "I'll tell you one thing, we're blessed to have Abby home safe and sound."

"I can tell you two are close."

Buck smiled. "Always have been. We've done everything from fishin', campin', and white-water raftin' to dance recitals, tea parties, and homework. I've tried to help fill the void of her daddy bein' gone. I've done it with the boys, too. But I've got a soft spot for Abby. We're just on the same page, if you get my drift."

Savannah came over to their table, holding a round tray containing a platter of something that looked and smelled delicious. "Benson made another Cajun favorite for y'all. Brown sugar cinnamon buns. They'll make your sweet tooth stand up and sing."

"Sounds mighty tasty," Buck said. "What's that on top?"

"Cream cheese frosting—prepared with a little extra something that makes them uniquely Benson's." Savannah set the platter in the middle of the table and gave them each a plate and fork. "They're still hot, so be careful."

Titus slid a cinnamon bun onto his plate. "Boy oh boy. These won't last long."

Savannah put her hand on Buck's shoulder and lowered her voice. "You doin' all right?"

"I'm holdin' *on*—to the One I know can bring Riley Jo home."

"Lots of prayers are going up for her," Savannah said.

"I know my church has our prayer chain on their knees." Buck moved his finger around the rim of his cup. "I doubt if Virgil slept a wink last night either. He's got his work cut out for him. I'm just grateful the authorities took a mouth swab from the girl to test her

DNA before she disappeared. No one in the family doubts she's Riley Jo, but we'll all feel better when it's official."

"Are you confident with Sheriff Granger running it?" Titus cut a piece of cinnamon bun and pierced it with his fork. "Doesn't sound to me like his people have exactly been on top of things over the years."

Savannah kicked Titus under the table, and Buck pretended not to notice.

"I'm not worried one whit about the sheriff," Buck said. "I'm confident that God's in control. If we're supposed to find Riley Jo, she'll be found."

Virgil yawned and turned to look out his office window. Glints of morning sun filtered through the leaves on the giant red maples that stood on the front lawn of the Raleigh County Courthouse.

On the sidewalk, a young woman pushed a stroller and held a schnauzer on a leash. Old Melvin Mayfield, clad in denim overalls and a yellow T-shirt, occupied a wrought-iron bench on the court-house grounds, just like he did most mornings, sipping on a large coffee and reading the *New York Times*.

Virgil had opted to sleep a couple hours on the couch in his office so he would be ready to go if any leads came in on Ella Tutt's whereabouts. But no breaks had come, and his sleep had been fretful. He couldn't quite shake the image of Micah fighting to his death, trying to protect his helpless daughter. How ironic that the skinny little neighbor kid who had idolized Virgil ended up dying a hero—murdered on Virgil's watch.

Virgil blinked to clear the image and turned his thoughts to Kate. He didn't want to let her down again. His deputies had worked through the night—gotten DCFS employees out of bed—but so far, none had offered his deputies anything useful. He refused to believe that Ella Tutt had vanished beyond their reach.

Virgil pulled the electric razor out of his drawer and turned it on just as he heard a knock at the door. "Come in."

Kevin, looking a little battle worn, his eyes bloodshot, came in and stood next to Virgil's desk.

"I'm about to make your day," Kevin said. "The maintenance supervisor at DCFS just discovered the night cleaning supervisor bound and gagged and locked in a closet. The victim said a middle-aged Caucasian man wearing a red bandana on his face accosted her shortly after she started her shift and threatened to hurt her unless she gave him the keys to the offices and the night entrance. She complied. The EMTs checked her over, and she wasn't harmed. We're bringing her in for questioning now."

"That had to be our perp," Virgil said. "He must've gotten into the files and found out where Ella Tutt was and gone after her."

Virgil, newly shaven and feeling more alert, sat with Kevin in the first interview room, across the table from Maria Diaz, the night cleaning supervisor accosted at DCFS. Introductions had been made and the woman given a bottle of water. She seemed to be at ease. Virgil decided to let Kevin take the lead.

"Ms. Diaz," Kevin said, "we truly appreciate your coming down to talk with us about what happened. As you know, we're in the middle of an investigation that includes a missing girl, whose whereabouts we believe were obtained by the man who accosted you."

"Sorry," Maria said. "I didn't want to give him the keys. He threatened to hurt me." Her lower lip quivered. "I have a son."

Kevin nodded. "We understand. You did the right thing. He probably *would* have hurt you—and forced you to give him the keys anyway. But now we need you to answer some questions so we can find this man. Can you do that for us?"

"Yes. Yes," Maria said. "Whatever I can do."

"Start by telling us what happened. I know you talked to deputies already, but we'd like you to tell us."

"Just after seven p.m., I got my supplies ready to clean the offices on the first floor when a big man with a bandana tied around his mouth grabbed me. He said he would hurt me real bad if I didn't give him my keys to the building. I was scared. So I did what he said."

"Okay, you gave him the keys." Kevin made a notation on his pad. "Then what happened?"

"He made me show him which key opened the main offices. And which key opened the night door. Then he forced me down the hall and into a tool closet. He tied me with rope and put duct tape over my mouth. He said don't make a sound, or he would come find me. And hurt me." Maria began to whimper and put her face in her hands. "I was so afraid. I didn't call for help or try to get untied—until I heard my coworkers calling for me."

"Do you know what time that was?"

Maria nodded and looked up. "They were getting ready to leave, so I knew it was around one a.m. I screamed for them until I ran out of air, but the duct tape muffled my voice. Nobody came. After they left, I prayed until I fell asleep. I knew someone from maintenance would find me in the morning."

"Okay, let's talk about the man. You told detectives he was Caucasian, right?"

"Yes. Definitely."

"What color was the bandana he wore?"

"*Rojo*. I mean red."

"Can you describe him?"

"Very big man. Tall. Big here." Maria wrapped her fingers around her upper arm. "His eyes were dark like mine. His hair was mixed—dark brown with some gray."

"So how old would you guess him to be?"

"Forty-five. Maybe fifty."

"I know the bandana hid much of his face, but could you tell if he had a beard?"

"I didn't see one."

Kevin wrote something on his pad. "What was he wearing?"

"I was so scared I didn't pay attention. But I *think* jeans and a blue shirt with no sleeves."

"You're doing great. Now, how tall was he?" Kevin stood. "Would you stand for a moment, please, Ms. Diaz?"

Maria did as he asked and stood facing him.

"I'm six feet tall," Kevin said. "Was the man taller or shorter than me?"

"Taller. He was a giant of a man. Not fat. Just thick. I'm not sure what is the right word to describe him."

"You're doing fine. You can sit now. Thank you." Kevin sat again and wrote something in his notes. "Okay, I need you to think really hard. Was there anything in particular that stood out about this man besides his size?"

"Yes, he sounded stuffed up, like he had a cold or allergies. He kept sniffing. It was disgusting."

"That's great information!" Kevin said. "Especially if we can apprehend him soon. Anything else?"

"His arms were hairy. And tan."

"Keep going," Kevin said.

"That's all I can think of at the moment."

Virgil cleared his throat. "Did your assailant say *why* he wanted the keys? Or did he say anything else directly to you or mumble anything under his breath?"

"He did mumble something." Maria seemed to be collecting her thoughts. "Something about his brother *frying*? I thought he sounded crazy. Does that mean something?"

Virgil's gaze collided with Kevin's. "Yes, ma'am. I believe it does."

CHAPTER 36

Virgil gripped the windowsill in his office, finally taking a breath after his minute-long rant that left Chief Deputy Kevin Mann red-faced and mute.

Virgil paused a few moments and then lowered his voice. "Good grief, Kevin. I thought you'd checked out Tutt's family."

"I … I don't know what to say, Sheriff. I didn't see this coming. We did check out Tutt's family. His only relatives that live in the area are an elderly mother and one brother, Walter, who kept the twins while Otha was being questioned. I met him when he came to the scene and picked up the boys. He seemed dazed and totally shocked that his brother was being accused of kidnapping Ella. I never once suspected Walter Tutt of anything."

"Yeah, well, he was *counting* on that."

"Duncan and Hobbs questioned him at his home. You saw the report."

Virgil exhaled. "Yeah, I saw it. Walter claims he hadn't seen Isaiah for a few years and then moved back to the area two years ago to help look after their elderly mother. Said he never met Isaiah's first wife, Ella, who died in childbirth. And that little Ella was five when he first met her."

"I'm guessing he really believes Ella is Isaiah's daughter."

"Which would give him all the motivation in the world to snatch her from foster care!" Virgil brought his hands down on the windowsill and swore under his breath. "I didn't see it either. I'm as upset with myself as anybody."

"How do you want to handle this?" Kevin said.

"We need to move quickly. Let's get Walter Tutt's driver's license photo and show it to Maria Diaz. I know he had a bandana around his face, but she might see a resemblance in his eyes and hair. Check what it shows for his height and weight, and see if it matches what she told us." Virgil paced in front of the window. "Send Duncan and Hobbs out to Otha Tutt's ASAP. See if she has a better photo of Walter. See if she can fill you in on the layout of his house. Ask her about his mental stability. His behaviors. Any history of violence at home. I want to know everything she knows about the guy—down to what kind of toothpaste he uses."

"I'll get right on it," Kevin said. "I'll check and see if any firearms are registered to him."

Virgil nodded. "Good. I'll have someone place a bogus call to his house and make sure he's home. If he's there, I'll set up a covert containment around his property until we can decide on a course of action. I'll update Chief Mitchell and ask him to help us with manpower."

"Should I get a warrant?"

"We clearly have grounds for exigent circumstances."

"I agree," Kevin said, "but I would hate to lose any evidence we find to some second-guessing judge who won't allow for any gray area in his black-and-white world."

"Right now, our job is to ensure the safety of that little girl."

"Can't we do both? Sir, this is a high-profile case. I don't think we should act in haste. There's no reason to believe Walter intends to harm the girl as long as he doesn't know we're on to him."

Virgil paused, then looked over at Kevin. "All right, start the ball rolling on a warrant in case we end up with a protracted containment. But I'm not waiting on a warrant if the situation requires we go in."

❧

Abby trudged down the back lawn at Angel View, passed by the cedar gazebo, and spotted Jay sitting on the bench under the sycamore tree. She waved, and he ran to meet her, his nose swollen and bruised, his face covered in cuts.

They threw their arms around each other, and Abby rested in her friend's embrace.

"I still can't believe Riley Jo's missing again," Jay said. "Any news?"

"Last I heard, a cleaning lady at DCFS was found locked in a closet. She told Sheriff Granger that some guy forced her to give him her keys. The sheriff thinks he got into the offices there and found out where Riley Jo's foster parents live."

"But they don't have a suspect?"

"Not by name. But they were taking the cleaning lady in for questioning and hope she can help identify him. Isaiah was smug about the whole thing and denied being involved."

Jay took her hand and led her to the bench, where they sat down side by side. He didn't let go of her hand, and Abby was surprised that she didn't mind.

"They're going to get Riley Jo back," Jay said. "That's all there is to it. We didn't risk our lives to have it end this way."

"That's for sure."

Jay glanced over at Abby and then looked out at the lake. "How's your mother?"

"Fragile. She's just got too much hurt going on. I think the news about Daddy caught her off guard. I hadn't seen her cry in a long time. It always breaks my heart whenever she does."

"I'd give anything to go back five years. If I'd told my mom about the shooting, maybe the sheriff would've made the connection and gotten your sister back—and none of this would be happening."

"You have to stop saying that," Abby said.

"I'm sure you wish I'd stop saying I'm sorry, too, but I really am."

Abby squeezed his hand. "I don't doubt that. At least now you know you didn't kill anybody. I think we should keep the focus on Isaiah, where it belongs. He's to blame."

"He *must* know who took Riley Jo."

"Says he doesn't."

"Like we can believe anything the creep says."

Abby turned and looked up at Jay. "Well, I believe he killed Daddy. He certainly enjoyed taunting us with the cruel details."

"Yeah, he did," Jay said. "That was horrible. It'll be a long time before either of us gets that image out of our minds."

The two sat in comfortable silence for a minute. Finally Abby said, "You told me on the phone that something good's come out of all this."

Jay smiled. "My dad came to see me. Mom told him what happened, and he wanted to make sure I was all right."

"That's wonderful!"

"We had the best talk we've probably ever had. He's really sorry that I was afraid he'd reject me if I told him the truth about the shooting. He blames himself for being an absentee father. He said things are going to change. That we have a lot of catching up to do." Jay paused and swallowed hard. "He said ... he was proud of me. That what I did to get Riley Jo back took guts. And that I was more of a man than he was."

"That must've meant so much," Abby said.

Jay nodded. "Never expected him to say he's proud of me—not in a million years. Of course, Mom reminded me how foolish it was to go after your sister, and I know she's right. I mean, we nearly got killed. But now that it's behind us, I'm glad we did it. But unless the sheriff gets Riley Jo back, it will all have been in vain."

"I still believe God's helping us."

"Somebody must be. We really dodged a bullet—no pun intended." Jay seemed lost in thought for a moment and fidgety.

"You seem ... different," she said. "What are you not telling me?"

Jay let go of her hand and leaned forward on the bench, his hands clasped between his knees. "Abby, I need to say something else. I don't know that this is the right time, but I believe we should stay completely honest with each other."

"I want you to be honest. What is it?"

Jay exhaled. "I don't think I can be best friends with you anymore."

Abby's heart sank. "Why not?"

"Because … my feelings for you have changed."

"What are you talking about?"

"After all we've been through, I feel a lot closer to you. I'm … *attracted* to you. I know that's the last thing you wanted, and I didn't plan it," he quickly added. "But the way I feel about you now goes beyond best friends, and I thought you should know."

Abby's heart and mind raced with the implications. "Are you saying you want to date me?"

Jay sat up and turned to her. "Honestly, I like things the way they are. I love being friends. But I also like holding your hand, and sitting close to you, and putting my arms around you. I've wanted to kiss you for days. I know that's not what we agreed on. But that's the truth. And if I keep it to myself for another second"—Jay slid his arm around her—"I'm going to explode." He gently cupped her cheek in his hand and let his warm, soft lips melt into hers.

Abby's heart pounded, her stomach feeling as if it were a trampoline with a million tiny gymnasts jumping up and down on it. She had been kissed a few times before, but never with this much tenderness.

Jay ever so slowly, almost reluctantly, ended the kiss. "Wow," he whispered.

Abby put her fingers to her lips, her cheeks scalded with a mixture of self-consciousness and sheer delight.

"I know this changes everything," Jay said.

"Definitely."

"I totally messed up, Abby. I promised this would never happen. I'm sorry."

"I'm not."

Jay stared at her blankly, surprise seeming to steal his voice. Finally he said, "So … you're okay with it?"

"Clearly." Abby smiled.

"I can't believe this." Jay hugged her tightly. "I didn't sleep at all last night, worrying that I'd lose you once I told you how I felt."

"No chance," Abby said. "Haven't you figured out by now that it's no accident we became friends? It had to be God who put us together. What are the odds you would befriend the daughter of the man you thought you killed? Or that you held the key to unraveling the mystery of Daddy and Riley Jo's disappearance? You were an answer to prayer."

"Whoa," Jay said. "That might be pushing the envelope a bit."

"Not really. I prayed and prayed that God would bring Riley Jo home. He used you to make that happen."

"But she's missing again."

"God knows where she is," Abby said. "She's not missing to Him. She never was."

"Why is He putting everyone through this?"

Abby shrugged. "I doubt we'll ever know why. But what I do know is that you and your dad have started over, which is very cool. And you and I have the beginning of something special because we've shared so much. And Mama will be free to let Elliot love her. I'm convinced he already does."

A shrill whistle caused Abby to jump, partly because she was suddenly aware of being in Jay's arms, and partly out of sheer terror.

"God, please don't let Riley Jo be dead," Abby murmured. "Come on, Jay. Come with me to the house."

He shook his head. "This is the wrong time. I'd be an intruder. I need to face your mother alone first."

"I have to go," Abby said.

He let go of her, except for her hand. "Call me."

"I will. Just as soon as I find out what's going on."

Kate rose from the kitchen table, feeling light-headed, and started to fall back in her chair.

Elliot grabbed her. "Just sit here a minute. You look pale."

"I need to tell the kids what's going on."

"Buck's getting them. Just take a minute and catch your breath."

"I'm afraid if I stop to think, I'll break." Kate's hands were shaking. "I can't lose Riley Jo again. I haven't even seen her. Or heard her voice."

"Virgil's deputies are trained for this. Have a little faith."

"I don't *have* a little faith."

"Maybe not in God," Elliot said, "but I know you trust Virgil. He's invested so much of himself into this investigation from the beginning. He's going to do everything humanly possible to make sure Riley Jo isn't hurt."

"What if it's not enough? It wasn't enough to save Micah."

Elliot pulled out the chair next to her and sat. "Kate, Micah was already dead by the time Virgil knew they were missing. It's nothing short of a miracle that Abby and Jay became friends, which led to their finding Riley Jo and discovering the truth of what happened. Or that Hawk found them just in time. Or that they narrowly escaped with minor injuries. By all accounts, they should be dead."

"I don't disagree," Kate said. "But Virgil had nothing to do with any of that."

Elliot smiled with his eyes, and Kate knew what he was thinking.

"Look, Virgil's people are in place, with a lot of prayer behind them," Elliot said. "They know how to handle people like Walter Tutt."

Kate heard footsteps and looked up as her dad ushered Abby, Jesse, and Hawk through the door, their eyes wide and questioning.

"I heard from Virgil," Kate said. "I want to tell you what's going on with Riley Jo."

Kate's family took their places around the kitchen table without anyone saying a word.

Kate took a sip of water. She told them everything Virgil had recounted to her about Maria Diaz's frightening encounter with Walter Tutt.

"Virgil also checked our phone records," Kate said, "and discovered the anonymous call came from Walter Tutt's residence and assume his mother made it. Sheriff's deputies and Foggy Ridge police officers have secretly surrounded Walter's house. He lives in the woods about a mile from Isaiah. They don't know if his mother's in the home now, but Walter definitely is because they placed a bogus call earlier, and he answered. He doesn't know they're out there yet. But he can't get away."

"What are they waiting for?" Hawk said.

"They don't think he's planning to harm Riley Jo. But if he's anything like his brother, it's hard to say what he might do if he's cornered. And if his mother's inside, they don't want to put her in harm's way either. Virgil is working on a plan."

"What reason would *Walter* have for takin' Riley Jo?" Dad said.

Kate folded her hands on the table. "Virgil thinks Walter's in denial about his brother's having kidnapped Riley Jo and murdered Micah. And still believes he's Riley Jo's uncle. He probably thinks he's doing the right thing by bringing her home with kin, rather than having her live in foster care." Kate glanced over at Elliot, calmed by his presence. "But Virgil did some further digging after he questioned Maria Diaz and found out Walter's divorced. And that three years ago, when he lived in Alabama, he had an eight-year-old daughter that was removed from the home and put into foster care. Neither he nor his ex-wife ever regained custody."

"Why'd they take her away?" Abby said.

"Virgil just said neglect. He didn't elaborate."

"So why would Walter want the *responsibility* of carin' for Riley Jo?" Dad said.

"Maybe it's his twisted way of wanting to redeem himself." Elliot leaned forward on his elbows. "If Walter believes his brother's innocent and will be cleared of the charges, he may have convinced himself that he did what he had to do to protect Riley Jo from getting swallowed up in the system—and that the law would see that and forgive it."

Hawk sneered. "Well, that's not gonna happen."

Abby twisted a lock of hair. "I wonder what the sheriff's going to decide."

"I don't know, honey," Kate said, dreading the thought of another long wait. "He said he'd call once he has."

"Why wait around here?" Hawk said. "I'll take you to his command post. We can stay out of their way."

Kate turned to Elliot. "That way I could catch a glimpse of Riley Jo—when they get her to safety. Surely Virgil can't argue with that. I'm tired of feeling like a bystander. She's my baby. My flesh and blood." Could she really handle it if something went wrong and Riley Jo were seriously injured—or worse? What could be worse than never laying eyes on her daughter again?

Kate moved her gaze from Elliot to Abby to Dad to Jesse and could almost hear their silent prayers going up.

Lord, if You're really there, just look at their faces—such hope. And faith. Please don't let them down.

CHAPTER 37

Virgil stood leaning on the hood of his squad car, where he had set up his command post for the operation to free Ella Tutt from her misguided uncle—hopefully without anyone getting hurt.

Virgil looked up just as Kevin Mann and Foggy Ridge Police Chief Reggie Mitchell walked over and stood next to him.

"Sheriff, the perimeter's sealed tight as a tick," Kevin said. "No way Tutt's getting through it. What's our next move?"

Virgil cleared his throat. "I've wrestled with each of the approaches we discussed. And since we really don't think Walter's intention is to harm the girl, and his mother may be in the home, I keep coming back to the simple ruse: I call Walter and tell him that we are intensifying our search for the missing girl and have some follow-up questions we want to ask him. I make it clear it'll be at least an hour before we get there. It's possible he'd buy the ruse and see that as an opportunity to flee. And if he does, we can catch him off guard and get the girl to safety, whether she's with him or still in the house." Virgil glanced over at Reggie, whose dark skin glistened with perspiration. "Thoughts?"

Reggie pursed his lips. "That could work if everything goes perfectly. But if your phone call makes him suspicious, he might decide to stay right where he is and devise a plan to keep us from getting Ella. That would give him the advantage. We both know he's far more dangerous in that house than away from it."

"Which is why if he doesn't flee within twenty minutes," Virgil said, "I'll use the bullhorn and try to talk him out while the SWAT team gets positioned. To buy us time, I can pass Walter off to Deputy Martinez. She can negotiate as well as the best of them. If she can't get him to surrender, the SWAT team will be ready to go."

"Sir, Tutt has several guns registered," Kevin said. "I think we have to presume he's armed and dangerous—and possibly unstable like his brother."

"I agree." Virgil looked from Kevin to Reggie and back to Kevin. "But I don't want us getting ahead of ourselves. Otha has never known him to be violent."

"Well, he sure had Maria Diaz convinced he was," Reggie said.

Virgil scratched the sandpaper on his chin. "I haven't forgotten, Chief. Could've been all for show. We just don't know. But believe me, the last thing I want is a dead body. All I'm saying is let's show restraint until we have cause not to. But protecting Ella Tutt is priority one, is that clear?"

"Crystal clear," Kevin said. "I'll inform the teams so we're all on the same page."

Reggie looked at the computer monitor, where Tutt's house was pictured, nestled in the trees about a mile from the command post. "This is your show, Sheriff. My officers are here to assist. Just tell us what you need."

Kevin heard voices and turned around. Buck Winters and Kate, Hawk, and Abby Cummings were approaching the command post.

"I could do without this right now," Kevin mumbled.

"Me, too," Virgil said. "But can you really blame them? After what they've been through, I'm not sending them home. Find Deputy Freed. Have her stay with them and give them updates when it's appropriate. Make sure they stay back far enough so they can't hear the decisions being made. And caution them about talking to the media."

"I'll take care of it." Kevin turned and left.

"Excuse me, Reggie," Virgil said. "I really should go say something. I've known the Cummings a long time, and we've been through a lot together."

"I understand." Reggie glanced over at the family. "I was fixin' to go check in with my officers. How long before you plan to make that call to Tutt?"

"Just as soon as I'm sure all teams are on the same page."

"My people will be. Don't you worry about that."

"I never have to worry about your officers." Virgil patted Reggie on the shoulder and then walked in the direction of Kate, Abby, Hawk, and Buck.

"There you are." Kate hurried over to Virgil. "Before you decide to try and turn us around, I—"

"Don't worry. I'm not going to send you away."

"You're not?"

Virgil shook his head. "You're welcome to wait here at the command post. All I ask is that you stay back and let us do our job. Deputy Roberta Freed will be here in a minute. She'll be giving you updates as we proceed."

"Do you know where my daughter is?" Kate said.

"We believe Walter has her inside his house. The perimeter's been secured. He's not going anywhere."

"What are you going to do?"

"I can't get into detail, but I have a plan. If it works, this thing will be over in a matter of minutes."

✣

"What's taking so long?" Kate glanced at her watch again, as if that would somehow move things along. "Why can't you tell us something?"

Deputy Roberta Freed put her hand on Kate's shoulder. "Try not to worry, Mrs. Cummings. The sheriff's chosen a conservative first approach, hoping to end this quickly and with minimal danger to the child. If we can catch Tutt off guard, we'll have the girl before he knows what happened."

"Are they going to kill him?"

"Not if they can help it. We'll do what we can to end this without violence. But Ella Tutt is our first priority."

"Her *name* is Riley Jo Cummings." Hawk threw his hands in the air. "Can't we stop playing games?"

Kate felt sure that, if Deputy Freed's skin wasn't dark, they would be able to see her blushing.

"Hawk, that's enough." Kate shot him a scolding look. "I apologize for my son's tactless remark, Deputy Freed. It's just that my family has no doubt who the child is."

Roberta nodded. "I understand, ma'am. I do. But it's not up to the sheriff's department to make that legal determination. A judge'll have to sort it out."

"I'm sorry I sounded rude." Hawk looked sheepishly at Roberta. "It's been a crazy few days. I just want my sister back and this whole nightmare to end."

"Understandably," Roberta said. "You've all been through a lot to this point. Now let us finish what we're trained for. We all want the same thing."

Abby linked arms with Kate. "Sheriff Granger won't take any chances with Riley Jo's safety, Mama. You know that."

Kate did know that. But so many things could go wrong. She noticed some activity at the command post, and Virgil talking to Chief Mitchell and Deputy Mann, but she couldn't hear what was happening. Her pulse quickened as Roberta walked away, her back to them, her walkie-talkie to her ear. What was going on?

Half a minute later, Roberta turned around and came back.

"I just got an update from the command post," Roberta said. "The suspect has not left the house as we had hoped. Sheriff Granger is moving to a different location. He's going to use his bullhorn and attempt to communicate with the suspect. You're free to stay here, but once the operation begins, you need to remain perfectly still. Everybody understand?"

Four heads bobbed in unison.

"Good."

"I can't speak for anybody else," Buck said, "but I think this'd be a good time to ask God for a little backup."

Buck took Abby's hand and held out his other hand to Hawk. "Come on, son. I'll do the talkin'."

Kate stood dumbfounded as Hawk joined hands with Buck and held out his other hand to her.

"Mama?" Hawk said.

Kate's heart nearly pounded out of her chest. Despite her doubts and audible renouncements of once-held spiritual beliefs, she felt herself walk over and take hold of Hawk's hand—and then Abby's. How long had it been since the family prayed together?

Kate was so self-conscious that she didn't hear much of her dad's prayer. But she felt the power of it—something else she hadn't experienced in a long time.

❖

Virgil stood hidden in the trees about fifty yards from the suspect's house. He put the bullhorn to his lips.

"Walter Tutt. This is Sheriff Virgil Granger of the Raleigh County Sheriff's Department. Your house is completely surrounded by law enforcement officers. We're not here to harm you or your mother in any way. We came to take Ella back into foster care until a judge reviews the facts of her family history. There's no way for you to escape, sir. We know you thought you were doing the right thing by bringing Ella home with you. We're all on the same side here. We all want what's best for that little girl. Come out, and let's talk about it. Open the front door slowly, and come out unarmed with your hands in the air."

Virgil stood quietly for perhaps a full minute, then put the bull-horn to his lips and repeated essentially the same message phrased a little differently.

"He's not going to cooperate, Sheriff," the SWAT captain said over the walkie-talkie. "Say the word, and we'll go in and get the girl."

"SWAT team, hold your position," Virgil said. "I repeat, hold your position."

Virgil turned to Deputy Julie Martinez. "I'm sure Tutt's mind must be reeling about now. Let's give him time to respond. This has to be intimidating, especially to a backwoods guy who's had little exposure to law enforcement and probably doesn't trust us."

Another minute passed with no response from Walter Tutt. "Okay, Martinez. You ready to take a stab at it?"

"Yes, sir."

Julie took the bullhorn. "Walter, this is Julie Martinez. I'm a deputy sheriff. I'm also a mother. I know how important it is that we make absolutely sure that Ella goes home to the right parents. I know you want that too, or you wouldn't have taken such a huge risk to remove her from foster care and hide her from the authorities. We understand why you did it. But, for Ella's sake, we need to be sure who her real parents are before we let her go home. Why don't you come out, and we'll talk about it. We want to hear what *you* have to say. I promise we'll listen. No one will harm you or your mother if you come out with your hands in the air. You're a smart man, Walter. You got our attention, and we're listening. But we need you to cooperate so we can all do the right thing for Ella."

Julie lowered the bullhorn and took a deep breath and let it out.

"You're doing great." Virgil patted her shoulder.

"Sheriff, he's opening the door," said Kevin, who was watching the monitor at the command post. "Just a crack, but it's definitely open."

"Copy that."

"What do you want me to do, Sheriff?" Julie said.

"Keep talking."

Julie raised the bullhorn. "Thanks for opening the door, Walter. That shows me you want to cooperate. Now, just come out unarmed with your hands in the air. No one will harm you. We'll talk about your brother."

"Y'all just want Ella," he hollered through the crack in the door. "You don't care nothin' 'bout me or my ma. Soon as you git Ella, you'll take us down. I know how you work."

"If you come out with your hands in the air, I promise neither you nor your mother will be harmed. Walter, we *want* to hear what you have to say. We have no desire to hurt you."

"Ella's our kin," Walter said. "You got no right to take her from us."

"Your brother, Isaiah, told you Ella was his daughter and that her mother died in childbirth. But that was a lie."

"So *you* say! He says it ain't."

"We checked the state and county records," Julie said, "and there's no record that matches the name and birth date Isaiah gave us."

"Them records could be lost," he shouted.

"They're not lost. We have good reason to believe that Isaiah killed Ella's real father, then took her home and pretended she was his."

"That's crazy talk! Why would he do that when he didn't have no wife?"

"So he could find a wife. Think about it, Walter. Wouldn't most women feel sorry for a man who was raising a little girl on his own? Otha admitted to us that the reason she married Isaiah is that she *did* feel sorry for him and wanted to take care of Ella. She believed Ella was Isaiah's daughter until yesterday, when he threw her down a hole with the two teenagers who came to rescue her. He threatened to kill all three of them. Told them he was going to feed them to his pigs."

"That's poppycock, pure 'n simple," Walter said. "My brother'd never hurt Ella. You'd spout anything to git me to surrender."

"I understand that you don't trust us, Walter. But there is one sure way to resolve whether Isaiah is Ella's father. We're awaiting the results of a DNA test—that's a scientific test—that will prove without any doubt whether Isaiah is really Ella's father. Even if you don't trust law enforcement, this test does not lie."

"I don't know nothin' about that."

"I'm telling you the truth. Ella's life is at stake here. We can't afford to play games. If you don't believe me, ask Ella yourself if Isaiah threatened to kill her. She told us she doesn't ever want to go back to him."

There was a long pause on Walter's end. Was he doing what Julie said—asking Ella?

Julie lowered the bullhorn and wiped the perspiration from her upper lip. "How am I doing?"

"Great. Keep him talking." Virgil put the walkie-talkie to his lips. "SWAT, hold your position."

"Copy, Sheriff. SWAT holding."

Julie took a slow, deep breath and exhaled, then continued. "Walter, what's it going to be? We need your cooperation in order to get Ella home where she belongs. Work with us!"

Another minute passed. Dead silence. Virgil squinted, his gaze focused on the house. What was Tutt doing? Should he send the SWAT team in or wait him out?

"Sheriff, the door is opening more," Kevin said. "I can see the girl. But I can't see Tutt."

"All teams, hold your fire!" Virgil said. "Hold your fire!"

A few seconds later, Virgil could clearly see Ella standing alone on the wooden porch.

"Tell her where to go before I change my mind!" Tutt shouted, still hidden inside.

Julie spoke into the bullhorn, her voice calm and steady. "Ella, honey, run straight ahead into the woods. Don't be afraid. I can see you. I'll be right here to get you."

Ella almost tripped rushing down the wooden steps.

"Kevin, is there any sign of Tutt?" Virgil said.

"Negative. The girl is crying her heart out, but I don't see any visible wounds."

"Agent Martinez," Virgil said, "be ready to get her out of harm's way."

"Yes, sir."

Everyone stood speechless as the scared little girl, dressed in a long pink nightgown, ran as fast as her little legs would carry her across the open area in front of the house toward the woods.

When Ella got close to the tree line, Julie stepped out from behind a tree and called to her. "Ella, over here, sweetie."

Julie opened her arms, and Ella ran into her embrace, clutching her tightly and sobbing. Julie pulled her behind some bushes and rocked her from side to side.

"Kevin, any sign of Tutt?" Virgil said.

"Negative."

"Copy that. SWAT team, move in," Virgil said. "We need Tutt *and* his mother alive. Go!"

"SWAT team on the move. Stand by ..."

Virgil glanced at the crying girl, and relief rushed through him. Now if the SWAT team could get Tutt into custody without bloodshed ... He waited patiently, knowing the team planned to enter through a rear window in the basement.

"SWAT has gained access," Kevin said. "Repeat, SWAT has gained access."

"Copy." Virgil lowered his walkie-talkie and smiled at Julie. "Good job. Call Deputy Freed and tell her to alert Kate that we have Ella Tutt in custody. And that I'll be bringing her to the designated location shortly."

Julie's face beamed. "I will, sir. Right away."

Virgil paced. He really wanted this thing to end peacefully.

"Sheriff, this is SWAT. We've completed our search. The mother is unharmed and in custody. But we can't locate the suspect."

"He's there," Virgil said. "We've got a visual on the entire house. He hasn't emerged. Doesn't the mother know where he is?"

"Negative. She was locked in her room."

Silence.

"Search the house again," Virgil said.

"Conducting second search. Over."

Virgil studied Julie as she talked on the phone, her arm still around Ella. He hadn't been sure when he picked a female deputy to try negotiating with Walter whether the man would be receptive to a woman. Julie had proven herself once again. Ella looked dazed, but she had stopped crying.

"Sir, this is SWAT. We've swept every room, including the attic and basement. The suspect is not in the house."

"He has to be," Virgil said, trying not to show his irritation. "The command post has maintained a visual of the entire exterior of the home. He never left."

"I'm not sure what else to tell you, Sheriff," the SWAT captain said. "He's not here."

"You've searched closets? Trunks? Cupboards?"

"Yes, sir."

"He didn't just vanish!" Virgil paused and took a deep breath. This was ridiculous. "All teams, maintain the perimeter. I repeat, maintain the perimeter." Virgil hit the speed dial on his cell phone.

"This is Mann."

"Kevin, what happened?" Virgil said. "Did you lose the guy?"

"Absolutely not, Sheriff. I've been watching the house from every angle. I assure you, if he'd come out, I would've seen him."

"Well, he didn't just disappear!"

"He must still be in the house somewhere."

"SWAT can't find him. They've searched twice."

"I heard. I have no explanation. I never took my eyes off the monitors. There's no way he slipped by me."

"All right. Maintain visual." Virgil disconnected the call and hit the speed-dial number for Billy Gene Duncan.

"Hey, Sheriff. This is Duncan."

"I want you and Hobbs to get inside Tutt's home and go over it with a fine-tooth comb. Check every conceivable place where there could be a hidden room or compartment. Proceed as if the suspect is still inside and armed and dangerous. SWAT will have your backs."

"Copy that," Billy Gene said. "We're on our way."

"Keep me posted."

Virgil turned to Julie. "I need you to try to talk Walter out of the house. If he keeps this up, he's going to get himself killed. There's no need for that."

"What about Ella?"

"I'm going to take her to meet someone." Virgil smiled at Ella. "A very nice lady named Miss Kate she can stay with until the social worker arrives."

"Has the social worker been called?" Julie said.

Virgil shot Julie a knowing look. "Not yet."

Julie rose to her feet and picked up the bullhorn. "Walter, this is Julie Martinez. Thank you for letting Ella go. You did the right thing. No one got hurt. Your mother is safe. Now, I need you to do another right thing. I need you to come out of the house with your hands in the air and come down to the station with us, where we can talk about Isaiah. I know you have questions. We want to answer them."

Virgil's cell phone buzzed. He heard a lot of static on the line and then a male voice.

"Sheriff, it's Billy Gene. We've got the suspect in custody. I repeat, we got him."

"That was fast," Virgil said. "Where in the world was he?"

"Winda' seat had a hidden door. He'd crawled inside and was holed up there."

"How'd you discover that?"

Billy Gene chuckled. "I just hollered 'fire,' and Mr. Tutt come a squirmin' outta that winda' seat like a wild hog from a mud pit."

Virgil felt a grin tugging at his cheeks. Leave it to Billy Gene to think of a simple solution. "Good work. Bring him in. All teams, suspect's in custody. Operation is complete. Repeat, suspect's in custody. It's over." Virgil looked at Julie. "You did great work. Thanks."

"I'm just glad it didn't get violent," she said.

"Me, too." Virgil lifted his Stetson and wiped his forehead with his sleeve. "I'll take Ella to meet Miss Kate. I want you to call Roberta and tell her to remind Kate of everything we talked about."

"I will."

Virgil held out his hand. "Come on, honey. You're safe now."

As Virgil walked the child to his squad car, his insides felt jittery—and not because of the standoff with Walter Tutt. He had waited for this moment for five long years. He couldn't imagine what Kate was feeling about now.

CHAPTER 38

Kate walked with Roberta out of view of the command post and stopped at a campsite near the unpaved roadway that wound through the woods and back to Summit Road.

"The sheriff thought this spot would work out nicely for you to have a few minutes alone with the girl," Roberta said. "He asked that you keep your promise not to reveal your suspicion that she's your daughter. He's bending the rules by sidestepping DCFS and letting you talk with her before the DNA results are back."

"Don't worry," Kate said. "The last thing in the world I want to do is confuse her even more. She needs time to assimilate what's happened. The only world she knows has been yanked apart."

Roberta flashed a bright smile, her dark eyes wide. "Can't imagine how you feel. Girl, if it were me, I know I'd have butterflies somethin' fierce."

"That's putting it mildly. I'm not even sure how long my knees can hold me up."

Roberta took Kate's arm and walked her over to the picnic table. "Why don't you sit? The sheriff should be here any moment. Have you thought about what you're gonna say to her?"

"A million times. But I don't remember any of it. My head is spinning. My heart is pounding. It's awkward that my daughter is a stranger. I don't know anything about her. I used to know everything about her."

"Maybe that side you knew when she was two is still there—just more developed."

"Truthfully, it scares me to think of what that child has seen and heard—and how it's affected her."

"Well, I know one thing"—Roberta held Kate's hands and looked into her eyes—"there's nothin' this side of heaven that's more powerful than a mother's love. When that child realizes how wanted she is and how long and hard you've searched for her, I think she'll come around quickly. Especially when the whole family welcomes her with open arms."

"I hope you're right. I'm so afraid she'll want to go home to Otha. And that DCFS will drag this out. I can hardly wait until a judge lets her come home. But I'm also scared to death. Does that make sense?"

Roberta nodded. "Of course it does."

Kate heard the sound of a vehicle approaching and looked up. A squad car had stopped on the dirt road about forty feet away.

"There they are," Roberta said. "I'm gonna step away and give you space to talk privately."

"Thank you."

Virgil got out of the car and walked around to the passenger door. He held it open, and a beautiful little girl—with long dark hair, huge blue eyes, and a bruised cheek—slid out onto her feet.

Kate sucked in a breath and forgot to exhale. Was it really happening? Was she really seeing her baby again?

Virgil, wearing his wide-brimmed hat, looked like a giant next to the tiny seven-year-old. He took her hand and walked toward Kate, whose heart hammered so hard it seemed to shake her entire being.

Kate stood, leaning on the picnic table, her knees shaking, unable to take her eyes off the little girl, who looked surprisingly like Jesse. In an instant Kate knew deep in her soul it was Riley Jo. Her eyes stung, and she blinked several times to clear away the tears of elation.

Virgil stopped in front of Kate. "Ella, this is Miss Kate, the nice lady I told you about. She'll take good care of you until your social worker gets here."

The girl flashed a shy smile. "Hey."

Kate returned the child's smile and struggled not to get emotional. "I'm glad you're all right," she heard herself say. "You're safe here with me."

Virgil's cell phone buzzed, and he glanced at the screen. "Excuse me. I've been waiting for this call." He quickly stepped away, his back to them.

Ella reached down and picked a black-eyed Susan and handed it to Kate. "I like these. We got lots of 'em where I live. Yeller is my favorite color 'cept for pink. Granny Faye sewed me a real pretty dress that's got yeller *and* pink. Otha don't want me wearin' it out to play. I'm savin' it for somethin' special."

"I'll bet it's beautiful," Kate said, aware that Virgil had walked up next to her.

He put his lips to her ear. "Stay calm and don't react. I called in a favor and got the DNA test fast-tracked. That was the lab on the phone. This little doll is definitely your daughter. But you can't be the one to tell her. Let's do this right so we can get her home to you."

Kate nodded, adrenaline rushing through her body.

Virgil bent down, eye level with Riley Jo. "I need to go check on your uncle Walter. Why don't you visit with Miss Kate, and I'll have Deputy Freed bring you something to drink? We have Coke, Sprite, water, Gatorade, and apple juice."

"Apple juice," Riley Jo said. "That's my favorite."

Of course it is! Kate thought. "That's a healthy choice. My girls love apple juice. I'll have one too."

"Apple juice it is. I'll have Deputy Freed get it for you. I need to leave now."

"Is Uncle Walter in trouble?" Riley Jo said.

Virgil wiped his perspiring face with a handkerchief. "Yes, he is—for taking you away from your foster home."

"He said I was kin and y'all don't have no right to take me."

"I know," Virgil said. "And he believes that's the truth. But that's not what Isaiah said, is it?"

Riley Jo shook her head and looked at Virgil with the saddest blue eyes Kate had ever seen. "The reason Uncle Walter let me go is 'cause I told him what Pa said to me and Abby and Jay. He said he killed my real pa and took me home with him so he could git a wife. He don't care nothin' about me. He ain't my real pa. And Otha ain't my real ma. Abby said I ain't really Ella Tutt neither." She sighed. "I don't even got a home now."

Yes, you do, Riley Jo! Kate swallowed hard and resisted the almost overwhelming desire to put her arms around her daughter. Instead she gently brushed the hair out of the girl's eyes and relished the first touch. "While we're waiting for our apple juice, let's sit at the picnic table, and we can talk about Abby."

"Okay. Abby's nice. She says she's my sister, but I don't remember nothin' about her."

Virgil stood and stretched his lower back. "You ladies have a nice time visiting."

"Mister Sheriff, you promise I don't hafta go back to Pa?" Riley Jo said.

"Absolutely. Isaiah's going to jail, honey."

"Good." Riley Jo folded her arms across her chest. "Now I won't hafta marry Bobby Lee Hoover. I really don't like him that much."

Kate tried not to show how appalled she was that a seven-year-old was already dreading her wedding day. Kate locked gazes with Virgil and mouthed the words *thank you*.

Virgil smiled and tipped his Stetson, then turned and walked back to his car. A few seconds later, he drove away, leaving a cloud of brown dust hovering over the road.

"I guess we should sit down," Kate said, suddenly afraid she might not have anything at all to say to her daughter.

Riley Jo sat at the table next to Kate, then reached down and grabbed a tall blade of wild grass and spun it between her thumb and forefinger. "The sheriff ain't mean like Pa said he was."

"I've known the sheriff a long time," Kate said. "He's a very good man."

"My pa ain't. He was gonna kill us." Riley Jo looked up at Kate. There were those sad eyes again. "I guess I ain't never gonna see him no more."

"Are you sorry about that?"

"Not really. But I'll be sad if I can't see the twins and Otha. And Granny Faye."

"I'm sure you'll be able to see them, honey. Everyone wants you to be happy."

"Then why can't I just go home?"

"What did Abby tell you?"

"She said my real family's been lookin' for me since I was two years old. But I don't know none o' them."

"When you do," Kate said softly, "maybe you'll like them, too. You don't have to stop caring about Otha and the twins and your granny Faye. I'll bet your heart is big enough to care about both families."

"But Otha might feel sad if I like my real ma."

Kate tilted Riley Jo's chin. "I think Otha would be happy to see you happy. And she would not want you worrying about this. Everything's going to work out. I promise."

Riley Jo seemed lost in thought for a moment. She replaced the blade of grass with a lock of her hair, which she twisted around her finger. Finally she said, "I had another baby brother. His name was Luke."

"Really? I didn't know that. Where is he?"

Riley Jo shrugged. "Pa said he died in the night. I heard him cryin' and cryin'. Pa hollered at him, and then he was quiet. The next mornin' when I got up, Luke was gone."

"Where was he?" Kate's heart nearly pounded out of her chest. Was the man a worse monster than she had imagined?

"Pa said Luke stopped breathin' so he had to bury him. Otha wouldn't talk about it. But I seen her cryin' when Pa weren't around."

"Did Isaiah take you to Luke's grave so you could say good-bye?"

"Nope. He wouldn't let us talk about him neither."

"How old were you when Luke died?"

"Six."

"Have you told anyone else about Luke?"

Riley Jo shook her head. "Pa got really ugly and made me promise never to speak of it, but I ain't ascared of him now. The sheriff said I don't hafta see him no more. I wish Luke didn't die. I think Pa shaked him. I seen him do it before."

Kate felt sick to her stomach. She would have to tell Virgil to add that to the charges he was mounting against Isaiah. And he'd have to question Otha about why she didn't report it.

"You were brave to tell me that," Kate said, blinking quickly to clear away the tears of empathy. "I'm sorry you lost your baby brother. I'll bet that was very hard."

"Yes'm. Powerful hard. I cried in my pillow sometimes, but I did what Pa told me and didn't say nothin'."

Riley Jo was quiet for perhaps a full minute. Finally she lifted her gaze. "Miss Kate, did you know my real ma's name is Kate too?"

"I did know that."

"Abby said she loves me lots and wants me to come home with her."

"Well, Abby's right."

Riley Jo mused, "Do you know Abby?"

Kate nodded. "Yes. I've known Abby all her life."

"Do you know her mama, too?"

"Yes. Better than anyone."

"Are you best friends?"

"Something like that."

Riley Jo turned and looked into Kate's eyes. "Is she nice?"

"She's not perfect. But she loves her children and tries very hard to show them every chance she gets. All she can think about right now is you coming home again."

"Did she tell you that?"

"She didn't have to," Kate said. "It's been that way for five long years. She's missed you with a love so deep there are no words for it."

Riley Jo paused as if she were processing, then cocked her head and looked up at Kate again. "If I ask you somethin', you hafta tell me the truth, right?"

"Of course, sweetie. What is it?"

"You *promise* you'll tell me the truth?"

"I will," Kate said. "I promise."

"Are *you* my real mama?"

Kate stopped breathing. She hadn't seen that coming. She felt hot all over, her heart racing, her temples throbbing. She'd promised Virgil she wouldn't go there. But Riley Jo had opened the door. And she wasn't about to lie to her.

"Yes! Yes! I'm your real mama. The sheriff just whispered in my ear a few minutes ago that the test you took proves it. I wasn't supposed to tell you until you had time to get over all the difficult things that have happened. But you asked me outright. And I'll never lie to you …" Kate's voice cracked, tears streaming down her face.

Virgil was going to be so mad.

Riley Jo cupped Kate's cheeks with both hands, just the way Jesse always did when he wanted to comfort her. "Don't cry. I'm happy. I like you."

Kate laughed and cried at the same time. "I like you, too. And I never ever stopped loving you—not for one minute."

"Not for a teeny-tiny second?"

"Not for a single heartbeat."

Riley Jo smiled—that beautiful, angelic smile Kate recognized! "So then, you're my mama and Abby's mama, and she really is my sister."

"For sure. And I know Abby's anxious to see you as soon as you get settled at your foster parents'."

"Why can't I just come home with you?"

"Because some really nice doctors will want to examine you first and make sure you're okay. And some other doctors, and probably a judge, will want to talk with you and see how you feel about everything."

"Well, I sure ain't feelin' happy about livin' with strangers."

"I know. But there are some things we both have to get used to. For example, what would you like us to call you? You've always gone by the name Ella, but we remember you as Riley Jo. You've never been to school, and we'll need to talk about that. And of course, you'll want to get to know your brothers and your grandpa Buck and Halo the cat. There will be more things like that we'll need to work out. We can take them one at a time."

"Can I see you while I'm with my foster parents?"

Kate smiled. "Definitely. This is going to have such a happy ending. After all you've been through, it's a miracle you're here with me now."

Kate heard someone cough, and Roberta came out from behind a tree, holding two cans of apple juice.

"Here you go, ladies." Roberta handed one can to Riley Jo and one to Kate.

"Thanks." Kate took a sip and studied Roberta's expression. "How long were you standing there?"

"Just long enough." Roberta winked. "I mean, how else is a mother supposed to answer that?"

CHAPTER 39

One week later, as the morning sun sat just below the horizon and turned the sky a blazing shade of hot pink, Buck sat at a table at Flutter's Café, having breakfast with Titus and reveling in the sound of Abby laughing with the customers at table six.

"Can you believe how good all this is turning out?" Titus said.

Buck smiled. "Actually, I can. Oh, I admit I started havin' some doubts. But God planned to bring Riley Jo home, even when we couldn't see it."

Titus's eyebrows came together. "But you have to wonder why He didn't save Micah."

"The Lord has His reasons," Buck said. "Far be it from me to question Him. Like the preacher said last Sunday, our lives are tapestries. It takes some dark threads to make a beautiful design. Losin' Micah was a dark thread, but I see each one in my family has grown stronger and even more beautiful because of it. And gettin' Riley Jo back is a real faith builder for me and Jesse—and most of all, Abby. When all she had was blind faith, she held on for dear life. And God did bring her *and* her baby sister home."

"When do you think Riley Jo will actually be coming to live with you?"

"Sometime within the next week." Buck folded Saturday's newspaper and set it aside. "The folks at DCFS think Riley Jo's about ready. The rest of us have been ready for five years."

"I can only imagine what this ordeal's been like." Titus took a sip of coffee. "Do Kate and Hawk seem less bitter?"

"They sure do," Buck said. "Kate's over the top with joy at the moment. She's givin' Virgil and Hawk the credit for savin' those kids. But I've noticed Hawk's real quiet. Seems like he's mullin' things over quite a bit."

"It was a really brave thing he did. Must be sobering to know you saved one person's life—let alone three."

Buck nodded. "He won't take credit for it, though. Insists he's not a hero."

"Maybe he's just being humble."

Buck laughed. "That's not usually Hawk's strong point. It's more than that. But I can't put my finger on it yet."

Titus spread strawberry jam on his last piece of toast. "What about Otha Tutt? Will she get to see Riley Jo?"

"Looks that way," Buck said. "The sheriff's questioned Otha at length and is convinced she had no clue that Isaiah had kidnapped Riley Jo and killed her real father. All that happened before they met. But just between us"—Buck lowered his voice—"there was another issue that had to be resolved. Seems Otha and Isaiah also had a baby boy, Luke, who died. The sheriff checked, and there's no record of Luke Tutt's birth or death. Riley Jo told the sheriff she heard Luke cryin' and fussin' one night, and then he was gone the next mornin'. She thinks Isaiah shook the baby because she saw him do it before."

"Couldn't the sheriff just ask Otha what happened?"

"He did." Buck stroked his mustache. "Otha told the sheriff that Luke had colic, and Isaiah was up late, tryin' to calm him down. She went to sleep and discovered the baby missin' the next mornin'. Isaiah seemed as upset as she was. Told her Luke had stopped breathin', and he decided to go ahead and bury him in order to spare her havin' to see her dead baby. Otha was devastated but never suspected he'd caused the baby's death. Neither of them spoke of him again."

"Just like that?" Titus said. "Without even calling the coroner?"

"That's the way mountain folk handle things. Otha said she didn't even know that births and deaths are supposed to be recorded with the state. She's gonna have to file delayed birth certificates on the twins and baby Luke, and a death certificate on Luke. The main thing is the woman seems like a right good mother to those boys. And she was good to Riley Jo."

"Are you going to call her Riley Jo?"

"That hasn't been decided yet," Buck said. "Kate wants the child to be comfortable with her name. They've been workin' on it together, but so far, they aren't sayin'."

Abby changed out of her staff shirt, then sat on her bed, reading a text message from Jay, who wanted her to take her to a movie later on.

A knock at her door caused her to look up. Hawk stood in the doorway.

"Come in," she said. "What's up?"

Hawk flopped on the bed next to her. "I've been meaning to ask you something and keep forgetting."

"What's that?"

"Didn't you tell us that Riley Jo said she saw an angel once? Had a strange name."

"Yes. Custos, why?"

"What did she say about him?"

"Well …" Abby thought back on her conversations with her sister. "She said he was humongous and strong. Then one time she fell out of a weeping willow tree into the pond and was choking on water. The next thing she knew, she was on the shore, and Custos was drying her with his wing."

Hawk shifted his weight. "She actually said that? He dried her with his wing?"

"Exactly that. Why are you asking?"

Hawk shrugged. "I just want to know everything about her. Anything else—like why she called him Custos?"

"She said he told her his name, that she didn't name him. He also promised that he was always watching out for her, even when she didn't see him."

"So … did she think this was her guardian angel?"

"Not in so many words. But that's how I see it. Jay and Grandpa think so too."

"Cool." Hawk stood. "So who are you texting … Jay?"

"Uh-huh. We're going to the movies this afternoon."

"I'm glad you two are together now, and not just best friends. I like him a lot. You seem like a good fit."

Abby felt her face warm. "Thanks to you, Jay's still breathing. I know I've probably overdone my thank-yous, but I can't thank you enough for saving him—and us. Isaiah really would have killed us."

"I believed it the second I saw him pointing his rifle at Jay's chest."

"You were *so* brave," Abby said.

Hawk shook his head. "I really wasn't. I didn't even think about it. I just aimed and shot the rifle out of Tutt's hand."

"Thank God."

"Yeah." Hawk cracked his knuckles and seemed to stare at nothing.

"Are you all right?" Abby said.

"I'm fine."

"You've been acting weird ever since you came to our rescue."

Hawk smiled. "I've *always* been weird, according to you."

"Well, for what it's worth, I think you're a cool kind of weird."

"Thanks. I'll let you get back to lover boy. See you later."

Hawk got up and left the room.

Abby sensed there was something on her brother's mind but wasn't sure what it was.

Kate put the last of the lunch dishes in the dishwasher and turned the dial to Normal Wash.

"Mama?"

Kate turned around. "Hawk. I didn't hear you come in. What is it?"

Hawk's expression was tentative and somewhat somber, his eyes animated. "Can we talk—just the two of us?"

"Sure." Kate dried her hands with a towel. "Everyone's gone at the moment. Let's sit here at the table. What is it?"

Hawk sat quickly at the table and waited to speak until Kate was seated across from him. "I ... I did a Google search of the word *custos*, the name of Riley Jo's angel."

"You mean her imaginary friend."

"Uh, actually, Mama, I meant her angel."

"Okay. And what did you find?"

"The name is Latin. Spelled C-U-S-T-O-S. Know what it means?"

"You know I don't," Kate said.

"Guardian! It's the Latin phrase for guardian. There's no way a seven-year-old who can barely read and had no access to TV or a computer could know that, unless ... what she told you and Abby and Jay is true."

Kate studied her son's face. He was serious. "Hawk, your sister could have heard that name anywhere. I'm not willing to decide a spiritual reality based on the story told by a little girl with a big imagination."

Hawk's eyes glistened. "Well, how about the testimony of your oldest son with the imagination of a tree stump?"

"What are you talking about?"

Hawk blinked several times to clear his eyes. "I haven't told anyone, but when I lifted my rifle to shoot Isaiah ... I felt something ... steadying my hand."

"Like what?"

"I know this is going to sound crazy, but you know I'm not crazy, right?"

Kate smiled. "You're not crazy, Hawk. What did you feel?"

Hawk swallowed hard. "It felt to me like … a wing. A *huge* wing. I felt the feathers and the weight of it."

"Don't you think in the adrenaline rush of the moment, there could be another explanation? After all, you were intent on stopping Isaiah from shooting Jay."

"Mama, I was shaking so hard I could barely aim. I just shot the rifle. I must've had a little help. I didn't imagine feeling that huge wing holding me steady. What if God wanted to show me that Riley Jo *did* have an angel with her the whole time she was missing? And that maybe I have one too? Maybe we all do."

Kate's heart pounded. Her son had a lot of strong qualities, but a good imagination wasn't one of them. She reached across the table and took his hand. He was trembling.

"I can't answer that," she said. "But it's possible that, in the confusion of the moment, you did imagine it."

"I *didn't*," Hawk said. "I know what I felt because it shocked the socks off me at the time. I wanted to tell the family right off, but I couldn't handle it if y'all thought I was nuts. Shoot, at first, *I* wondered if I was nuts. But it was real, Mama. Just as real as you sitting here holding my hand."

Kate decided not to try and talk him out of it. "You say the name means guard?"

"It's the Latin phrase for guardian. Google it yourself. You'll see."

"But how do you even know it's the correct spelling?" Kate said. "It could just be coincidence."

"I looked it up every which way, and this is all I found. It can be spelled with a *k*, too, but it means the same thing. That'd be some pretty amazing coincidence, don't you think?"

Kate considered the implications if this were true. Was it possible that God really had been listening to their prayers? That He really did use angels to accomplish His purposes? That Hawk and Riley Jo had indeed encountered at least one of them?

Kate looked into Hawk's eyes, her mind racing with clever ways to discount his experience, but none of them were adequate.

"This was very real to you," she said, letting go of his hand. "I can see that."

Hawk smiled. "About the most real thing I've ever experienced. I think maybe God wants to call a truce. I've shut Him out for five years. Maybe it was His way of showing He hasn't given up on me—and doesn't want me to give up on Him."

"Is that why you joined hands with Grandpa and then pulled me into the prayer circle that day at the command post?" Kate said.

Hawk nodded. "Yeah. I don't really know how to get back to God. But I knew I had to stop running." Hawk's eyes turned to dark pools. "Think about it. What if God actually sent an angel to help *me*? I wasn't even speaking to Him. I bad-mouthed Him up one side and down the other. Yet He helped me, even when I didn't ask for help. And He helped Riley Jo when she was so vulnerable. He's been right there all along. You and I were just too hurt and mad to accept it."

"You know this is a lot for me to take in." Kate sighed. "I just assumed Riley Jo had imagined it. I do believe what you're telling me. Obviously, it made a huge impact on you. I just don't know what to do with it."

"Me, either," Hawk said. "I thought maybe, together, you and I could figure it out."

CHAPTER 40

The following Monday, Kate sat in the office of Stella Rhodes, Riley Jo's caseworker, at the Department of Children and Family Services.

"I've started preparing your daughter for the idea of moving to your home," Stella said. "As we discussed on the phone, the results of her tests were encouraging. There's absolutely no indication of sexual abuse. What physical abuse there was left no permanent injuries. And her psych evaluation indicates she handles stress well and has a remarkably bright outlook, considering all she's been through. From what I can see, she's eager and ready to join your family."

Kate felt almost giddy. Was it finally going to happen? "I'd like to think it helps that our family loves her and can hardly wait to have her back with us."

Stella nodded. "Yes, that's a huge part of it. I don't see any reason to draw this out much longer. It'll be better for her when she's settled. My only real concern now is that the two of you haven't decided on her name."

"She said she would have her mind made up the next time I see her. And that's today."

"Good." Stella squeezed Kate's hand and smiled. "Go. Talk to your daughter. I'm dying to know what she's decided."

Kate took a slow, deep breath, then got up and walked across the hall. She turned the knob and slowly pushed open the door to the pleasant room with pale blue walls painted with white clouds and colorful balloons.

Riley Jo jumped up and ran to the door, throwing her arms around Kate's waist. "Hi, Mama!"

"Hello, sweet girl. Miss Stella just told me that it won't be long until you can come home to us. Abby's already got your side of the room ready with the pink-and-yellow comforter and matching curtains you picked out."

"Yippeeeee!"

Her daughter's bright blue eyes sparkled with delight.

"Let's sit at the table," Kate said. "We have a very important issue to deal with today."

Riley Jo nodded. "My name."

Kate sat facing her daughter, her heart pounding. Would she be able to handle it if her daughter wanted to keep the name Ella?

"Have you decided?" Kate asked.

Riley Jo drew an imaginary circle on the table with her finger. "I been thinkin' lots and lots about it. I know I ain't gonna be Ella Tutt no more. I don't wanna be Ella neither, 'cause that name was given to me by Pa, and it was a lie."

"So what are you thinking?" Kate tried not to look or sound relieved.

"Well … can Micah be a girl's name?"

"It can if you want it to."

"Then how about … Riley Micah Cummings? I ain't never had a middle name before. That way I'd be named for my real pa who really *did* care about me."

Kate blinked to clear her eyes, but a tear spilled down her cheek.

Riley's lips turned down. "If you don't like it, I might could think of somethin' else."

"No, I *love* it!" Kate gently took her daughter's wrists. "It's *perfect*. You just caught me off guard, sweetie. These are tears of joy. I think it's so special that you'll have your real daddy's name now."

"You can just call me Riley—and not Jo. I might miss the name Ella some. But I'll git used to it."

Kate studied her daughter's china-doll face, remembering the day she and Micah dedicated their baby girl to the Lord. How could she possibly have imagined that, after five agonizing years, Riley would come back to her, changed and wanting to use her father's name as part of her own?

"Riley Micah Cummings," Kate said aloud for the first time. "It's just right. And beautiful—like my precious daughter." She brushed Riley's soft dark hair out of her eyes and relished the glow of excitement on her face.

"I ain't sure my forever family'll like it."

"They will," Kate said. "It's a wonderful choice. I had never even thought of it. But I'm glad you did."

"Now I got a name. Can I go to your house with you?"

"Not today," Kate said. "But very soon. And you need to think of it as *our* house. It's yours, too."

CHAPTER 41

That same afternoon, Abby sat out in the grass, several yards from the shady oak tree where she had sat with Jay on all their previous encounters on the slope. Jay had brought his easel and paints and positioned Abby so Beaver Lake would be the backdrop for the portrait she had agreed to let him paint.

"You're a good sport to let me do this," he said. "This is the right spot. I love the way the sun makes your hair look almost copper."

Abby rolled her eyes. "I hope you know I'm not doing this just for you. Once Mama sees what a good artist you are, she's going to want you to do a family portrait with Riley Jo in it."

"I can do that from a good photo," Jay said. "I won't need everyone to pose every day."

"Then why don't you just use a photograph to paint *me*?"

Jay grinned, his shadowy beard looking masculine—and rather artsy. "Because I love looking at you. And being with you."

"Mama's worried we're too young to be this crazy about each other."

"I can't help what I feel," Jay said. "I think it might ease her mind if we had a face-to-face. But in the meantime, Hawk made me promise to treat you with respect and not do anything I'd be embarrassed to tell my grandmother."

Abby laughed. "He made me promise the same thing and reminded me that I've still got my senior year ahead of me and that you're just starting junior college. You have to admit the timing's not ideal."

"I know. But this is so much more than just the boy-girl thing. What we've been through together was life-changing. And I saw a side of you no one else has. I admire your courage—and your faith. You're a strong person. And you're still my best friend."

"I feel the same way. I hope nothing ever changes that."

"My mom insists it won't last," Jay said. "She said we'll outgrow each other eventually. Like she ever held on to anyone in her life. Though she does seem crazy about the Stump."

"You've got to stop calling her husband the Stump. It's disrespectful."

"I don't mean it that way, Abby. I'm just afraid of getting too comfortable thinking of them as Mr. and Mrs. Richie Stump. About the time I do, Mom'll divorce him."

"At least you've got your real dad back in your life."

"Yes, but you don't."

"Coming to grips with Daddy's death is hard," Abby admitted. "But I'm grateful we finally know what happened to him. I'll be glad when the time is right for you and Mama to talk. I know she doesn't hold you responsible for anything. She just needs time to let everything sink in first. I think she'll be in a better frame of mind after Riley Jo is home with us."

"That's all right. I'm not in a big hurry to face her. I'm still freaked out about it."

"Don't be. You suffered too. Mama understands why you did what you did."

"I hope so. The regret is just something I have to live with." Jay seemed to study her. "Turn your head slightly to the left. There. That's good. Ready? Here goes."

Abby watched Jay as he dipped his brush in the paint and made the first strokes on the canvas. He was silent for a long time and appeared to be intensely focused. He chewed his lip the way he always did when he was deep in thought.

"What are you thinking about?" she said. "Please don't tell me we have to move again."

"Nope. This is the perfect spot." Jay dabbed his brush in paint and continued working. "Abby, be honest with me. Do you think your mother will be able to find peace if we never discover what Isaiah did with your dad's body?"

"Truthfully, I'm not sure that discovering what Isaiah did with Daddy's body will bring any of us peace. We're probably better off *not* knowing."

❧

Virgil scanned the preliminary report regarding the remains of at least eleven bodies found in the mass grave. It was the consensus of the experts that the remains had been buried between three and five years. The skull sizes and shapes suggested Hispanic descent. And several artifacts discovered—a silver necklace, buttons, and a turquoise and silver ring—supported that idea.

Virgil heard a knock at his door and looked up into the eyes of Kevin Mann.

"You reading the prelim?" Kevin said.

Virgil nodded. "Sounds like they're on to something. But it's too soon to tell us much."

"Not necessarily." Kevin walked in and handed Virgil a fax.

"What's this?"

"Seems news of our mass grave got back to a Mexican priest in Laredo who's been trying to track several families who left there illegally four years ago to find work. Each had paid their life savings to be transported across the border and into Eureka Springs to work for some wealthy landowner. Family members in Mexico never got word that they had arrived and feared that the contact in the US was bogus. The Eureka Springs PD has had a missing-person report on file for each of these folks, and we're getting that information faxed to us shortly. Sure sounds possible that we've uncovered their remains."

Virgil scanned the fax. "Unfortunately, it wouldn't be the first time a group of undocumented workers have been conned out of their money and then disposed of. As if it wasn't hard enough just being poor. Make sure the medical examiner's office has all the pertinent information."

"I will." Kevin stared at his hands. "Sir, we also made another discovery. This one could be definitive."

Just as the sun dipped below the horizon, Kate stood at the front door and waited as Virgil pulled his squad car into the Cummings'

driveway and turned off the motor. He got out of the car and walked up to the front door of their log house and removed his Stetson.

Kate opened the door and let him pass. "When you called and said you were on your way up here, my mind was all over the map. Please tell me there's not a problem with getting Riley back. Our court date is next Tuesday."

"No, no. Nothing like that. I've got some news I didn't want to give you over the phone."

"Let's sit out in the kitchen." Kate led the way and flipped the light. "Make yourself comfortable. Can I get you something to drink?"

"No, thanks. I'm good. I can only stay a few minutes."

Kate got a bottle of water out of the fridge and sat across from Virgil. "What was so important you couldn't tell me on the phone?"

"I waited to say anything until I was sure." Virgil spoke softly. "Kate, we found Micah's remains buried in a wooden box under the root cellar at the Tutts'—several feet under the room where the kids were held hostage and where Isaiah told Abby he had thrown Micah's body. The dental records match."

Kate stared at Virgil and let the gravity of his words sink in. "You're *sure*?"

"Absolutely. There's no doubt. We recovered his entire skeleton. And his gold wedding band—his initials and yours were carved on the inside of the band, along with your wedding date, just the way you told us."

Kate put her fist to her mouth and pushed down the emotion that she desperately wanted to hold in and release privately.

"We immediately confronted Isaiah with this new information," Virgil said, "and he admitted that he buried Micah there but still contends that Jay shot him. However, the medical examiner found a distinct scrape on Micah's breastbone, consistent with a deep stab wound. If it's the last thing I ever do, I'm going to get Isaiah to confess to Micah's murder. I'm going to nail him, Kate."

"I know you will." Kate met his gaze. "At least now we can *finally* close this chapter, though it doesn't seem real yet."

"After all you've been through, it'll take time for this to sink in. But it's definitely Micah's remains we found. It's over, Kate. It really is."

Over. How many times had she longed for it, only to have her hopes dashed? "So … can I bury my husband's remains?"

"We'll release them to you just as soon as the ME is finished with his analysis and the DA's office has what it needs to make the case."

Kate wiped the tears off her cheeks. "I can't believe it's really over. Soon Riley will be home—and so will Micah, though it's not at all the way I would've chosen."

"I know. I wish I'd been able to find them both alive and spared Riley those years with the Tutts."

"I just hope you're able to find out who those people are in the mass grave," Kate said. "I'm sure their families are suffering like mine did."

"Actually, I think we may have that solved too."

Kate listened as Virgil told her about twelve missing people from Mexico and the suspicion that they had fallen into the hands of con artists who took their money, smuggled them across the border, and then did away with them.

"We found a silver necklace among the remains," Virgil said. "This afternoon, we sent a picture of it to the parents of a young girl listed among the missing, and they verified it was a confirmation present from her grandparents. A lot more testing has to be done to identify the dead from the remains, but we're hopeful these are the folks the priest has been looking for."

"I hope so. No family should have to go through what we did." Kate put her hand on Virgil's. "I can never thank you enough for all you did for this family over these five years. You invested far more of yourself than you had to. It helped to know you cared."

"I sure did. Still do." Virgil put on his hat and stood. "I'll say one thing: your kids must've had someone watching out for them. It's a miracle that Hawk, Abby, and Riley are even alive."

"I know." Kate blinked the stinging from her eyes. She really did know.

⚜

Two weeks later, in Blessed Redeemer Cemetery, high atop Sure Foot Mountain and in the midst of a protective fortress of giant hardwood trees, Kate stood silent as the spirit of her beloved Micah was ceremonially given back to the God whose motives she had ceased to question. Even as she stared at the silver casket with a mound of summer flowers draped over it, there was no doubt in Kate's mind that it contained only earthly remains, that Micah was in the presence of his Lord and Savior.

Pastor Austin Windsor and the good people of Praise Chapel displayed a respectful melding of solemnity and jubilation over Micah's earthly fate and his heavenly one. Hundreds stood with her in the sticky summer morning for the graveside service she had long been denied.

Kate fought hard to erase the awful image of Micah's last moments by holding tightly to Riley's hand. What must her little girl be thinking? She had no memory of her father. No firsthand understanding of the pain caused by the five years she and her daddy were missing. Riley would never know what it was to be loved by her biological father—the kind and decent man who adored her as a toddler and who fought to the death trying to protect her from Isaiah Tutt.

Kate would make sure Riley knew all about her father. That she carried with her the truth of his character and devotion.

It seemed almost surreal, saying good-bye *again* to the love of her life. But this time would be the last. Kate finally had the closure she so desperately needed—a dichotomy of relief and angst. It was finally over.

Pastor Windsor's voice seemed to glide on the breeze. "Heavenly Father, no one understands a father's love more than You, who gave your Son as a sacrifice to save us from eternal death. You alone know the reason that Micah was called home to glory. In our timing, it seems far too soon. But in Yours, there are no mistakes. We pray for the poor soul who took Micah's life and trust You to deal with Him justly.

"We pray that these children, who will grow up without the father who gave them life, will not grow up without his influence. Nor will they grow up without the love and care of their heavenly Father, in whose presence Micah now resides for all eternity.

"Father God, we waited five agonizing years, not knowing what happened to Micah. What a joy now to know he is with You because he trusted Jesus Christ as his Lord and Savior. But despite that joyful knowledge, we are left to deal with the sobering reality of his murder and the aching void of his absence.

"I ask you to be with Kate. And Hawk. With Abby, Jesse, and Riley. And with Buck as they walk into the future, now able to put this chapter of uncertainty behind them. Make real to them the words of Jeremiah 29:11: 'For I know the plans I have for you,' declares the LORD, 'plans to prosper you and not to harm you, plans to give you hope and a future.'

"Grant them healing and new joy as You fill the void in their hearts with more of Your Holy Spirit. Make Your presence real to them. And let them rejoice with the angels that their beloved Micah is in that blissful place where sorrow and tears will be no more. And where all of us believers will one day see him again. For it's in the Name of your Son and Our Savior, Jesus Christ, that we pray. Amen."

Pastor Windsor asked everyone to stand as he motioned for the family to come forward. One by one, each member approached the casket in silence and lingered for a moment in the privacy of his or her thoughts, each placing a single rose on Micah's casket before stepping back.

When Kate's turn came, she decided there was something she needed to do first, something she'd been unable to do until now. She turned around and put her arms around Jay, who stood in the second row next to Elliot. How difficult it must be for Jay to have come, and how alone he must feel with his regrets. Even though Abby had assured him that Kate didn't hold him responsible for the grief her family had endured, she hoped this gesture would remove all doubt.

"Thank you for coming," she whispered. "It means more to me than I can possibly express."

Jay nodded but seemed too choked up to say anything.

Kate comforted him for a moment and then turned her attention to the silver casket draped with a spray of orange orchids, white roses, red gladioli, lilies—and a white ribbon with the word *husband* imprinted in gold. This was the final farewell. The moment no one thought she would ever have. She stepped up to Micah's casket, her defenses starting to give way to the powerful surge of emotion that begged to be released. How was she supposed to say good-bye to the other half of herself? What words befitted such a moment, what lamentation was adequate to give voice to the agony she felt in the depths of her soul?

Kate began to perspire, her temples throbbing, her heart pounding. She twisted the rose in her hands and bowed her head, teardrops falling on her wrist.

I will always love you, Micah. I will keep your memory alive in the hearts of our children. It's time to move away from the grief and begin to live again. That's what you would want—for them and for me. But I'm not going to say good-bye. I can't. You will always be a part of me. Now and forever.

Kate paused to consider what forever really entailed. It was an issue worth revisiting. But not here. Not today. Kate laid the white rose atop Micah's casket and struggled for a moment to turn loose of it. But when she did, she felt her strength return and Riley's tiny hand slip into hers.

Kate looked upward into the blue summer sky as a white dove was released and the choir director led those gathered through each stanza of "I Can Only Imagine."

She didn't know the words but listened intently as her father and Abby joined in, singing with all their hearts. Jesse linked arms with her, and Hawk laid his hand on her shoulder, and for the first time in five years, something stirred deep in her spirit ... and she longed to reclaim her faith and the joy that pain and bitterness had stolen from her.

CHAPTER 42

Five months later — Thanksgiving Day

Abby looked out the huge dining-room window in the Cummings' log house, the billows of morning fog on Beaver Lake not quite dissipated in the chilly November air. High above the sea of white, a flock of Canada geese moved in a perfect V formation, the white in their wings dazzling in the sun as they flew southward.

Warmed by the crackling fire, the beauty of Mama's Thanksgiving table, and the presence of those she loved, Abby lingered for quite some time over her empty plate. What a blessing it was having Riley with them again.

"I keep thinking I want thirds," Abby said. "But I can't eat another bite. I'm sure I'll want leftovers later."

"Mrs. Cummings, that was the best fried turkey dinner I ever sunk my teeth into," Jay said. "Just don't tell my mom I said so. She really hates to cook. Richie took her out to Mrs. Simm's Back Porch."

"Mama's fried turkey is the juiciest in the world!" Jesse exclaimed. "But I also love her cornbread dressing. Mashed potatoes and gravy.

Sweet potatoes with marshmallows. Frozen fruit salad. Those awesome green beans with the crunchy onions. And I ate *four* homemade rolls."

Hawk stood. "So who's ready for pie?"

"Are you kidding me?" Kate said. "You couldn't possibly *enjoy* dessert this soon after eating all that food."

Hawk laughed. "Y'all are wimps. I'm ready for a piece of Dutch apple, lemon meringue, blackbottom, *and* pumpkin pie!"

"Well, you're going to have to wait for the rest of us," Kate said. "And we're waiting for Elliot. He's having Thanksgiving dinner with his sister's family but promised to have dessert with us and to watch *Home Alone*."

"I know," Hawk said. "I'm just messin' with you, Mama. It wouldn't be nearly as much fun without Elliot, now would it?"

Kate smiled, wondering if she was as transparent to everyone else in the family.

"I ain't never had Thanksgivin' before," Riley said, looking adorable in her brown-and-white gingham dress and the matching bow holding her long ponytail. "It's the funnest day."

"It's fun all right," Buck said, a smile appearing beneath his white mustache. "But there's still Christmas."

"Yay, I love Christmas!" Jesse exclaimed. "We get to make a gingerbread house."

"I ain't never seen one," Riley said. "Is it bigger 'n this house?"

Jesse shook his head. "It's just a wee little house we make with walls of gingerbread and icing and candy and sprinkles. It's so much fun. It's just for decoration. You'll see."

"We string a gazillion colored lights on the outside of Angel View," Abby said, "and all across the back deck. And a huge white star on the very top of the roof. People can see it from Beaver Lake. It's so cool."

"*And* we get to cut down our own Christmas tree that goes all the way to the ceiling"—Jesse's eyes grew big and round—"and put it in front of the big window in the living room so Santa can't miss it. Right, Mama?" He winked at Kate.

"That's right. I told Riley we're going to celebrate Jesus's birthday properly this year. But we also look forward to whatever Santa brings us. We seem to get lots of presents."

Riley grinned, exposing a gap where her front teeth had been. "I love presents!"

"As long as we're waiting on Elliot," Hawk said, "I think I'll drive down the mountain to Foggy Ridge and wash my jeep."

"Tell Laura Lynn we said hey." Abby shot her brother a knowing look and laughed at his red cheeks.

"Man, is nothing sacred around here?" Hawk sat back in his chair, his arms folded across his chest.

"Why don't you invite Laura Lynn to join us for dessert and the movie?" Kate said. "There's always room for one more."

Hawk smiled sheepishly. "I knew you'd say that. I already did."

"After I help Mama clean the kitchen," Abby said to Jay, "why don't we go for a walk and burn off this amazing meal?"

"I may have to run to get this off." Jay put his hands on his full belly.

"As for *this* ol' duffer," Buck said, "I'm gonna snooze a while, right there next to that warm fire."

Jesse tore off a piece of a hot roll and popped it into his mouth. "I'm gonna play video games."

"Before you go, would each of you bring your dishes to the kitchen?" Kate said.

"I'm fixin' to help Mama dry the pans and platters," Riley proudly announced. "I know how to be real careful so I don't break nothin'."

Abby thought back on memorable conversations she'd had with her mother while cleaning up the kitchen on holidays past. She looked over at Riley. "Thanksgiving cleanup is a special time only we girls get to enjoy."

"And we guys are more than happy to let you." Hawk laughed. "See y'all later."

Abby got up and carried her dishes into the kitchen. She hugged her mother and whispered in her ear. "I love you. This is the best Thanksgiving ever—for so many reasons."

Kate nodded. "It's been a long time since there's been this much laughter in the house. Why don't you and Jay go for that walk. Riley and I can handle the kitchen."

"You sure?"

Kate smiled. "I'll load the dishwasher, and whatever's left, I'll wash and she can dry. It'll be fun."

"Okay, see y'all later." Abby linked arms with Jay. "Guess we're good to go."

Abby opened the front door and stepped into the crisp November afternoon, marveling at the ways God had honored her mustard-seed faith when that's all she had. He had done a lot more than just bring Riley home. He had given her back her family.

Kate ran the fully loaded dishwasher on the china-and-crystal setting, and then handwashed the pots and pans and serving pieces.
She was tickled that Riley seemed to take great pride in drying them
thoroughly and setting them aside neatly on the countertop, as if to
display her handiwork.

"Mama, can we spend time lookin' at the pictures now?" Riley
said.

"Sure."

"I wanna see the ones of me when I was little. And of Daddy
and me."

"Come on," Kate said. "We're about done here. Let's go look at
pictures while the house is quiet."

Kate went into the living room, where her father snored con-
tentedly in his easy chair next to the crackling fire. She picked up the
least heavy of the brown leather photo albums and sat on the couch
next to Riley. She opened the album, which was filled with pictures
taken of Riley shortly after she was born. They had looked through
this album more in the past six months than in the entire five years
her daughter was missing.

Riley studied each picture, smiling with her eyes. "Daddy looks
nice. I look kinda weird."

"You were a beautiful baby."

"Why do you think that?"

"Oh, sweetie, look at all that dark hair," Kate said. "And those
pretty almond-shaped eyes. And fair skin. You looked like a little doll."

"Is that why you and Daddy loved me?"

Kate slipped her arm around Riley's shoulder. "You were adorable, but that's not the reason. There's a very special love that happens

between a parent and child. Your daddy and I didn't even have to try—we just loved you the minute we saw you. Of course, we'd been waiting patiently for nine months to meet you."

"And y'all weren't disappointed?"

"Not even slightly. We were thrilled."

"I wish I could remember Daddy. I can't remember nothin' before I lived with Pa and Otha."

Kate stroked Riley's ponytail. "Well, most kids don't remember much before the age of five anyhow. But you can count on me and Abby, your brothers, and Grandpa Buck to tell you about it. All of us remember."

"I wish Pa didn't kill my real daddy."

"Me, too," Kate said. "Micah was a fine man. He loved us all very much. And we loved him with all our hearts."

Riley paused and seemed to be thinking. "Maybe if *I* woulda got killed instead, you wouldn't hafta miss him so much."

"Sweetie, don't ever think that. We would miss you the same way." Kate looked into her daughter's innocent blue eyes. "We already know what missing you feels like. It was the most awful hurt in the world."

"And now it don't hurt no more?"

"Not at all." Kate pulled Riley closer. "And having you home is the greatest blessing of this Thanksgiving."

Kate noticed the corners of her father's mouth had curled up, as if to say it didn't hurt that Kate had stopped blaming God and decided to move on with her life.

"I'm glad you're my real mama," Riley said. "You make me happy every single day."

"I feel the same way about you." Kate tapped her on the nose. "You make me happy from the inside out."

"'Cause you like me?"

"Yes. And because I've never ever stopped loving you—not for one minute."

"Not for a teeny-tiny second?" Riley cocked her head and flashed an elfin grin.

"Not for a single heartbeat." Kate took her daughter's hand and kissed it, relishing this daily mantra that reminded her that the ending of the story was still in the making.

Riley went through all the photos in the album two more times, never seeming to tire of seeing the same pictures and hearing Kate repeat the stories behind them.

Kate glanced at her watch. An hour and forty minutes had flown by. Soon her other children would return, Elliot would arrive, and the Cummings household would be bustling with love and laughter and crazy chaos. But for now, Kate nestled with Riley for a few sacred moments, words totally unnecessary, and affixed this sweet memory onto a new page of her mental scrapbook, all too aware of the five years of empty pages stained with tears.

"For I know the plans I have for you," declares the LORD, *"plans to prosper you and not to harm you, plans to give you hope and a future."* The words of Jeremiah 29:11 raced through her mind with newfound clarity and hope.

Kate would never again take these intimate moments for granted or assume there would be another. Every day she was still breathing, she would be intentional about embracing her blessings—great and small, past and present. And she would leave the door open to the future—to the happier days God still had in store for her.

Kate heard a car door slam just as Jesse slid down the staircase banister and landed on his bare feet.

"Elliot's here!" Jesse announced, his voice booming about three decibels louder than was necessary. "He's *exactly* on time!"

Kate smiled at the understatement and relished the warm glow that seemed to melt through her at the mention of his name. *Yes, he's exactly on time. But then, God's blessings always are.*

... a little more ...

When a delightful concert comes to an end,

the orchestra might offer an encore.

When a fine meal comes to an end,

it's always nice to savor a bit of dessert.

When a great story comes to an end,

we think you may want to linger.

And so, we offer ...

AfterWords—just a little something more after you

have finished a David C Cook novel.

We invite you to stay awhile in the story.

Thanks for reading!

Turn the page for ...

- **Discussion Questions**
- **An Interview with the Author**

A NOTE FROM
THE AUTHOR

Without faith it is impossible to please God,
because anyone who comes to him must believe that he exists
and he rewards those who earnestly seek him.
Hebrews 11:6

Dear reader friend,

Deep, abiding faith is rarely easy to come by. We aren't "born again" with our faith already mature and strong and tested. But we usually begin with a childlike faith that trusts our Father to hear and answer our prayers—that believes with all our heart that He can do anything. Abby did. She chose to trust Him even when the path was dark and scary and uncertain. It wasn't because she had no other choice. She could have chosen to blame God for the woes that had befallen her family. Allowed anger and bitterness to consume her life and steal her faith. But she saw firsthand what that kind of attitude had done to her mother, and she chose better.

I'm not one to walk away from God when things get tough. But I admit I have been guilty, from time to time, of reacting to adversity out of the flesh when circumstances were overwhelming, and not really believing deep down that God was going to help me. I knew He *could*. But would He? During those times when I didn't exercise faith, the struggle was significantly more difficult. Attitude is everything! Every painful trial I've faced without faith has left a dark, ominous memory. But those trying times when I chose to believe God's promise never to leave or forsake me, and trusted Him to help me through, often resulted in a blessing for me and/or someone else.

It's impossible to overrate the peace of God that passes understanding. But it's also impossible to have that confident peace without faith in the One who provides it.

Kate suffered immeasurably, to be sure. And her faith was tested beyond what most of us will ever be forced to endure. But in the end, she came back to faith, back to the spiritual realities she had discarded as myth and the God who had disappointed her. In her suffering, Kate's perspective had changed. She realized that it was better to forge ahead in blind faith than to forge ahead merely blind. She couldn't control the outcome either way. But choosing to have faith in the One who *could*, had the power to make the journey infinitely more bearable.

Well, friend. I hope you're hooked on these characters after this first book, and I invite you to join me for book two in the Ozark Mountain Trilogy. We will watch several budding romances and go on a roller-coaster ride of emotions after Jesse witnesses the drowning of an elderly woman while he's fishing from the riverbank—more nail-biting suspense involving the entire Cummings family.

I would love to hear from you. Join me on Facebook at www. facebook.com/kathyherman, or drop by my website at www.kathy-herman.com and leave your comments on my guest book. I read and respond to every email and greatly value your input.

In Him,

Kathy Herman

DISCUSSION GUIDE

Not by Sight

1. This story is based on 2 Corinthians 5:7: "We live by faith, not by sight." Can you think of a time in your life when you found yourself in circumstances that required blind faith? Did you, like Abby, have a quiet thrill of expectation, believing God would act? Did He? Or were you, like Kate, disappointed that He seemed silent? If you were disappointed, could you see His hand in the situation later on?

2. Would you agree that God lives outside the constraints of time? Do you think it's possible that sometimes He answers our prayers, but it takes us years of our life's journey to get to the answer? Can you think of an example of that in your own life?

3. Do you think that having genuine faith makes confronting life's difficult issues easier? Why or why not? How might Kate's life have been different had she embraced the same kind of faith Grandpa Buck had? Or Abby?

4. Can you understand how Kate must have felt when it seemed as though God had turned a deaf ear to her cries for help in the search for Micah and Riley Jo? Have you ever been in a situation that was dire and experienced answered prayer that changed everything? Have you been in dire circumstances that never seemed to change, no matter how hard you or anyone else prayed? Were you able to hold tightly to your faith? Or did you find yourself slipping into unbelief? If so, did you eventually come back to faith in God? Can you pinpoint the reason why you did or didn't?

5. Hebrews 11:1 tells us, "Now faith is confidence in what we hope for and assurance about what we do not see." Can you put this into your own words? Can you name some spiritual truths that you believe strictly by faith?

6. "And without faith it is impossible to please God, because anyone who comes to him must believe that he exists and that he rewards those who earnestly seek him" (Heb. 11:6). Why do you think it's impossible to please God without faith? Has there ever been a person who has put his or her faith in you to accomplish something? How did it make you feel to have their trust? Has anyone ever treated you with a complete lack of faith? Did their lack of trust and confidence in you do anything positive to build a closer relationship? Do you think that our faith in God helps to build our relationship with Him?

7. Are you comfortable leaving every detail of your life in God's hands? Or does it make you a little nervous? Are there some things (or people) you find harder to trust God with? If you had been in Kate's shoes and had to go forward, not knowing if your spouse

and baby daughter were alive or dead or whether your spouse had left you, do you think you would have handled it better?

8. Has God ever tested your faith by allowing a family member's life to hang in the balance? Were you able to let go of that loved one, believing that God knew what was best? Or was it a difficult struggle for you, coming to grips with your helplessness in the matter?

9. Do you think that having faith means never asking *why*? Do you think that having questions negates your faith? Is it possible to choose faith, in spite of questions and doubts? Have you ever done that? What do you think the father of the deaf-and-mute boy meant (Mark 9:24) when he said to Jesus, "I do believe; help me overcome my unbelief!"?

10. How do you think faith grows? Do you believe Grandpa Buck, that faith isn't really faith until it's tested? In what ways has your faith been tested? Did the trial make your faith stronger? Did it make you trust God more? If not, how did it affect your relationship with Him? Is there something besides adversity that has grown your faith?

11. Who was your favorite character in the story, and why? Who was your least favorite character, and why? What was the takeaway for you?